Praise for *Brothers in Blood*

'A brilliant debut'
    —*Sunday Times*, Crime Club

'Tense and pacey ... fast and furious'
    —*Guardian*

'A fresh and exciting new voice to the genre'
    —Ann Cleeves

'Gritty, compelling and authentic, with an engaging hero and a hugely enjoyable plot'
    —*Daily Express*

'Have never read anything so action-packed and tense! A fantastic read!'
    —Ausma Zehanat Khan

'Gritty, startlingly original and great fun'
    —Robert Bryndza

'The finest storytelling finds the epic in the intimate and the intimate in the epic. *Brothers in Blood* introduces new voices and new communities into the world of crime fiction ... you won't be putting this book down'
    —Hardeep Singh Kohli

STONE
COLD
TROUBLE

Amer Anwar

dialogue
books

DIALOGUE BOOKS

First published in Great Britain in 2020 by Dialogue Books

10 9 8 7 6 5 4 3 2 1

A CIP catalogue record for this book
is available from the British Library.

ISBN 978-0-349-70034-2

Typeset in Berling by M Rules
Printed and bound in Great Britain by Clays Ltd, Elcograf S.p.A.

Papers used by Dialogue Books are from well-managed forests
and other responsible sources.

Dialogue Books
An imprint of
Little, Brown Book Group
Carmelite House
50 Victoria Embankment
London EC4Y 0DZ

An Hachette UK Company
www.hachette.co.uk

www.littlebrown.co.uk

For my mother, Shahnaz,
and for Lana,
with love, always.

Chapter One

Zaq was sitting in traffic going nowhere fast when his phone rang. He saw Jags' name on the screen and hit the green button. 'Hey, how you doing?'

'All right. What you up to?'

'Not much. I'm stuck in traffic near Ealing Common.'

'Shouldn't you have finished work already?'

'Yeah, but that idiot Sid sent me out on another drop last thing and now I've hit the Friday evening rush. I knew this'd happen.'

'You should've told him to stick it.'

'Wish I had. But he said he had this urgent delivery that had to go out today. Shits wasn't back – probably parked up somewhere having a joint – so I had to do it.'

Shits was the other driver at Brar Building Supplies, whose family nickname, Bits, had been bastardised to Shits by his workmates.

'Bummer,' Jags said. 'What you up to this evening? Fancy coming to mine? Uncle Lucky's here, says he needs to talk to us.'

'Us? Why me?'

'Don't know. He said to call you round, though.'

'You don't suppose they've finally found a girl dumb enough to marry you, do you? Maybe he wants me there to help convince you.'

'Get out of it. Better not be. And anyway, why would my mum and dad send my uncle? Why not come themselves?'

'True.' The traffic crept forward a few car-lengths. What was going on? Had there been an accident up ahead at the lights? 'The yard'll be shut by now,' Zaq decided. 'I might as well head straight to yours and drop the van off later. Dunno how long I'll be, though.'

'That's cool. See you in a bit.'

The traffic inched forward again. There had indeed been an accident: two cars had collided at the main junction by the common. Once Zaq made it past them, there was just the usual rush-hour grind to contend with. He thought about cutting through the back of Ealing over to the A40 but figured it'd probably end up taking just as long, so he stuck to the straight route along the Uxbridge Road, passing through Ealing and Hanwell before he hit his home turf of Southall.

Zaq had been born and brought up in the large, close-knit Asian community there, and it was where he'd lived practically his whole life, except for eighteen months in his own place in Greenwich and five years at Her Majesty's pleasure. When he'd bought his flat he couldn't wait to get away from Southall, but when he was banged up all that time he couldn't wait to get back to it. It was a strange feeling to be back now. Though it was still home, he couldn't help feeling a bit of an outsider. So much had changed while he'd been away – not least of all himself.

Now he was back, he appreciated all the things he'd thought he wanted to leave behind. The too-familiar sights and sounds, places and people. Turned out those were exactly the things he'd missed the most. As he drove along the Broadway, he took in the bright, bold colours that assailed the eye from window displays, signs, lights, and the Asian clothing worn by so many of the area's inhabitants. The Bhangra and Hindi music blaring out from the Indian shops and street stalls competed with raised voices speaking a myriad languages, the most common being Punjabi and English; and hunger-inducing smells emanated from the restaurants and takeaway joints – onion, ginger, garlic and chillies, mingling with the aroma of chicken and lamb curries, French fries and pizza. To top it all off, the glitter and sparkle of Indian gold and jewellery gave the whole place a magical, otherworldly feel. In the dusk and summer heat, it felt like a high street plucked from the heart of the Punjab itself and dropped into west London.

Zaq couldn't help but feel uplifted as he drove through it all – like a battery being recharged. No matter what had changed, this was where he belonged. It was where his heart felt at home.

He passed the place where the Hambrough Tavern used to stand, a landmark from the riots in 1981, and left the Broadway behind, heading on into Hayes, where Jags lived.

'You made it, then?' Jags said, when he opened the door. Zaq and Jags had been best friends since childhood and were still pretty much permanent fixtures in each other's lives. Jags was about the same height as Zaq, though slightly leaner in build. His dark hair was stylishly ruffled, his beard shaped and trimmed close. His brown eyes held their usual mischievous glint, though if ever there was trouble they'd turn hard as shards of iron. He was dressed in lightweight grey sweatpants and a Batman T-shirt. 'Fancy a drink?'

'I could murder a beer.'

In the L-shaped lounge-kitchen-diner, Jags' uncle Lucky was sitting on one of the sofas, looking unusually serious. He was a stout, generally jovial character, athletic in his younger days, his body now padded out by a fondness for drink and easy living. His hair was cropped short, more grey than black, and he was dressed in dark jeans and a dark polo shirt. His name was actually Lakhbir, but he'd been called Lucky all his life.

'*Kidaah*, Uncle?' Zaq said, and shook his hand. Even though Lucky was Jags' relative not Zaq's, Zaq called him Uncle too, partly out of respect for an elder, but mainly because he and Jags had grown up so closely that they were practically part of each other's families.

'*Teek uh*,' Lucky said, though he sounded anything but OK.

'Uncle, you want another beer?'

Lucky looked uncomfortable, the lines in his face suddenly deeper, more pronounced. 'Got anything stronger?'

Jags raised an eyebrow. 'Might have a bottle of Black Label somewhere.'

Lucky nodded, and Zaq sat down on the sofa opposite him. 'How's business?' he asked.

Lucky had left school at sixteen with no qualifications and got a job at a garage as a trainee mechanic. He'd been rubbish academically, but out in the real world he'd discovered he had a natural affinity for cars and engines. In those days, in Southall, everyone had had a car but no one had much money, so before long Lucky was fixing up his mates' cars outside of work. Soon he'd had so many people coming to him, he'd been able to convince his dad to lend him the money to set up his own garage. Now he owned three large garages, in Southall, Hounslow and Hayes, as well as a showroom for buying and selling cars.

'Business is good,' he said. 'All this austerity bullshit means people are holding on to their motors longer, which means they need to get them fixed more. Works well for me, if not everyone else. Saw your name in the papers a while back ... what's happening with that court case you were involved in?'

'Nothing right now. The guys are all banged up on remand until the actual trial. It'll be the end of the year some time, I think. There's a lot of them involved, so I suppose there's a pile of evidence to go through and get straight.'

Lucky nodded. 'You have to go court too?'

'Yeah, as a witness. Not that I know much. I just got caught up in things at the end.'

This wasn't strictly true, but Zaq was circumspect. There were only four people who knew the truth about what had really happened with the Brar brothers and Mahesh Dutta's gang. Two of them were in the house – and Jags' uncle wasn't one of them.

'Way it looks,' Lucky said, 'those fuckers are going down for a long time.'

Zaq shrugged. Jags came back carrying two bottles of beer in one hand and a tumbler of whisky in the other. He set the drinks down on the coffee table between the sofas. Lucky held up the tumbler. 'What's this?'

'Black Label, like you wanted,' Jags said.

'I mean, what sort of shot is it? Just bring the bottle – and get some ice too.'

Jags rolled his eyes at Zaq, who knew exactly what he was thinking, and headed back to the kitchen. The last thing he wanted was for his uncle to get drunk here and then have to take him home. Jags' aunt would not be impressed, and Lucky would deflect any blame on to his nephew. It wouldn't be the first time.

Jags returned with a half-full bottle of Black Label and a bowl of ice with a spoon. He put them close to his uncle, picked up his beer and sat down next to Zaq.

Lucky tripled the measure Jags had poured. 'Now that's what you call a proper shot.' He raised the tumbler in salute and knocked the whole lot back in one long swallow, exhaled a slow appreciative breath, and put the glass down. He refilled it to the same level. This time he added an ice cube and let the drink sit in front of him. Its presence seemed to have a calming effect on him.

'So, Uncle,' Jags said. 'What did you want to talk to me and Zaq about?'

Lucky picked up his drink and took a hefty swallow. He kept hold of the glass and breathed deeply before he spoke. 'I need your help.'

The way he said it, Zaq figured it had to be more than just some simple building or decorating project, which was what he usually roped them in for.

'OK . . . ' Jags said. 'What with?'

Lucky was clearly trying to work out what to say. 'Your auntie and me,' he began, 'we went to a wedding last week. You know Diggy?'

'Yeah, he runs your place in Hayes, don't he?'

Lucky nodded. 'Well, it was his youngest boy's wedding. Big do – he invited a load of us from work.'

Sounded to Zaq like the perfect excuse for a piss-up.

'So,' Lucky continued, 'I got drinking with some of the guys from the girl's side too, having a proper party and all that. Later on, we were still sitting around having a few shots, and they started talking about a card game . . . '

Uh-oh. As soon as Lucky mentioned a card game Zaq thought he knew where it was going. Jags' uncle might've been Lucky by name, but when it came to gambling he was nothing of the sort. He'd probably lost money and needed to borrow some to help cover whatever he owed and keep it quiet from his wife, who was well aware of his gambling problem. Either that, or he wanted their help with some sort of dubious scheme to make a bit of quick cash.

'A bunch of them,' Lucky went on, 'get together once a month for a poker night, at one of their houses – get some food in, drinks, you know, make a night of it. Their next game was the day after the wedding, and they invited me and a couple of the other guys along. I thought, why not? Go along, have a drink, something to eat, bit of a laugh, play some cards, no big deal.' He took another swig of his whisky. 'Well, it all started off friendly enough, but then I guess the more we drank and played, the more serious it got.'

'Serious how?' Jags asked, though Zaq was sure they both knew.

'We ended up playing for silly money.' Lucky didn't look happy; he must've lost a significant amount. He took another hit of whisky. 'But I was on a roll, I'm telling you, proper winning streak. End of the night, just a few of us left, we decided to have one last game. The stakes kept getting higher and higher. I had a fucking *great* hand – all four aces and a jack. It was a winning hand, I was sure of it.'

'So, what happened?'

'Ended up just two of us left, me and this guy Shergill, whose house it was. Everyone else had dropped out.'

'And . . . ?'

'I ran out of money.'

'What? You just folded and gave it all away?'

A strange expression passed over Lucky's face. He seemed a bit peaky, as though he wanted to be sick. 'No, I didn't,' he said, looking like someone who'd just discovered they'd shat their pants.

Zaq and Jags waited for him to tell them what he had done. He took another belt of whisky.

'You know your auntie's necklace . . . ?'

'Which neck—?' Jags started to say before it hit him. 'You mean the antique one, the family heirloom? With the emeralds and the other big stones and that?' They could tell by Lucky's pained look that he did. 'What the hell have you done? Auntie'll kill you if she finds out!' It wasn't just a figure of speech. OK, so she might not actually kill him, but there was every chance he'd end up needing hospital treatment.

'It was Monday night,' Lucky said, holding his hands out, palms up, gesturing like it wasn't his fault. 'She'd worn the necklace to the wedding, wanted to show it off. We don't keep it at home, not with all the fucking break-ins happening all the time, fuckers after all the Indian gold and jewellery *desi* families have. We keep it in a safety deposit box at the bank. I took it to work with me on Monday, so I could put it back during the day. Only things got bloody hectic and I didn't have time. Then it got too late. So I figured I'd just do it the next day. I had it with me when I went to the card game.'

'You didn't just bet it away, did you, Uncle?' Jags asked.

'I'm not that stupid,' Lucky growled. 'I just used it as a marker to cover me for the game. I needed five grand to stay in.'

'Five grand!'

'And another five to see him, so ten in all. The necklace is worth way more than that, so it easily covered the bet.'

'Then what happened?'

'He played his hand. Fucker only had a straight flush, king high.' Lucky must've seen the blank looks on Zaq and Jags' faces. 'A straight flush beats four of a kind.'

'Shit,' Jags said.

They were quiet for a moment.

'But you only put the necklace down as a marker,' Zaq said. 'So, all you got to do is give the guy the ten grand and get it back.'

Lucky's queasy expression transformed into a sour look. 'I tried that already.'

'And . . . ?'

He shook his head. 'Bastard said he'd changed his mind. Decided to keep the necklace.'

Zaq frowned. 'He can't do that, can he?'

'Well, he has. Told me it was up to him, as he won. Said I could keep the money. I told him the necklace is worth a lot more and he knows it. Probably shouldn't have said that. Anyway, I started to get mad and he fucking threw me out of his house.'

'So what do you want us to do?' Jags asked.

'I thought we could go and see him again, try and get him to give back the necklace for what I owe. I'll even throw in a couple of grand extra, as interest or whatever. I was hoping you'd come with me.'

Jags looked at Zaq. 'What d'you think?'

Zaq shrugged. 'Sure, why not? Might help if you don't lose your temper this time though, Uncle. Just try reasoning with him. Hopefully, he'll see sense and take the money.'

'OK. Shall we go tomorrow? I need to get it back as soon as possible.'

'I suppose we could go after I finish work,' Zaq said. 'I should be done by about five, so let's say six o'clock.'

'I'll pick you both up.' His mood lightening, Lucky lifted his glass only to find it empty. He grabbed the bottle, poured himself another finger of whisky, knocked it back and looked at them, concern tightening his features. 'Let's keep this just between us, right? Don't mention it to anyone, especially not your auntie, or your mum and dad.'

'Sure, no problem,' Zaq said. Jags agreed too.

'Thanks, boys,' Lucky said with a grin. He got to his feet. 'I better get home for dinner. See you tomorrow.'

'You sure you should drive after those whiskies, Uncle?' Jags said. 'I can call you a cab.'

'Aw, *jah purreh*,' Lucky said, waving him off. 'Those were nothing, just little pegs. I'll be home before they have any effect. You youngsters don't know what real drinking is.'

'I know what drink-driving is.'

'I've never been pulled over for that.'

'Maybe that's where all your luck went.'

'Cheeky bugger.'

Jags showed his uncle out then came back to the lounge. 'Why d'you say we'd go tomorrow? We're going out with the girls, ain't we?'

'Yeah, but we're meeting them at eight, right? I'll get home, shower and change, then we'll go with Lucky and sort his shit out. He can drop us off in Ealing straight after, in time to see the girls.'

'Why not do it Sunday?'

'Man, I'd rather just get it out of the way tomorrow and chill on Sunday.'

'All right. What d'you want to do now?'

'It's gone eight. I'm going to head home. The guys'll have got some food in, so I'll probably just eat, have a drink and go to bed.'

'We can always order something here.'

'I know, but I'd still have to drive back later, which'd be a drag. And I got to get up for work in the morning. Least if I go back I'll be able to have a couple of beers, and the guys'll do my head in so I won't stay up too late. Don't get me wrong, you do my head in too, it's just they'll do it a lot quicker. Besides, I'm seeing you tomorrow anyway ...'

'Yeah, yeah, OK. Go on, get the fuck out of my house.'

Zaq smiled. 'I love you too, mate.'

Chapter Two

Zaq followed the aroma of food to the communal lounge-kitchen at the rear of the house and stuck his head through the open doorway. All five of the guys he shared the place with were seated at the dining table. 'Leave some for me, you greedy sods.'

His housemates, who were all Sikh, looked around. Zaq was the only Muslim in the house, and even though he wasn't religious in any way it had caused some friction when he'd first moved in. It had been a bigger deal than the fact he'd just been released from prison. But over time they'd come to accept him as one of them and now, most of the time, the matter of religion never even came up.

'Where the fuck you been?' Bal said, round a mouthful of *naan*. 'Weren't sure if you were coming or you'd gone out.'

'Well, I'm here now. I'll just dump my stuff upstairs.'

'*Phudi da*, better hurry up then, innit.'

Zaq took the stairs two at a time. His was a double room at the front of the house that he paid extra to have to himself. After five years of sharing cells, he valued his privacy. The room was clean, tidy and basically furnished. A bed and nightstand on one side, a double wardrobe, drawers, clothes rail and a full-length mirror on the other. Over by the bay window was a chair with a pile of folded clothes, and a small IKEA desk with his laptop on it. On the floor near the desk were several sets of dumbbells, and a punchbag that he kept meaning to hang somewhere.

Downstairs again, he grabbed a plate and fork and dished himself some *seekh kebab*, *karahi* lamb, chilli *paneer* and butter chicken, along with *jeera* rice and a *tandoori naan* from the various containers laid out on the table. He and his housemates usually took turns to cook during the week, but Friday and Saturday nights they'd invariably opt for a takeaway and some booze. They'd all chip in some cash and order from their favourite Indian place, some of the guys not being at all adventurous about food, though on occasion they'd have a Thai or Chinese. The alcohol would be beer, whisky, Bacardi and vodka; no gin or any other more exotic liquors for these guys – they weren't exactly what anyone would call sophisticated drinkers. As usual, they'd ordered too much, so there was still plenty left. It wasn't as piping hot as Zaq liked, so he gave it a blast in the microwave. While it was heating up, he grabbed a beer from the fridge and poured it into a pint glass. The fact that he liked a drink was a major point in his favour as far as his housemates were concerned.

'*Kidaah?*' Manjit greeted him. The big Sikh builder was out of his work clothes and highly colour-co-ordinated in black Adidas tracksuit bottoms, a black T-shirt and a pristine black turban, all of which matched his thick black beard.

'I'm good,' Zaq said, sitting down at the end of the table. 'Bloody starving though.' He grabbed a piece of *seekh kebab* in a bit of *naan* and started to eat. It was a favourite of his: he'd been thinking about it since lunchtime. Damn, it tasted good. He finished chewing, swallowed and washed it down with a few gulps of cold beer. 'Ahhh,' he sighed, expelling some of the stress of the day. 'I got held up in traffic then had to go see Jags.'

'Left it any later, you'd have been cooking your own dinner.'

'Shut up, we always order too much.'

'Yeah, but we don't waste it, though. We keep going till it's all gone. Talking of which . . . ' Manjit reached over and spooned more rice and butter chicken on to his plate.

'Seconds?' Zaq asked.

'Thirds, mate. Still got some room left.'

After they'd eaten, they all sat around with full bellies, shooting the shit, taking the piss out of each other and gossiping. Zaq had another beer, knowing the others were waiting for their food to go down before starting on the spirits. They'd usually wait for either Manjit or Bal to crack open a bottle: Manjit because he was the biggest of the bunch and they kind of deferred to him because of that, and Bal because he was the loudest and meanest, and no one wanted to get on the wrong side of him. Zaq figured he must have a metabolism like a goddam furnace; he ate and drank whatever he wanted, in no small quantity, and it never seemed to affect him. He didn't even put on any weight. An inch or so shorter than Zaq, and broader, Bal was as solid as a lump of rock that had been chiselled to resemble a stocky Asian plumber.

It wasn't long before Bal got Lax to pass him the bottle of Chivas Regal. He broke the seal on the bottle and held it up, offering to pour shots for everyone else. They all knew better than to accept. Bal's measures were the complete opposite of what you'd get in a pub – three-quarters of a glass of whisky with a splash of Coke, instead of the other way round. And if he poured it for you, you *had* to drink it. Bal gave a shrug, poured himself a mega-shot, dropped in some ice and added so little Coke it hardly seemed worth bothering. '*Chak de phatte,*' he saluted, and took a drink.

Once Bal was sorted, it seemed to be a signal for the others. Lax grabbed the whisky and poured normal shots for himself and

Dips. Pali, the oldest of the housemates by several years, opted for vodka and got up to get some tonic water from the fridge.

'Zaq, OK if I use some of your lime?'

'Yeah, go ahead.' Zaq always kept some limes handy, to cook with and also to squeeze into his Bacardi and Coke. For now, though, he was happy to finish off his beer. 'You not having a shot?' he asked Manjit, who still had a beer too.

'Might have one in a bit, but I got work tomorrow and I want to hit the gym after. I'll have a proper drink tomorrow night.'

'Yeah, I got work too, then I'm out tomorrow night. I'll have a few then.'

None of the guys had cushy office jobs. They either worked shift patterns or had jobs where they needed to go in on a Saturday, which meant most of them had to be up for work the next morning, so they wouldn't drink too much tonight. All except Bal, who didn't give a shit what day it was and would happily put away a bottle of whisky any night he felt like it. Six or seven years ago it wouldn't have worried Zaq either. For one thing, he'd had a well-paying job that didn't require him to work weekends, and in any case he never used to think twice about having a few mid-week drinks and going in to work slightly hungover. It was all par for the course back then.

Now things were very different. Prison had that effect.

'Oi, who's doing the dishes?' Bal demanded, from the other end of the table.

With the dishwasher out of order, they took it in turns to wash up after they all ate together. If you cooked you were excused, and anyone cooking for themselves had to clean their own stuff. All eyes turned to Lax. The skinny twenty-three-year-old was treated by the others rather like an annoying younger brother.

'What?' he said. 'Ain't my turn. I did it last time.'

'No, you didn't,' Pali said. 'I did.'

'Yeah, that's right,' Manjit agreed. 'And it was me and then Zaq before that.'

'What about Dips?'

'Don't even go there,' Dips retorted. 'You know I took my turn, 'cause you slipped in a mug and plate from upstairs you should've washed yourself.'

That only left Bal. Lax looked at him. 'What?' Bal barked.

'Nothing.' Lax got up and started collecting the dishes.

Zaq didn't know why Lax was making such a big deal of it: the takeaway containers would all go in the bin, so all he had to do was wash their plates, glasses and cutlery – no pots and pans. He was a right lazy shit at times.

'Seeing as you're doing all that,' Bal said with a smirk, 'there's some plates and glasses next to my bed. You might as well run up and get them too.' Bal and Lax shared a room, as did Dips and Pali.

Lax grunted and took the pile of plates to the sink. Then he went off upstairs. Zaq and the others carried on drinking and chatting. Lax came back carrying a small stack of dirty dishes that couldn't all have been Bal's.

'You going to have a shot?' Bal asked when he saw Zaq had finished his beer.

'Yeah, *one*,' Zaq said. 'Manj?'

Manjit had finished his beer too. 'I'll have one of yours.'

Zaq took their pint glasses to the sink and deposited them there for Lax to wash.

'Thanks,' Lax said, his tone stripping the word of any gratitude at all.

Zaq got two tall glasses from the cupboard and returned to the table where he half-filled each with ice. He opened the Bacardi and poured two sensible but generous shots, topped them up with Coke, then grabbed two quarters of lime from the plate in front of Pali and squeezed one into each glass. Theirs being a classy joint, he used a clean knife to stir the drinks before passing one to Manjit. They clinked glasses then raised them to the others. 'Cheers.'

'Fucking girlie drinks,' Bal grumbled.

'It tastes good,' Zaq said. 'What's wrong with that? I want to enjoy it. I ain't trying to teach my liver a lesson.'

Bal just huffed. As far as he was concerned, if alcohol didn't scorch its way through you, you weren't doing it right.

Dishes done, Lax rejoined them. He'd finished his whisky while washing up so Dips poured him another and told him to stop being such a grumpy *bhen chaud*. They sat around, drinking and taking the piss, first out of Lax then out of each other, laughing and cursing in a mash-up of English and Punjabi. It would have been quite easy to stay and carry on, but Zaq was tired and had to be up early. He finished his drink and stood up.

'Where you going? Have another one,' Dips said.

'Nah, I got to get up for work.'

'So do we.'

'Yeah, but I got to drive all day, so I better not have any more.' Zaq washed his glass and left it on the dish rack to dry. 'See you guys tomorrow,' he said, and went up to bed.

Chapter Three

He was woken by his phone ringing, pulling him from the depths of sleep. He forced an eyelid open. It was still dark. What the hell time was it? He grabbed the phone. The time on the screen read 02.56. Who the fuck was calling him at that hour? He didn't recognise the caller's number. It had to be a mistake. He rejected the call and closed his eyes, hoping to fall straight back to sleep.

A few seconds passed ... and his phone rang again.

What the hell? The same number was calling again. He was sort of awake now anyway, so this time he answered it. 'Hello.' His voice was still thick with sleep.

'Is that Zaq?' an urgent male voice wanted to know. 'Tariq's brother?'

'Yeah,' he said, his tone making his annoyance clear. 'Who's that?'

'My name's Prit. I'm a mate of Tariq's.'

'What d'you want? You know what time it is?'

'Yeah, sorry. Look, it's Tariq – he's in hospital.'

Zaq was instantly wide awake. 'What's happened?'

'We got jumped by some guys. They really fucked him up.'

'Where are you? Which hospital?'

'Hillingdon.'

'Stay there. I'm on my way.'

Zaq rushed to the bathroom and splashed some cold water on his face to wake himself up. Then he threw on a pair of jeans, a T-shirt and a scuffed pair of Nike Air Max, grabbed his phone, wallet, keys and a tracksuit top, bounded downstairs and left the house.

Outside, everything was quiet. The stark white LED street-lights cast harsh shadows. Zaq pulled on his black Adidas tracksuit top as he strode out of the drive, past Bal's and Manjit's parked vans to his own recently bought car, a ten-year-old Volkswagen Golf. It needed work but the engine was fairly sound and it got him around, which was all that mattered. He could have bought something better with the money Jags had given him, which he had stashed in his room, but he didn't want to blow it all on a flash motor, or draw any attention to himself. He gunned the engine and took off towards the Broadway.

The streets were practically deserted and he was able to make his way unhindered, unlike daytime when he spent far too long sitting in traffic in this part of west London. As he approached the top of Lady Margaret Road, the light ahead changed to amber. His first instinct was to floor it and streak through the junction as it turned red, but then he remembered he'd had a few drinks earlier and braked instead. He was pretty sure he was OK to drive now, but he didn't want to risk getting pulled over by the cops. The lights seemed to take an age. Zaq went on amber.

Having spent nearly all his life in the area, he knew the roads well – where you could speed up, where to slow for cameras. He knew he could get there faster but forced himself to stick to the speed limit all the way. When he reached the hospital, he parked, got a ticket from the machine, locked the car and jogged to the entrance.

Almost every seat in the waiting area was taken, people of

a wide spectrum of colours, nationalities and ages, all waiting to be seen. The harsh clinical glare of the fluorescent lights desaturated their faces, making them look sick even if they were only there accompanying someone. The scent of antiseptic and disinfectant was only marginally stronger than that of body odour and sweat.

Zaq joined the end of the queue at the reception desk. Immediately in front of him were two men, both clearly having difficulty standing up straight, speaking what sounded like slurred Polish. One of them had a bloody nose and mouth, probably the result of a fall or a fight. Ahead of them was a young Asian couple with a crying infant. At the front of the queue was a middle-aged Somali man who seemed to be holding things up due to communication difficulties; his English was as threadbare as his crumpled brown suit, and the reception-ist was having a hard time getting the necessary information out of him.

Zaq had to chew his lip to stop himself swearing. This was a waste of time: he didn't need to be booked in for treatment. Looking around, he saw double doors at the far end of the wait-ing room that had to lead to the treatment area. He could see movement through the small window – a nurse about to come out – so he left the queue and made for the doors.

'Excuse me,' he said, 'I'm here to see my brother. He was brought in by ambulance a little while ago. His name's Tariq Khan.'

The dumpy blonde nurse gave him a harried look. 'OK, just a minute.' She called out the name of the next patient. When that person rose from a seat and started towards her, she turned back. 'What was the name again?'

'Tariq Khan.'

'Wait here. I'll try and find out where he is for you.'

He thanked her, and she escorted her patient through the doors to the treatment area.

'Are you Zaq?' a voice behind him said. He turned to see a young Asian guy with a heavily bruised face, white Steri-Strips dressing his cuts. He looked to be in his mid-twenties, shorter and slimmer than Zaq, in clothes that would've looked smart if they hadn't been so crumpled and dishevelled. He couldn't tell if the guy's hair was messed up or if it was meant to be that way. 'I'm Prit. I called you.'

He looked familiar. 'I know you . . . '

'I been mates with Tariq since high school.'

That was it. He should've known, but it'd been years since he'd seen any of his brother's friends. 'What the fuck happened?'

Prit swallowed and shook his head. He took a moment to compose himself but, just as he was about to speak, the nurse came back out.

'Tariq Khan's brother?' she asked Zaq. 'Come with me.'

Zaq turned to Prit. 'Stay here. I need to talk to you. Let me see Tariq and I'll come back out.'

He followed the nurse through the doors, past a couple of treatment rooms then on through a larger, more open space lined with bays that housed beds and racks of equipment. Every bay had a patient being treated or waiting to be seen. Zaq looked for Tariq but the nurse led him on to another set of doors, with a sign above that said RESUS ONLY. Zaq knew that wasn't good. 'What's going on?' he said.

'The doctors are still treating your brother,' she told him, sounding more sympathetic now, as she led him through the doors. 'If you take a seat here—' she opened a door marked RELATIVES ROOM and ushered him inside '—one of them will come and talk to you soon.'

'Can't I see him?'

'Best talk to the doctor first.'

She left him to wait. The room was about the size of a prison cell, only cleaner and more sparsely furnished: some chairs, a coffee table and a drink vending machine. Grey walls and a dark linoleum floor heightened the institutional feel. He found it difficult to sit still, worry making him fidget and move. He ought to be doing something, not sitting around like a lemon. If only there were a punchbag around, something to hit to relieve the stress.

After what was probably only a few minutes but seemed a lot longer, the door opened and a doctor and nurse entered, accompanied by two police officers. The room was suddenly crowded.

'What's going on?' Zaq demanded.

'Mr Khan? I'm one of the doctors looking after Tariq.' He took the seat next to Zaq. The nurse sat opposite but the cops remained standing. 'I'm sorry to have to tell you that your brother's sustained some serious injuries as the result of an assault.'

'What sort of injuries?'

'We still need to do some scans, but X-rays confirm he has a broken jaw, a broken nose, a fracture to the cheek and several broken ribs. He had a collapsed lung, but we've managed to stabilise it. He also has a broken wrist and a broken femur.'

Bloody hell. Zaq took it all in and tried to process it.

'We still have some concerns regarding any internal injuries, and haven't yet ruled out the possibility of head or neck trauma.'

Fear started to claw at Zaq. The mention of head trauma made him think of Rahul Dutta – only he'd died straight away, on impact, when his head hit the pavement. Tariq was still alive and breathing ... at least for now.

'The fact that he hasn't woken up since he was brought in is a worry,' the doctor was continuing, 'so we've put him into an induced coma for the time being, to be on the safe side, until we can rule out any further complications.'

'Can I see him?'

The doctor stood up. 'Yes, I'll take you through. Be prepared, though – with the extent of his injuries, he looks in a bad way. But we're doing everything we can for him.'

One of the cops held the door open as everyone filed out of the room. The doctor led them to a bay full of medical staff buzzing around a motionless figure on the bed.

If the doctor hadn't said he was taking him to see his brother, Zaq doubted he would have recognised Tariq. His face, where it wasn't obscured by breathing apparatus, neck brace and head supports, was puffed up like a balloon, crusted with dried blood and covered in bruises. Both his eyes were swollen shut. A multitude of tubes and wires snaked over his body, connected to an array of monitoring equipment.

'Fuck . . .' Zaq felt himself start to well up and blinked rapidly.

'He's stable at the moment,' the doctor said. 'We're just about to take him for a CT scan. As I said, our main concern's with any internal injuries or head trauma. Once we've ruled those out, we'll move him up to the Intensive Treatment Unit. Then we'll consider how bad the break to his wrist is and see if it requires surgery or just a cast. I'm afraid he's definitely going to need surgery for his femur, probably later today.'

This was more than just some random fight. It seemed as though someone had wanted to kill him.

'Can I stay here?' Zaq said.

'Yes, of course. The CT shouldn't take long, and they'll bring him back here until a bed's available upstairs.'

'Thanks.'

The doctor gave him an encouraging smile and went to talk to his colleagues. Zaq looked down at his bruised and beaten brother. Fucking hell. He knew better than anyone what a pain in the arse Tariq could be at times, but nothing warranted *this*.

Recalling the injuries the doctor had reeled off to him, Zaq felt sure that whoever had inflicted this on his brother had wanted to cause him serious fucking harm, probably even kill him. But why?

The squawk of a radio made him look over his shoulder. The two policemen who'd been in the relatives' room were standing just outside the treatment bay, one talking quietly into the radio clipped to his shoulder. Zaq caught the other one's eye. 'You know what happened?'

The policeman came over, hands tucked into the top of his equipment-laden stab vest. 'No details yet, I'm afraid,' he said. 'We were called to a fight near a pub in Uxbridge. When we got there we found your brother unconscious, his friend with him. They'd both been attacked but your brother got the worst of it. The attackers had made off.'

'Anyone see anything?'

'The only witness at the scene was your brother's friend. He didn't see much as he was attacked as well. Could have had something to do with an altercation inside the pub earlier but we don't know at this stage. Other officers are there talking to people, trying to find anyone who might've seen something, and we'll be checking CCTV in the area, see if we can get anything from that. You don't happen to know of anyone who might have done this, do you?'

'No.' But that wasn't entirely true, was it?

'We were hoping to talk to your brother, see if he could tell us anything, but he's in a pretty bad way. It'll have to wait till he's awake.' The policeman took out a card, jotted a reference number on it and handed it to Zaq. 'You can contact the incident room directly, if you need to get in touch with us or have any information. Just give the reference number at the top there.' He gave Zaq a sympathetic half-smile. 'I hope he gets better soon.'

'Thanks,' Zaq said.

The two cops went and spoke to the doctor briefly, then left.

There was a single blue plastic chair in the bay. Zaq pulled it next to the bed and sat down, watching the shallow rise and fall of his brother's breathing. He reached out and placed a hand on Tariq's arm. It was the most physical contact he'd had with his brother since he'd got out of prison. They didn't even shake hands any more.

A confusion of emotions swept through him: shock, grief, helplessness, even fear. But one slowly overrode them all – anger. It bloomed in the pit of his stomach, then spread to rage within him like a forest fire in a hot, dry summer. It was only when he realised he was grinding his teeth and gripping Tariq's arm too tightly that he let go, took several deep breaths and managed to smother the blaze for the time being.

Shit! He'd have to tell his parents what had happened. They'd be absolutely distraught. Would they blame him? Think it was somehow his fault? Why not? Hadn't he already wondered the same thing himself? He decided to put it off, at least for a little while. He'd call them later. Better to let them sleep and break it to them at a more reasonable hour. Unless Tariq's condition deteriorated ...

A porter came into the bay, along with a couple of nurses and the doctor he'd spoken to earlier. 'We're just going to take Tariq for a CT scan,' the doctor told him. 'It won't take long. You can wait here, or go get a coffee if you like.'

Zaq remembered he'd told Prit to wait for him. 'I might go out and get some air,' he said. 'Will I be able to get back in here?'

'Just buzz and give Tariq's name. Say he's in Resus. They'll let you in.'

Zaq watched as they wheeled Tariq away on the gurney. Then he followed the signs back to Reception and the exit.

He let himself out through the double doors and scanned the waiting area.

Prit saw him at once and stood up 'How is he?'

'Not good,' Zaq said. 'Let's go outside and talk.'

Chapter Four

It was the middle of summer and a warm night. Zaq led Prit away from the smokers and people on their phones to get some privacy. 'What the fuck happened?'

'I don't know, man. We'd just left the pub, and a bunch of guys jumped us.'

'What guys?'

'I don't know ... but they might've been the same fuckers that started on T in the pub earlier. They were looking for trouble.'

'What d'you mean, they started on him earlier?'

'I told it all to the cops.'

'Well, now you can tell me.'

'We was out for a quiet drink at the Slug and Lettuce, in Uxbridge, just hanging out, chatting, minding our own business, when this guy comes over.'

'You know him?'

Prit shook his head. 'Never seen him before.'

'Then what?'

'He asked if we were DJs.'

Tariq and a couple of his mates had a DJ business on the side, playing weddings, birthdays and clubs at weekends. His brother had always been into music but Zaq didn't know much about the DJ business, as it had all taken off while he was in prison.

'We said yeah, we were,' Prit continued. 'Thought maybe he

was interested in booking us. But then he asked if we played a wedding in Slough recently.'

'Did you?'

'We play weddings all over the place, man – Southall, Hounslow, Slough, Uxbridge, wherever. Then he asked about this one particular wedding, that T and Bongo DJ'd.'

Zaq raised an eyebrow. 'Bongo?'

Prit shrugged. 'Yeah, his real name's Kushwant Bangar. He used to have *tabla* lessons after school, had to lug his *tablas* with him. The other kids said his family were so hard up they couldn't afford phones, used the bongos to communicate with each other. Started calling him Kushy Bongo. Bongo stuck.'

'OK, then what happened?'

'T said, yeah, he played the wedding, and the guy just looked at him, nodded and went back to his table.'

'He on his own?'

'No, he was sat with a group of other guys.'

'You recognise any of them?'

Prit shook his head.

'The guy that came over to you – what did he look like?'

Prit thought about it. 'He was big – not tall, pumped up though like he did a lot of weights. Same age as me and T, I'd say. His hair was all kind of styled up on his head—' he demonstrated with his hands '—black but with like copper highlights or something. Oh, and one of his front teeth was gold.'

It was a good description. 'You catch his name?'

'No.'

'So he went back to his table – then what?'

'We thought it was a bit weird but just carried on drinking and forgot about it, until later when T went to the bar to get a round in, and it all kicked off. I was on my phone so didn't see how it started, but I heard arguing and swearing, and next thing

T was surrounded by that guy and his mates. I went over and one of them grabbed me. We was about to get into it when security came over and told that lot to fuck off. Apparently they'd seen them knock the drinks out of T's hands on purpose, trying to start something.'

'Did they leave?'

'Yeah. Gave us cut eyes as they went, but they left.'

'What you guys do?'

'T was vexed but we didn't think it'd be a good idea to leave right after those wankers, so we stayed and got another round.' Prit stopped, looking off into the distance somewhere. Zaq didn't say anything, letting him continue in his own time. 'We left at closing time, to go get something to eat then cab it home. We were just walking along. Fuckers must've been waiting for us. They came at us out of nowhere, bundled us behind some shops and went to work on us.

'One of them got me round the neck while another smacked me in the stomach. I couldn't breathe. Then they threw me down and started kicking me. Tariq was down too. I saw the rest of them laying into him.' Prit swallowed a lump in his throat. 'They were kicking and stamping on him, fucking bad ...'

Zaq's hands balled into fists as he listened, rage building like thunderclouds before a storm. He forced himself to breathe deeply, exhaling slowly, releasing as much of the anger as he could. There was no point getting mad now. Better to lock it away and save it for when it mattered.

'I must've blacked out or something,' Prit continued. 'Next thing I knew, they'd gone. T was just lying there, not moving. I managed to get over to him but he was totally fucking out of it, blood everywhere. I thought he was dead. Then I saw he was breathing. I called 999 and told them to send an ambulance. Cops turned up too.'

They were silent for a moment. 'Thanks for staying with him,' Zaq said finally, 'and for coming here and calling me. How d'you get my number?'

'I already had it. Tariq gave it to me a few months back, when there was some trouble. He said some guys were after you and maybe him too. Told me if anything happened to him, to call you straight away.' Prit looked at him, frowning. 'You don't think it's the same guys, do you?'

'I don't know,' Zaq said. 'I thought that was all taken care of . . . only now I ain't so sure. But I'm going to find out.' All he had to go on so far, though, was the wedding and the arsehole with the gold tooth. 'This wedding the guy was on about in the pub – you know where, or whose it was?'

'No. Like I said, I didn't work that one. We should have a booking form for it somewhere, though. Bongo would probably remember.'

'You got his number?' Prit nodded. 'Let me have it. I'll call him later.'

Prit took out his phone and read off Bongo's number, which Zaq saved to his own phone. 'Thanks, Prit. I better go back in and check on Tariq, see what the doctors are saying. How you getting home?'

'Cab.'

Zaq stuck out his hand. 'Thanks again, man, for looking out for him.'

They shook hands. 'I just hope he's going to be OK,' Prit said.

'You and me both.'

Chapter Five

Zaq got back to Resus as Tariq was being brought back from having his CT scan. The porter manoeuvred the bed into place in the treatment bay. The doctors and nurses moved quickly and purposefully, doing what they needed to do, the atmosphere one of quiet determination.

Zaq approached the doctor he'd spoken to earlier. 'What did the scan show?'

'We're waiting for a consultant to take a look and give us a verdict, then we'll be able to decide what to do next. For now, we'll keep an eye on Tariq here until there's a bed in the Intensive Treatment Unit, then we'll move him up. Sorry not to have any more for you just yet.'

'Can I still stay with him?'

'Of course. You can go up with him too, when he's moved.'

'Thanks.'

Zaq sat down in the chair beside the bed. The medical staff were now busy with other patients, apart from a nurse who was checking Tariq as he lay there, still as a paving slab. The warm brown of his skin contrasted with the cold white of the bandages and dressings, punctuated here and there by dark red where blood had seeped through.

Now the initial shock of seeing his brother's battered body

had passed, Zaq took a long, hard look at him. *Who the fuck's done this to you? And why?*

The answer that pushed its way to the front of Zaq's mind, now as earlier, was that it might be connected to *him*. Tariq had been targeted before, simply for being his brother. Was this attack related to that? Had Mahesh Dutta, sitting in his prison cell, finally figured out who might've put him there and sent people to get payback? Or was it completely unrelated, a problem Tariq had with someone else? Zaq didn't know. He needed to find out though, one way or another. But then what? The answer was simple – track down whoever was responsible and deal with them, any way he had to, so it didn't happen again.

He still had to tell his parents what had happened. It wasn't something he was looking forward to. His mum would fly into hysterics, weeping and wailing all over the gaff. His dad would be the complete opposite, bottling everything up, stoic as a brick wall. Zaq was sure he'd wind up bearing some of the blame, even if it was nothing to do with him. He had to find out who was behind the attack, to be sure if it was because of him or not. If it had nothing to do with him, at least his conscience would be clear and he could tell his parents it wasn't related to him. Whatever the reason, he'd give the fucking scumbags that did it a taste of their own medicine, see how they fucking liked it.

That was for later, though. Right now, he had to think of the best way to break the news to his mum and dad. He could picture the look he'd get from his parents when they got here: the combination of pain and disappointment they could never really hide whenever they looked at him, their ex-con son who'd ruined his own life, and by extension theirs, through a split-second reaction that had resulted in a death. And now, when they saw what had happened to Tariq, that pain and disappointment would be amplified even more.

They'd feel that as the elder brother he should've been looking out for Tariq, keeping him out of trouble, ensuring he didn't make the same mistakes Zaq had. But how was he meant to do that when he and Tariq hardly saw each other? It wouldn't matter to them that he still had his own life to lead and try to do something with. Just thinking about it made him feel tense, the way he usually did these days when dealing with his family. It was why he didn't live at home.

He'd just have to grit his teeth and accept whatever criticisms they levelled at him. What else could he do – for now?

It was still too early to ring them, though he knew what they'd say if he didn't – that no matter what time it was, he should've called straight away.

Zaq decided to fudge it. He took out his phone, brought up his dad's mobile number on screen and pressed the button. He listened carefully and, just as he heard the connection made but before it started to ring, he abruptly ended the call. He knew that if you were quick enough the phone at the other end wouldn't ring, but the call would still show up as missed. He waited a couple of minutes then repeated the procedure, and did it a few more times. Then he sent a text message saying to call him urgently. When his dad eventually woke up and checked his phone, it would look as though Zaq had tried calling him repeatedly and, when no one had answered, had given up and sent a text. It would give his parents a few more hours of sleep and himself some more time to sit with his brother and think.

A short time later the doctor came to talk to Zaq again.

'We've had the results of your brother's CT scan. Fortunately his neck and spine are OK, so we can remove the neck brace. However, we're quite concerned about some bleeding and swelling around his brain. It's nothing to worry about necessarily, but we'll need to keep him in for a few days, to monitor his situation and keep an eye on him. That way, if anything should happen, we'll be able to assess him straight away and treat him accordingly.'

'OK,' Zaq said. What else could he say?

'A bed's opened up in the ITU, so we're going to move him to the unit as soon as a porter arrives. You can go up and stay with him if you like.'

Zaq was glad when the neck brace and head supports were removed. Although he still looked pretty terrible, Tariq wouldn't look quite as bad when his mum and dad eventually arrived and saw him.

It took twenty minutes for the porter to show up. The nurses packed the equipment that needed to go with Tariq on to the bed with him, then the porter released the brake and wheeled him out of Resus. Zaq followed, carrying a clear plastic bag containing Tariq's wallet, keys and mobile phone. A nurse came with them. They took a lift to the first floor. In the Intensive Treatment Unit, the lights were turned down and the atmosphere hushed. A new group of nurses, working quickly and quietly, slid Tariq into a freshly made-up bed and hooked him back up to various monitors and screens. Once they had him sorted and the handover was complete, they dispersed to check on other patients.

'He'll be well looked after,' the nurse who'd come up from Resus told Zaq. 'And hopefully he'll be right as rain in no time.' She left with the porter, leaving Zaq alone with his brother. He took off his jacket and sat down. The chair here was bigger and heavier than the one downstairs, and padded ... a little more comfortable ...

*

He came awake with a start and for a split second didn't know where he was. Then he remembered. He must have dozed off for a bit. His phone vibrating in his pocket was what had woken him. It was his dad. The time was almost seven a.m. Zaq swallowed, took a breath, and answered. 'Hey, Dad.'

'What's the matter?' his father said, without preamble. His English was very good, with just the hint of an accent. 'You've been calling. I just saw your message. What is it?' He knew something was up. Zaq didn't ring him all that often, and especially not late at night.

Zaq took another breath. 'It's Tariq.'

'What about him?'

'He was beaten up last night. He's in the hospital.'

'What? Where? Which hospital?'

'Hillingdon. I'm here with him now.'

'What happened?'

'He was attacked by some guys, in Uxbridge. That's all I know.' He heard his dad swear in Punjabi. 'Dad ... we're up in the Intensive Treatment Unit.' There was silence at the other end of the phone. His dad understood that meant it was serious. 'Just give Tariq's name when you get here and they'll let you in.'

'We'll be there as quickly as we can.'

Chapter Six

Zaq got some coffee from a machine. It wasn't very good but he drank it anyway, to wake himself up. He found he couldn't sit still, so he paced around instead. He was nervous about his dad's arrival and how he'd react when he learnt the extent of Tariq's injuries. A nurse came in to check on Tariq and made notes on a chart at the end of his bed. A doctor would be around in a while, she said, to assess him more fully.

Just under an hour later Zaq heard his dad's voice, asking for Tariq Khan, then he and Zaq's mum came hurrying in, concern etched on both their faces. It was evident from their slightly rumpled appearance that they'd rushed to leave the house.

'Hi, *mera moondah!*' his mother gasped, her hands flying to her mouth as tears filled her eyes and began to roll down her cheeks. She started to shake her head, as if hoping to deny the reality of what was in front of her.

His dad's reaction was completely the opposite, still and silent, whatever he was feeling smothered and internalised. The concern he'd worn as he entered the room was replaced by an inscrutable mask behind which his emotions were hidden. Only his eyes gave anything away. They were focused on Tariq in a hard, flat stare, devoid of their usual warmth and good humour, sharpened instead by anger and a father's pain.

Zaq's mum placed her hand on Tariq's, tears dripping from her face on to the blanket.

'What happened?' his dad asked, in a choked voice.

'He was out in Uxbridge with a friend. Some guys attacked them and beat them up.'

'Why?'

Zaq shrugged. 'I don't know.'

'Do they know who it was?'

'No.'

'Were you there too?'

'No, I was at home in bed.'

'How did you find out about it?'

'Tariq's friend, the one who was with him, phoned me. I came straight here.'

'Where is this friend?'

'He went home.' His dad glanced at Tariq then back at Zaq, with a frown. 'He wasn't hurt that bad. They let him go.'

'Then why is Tariq here like this?' he said, emotion amplifying his voice.

'I don't know,' was all Zaq could say.

'What about the police? Did they arrest anybody?'

'No. Whoever did it had run off before they got there.'

His dad swore violently in Punjabi, then switched back to English. 'Who the fuck, bastards, would do this?' His eyes narrowed. 'Is this anything to do with you?'

'No, course not,' Zaq said, though he'd wondered the same thing himself.

'Nothing to do with that court case you're involved in?'

'If it was anything to do with that, it'd be me lying there, not Tariq.' That wasn't entirely true – his brother had been targeted before because of him, only that time Zaq had managed to foil the attack. His parents knew nothing about that, though.

'What have the doctors said?'

Zaq told him about Tariq's injuries and heard his mum's sharp intake of breath.

'When will he wake up?'

'They're not sure. They want to make sure everything's OK before they bring him round.'

'*Hi, hi, hi,*' his mum intoned. She was rocking back and forth, probably reciting a silent prayer.

'Where's the doctor?' his dad demanded.

'Doing his rounds or something. The nurse said he'd be here in a while.'

Needing to do something, his dad dragged the heavy chair closer to the bed and told Zaq's mum to sit down.

'Let me go and see if I can get another chair,' Zaq said, and went to the nurses' station to ask. A nurse helped him find one. He thanked her and carried it back to the room, placing the chair beside the bed next to his mum and gesturing for his dad to sit.

For a while they all sat and stood in silence, each contemplating Tariq's state. After a few minutes, Zaq's dad looked up and caught Zaq trying to stifle a yawn.

'What time did you get here?'

'About three.'

'Have you been awake since then?'

'Yeah.' Zaq checked the time on his phone. 'Shit, I'm supposed to be at work in a while. I'll have to go and tell them I need the day off. I can't drive all day if I haven't slept.'

'When you've done that, go home and get some sleep. We're here now. We'll stay with Tariq.'

'I'll come back later,' Zaq said. 'I'll call first, see if you need me to bring anything.'

His dad nodded. '*Haah.*'

Zaq put a hand on his mum's shoulder. 'See you later, Mum.'

She looked up at him and gave a brief nod, light from the window glistening off the tracks of her tears. Then she turned back to Tariq.

His dad got up and followed Zaq into the corridor. 'Zaq, *ter ek* minute,' he said. He put a hand on Zaq's back and urged him along the corridor. 'I know you and your friends might be able to find out something about this,' he said in a low voice. 'Who did it and why.' Zaq started to say something but his dad held up a hand to silence him. 'You should find out if you can. Find out who did this to your brother, and then go to the police and tell them. Don't do anything stupid and get into trouble yourself.'

'I won't. *If* I find anything out, I'll do as you say and go to the police.'

His dad looked at him a moment longer, then nodded, turned and went back to Tariq's room.

And Zaq uncrossed his fingers.

Chapter Seven

It was a little after eight a.m. when Zaq got home, and both Manjit and Bal's vans were gone, which meant they'd already left for work, so Zaq was able to pull into the driveway. He let himself in, heard sounds from the kitchen but ignored them, and went charging up the stairs to get the van keys from his room. He came back down again and left the house, crossed the driveway and went right, to the cul-de-sac where he'd parked the van overnight. He'd got back from Jags' too late to bother dropping it off at the yard, thinking he'd just drive it in this morning instead, which was what he did.

Five minutes later he turned into the service road behind Brar Building Supplies. The other guys were still waiting by the shutter beside the gates, which meant he'd beaten Sid, the yard manager, in. He received nods and waves as he went past and parked the battered flatbed van further up the road. He got out and joined the group outside the shutter.

'*Kidaah?*' Ram, one of the yard workers, greeted him. 'You look a bit rough.'

'Thanks,' Zaq said. 'I didn't really sleep last night. Listen, I'm going to have to take today off, so you'll probably have to take the deliveries out.'

'Fine by me,' Ram said, grinning. He was the back-up driver, not because he was any good at driving but simply because he had a licence. He'd been one of the regular drivers before Zaq started working there. The problem was, he had no sense of direction and couldn't read a map for shit, so Zaq had replaced him; it had caused some friction at first but things had soon blown over. The company being too cheap to fit sat nav in the vehicles, drivers had to either look up where their drops were in tattered copies of the *A–Z* or rely on their own phones. It wasn't an issue for Zaq, who knew his way around and was good with maps, but it was different for Ram. He just couldn't process how a map related to the world around him. He even had trouble following directions on his phone. It didn't help that he used most of his data allowance watching dodgy videos so that half the time he couldn't even use his phone, and was too tight to pay for a higher data plan. His preferred method of navigation was to stop and ask people for directions, which meant he regularly got lost and always took ages to get to his drops.

The sound of Hindi music announced Sid's arrival before his Mercedes turned into the service road. The windows were down and the bright morning sun shone off the dark red paintwork, the colour of congealing blood.

'I just have to sort it out with that idiot,' Zaq said.

Sid cruised regally past them and parked at the end of the road, beside the garages that belonged to the flats opposite, on the other side of a small green. He put his windows up, opened the door and levered himself out of the car. He grabbed his stuff – a packed lunch and a newspaper – locked the vehicle, and sauntered towards them, a large bunch of keys dangling from his other hand. He had the chunky build of a wrestler gone to seed, with a bowling-ball belly and a thick black moustache that might have been admired in the '70s but not so much now. '*Moondehaw*,' he greeted them, even though none of the guys waiting were kids, and received grumbled responses. 'Hari, *eh le*. Shutter *kohl de*.' He threw the keys to Hari as usual, getting him to open up.

Hari, the youngest of the workers, caught the keys and began taking off the six heavy-duty padlocks that secured the shutter. His hands were full when he got the last one off, so Mohinder squatted down and threw the shutter up with a clatter. Hari dropped the padlocks into a plastic box just inside the entrance. Zaq followed him and the others inside, across the saw room, heavy with the scent of timber and sawdust, and through the thick plastic partition into the warehouse. While Hari sloped off to unlock the yard gates – something else Sid got him to do – most of the others headed for the kitchen to make themselves something approximating tea.

Zaq followed Sid into the manager's office and waited as he went around his desk and eased himself into his seat. When he saw Zaq standing in the doorway, he said, 'You getting back late yesterday,' mangling the language with his thick Indian accent. 'Hurry and load van to take out for today.'

'You'll have to get Ram to do it. I need to take the day off.'

'*Kee?*' Sid's tone was one of disbelief.

'I need the day off,' Zaq repeated. 'My brother got beaten up last night. He's in the hospital – *Intensive Care*.' Zaq emphasised the last bit so even Sid would understand it was serious. 'I've been there all night, came straight here to let you know. I need to go home and get some sleep before I head back there.'

Zaq read a combination of annoyance and confusion in Sid's frown. Annoyance, because if he allowed Zaq the day off he'd have to let Ram take the deliveries out, and confusion, because, much as he might not like it, under the circumstances he probably should give Zaq the time off. In the end, he shirked responsibility by saying, 'Brar *sahib nu puchi*.'

'But he doesn't get in till ten.'

'Then you load fucking van while you wait,' Sid told him, his expression changing to a satisfied grin. Morning deliveries were normally loaded the evening before, so they could go out first thing in the morning, and the drivers could get back and take out more orders in the afternoon. But because Zaq hadn't made it back in time yesterday, his deliveries for this morning had yet to be loaded.

Tosser, Zaq thought. It might work to his advantage though. If he got the van loaded and made sure Ram was ready to go out on the road before Mr Brar turned up, maybe he'd have a better chance of getting the day off. Come to think of it, if he was going to have to ask Mr Brar, he might well see if he could get more than just today off. After all, family was very important in the Asian community – and especially to Mr Brar, who had his own worries in that regard at the moment – so there was a chance he might be a little more understanding. There was also that business from a few months ago, when Zaq had been questioned by the police in relation to Mr Brar's sons, who were now banged up in Wormwood Scrubs. He'd done his best to defend them both – at least, that was how it would've appeared – and it had certainly helped put him in Mr Brar's good books. Maybe that would work in his favour now.

'Are the orders ready?' he asked Sid.

'*Haah, haah.* Warehouse *wich.*'

'All right, give me the loading sheets and I'll get them on the van.'

Sid handed him a clipboard with the paperwork and Zaq left the office.

'*Kidaah?*' said Hari, who had opened the gates and was now taking the keys back to Sid.

'All right,' Zaq greeted him.

'See you later,' called Shits. He gunned the engine of his already loaded van and took off through the gates.

Zaq waved away the dust left in Shits' wake and went to get his own van. He reversed back into the yard and jumped out to drop the side panel of the flatbed, to make it easier to load. Then he got a pallet truck and heaved out the pallets with the orders on them. He checked the addresses on the paperwork and worked out the best order to deliver them in. After that, he went and got Ram to help him load up.

'Am I going out, then, or not?' Ram wanted to know.

'Sid's being a tit, as usual,' Zaq told him. 'Says I have to ask Mr Brar about taking the day off. But we get this lot all loaded and ready to go, I'll tell him he's wasting time just having it sitting here and that he might as well send you out now.'

Ram liked the sound of that and it encouraged him to put his back into it. Once all the stuff was loaded, and before he went to let Sid know, Zaq got out the map book and did his best to explain to Ram the route he'd planned. Ram was a decent enough bloke. He knew his way around Southall and maybe a little of the surrounding area, and getting to Northolt, Hayes, Ruislip and places like that he could manage by following road signs. But anything other than that, like finding an actual address, was what he had a problem with. Zaq showed him the roads to take and mentioned various landmarks to look out for, but, although Ram was nodding as though he understood, the look in his eyes was completely vacant.

Zaq shook his head and put the map book back in the van. 'Wait here,' he said. 'I'll go and see what Sid says.' He found the manager drinking tea and reading the newspaper. 'Van's all loaded,' Zaq said. 'What now?'

Sid looked at him over the top of the paper. 'You take deliveries.'

'I already told you, I been up all night at the hospital. I can't drive. I need to take the day off.'

Sid put the paper down on the desk. 'You here, awake.'

'I came in *because* I was still awake, but I need to go home and sleep.'

'You must ask Brar *sahib*.'

'I know, and I will. What about the deliveries, though? They're all loaded and ready to go. Don't think Mr Brar'll be too happy if he comes in and sees them just sitting there in the yard.'

'*Au, thu lehja phir.*'

'Not me. I'm waiting here to talk to Mr Brar, remember? Just like *you* said.' He could see Sid was getting wound up. 'Ram's ready to go, though. He can take them.'

They both knew the deliveries would take longer if Ram was driving, but it would be better than Mr Brar turning up to find them just sitting there.

'*Chunga, bhen chaud.* Ram can take. You tell him, go. Then you come see me. I have job for you.'

'Not another blow job from your missus, is it?' Zaq said as he left.

'FUCK OFF!' Sid yelled after him. That was one English phrase he had no trouble pronouncing. Whatever he had lined up for Zaq, it wouldn't be anything good, that was for sure.

Outside, Ram was still waiting by the van. 'Here,' Zaq said, handing him the keys, along with the clipboard of delivery sheets. 'Off you go.'

'Wicked.' Ram took them, and jumped in behind the wheel. The engine roared to life and the van started moving even before Ram had his seatbelt fully on. 'See you later,' he shouted, and sped off through the open gates.

'Not if I can help it,' Zaq muttered.

Chapter Eight

Inside the warehouse, six large pallets were lined up against the wall, three stacked with bags of cement, three with bags of plaster. When bags were required for an order, whoever was getting them would invariably grab one from the highest pile – it was easier to haul a bag off the top than to squat down and lift it. That meant the lower bags were always left till last. All six pallets were now down to about waist height. With a new delivery due, there was no room for four new pallets. So Zaq had to consolidate all the bags down to one pallet for the cement and one for the plaster, and he had to do it by hand. It was a proper bit of labouring.

He wasn't about to bust a gut doing it, though. He had about an hour and a half until Mr Brar arrived, so he strung it out, going for a drink of water, resting and taking a couple of toilet breaks, in between hefting the bags from one pallet to another.

Zaq had moved all of the cement and most of the plaster when he saw Mr Brar coming through the warehouse, calling out a greeting to Sid as he made his way to the stairs that led up to his office. The owner of Brar Building Supplies was a big man, like a bodybuilder who'd given up competing a long time ago but still maintained his bulk. His clothes always seemed a touch too tight, stretched over his broad frame, and though he had to be pushing sixty he moved with a strength and purpose that belied his age. His brow furrowed into a frown when he saw Zaq.

'What are you doing here? Why aren't you out with the deliveries?'

'Ram's taken them.'

'*Kyoh?*'

'I was going to come and see you about that when I finished doing this.' Zaq waved a hand at the pallets. 'My brother was beaten up last night. He's in Intensive Care. The doctors have put him into a coma and don't know if he'll be OK. I was at the hospital all night then came straight here, to see about getting some time off. Sid said I had to ask you.'

There was no change in Mr Brar's expression, no way of knowing what he was thinking as he absorbed what Zaq had told him. Finally, he nodded a fraction. 'How many days you want off?'

Zaq wasn't sure. 'Three or four,' he ventured. 'If he comes round sooner and he's all right, maybe less.'

Mr Brar considered, then said, 'OK. Finish this and then you can go. Tell Sid when you leave.'

'I will. Thanks.'

'And Zaqir . . .' Mr Brar said, using Zaq's given name, 'I hope your brother is better soon.'

Fifteen minutes later Zaq, slapping cement and plaster dust off himself and leaving faint clouds in his wake, made his way to the warehouse office where Sid, pen in hand, was poring over the racing pages of the newspaper. 'Hard at it, I see,' Zaq said.

Sid looked up. '*Kee?*'

'Nothing. I've sorted all that shit out. The empty pallets are stood up out of the way, against the wall. Right, I'm off.'

Sid screwed his face up like he'd just smelt a fart. 'Where you going?'

'Home, to sleep.'

'Heh? *Bhen chaud*, sleep? I not say you can go.'

'You said to ask Mr Brar. He said it was OK. Gave me a few more days off, too.'

'Few days?' Sid spluttered. 'Few days? Who taking fucking deliveries next week?'

'Ram, I guess. Unless you want to do them?'

'*Meh?*' Sid said, pointing to himself, eyes wide in disbelief as if Zaq had just told him to stick the pen in his hand up his arse.

Zaq shrugged. 'Send whoever you want. You're the manager, so manage.'

Sid cursed him at length in Punjabi.

'Yeah, whatever. You got a problem with it, talk to Mr Brar.' And, with Sid still ranting behind him, Zaq left the office to go home and sleep.

Chapter Nine

His alarm woke him several hours later. He'd set it to wake him at four o'clock so he wouldn't sleep the whole day, but it felt as if no time at all had passed since he'd put his head down. And now the alarm – a piece of classical music, Satie's *Gymnopédie* No.2 – was pulling him out of sleep.

He reached for his phone to turn off the alarm, and saw he had several missed calls from Jags, and a couple from his dad. Shit. He rang his dad back.

'Where are you?' his dad asked. 'What are you doing?'

'Sorry, I've been asleep. What's happened? How's Tariq?'

'He's the same. They operated on his leg, put some metal plates in but other than that, there's been no change. Are you coming back here?'

'Yeah, just let me get showered and dressed and I'll head straight over. Have you spoken to a doctor?'

'Yes. He said they will wait for a day or two and then do another scan. Until then, they will just keep monitoring him. He didn't tell us any more than that. *Oh, suni*, pick up some food on your way. Your mother and me could do with something to eat.'

'Yeah, sure. What d'you want?'

'Anything.'

'OK. See you in a while.'

No change in Tariq's condition. Was that good or bad? Zaq

decided to give Jags a quick call before he got up. 'All right? What's up?'

'Nothing much,' Jags said. 'What time you reckon you'll finish work and come over, so we can go sort that thing out for Uncle Lucky?'

'Oh shit, I totally forgot about that. I ain't going to be able to do it today.' He told Jags about Tariq.

'Fuckin' hell. That's well bad. I'm so sorry, mate.'

'I took the day off work to sleep, and just woke up. I'm going back to the hospital soon as I'm ready.'

'Course, man. Don't worry about my uncle's thing. We'll do it another time. I'll let him know. Where is he? Tariq, I mean. I'll come to the hospital too.'

'Thanks, mate.' Zaq told him how to find his brother's room. 'See you there.'

Chapter Ten

On the way to the hospital, Zaq stopped at a petrol station with an M&S shop attached and bought sandwiches, snacks and water. He opened a sandwich and placed it on his lap so he could eat as he drove.

He found a space in the hospital car park, where he sat and wolfed down the remainder of the sandwich. It was egg and bacon, so he wanted to finish it before he went in and saw his parents. They knew he ate bacon and pork, but didn't say anything as long as he didn't bring it home or do it in front of them. It was his mum who had more of a problem with it, having become slightly more religious in recent years. If she wasn't around, his dad would probably want a bite himself.

His parents were exactly as he'd left them, sitting beside his brother's bed. Even though Zaq was more prepared, Tariq still looked fucking awful. If anything, he looked even worse than before, his face mottled with bruises, swollen almost beyond recognition. There was bruising on his arms and chest too.

'How is he?'

His dad looked up. 'The same. The doctors have said he's stable, though.'

His mother sat gazing silently at her youngest son. She had pulled the thin material of her *chunni* up over her head. Her face looked drawn, her eyes tired and red, and the residue of tears was still evident on her cheeks.

Zaq watched the shallow rise and fall of his brother's breathing as a machine pumped air in and out, and heard the rhythmic beep of the monitors. Anger began to churn inside him like a cement mixer. Someone had done this to Tariq on purpose; it had been targeted and deliberate. That was bad enough, but it was having a devastating effect on his parents, and on Zaq too. Thinking about it hardened his resolve to find the motherfuckers responsible, and pay them back in kind.

'Here,' he said, handing the M&S bag to his dad. 'There's an egg mayonnaise sandwich, a cheese and salad roll, and some other snacks and drinks.'

His dad gave him a strained smile. He took out the sandwich and roll, and offered both to Zaq's mum, breaking her trance-like state. She looked at the items blankly, as if she didn't know what they were or what she was supposed to do with them.

'*Kuch kahlo*,' Zaq's dad said gently, urging her to eat something. She took the roll, which she held in her lap as she returned her attention to Tariq. She'd eat in a while, Zaq hoped. He stood leaning against the wall, not knowing what to say or do, feeling like a bit of a spare cog. He had to be here, though, even if there was nothing he could do. This was a family emergency and, even though he'd been distanced from them since he'd gone to prison, he was still a part of the family and always would be. He was relieved and grateful when Jags walked in a short while later.

Jags went straight to Zaq's parents. '*Kidaah*, Uncle? Auntie *ji*.' He bent over and put an arm around Zaq's mum's shoulders. She looked up, wiping her eyes with her *chunni*, and gave him a weak smile. Then he joined Zaq by the wall. 'Shit, man,' he said in a low voice. 'He looks well bad. How is he?'

'Pretty fucked up.' Zaq said. He led Jags outside and filled him in on the full extent of Tariq's injuries.

'Bloody hell!'

'Whoever did it really went to town on him. Thing is ...' Zaq hesitated before continuing. 'I think he might've been targeted. Something his mate said.' Zaq relayed everything Prit had told him earlier.

'Why, though? You don't think it's anything to do with ...?' Jags didn't finish. He didn't need to.

'I wondered the same thing. I'm not sure ... but I'm going to find out.'

'Cool.'

In the unspoken language of their lifelong friendship, Zaq knew Jags wasn't simply saying it was a good idea; he was also saying he'd help him find the answers he wanted, whatever it might entail. Then he remembered something else. 'Shit ... we're supposed to be meeting Nina and Rita tonight.'

'It's all right – I called and told them. They're shocked, and both said to tell you how sorry they are. They wanted to come here. But I said I'd check with you first and let them know.'

The circumstances were far from ideal but it would be good to see them. Zaq said, 'Mum and Dad have been here all day. I'll tell them to go home – I can stay with Tariq while they get some rest. Then maybe the girls can pop by for a bit if they still want to.'

Jags nodded, and they returned to the room.

Zaq's parents' initial reaction was to protest. That was no surprise. 'But there's nothing you can do for him right now,' Zaq told them. 'You're just going to make yourselves ill if you don't get some proper rest, and that won't help anyone. I'll stay with him. If anything changes, I'll call you straight away.'

Reluctantly, they agreed. They gathered their things, and Zaq put an arm around his mum's shoulders and gave her a gentle hug. She acknowledged it with about as much energy as a fading light bulb, suddenly frailer than he ever recalled her being.

His dad gripped his arm. 'I'll leave my phone on. Call if anything changes.'

Zaq walked his parents into the corridor, watched them leave through the double doors, then returned to the room, where Jags was still leaning against the back wall, watching the machines that were keeping Tariq alive.

'This is fucked up, man,' he said gravely.

'Damn right.'

Chapter Eleven

After a while, Jags said, 'So – shall I call the girls, tell them to come?'

'Yeah, if they want to. Visiting time's till eight but they'll probably be able to stay a bit longer. Listen, do me a favour?'

'Sure. What?'

'Move my car. It's in the car park but if I'm here all night it'll cost me a fortune. There's a dead-end street on the other side of the main road. You can park there and cut through on the footpath back to here.'

'OK, no problem.'

Zaq fished out his keys, the car park ticket and some cash.

'Don't worry about it, man,' Jags said. 'I got it.'

When Rita and Nina knocked and hesitantly entered Tariq's room, Zaq read the shock on their faces as they took in his brother's condition. Both girls came over and hugged him.

'I'm so sorry,' Nina said.

'Me too,' Rita agreed. 'Oh, my God, it's terrible.'

Jags greeted both girls with a kiss on each cheek.

Zaq was glad to see the girls. Even though they'd dressed down a little to come to the hospital, they both looked amazing. Nina would have worn a dress to go out but was now in black jeans and a black top, with a long, thin grey cardigan. She'd straightened her hair for tonight, and it was smooth and shiny as a model's in a shampoo advert.

They'd been seeing each other for a few months – just meeting up now and again, nothing official – but he felt comfortable with her, and being around her always had an uplifting effect on him. Somehow, it felt *right*. He was conscious that he didn't have much going for him at the moment – an ex-con with a menial job, not much money and no immediate prospects, and who shared a house with a bunch of *desis* – but none of that seemed to bother Nina. Part of that was down to what had happened the night they'd first met, when he might very well have saved her life. It was Rita who'd told him afterwards that he'd made a good impression and should ask Nina out.

'Sorry about this evening,' he said.

'Don't be silly,' Nina told him, squeezing his hand gently. Five years inside, plus a year out, meant it had been a long time since he'd experienced contact of this sort. It sent a tracer of electricity through him every time, made him feel like a teenager all over again.

Rita looked as good as ever, though Zaq was well aware that behind her bright amber eyes and dazzling smile she was still dealing with the loss she had suffered a few months ago. It was going to take her time to properly get over it. She'd thrown herself back into her work – fortunately the company she worked for were very understanding and, with a high proportion of Asian staff, they were sympathetic towards any *cultural issues*, as they put it. It wasn't as if she'd just gone off on a two-week jolly to Ibiza without notice. There'd been rumours of a boyfriend and a possible forced marriage but, when everything else hit the news, her employers and colleagues had realised there was a shedload more going on and given her some space.

The four of them here now at the hospital bedside were the

only ones who knew the whole story of what had really gone down between Rita's brothers and Mahesh Dutta at the house in Southall.

The girls sat down, and listened as Zaq told them about Tariq's injuries.

'Why would anyone do that?' Nina asked when he'd finished.

'You don't think it's anything to do with ...?' Rita didn't finish. She didn't need to. They knew exactly what she meant.

'That's what I thought at first, but I doubt it was your brothers.' Raj and Parm Brar were currently banged up in Wormwood Scrubs awaiting trial. 'They wouldn't have bothered with Tariq; they'd have sent someone straight after me. I doubt I'd still be working for your dad, either. First thing they'd have done was make sure I got sacked, then had their guys do me over.'

'You think it could've been Dutta, then?' Jags asked.

'Well, he's got form for it. He went after Tariq before, remember? A brother for a brother. It'd be just his style. He's had plenty of time inside to work out who put him there, or maybe he's still out to settle the score from before.'

Mahesh Dutta, currently in prison awaiting trial on a number of charges similar to Raj and Parm Brar, wanted Zaq dead. He believed Zaq was responsible for the murder of his brother Rahul, even though it had clearly been a case of self-defence. The murder charge against Zaq had been dropped, but he had still been convicted of manslaughter. Dutta had been incensed that Zaq had only got five years in prison. As far as he was concerned, it was nowhere near enough, and he'd tried to enforce his own form of punishment.

'Whoever did it,' Zaq said, 'I gotta find out who they are and make sure they don't come after Tariq, or any of us, again.'

'You're not going to do anything silly, are you?' Nina asked. 'Don't get into any trouble.'

'Not if I can help it, but I need to get this sorted. If it is any-thing to do with Dutta, it could well be me, or even you, lying in here next, and that ain't a chance I want to take.'

'What if it wasn't him?'

'I still need to find out who it was and make sure.'

'Promise me you won't try to deal with it all yourself?'

'Nah – better to let the cops handle it, with *the full weight of the law*. I know what that's like, remember? I been on the receiving end.'

Zaq was glad Nina was here, even if only for a short time. He hadn't expected the girls to stay for as long as they did – no one wanted to spend their Saturday night at a hospital – and he didn't want to keep them. 'Thanks a lot for coming, I really appreciate it ... but you guys can go now.'

'Are you sure?' Nina said.

'Yeah. It's past visiting time anyway. A nurse'll probably be in any minute to chuck you all out.'

'What about you?'

'I'm staying here the night.'

'If there's anything you need ... ' Nina gave him a hug.

Rita hugged him too. 'I really hope Tariq gets better soon.'

'You might as well shoot off too, mate,' Zaq told Jags.

'You want me to get you anything?'

'I'm good for now, thanks.'

The girls got up and gathered their things. As they started out of the room, Jags hung back. 'You serious about finding out who did this, and then letting the cops handle it?'

'Only after I kick the shit out of them first.'

'That's what I thought.' They bumped fists, and Jags left to catch up with the girls.

Chapter Twelve

Zaq sat by his brother's bed, willing him better. But it didn't make any difference.

His mind wandered and eventually settled on the question that kept nagging at him: who was responsible? Was it really just some trouble at a wedding, or was there something else behind it? As far as Zaq was concerned, the targeted nature of the attack, and the fact that he'd gone after Tariq before, meant Mahesh Dutta was prime suspect. Even though he was currently stewing in prison, his hatred of Zaq was very likely still festering and growing unchecked. It'd be just like him to send people after Tariq, and then Zaq.

If that was the case, then they'd made a big mistake going after Tariq first. What was that saying – forewarned is forearmed? Well, now that he was forewarned, he'd make goddamned sure he was forearmed and ready for the motherfuckers. He'd be actively looking for them, too. If they attacked him like they did Tariq, he'd go all out to break their bones and make them bleed. He could feel himself getting riled just thinking about it, his fighting instincts firing like spark plugs.

After everything that had happened a few months ago, he'd picked up his training again – not as hard as when he'd trained with the other fighters in prison, but enough to be able to look after himself. He'd learnt the hard way that being back on the streets was just as dangerous as being banged up inside.

But finding the bastards who'd done Tariq over was easier said than done. He had no idea who Dutta's friends or associates were, or how he was meant to track them down. Could they have been at the wedding, seen Tariq, and relayed the information to Dutta? Tariq's mate, the one with the stupid name – Bongo – was at the wedding; maybe he'd know something useful.

Zaq looked up the number Prit had given him for Bongo and hit the call button. After a bit, the call went to voicemail and a recorded greeting kicked in. He didn't like leaving messages, so he hung up. Just after nine on a Saturday night – prime time for weddings, parties and club nights. Chances were Bongo was busy DJing somewhere.

Prit had described one of the guys pretty well, though Zaq's mind had been a little elsewhere at the time. He tried calling Prit and had more luck.

'Listen, describe that guy to me again, the one that came over to you and T in the pub.' He wanted to get the description of this motherfucker straight.

'Er ... he was about our age, I reckon, and the same height as T. He was broad, though, beefy, like he does a lot of weights. Had a funky kind of hairstyle, dark but with copper or brown highlights – yeah, and he had a gold tooth. One of his front ones.'

'Beard or clean-shaven?'

'He had a kind of beard, really trimmed down though.'

'Earrings?'

'Didn't really notice. He might've had two hoops.'

'Fair or dark?'

'Average ... just brown.'

'OK.' Zaq said. 'Thanks.' He now had an image in his mind

of the guy he wanted to find, question and beat the fuck out of. 'I tried getting in touch with Bongo just now . . . '

'He's DJ'ing a thirtieth birthday party. I was supposed to do it, but I couldn't, not after last night. I'm still a bit battered and bruised, and I keep seeing what they did to Tariq, can't get it out of my head.'

'Good thing you were there to call for help. Otherwise, who knows what could've happened?' He wasn't just saying it to make Prit feel better. It was true.

'OK if I come and see him tomorrow?' Prit asked.

'Yeah, course. My parents'll be here during the day but I'll be here in the evening if you want to come then.'

'I'll come during the day if I can, and see your parents too.'

It struck Zaq that just because he didn't know Prit, it didn't mean his parents wouldn't. Tariq lived at home, so they probably knew his friends. Five years in prison had created a distance between Zaq and his family – between Zaq and his former life – that he felt particularly keenly just at that moment.

He told Prit how to get to Tariq's room, and ended the call. Then he typed the description Prit had given him into his phone and saved it, so he wouldn't forget anything. He'd try calling Bongo again tomorrow.

Chapter Thirteen

Sleep proved elusive. He couldn't get comfortable in the hospital chair; he'd never been good at falling asleep in any other position than lying flat. The buzzing and beeping of the equipment didn't help either. He tried tuning in to the rhythm of a particular piece and using it to lull him to sleep, but just as he started dozing some other discordant sound would jab him awake. Nurses came in every so often to check on Tariq, bringing Zaq out of whatever dozing state he was in, no matter how quiet they tried to be. Prison had made him a light sleeper, quick to wake and alert to threat.

Time seemed to behave randomly. At first it crawled by; every time he closed his eyes and thought he'd managed to snatch some sleep, he'd find it had only been a few minutes. He spent longer trying to get to sleep than actually sleeping. Next thing he knew, the sky, through the gaps in the blinds, was already lightening with the approach of morning. He was knackered and in need of a toothbrush. He gave up hope of any more sleep.

Even though it was early, he could hear sounds of activity in the unit. Rubbing his eyes, he sat up and slipped his feet back into his trainers. Tariq hadn't moved. He lay in an enforced sleep so deep that Zaq wondered if he could even dream. But his wasn't a peaceful, restful sleep. Beneath the stillness, his body was struggling to repair itself and survive.

'Get better, you idiot,' Zaq urged, under his breath. 'Come on, you can get through this. Don't wimp out on me.'

A nurse came in to check on Tariq and update his chart. She gave Zaq a smile. 'Manage to sleep OK?'

'Not really.'

'They're not the most comfortable chairs in the world.'

'Tell me about it.'

'There's a small kitchenette where you can help yourself to tea or coffee and usually some bread for toast too if you like. The doctors should be doing their rounds soon, and they can answer any questions you might have.'

Zaq followed her suggestion, and made himself a mug of builder's tea and a slice of toast. When his tea was nice and strong, he took it to the family room and drank it with a Yorkie bar he'd saved from the night before. Not exactly a healthy breakfast, but it did the trick.

Back in Tariq's room, he sat beside his brother as the day brightened outside.

When his parents arrived just after eight-thirty, carrying a couple of large carrier bags, the doctors still hadn't been by on their rounds, so Zaq had no news for them. They looked a little better than they had the previous evening – rested, at least, if nothing else. His mum's eyes were still red and puffy, and she seemed slightly drawn. Any shock and emotion his dad had shown the previous day remained locked away behind a rigid masculine demeanour. It was pure old school. What was wrong with showing how you felt, especially if your child was in the state Tariq was? Then again, maybe he was doing it for their mother's benefit. If he was an emotional wreck too, how would that help her?

'You look tired,' his dad said. 'Go home, get some rest. We'll be here today, and we've brought food this time.' He hefted the bag in his hand. 'There's a little kitchen where we can warm it up, so we'll be all right.'

Zaq wasn't about to argue. 'I'll come back later.'

'Don't you have to work?'

'No, it's Sunday, and anyway I managed to get a few days off. Call me if you need anything, or if there's any news.'

His dad said he would. Zaq put an arm around his mum's shoulders, giving her gentle squeeze. She looked at him and nodded, the lines in her face deeper than he remembered. He hugged his dad, who hugged him back fiercely, demonstrating physically, perhaps, the emotions bottled up inside him. When they separated, his dad rubbed his eyes, as though he'd got something in them.

Chapter Fourteen

It was Sunday morning, and Zaq got in just as the rest of his house-mates were starting to stir after their late Saturday night. Quiet and considerate they were not. Zaq dozed fitfully at first, with the crashing, banging, slamming and talking of the others, but he must eventually have managed to drop off, because when he did wake from a deep, dreamless slumber it was the middle of the afternoon.

As he went to the bathroom, he could hear the guys chatting and laughing downstairs in the lounge. He decided to give his parents a quick call, to see if everything was OK. There was nothing new. The doctors had come on their rounds and said that Tariq was stable and they'd continue to monitor him. 'Did you sleep?' his dad asked.

'Yeah, a bit. I just got up. How's Mum?'

His dad's response was a non-committal 'Hmm,' which told Zaq that she could hear him and that she was still in a bad way.

'Shall I come and take over from you?'

'Will you stay the night again? If so, come later, maybe seven or eight. We are OK for now.'

'All right. I got a few things to do then I'll come. Let me know if anything changes.'

Zaq sat on his bed and thought. He still wanted to talk to Bongo, and now was probably a good time to catch him. He found the number on his phone and made the call.

'Hello,' answered a voice full of confidence.

'Bongo?' Zaq couldn't help feeling slightly silly saying the name out loud. 'I'm Zaq, Tariq's brother.'

'Oh, shit, man. Look, I heard what happened. Prit called and told me. It's fucking out of order. How's he doing?'

'Not so good. Whoever jumped him really did him over big-time.'

'That's bad, man. I'd come and see him today but I got a gig tonight, you know? Got to get my gear ready and that. I'll come by after work tomorrow, though, if he's still going to be there.'

'Yeah, fine. He won't be going anywhere for a while yet. Look, I wanted to ask you something – Prit said one of the guys that jumped them came over and asked about some wedding you and Tariq played at a couple of weeks ago, in Slough. You know which one he was on about?'

'I think so. Prit said something about it.'

'He describe the guy to you?'

'Yeah, didn't ring any bells, though. I was just shocked about what had happened to T.'

'Well, have a think about it and see if it jogs your memory. What about the wedding? Anything happen there – a fight, some trouble, anything like that?'

Bongo thought for a moment. 'No, nothing like that.'

'Whose wedding was it?'

'Don't know off the top of my head. Can dig up the booking form though; that'll have the info.'

'Cool. How soon can you do that?'

'Er ... I might be able to have a look for it before I go to the gig.'

'All right. What time you leaving?'

''Bout five.'

'I'll come by and see you before you leave.' Bongo gave Zaq

his address, and Zaq jotted it down on the back of an envelope. 'Thanks. See you a bit later.' He'd run the description of the guy with the gold tooth past Bongo when he saw him, see if it did jog his memory.

Next he called Jags. 'What's going on?'

'Nothing, man. How's Tariq?'

'Same as yesterday.'

'What you been doing?'

'Trying to sleep. Still knackered, though. You want to go sort this thing out for Lucky today? My dad said to come to the hospital this evening, so I got time.'

'That'd be great. Be good to get it done, and get my uncle off my back. He's been doing my head in about it. Got flippin' ants in his pants or something.'

'All right. I'll come over to yours in a bit. You might as well give Lucky a call and tell him.'

Chapter Fifteen

Before heading over to Jags' house, Zaq made himself do a quick workout in his room. He spent five minutes shadow-boxing, holding a pair of light dumbbells, as a warm-up, followed by some stretches. After that he went through a short but intense full-body weights routine with a heavier set of dumbbells. He rounded it all off with another few minutes of shadow-boxing and some more stretching, this time pushing each stretch further and holding it for longer.

If he hadn't had other things to do, he would've spent longer shadow-boxing, working on his speed and technique. Since he'd got back into the habit of training, he tried to do at least a little bit every day. All that stuff with Rita's brothers and Dutta had made him realise how much he'd let himself go and allowed his reflexes to dull. It had brought home to him that even though he was out of prison he still needed the skills he'd learnt and practised so hard while inside. Being back in Southall wasn't so different from being banged up; there were still plenty of arse-holes around, and you never knew when they'd want to start some trouble. It paid to be ready.

He showered, dressed in jeans and a T-shirt, grabbed his cards, money, phone and keys, and went downstairs to get something to eat. His housemates were lazing in the lounge.

'Fuckin' hell,' Bal greeted him. 'You just getting up now, you lazy shit?'

'If you was hoping some beauty sleep would make a difference, I got bad news for you,' Manjit said.

'Maybe he was out with his girlfriend?' put in Lax. He was the youngest of the housemates and the one with the biggest mouth. He'd happened to see Zaq with Nina one time, and had blabbed to the others.

'I been at the hospital Friday night. Got back this morning and was trying to get some sleep, despite you lot making enough noise to wake the dead.'

'What were you doing at the hospital?' Manjit asked.

'My brother got jumped Friday night.' The laughter petered out, like water soaking into sand. Zaq told them all what had happened. When he finished, the atmosphere had turned from joviality to grim silence.

'Shit,' Lax said.

'You know who did it?' Bal demanded. 'We can go find them, stick them in the fucking hospital too, *ma chauds.*' His eyes gleamed with brute intelligence at the possibility. Always up for a fight, Bal was stocky, muscular and strong as an ox. What he lacked in height, he more than made up for in breadth. Sure, he'd never win *Mastermind*, but it'd be a mistake to write him off as thick. 'You need a hand busting their fucking heads, just let us know, innit.'

'I will.' Zaq went through to the open-plan kitchen, to grab something quick to eat before he headed to see Bongo on his way to Jags'. He opted for toast and had just put two slices of bread in the toaster when Manjit came and joined him.

'Sorry to hear about your brother,' the big Singh said. Tall, broad-shouldered, bearded and turbaned, he was the very picture of a Sikh warrior. He was a builder by trade, and the physical nature of his work helped keep him fit and his thickly muscled frame lean. 'I'll mention it at work tomorrow,' he said. 'Put the word out, see if anyone's heard anything about it or who might've done it.'

'That'd be cool, thanks.'

'You know what the *desi* grapevine's like, innit?' Manjit went on. 'Someone'll hear something sooner or later.'

'Yeah, but I ain't going to sit around and wait. I'm following up a couple of things to try and find the bastards myself.'

'What about the cops?'

'What about them? Violent crime stats are going through the roof and they ain't got enough money or men to deal with it. This'll get shelved as just another Asian-on-Asian thing, unless the evidence falls right in their laps. Well, if I find any I'll drop it right there for them – otherwise I'll sort it out myself. Fuck the cops and the courts; I'll do it our way.'

Manjit nodded. 'I hear you. Like Bal said, you need any help, just ask.' He drifted back to the lounge.

Of all the guys in the house, Manjit was the one Zaq got on with best, which might've seemed odd to some, seeing as how Manjit was the most visibly Sikh of the housemates and they all knew from his very name that Zaq was a Muslim, or at least supposed to be. But Manjit was more spiritual than fundamental in his beliefs, and Zaq was about as religious as a sack of cement. That, and the fact they shared a similar sense of humour as well as an interest in books and history, meant they'd become good friends.

Zaq buttered his toast, then spread Marmite and peanut butter on one slice and strawberry jam on the other and wolfed them down. He didn't have time to make tea, so had a glass of water instead.

'Laters,' he told the guys on his way to the front door.

Outside it was hot, the sun's heat simultaneously pressing down from above and rising from the ground in waves. Zaq's car felt like an oven. He started the engine, wound all the windows down, turned the fan up to max and got out again, wishing he'd stumped up for a motor with air-conditioning. But how often did you really need it during a summer which usually only amounted to two or three weeks of hot weather anyway? In the end, he hadn't bothered. He also hadn't wanted to get anything too flash, that might draw attention to him and raise questions – like, how could he afford it? He'd paid about three grand for the car, almost another grand for road tax and insurance, and had bought himself a MacBook Air. That was all he'd allowed himself for the time being. The rest of the cash – just under twenty-five grand – was safely hidden under a floorboard by the wall, beneath his bed.

Once the car had aired out enough to be just about bearable, he got in and drove off to see Bongo.

Chapter Sixteen

The houses in Woodlands Road were compact three-bedroom terraces, set behind walled front gardens that were too small to fit a car into, so had all been left as they were instead of being turned into driveways.

The pale blue edifice of the old gas tower, which had once reared up behind the houses like a sentinel keeping watch over Southall, was now being dismantled. It was strange to see something that had been there his whole life, a landmark that had become a symbol of home, coming down. Its absence would feel like the loss of something personal. The whole site and the area around it were being redeveloped and replaced by flats. The skyline would be changed beyond recognition. In a way, it mirrored how his own life had changed from the way he'd thought it would go, especially being sent to prison. No matter how much you wanted things to stay the same, shit happened, life moved on, and sometimes it kicked you in the teeth.

When Zaq spotted the right house, about halfway down, he drove on past it, to the first available parking space. The roads were all permit parking these days, which was a pain in the arse, but he wasn't going to be long and would keep an eye out for parking attendants.

He locked the car and walked to the house, opening the gate and going up the short path to press the doorbell. He heard movement from inside, then the inner door opened and a figure leaned out to unlock and open the porch door.

Bongo didn't look anything like Zaq had imagined – but then, what had he been imagining? This guy was clean-cut, neat, and clearly looked after himself. His dark hair was cropped close, with a fade around the back and sides, and a fashionable tramline cut in at the front. His jaw was smoothly shaved and he had good skin and gleaming teeth. Probably spent a few quid on grooming and looking after himself. He was dressed in dark jeans and a form-fitting navy T-shirt that showed off gym-toned arms. A jewelled stud glittered in each earlobe.

'I'm Zaq, Tariq's brother. We spoke earlier. You manage to find that booking info?'

'Yeah, I did,' Bongo said, nodding. 'Just hang on a sec . . .' He left the door open and disappeared inside and up the stairs, returning a few moments later with a piece of paper. 'Here it is.' He looked at the sheet, but made no move to hand it to Zaq.

'Can I have a look?'

Bongo hesitated. 'I ain't being funny or nothing, but I don't know if I can just show it to you. All this GDPR, data protection shit – know what I mean?'

'Listen,' Zaq said, 'someone tried to kill my brother last night. He's in Intensive Care, in a coma, and we don't know how bad it's going to affect him. What I do know, though, is that one of the guys who did it was asking about this wedding. There's a link there. Someone at the wedding might know who he is and where I can find him. Whoever booked you for it will be a good place to start. Now, you going to help me or not? I'm not going to tell anyone how I got the details, if that's what you're worried about.'

Bongo hesitated a bit longer, then said, 'OK, here . . .' and handed the sheet to Zaq. 'I can't let you keep it, though.'

'That's fine.' Zaq cast his eyes over the form, then took out his phone and snapped a picture that was converted into a crisp black and white scan.

'Hey, I ain't sure you can do that,' Bongo protested.

'It's OK, I just have. Don't worry about it. Thanks.' He handed the form back. 'Just saves me having to type it all out.' He saved the scan then swiped to the notes on his phone. 'While we're here, do you remember this guy from the wedding?' He read out the description Prit had given him. 'Sound familiar?'

Bongo shook his head.

'Do me a favour then and ask around? Let me know if you find anything out.' Bongo said he would. 'Cool.'

'I'll try and swing by to see T after work tomorrow,' Bongo said.

'OK.' Zaq stuck out a hand and they shook. Then he went back to his car and drove off, heading for Jags' place.

Chapter Seventeen

Lucky was already at Jags' when Zaq arrived. As soon as he saw Zaq, he said, 'Good, you're here. Let's go,' and was out of his seat, heading for the door. Jags rolled his eyes at Zaq and shrugged. Outside in the driveway, Lucky said, 'I'll drive.' So the three of them got into his Mercedes, Jags in front, Zaq in the back, and off they went.

Zaq was glad of the air-conditioning, which kicked in fast. 'Where exactly we going?' he asked.

'Out towards Slough,' Lucky replied. 'That's where the guy lives.'

Zaq knew the area a little, having made deliveries out that way before.

'Listen, boys,' Lucky said, 'I've got to get that necklace back, OK? It's really important. I've got the money I owe the fucker from the card game, I even added another two grand, as a bonus or whatever. Just make sure you get the necklace.'

'Yeah, all right.' Zaq thought Lucky was being a bit over-the-top about it. If the guy got the money, plus some extra, what was the problem?

Lucky drove to Uxbridge then turned west on to a smaller road heading away from the urban sprawl that marked the edge of London's expansion. After a while, the terraced houses lining the road thinned and then disappeared altogether, replaced by trees and thick greenery on either side, open sky above. It was amazing how quickly you could leave London behind and feel you were in the country. Every so often they'd pass a large, impressive house, set well back from the road, hidden behind walls, fences and security gates. The number of properties increased as they neared the village of Iver, but were still relatively spread out. It felt a million miles from the noise and colour of Southall.

They passed a pub called the Black Horse, which made Zaq think of another pub in Hounslow with the same name, where he'd met Rita's ex-boyfriend a few months ago. That hadn't turned out so well. He tried to think about something else.

Iver itself was a little more built-up, but they soon passed through it and left it behind. They turned left at the Five Points roundabout and, if anything, their surroundings became even greener, branches meeting overhead in places to create a natural tunnel through which they drove.

A little further on Lucky slowed down to let a car pass in the opposite direction, then pulled across the road and stopped at a driveway that led to some security gates. A huge brick and timber house could be partially glimpsed through the trees behind the wall that flanked the gates.

'Here we are,' he said. 'This is the guy's place.' He'd stopped the car across the driveway rather than facing the gate.

'Come on, then,' Zaq said, 'let's go in and see him.' Lucky just looked at him and Jags. 'Are we going in, or what?'

'It might be better if you go in by yourselves,' Lucky said. 'I'll wait here.'

Zaq frowned. 'What're you talking about?'

Lucky hesitated. Finally, he said, 'When I came myself last week to get the necklace back ... I might have told him to go fuck his sister. And his mum. And a few other things.'

'Bet that helped,' Jags said.

Lucky leaned across Jags to open the glove compartment, and took out a thick white envelope. 'Here,' he said, handing it to Jags. 'There's twelve grand in there. The ten I owe, plus the extra two to sweeten the deal.'

'Twelve grand?' Jags said. 'That's some crazy money to be betting.' He opened the envelope and thumbed through the wad of fifty-pound notes inside.

'*Bhen chaud*, I was positive I had a winning hand,' Lucky told them. 'So maybe I got a bit carried away with the betting.'

'You'll get carried away all right,' Jags said. 'In a pine box, if Auntie ever finds out.'

'Well, if you get the fucking necklace back, she won't have to, will she?' Lucky was petulant, like a kid old enough to know better getting told off for still taking a shit in his pants.

'Come on,' Zaq said. 'Let's just go and do it.'

Jags got out, folded the envelope in half and stuffed it into the front pocket of his jeans.

'You walk in looking like that,' Zaq said, indicating the bulge it made there, 'they'll think you're really happy to see them.'

'I'll be happy to get this done and get out of here,' Jags grumbled. 'What's the guy's name again, Uncle?'

At the security gates, an intercom system was affixed to one of the chunky brick gateposts. Jags pressed the button and after a moment the speaker crackled to life and a gruff voice said, 'Yes?'

'We're here to see Mr Shergill,' Jags said.

'Who're you?'

'My name's Jags and this is my friend Zaq.'

'What do you want?'

'I told you . . . we'd like to see Mr Shergill.'

'What about?'

'We've got some money for him.' The speaker went dead. Zaq and Jags looked at each other, unsure what to do. 'We meant to wait, or what?'

Zaq shrugged. 'Might as well. Can always buzz again if nothing happens.'

They waited. Just as Zaq was about to tell Jags to try again, there was a loud buzzing sound followed by a click, and the gates started to open.

Chapter Eighteen

'About time,' Jags said. 'He didn't even ask what the money was for.'

'Size of this place, maybe they're used to people just dropping money off.'

The house, seen properly now they were past the screening trees and hedges, was huge, a sprawling modern two-storey construction of red brick and timber, with plenty of large windows, and a third floor built into the ample roof space, judging by the number of skylights. The driveway made a gentle S-curve between well-tended lawns planted with shrubs and mature trees, and opened out into a wide parking area in front of the house. Zaq noted the cars that were there: a Range Rover, a Jaguar SUV, a Mercedes and a BMW Z4, all the latest models and gleaming in the sunlight.

'I should've driven us in my motor,' Jags complained, as they trudged along. 'Least then we could've driven up like you're supposed to, instead of walking like a couple of saps. Lucky could've flippin' waited for us out there like the lemon he is.'

'We're here now. Let's just get this sorted.'

As they approached the high, wide double front doors, one of them opened and a man stepped out. Zaq didn't need to catch Jags' eye; he was pretty sure Jags was thinking the same thing he was. The guy was huge, seven foot at least, and put together like he'd give Thor and the Hulk a hard time. He was dressed all in black – black sports shoes, loose black bottoms and a V-neck T-shirt stretched so tight across his upper body it looked set to rip at any moment.

When they were close enough that he didn't have to raise his voice, the guy held up a hand and said, 'Stop there.' His voice was deep, like the rumble of a tipper truck. When his balls had dropped, they must've hit the ground, Zaq thought to himself. He also detected the faint hint of an accent, which had to be Indian. There was something distinctly Indian about his features too. '*Kidaah*?' he said, to test his theory.

The guy responded with the slightest of nods, enough to let Zaq know he was right. He was fairly young, early twenties maybe, and his hair was cropped short all around, a little longer on top, where it was gelled and swept to one side. He watched them with sharp eyes.

'You said you're here to drop off some money?'

Zaq and Jags nodded.

'Where is it? Let me see.'

Jags shrugged and moved to take the envelope out of his pocket. The big guy shifted position, his right hand going behind him as though he was reaching for a weapon.

'Whoa!' Zaq raised his hands, palms out, in a calming gesture. He'd seen people move like that in films. It seemed a bit surreal here though, on a Sunday afternoon in Buckinghamshire. Why the hell did this Shergill guy need armed guards at his house? Zaq felt tension humming through him.

Jags slowly took out the envelope, unfolded it, and held it open, flicking through the banknotes with his thumb. 'See?'

'OK, come here,' the guy said, beckoning Jags forward.

Jags approached him.

'Stop. Arms out.'

'What?'

'Arms out,' the guy said, more forcefully.

Jags shook his head, but raised his arms. The big guy frisked Jags, his eyes all the while flicking over to watch Zaq. When he was satisfied that Jags wasn't carrying anything he shouldn't be, he signalled for Zaq to come forward. 'Your turn.'

Zaq couldn't believe it. He'd never been searched going into someone's house before. It was like something out of a gangster movie. He stepped forward, raised his arms and allowed himself to be frisked. The guy had big hands and wasn't the least bit shy in using them to pat him down.

When he was done, the guard stepped back and nodded towards the open front door. 'Inside.'

They stepped into a large marble-floored entrance hall, tastefully decorated and furnished with what must have been antique armchairs and ornate side tables. Paintings and photographs were hung on broad expanses of white wall. A staircase led up to a landing that looked as big as the hall they were in, with a corridor off to either side, and one leading back towards the rear of the house. Zaq saw furniture up there too, sofas and armchairs.

Behind them, the guy closed the door. 'That way,' he said, pointing to the rear of the hall and a wide entrance through which Zaq could see an open living area.

The space they walked into was huge and spanned the whole width of the house. Zaq couldn't help but be impressed. The room was the size of four or five normal houses combined. To Zaq's left was a state-of-the-art kitchen, and beyond it a dining table with what looked like twelve chairs around it. Past that was an open set of bi-fold doors through which Zaq could see a well-tended landscaped garden.

The big guy steered Zaq and Jags towards a massive lounge, full of light-coloured sofas and armchairs and the biggest TV

Zaq had ever seen. Two men were sitting there, one watching a cricket match on the TV, the other watching him and Jags.

The one watching them looked to be about average height and build, and had a black moustache along with an unruly tangle of dark hair. His skin was a deep brown, only a few shades lighter than the black T-shirt and bottoms that he wore. What was with the black outfits? Was it some sort of uniform? The other man didn't bother to look around. Chunky rather than muscular, he was wearing a pink short-sleeved shirt and shorts, and had one arm casually draped across the back of the sofa. His head seemed rather large, and his big nose, thick lips and broad forehead made his eyes seem small in comparison. His thick, dark hair was shot through with grey.

'This is them,' the giant informed the man, who had to be his boss. He must have heard, but he continued to watch the cricket. The hand that wasn't on the back of the sofa was holding a large tumbler full of what Zaq guessed was whisky, with ice. Zaq remembered having to stand and wait like this in the prison governor's office until the governor had finished whatever he was doing, to demonstrate his power rather than because he was actually busy. This was a slightly more obvious version of the same game.

On the TV, the bowler made his delivery, which the batsman took on his bat, allowing the ball to roll away to one of the closer fielders. That was the end of the over, and the players milled around while the new bowler got ready. Zaq saw from the scorecard that England was playing India.

The man in the pink shirt looked up at last. 'I don't know you,' he said. 'Who are you?'

'Mr Shergill?' Jags asked. 'I've got some money for you ... and I'm here to pick up a necklace in exchange.'

Shergill turned his attention back to the TV for a moment.

Then he shifted position, picked up the remote control and turned down the volume. 'I asked who you were.'

'I'm here for my uncle, Lucky. I've got what he owes you from the card game.'

'Oh, so you're his nephew, huh?' The way Shergill said it, that wasn't a good thing. 'He hasn't got the balls to come himself after last time, is that it?'

'He mentioned he might've said some things he shouldn't have. He's really sorry about it.'

'He's *lucky* I let him walk out of here, talking to me like that in my own house.'

'Yeah, well, like I said, he's sorry, and he wants to make up for it.' Jags held up the envelope. 'This is the money he owes, along with an extra two grand, by way of apology and thanks for being so understanding.'

Shergill let out a laugh and looked at the guy on the other sofa, jerking his head towards Jags as if saying *Get a load of this guy*, before returning his attention to the TV and turning the volume back up. He swirled the ice around in his whisky, then took a long swallow. Without looking at them, he said, 'I'll tell you the same thing I told your uncle – that necklace is forfeit. It's mine now, and I'm keeping it. If anything, him offering more money for it makes me think it might actually be worth something.'

'It belongs to my aunt and any value it's got is probably just sentimental. I've got the money my uncle owes, and more. How's it forfeit?'

'My house, my rules,' Shergill stated. 'If he couldn't afford to lose it, he shouldn't have bet it, simple as that.'

'But he's paying the bet now.' Zaq could see that Jags was getting annoyed.

'He had twenty-four hours. He should've brought the money the next day, but he didn't. So it's up to me if I decide to keep the necklace. The way he acted when he did show up, and now sending you two . . . I think I'll hold on to it, see what it's worth, maybe take what he owes out of that.' Then Shergill said, 'That's all,' dismissing them both with a wave of his hand.

'Hang on a minute . . . ' Jags began.

'No, *you* wait a fucking minute. Who the hell are you, coming into my house, on a Sunday, and trying to tell me what to do? I've heard what you had to say and given you my answer. Now fuck off.'

Zaq just prayed Jags wouldn't explode. Shergill said in Punjabi, '*Eh dono nikahl de.*' And Zaq and Jags were both grabbed by the backs of their T-shirts, yanked violently around and shoved in the direction of the hallway they'd come in from.

'Get the fuck off me!' Jags snapped.

The giant glared down at them with a malevolent frown, his hands curled into fists the size of melons. Beside him stood Moustache Guy, looking small in comparison but just as unfriendly.

Zaq hadn't come for a fight. 'Come on,' he said, turning Jags by the shoulder. 'Let's just go.'

Chapter Nineteen

'Fucking arseholes.' Jags spat the words out, barely keeping a lid on his temper, as he and Zaq strode back down the drive. 'Who the fuck does that prick think he is?'

'Just some rich wanker who likes to throw his weight around.' Zaq glanced back over his shoulder to see the giant standing at the front door, watching them.

'I'd like to throw his weight around all right . . . bounce him off the fucking ceiling. Telling those idiots of his to throw us out. We should've slapped them up, then done the same to him. Prick.'

'You see the size of the big one? Would have taken both of us to put him down. And that other geezer looked the type to knife you given half a chance. That's what they're there for: so Mr Big Mouth can say whatever the fuck he wants and they take care of anyone that don't like it.'

'Still, should've given them something to think about.'

'We didn't come here for a fight. Probably just as well we didn't have a punch-up and ruin any chance of trying again.'

Jags grunted in sulky agreement.

'Besides,' Zaq continued, 'now we know what the score is, we'll be better prepared next time. Let's just get out of here and then decide what to do.'

As they approached the gates there was a buzz followed by a click, and the gates began to swing open. Zaq noticed a pair of small CCTV cameras mounted on one of the gateposts, one facing out of the property, the other in, straight at them. Seeing Jags' arm start to move, Zaq warned, 'Don't.'

'Don't what?'

'Don't give them the finger.'

'How'd you know that's—?'

'How long have I known you? Save it for next time, in case we do come back.'

'When did you get so sensible?'

'One of us has to be.'

'Let's just get the fuck out of here,' Jags said, casting a last sneering look at the camera and stalking out through the opening gates.

Lucky had turned the car around and was pulled up on the footpath just past where the drive met the road. Jags got in the front, Zaq in the back again.

'Did you get it?' Lucky asked before they'd even shut the doors.

'No,' Jags snarled, slamming his shut.

'What do you mean, no?' Lucky demanded. 'Why bloody not? That's what you went in there for.'

''Cause he didn't want to give it to us. Said you were supposed to give him the money the day after.'

'That's bullshit. I told him I needed a couple of days to get the money together, then I'd pay him.'

'He say that was OK?'

'He didn't say it wasn't.'

'Did he actually agree, though?'

Lucky shut up and thought about it. 'He didn't say anything. But he didn't say no, so I thought he was all right with it.'

'He let you think what *you* wanted,' Zaq said, 'so he could turn around and do whatever *he* wanted.'

'*Bhen chaud*,' Lucky cursed. 'OK, but I still need that necklace back. Can't you go back in and ask him again?'

'We've only just been chucked out,' Zaq said.

'And you never said anything about him having a couple of bodyguards, either,' Jags added.

Lucky gave them a weak smile.

'I think the big one might've been armed,' Zaq said. 'Maybe both of them.'

'With a gun?' Lucky looked shocked.

Zaq shrugged. 'Not with a cuddly toy, that's for sure.'

Lucky groaned. 'I *have* to get that necklace back – and soon. If your auntie finds out I lost it in a card game, she'll cut off my *tutae*.' He made a chopping motion at his balls.

'I thought she already had,' Jags muttered.

'*Kautha, jeya*.' Lucky raised a hand, threatening him with a slap.

'Get out of it.' Jags brushed him off with a laugh, knowing it was just an empty threat.

'Let's just go,' Zaq said. 'Ain't no point sitting out here like a bunch of *lulloos*.'

Lucky pulled out on to the road. They drove in silence for a few minutes, then he said, 'Let's find a pub. I need a drink.' They followed the road as it snaked its way through the countryside until they eventually reached the roundabout and a pub there called the Crooked Billet.

Inside, the place was done up in bold colours, with lots of film-related photos on the walls, a nod to the nearby Pinewood Studios. Zaq and Jags slipped into an empty booth, while Lucky went to the bar. He returned with three pints, put them on the table and squeezed in beside Jags.

'Cheers.' He picked up his beer and downed half in a few hefty gulps. 'Listen, boys, what are we going to do? I got to get that necklace back. It's been a week already. Your auntie thinks it's in the safety deposit box at the bank. I can't risk her finding out it isn't.'

'How would she do that?' Jags said.

'I don't know – people talk. If anyone mentions the card game, or Shergill starts telling people about the necklace, she might hear about it . . . and then there'll be hell to pay.'

Only for you, Zaq thought.

'How often does she wear it?' Jags asked.

'Not that often. Only if it's a special occasion and she's wearing something that the emeralds will go with.'

'Maybe he's just holding out for a better offer,' Zaq said. 'You think maybe he just wants more money?'

'What for? The dickhead looks pretty fucking loaded already,' Jags replied.

'Yeah, and how d'you think he got that way?'

Jags looked at his uncle. 'Can you get any more money?'

Lucky didn't look happy about it. 'I suppose . . . but I'll have to do it without your aunt knowing.'

'All right,' Jags said. 'You get some more money and we can go back in a day or two, see if that does the trick.'

'What if he still says no?' Zaq said. 'Then what?'

Lucky ran a hand over his face and held up the other as if to ward off the suggestion. 'I don't even want to think about that.'

'What about just going to the police and telling them about it? Maybe they could do someth—'

'No,' Lucky snapped. For a second he seemed more scared of the police than worried about his wife. Then he regained his composure.

Zaq glanced at Jags. He'd noticed too. 'Why not?'

'Just no police, OK? I don't want them involved. It's . . . family stuff.' Lucky waved a hand, as if trying to brush the issue away.

'Plus, then your auntie would definitely find out, and everyone else would know too. Let's just try and sort it out ourselves, huh?' He looked from one to the other, searching for agreement.

'OK, sure,' Zaq said, though something didn't sit quite right with him about it. Lucky was worried about getting the police involved even more than he was worried about Jags' aunt finding out. Zaq wondered what the 'family stuff' he'd referred to could be?

'Fine,' Jags said. 'You get some more cash, and me and Zaq'll go try again.'

Chapter Twenty

Lucky dropped them back at Jags' place, asking again that they keep everything about the debt and the necklace between themselves. They promised they would.

'You coming in?' Jags asked, as Lucky drove away.

'For a bit, then I have to get to the hospital.'

'Oh, shit, yeah.' Jags let them into the house. 'You want a cup of tea?'

'Nah, I'm good. What did you make of what Lucky said back there, when I said maybe he should tell the cops?' They sat down opposite each other, a coffee table between them. 'He seemed pretty jumpy about it.'

'Yeah, like someone had stuck a poker up his arse.'

'So what was that about?'

Jags shrugged. 'He's probably just shit-scared of my aunt finding out.'

'Didn't seem like that was his first thought. He said there was some "family stuff" to do with the necklace. You know what that might be?'

'Always some family drama about something. Could be anything. Unless it's something to do with Lucky having got it, instead of my dad or Uncle Dee.'

'Hang on, so it's Lucky's, not your aunt's?'

'It's hers now – he gave it to her when they got married. But it was passed down through his side of the family, from my grandparents and great-grandparents.'

'Why would it be an issue, if your grandparents gave it to him?'

'I don't know. Lucky's the eldest, so he was always likely to be the first to get married, and it was probably always going to go to him. If there was an argument about it, maybe he just doesn't want to bring it all up again.'

'Yeah, maybe.'

'Let's just wait for him to scrape the extra cash together, then we'll go back and see that stuck-up dickhead again and get him to give it back.'

'And this time we'll know what to expect.'

'We'll take my flippin' car too. I ain't doing that walk of shame up the driveway again.'

Zaq took out his phone and checked the time. 'I better get over to the hospital,' he said, getting to his feet.

Jags stood too. 'There been any news? How's he doing?'

'Doubt there's been any change, otherwise, my dad would've called. I'll find out the latest when I get there.'

Jags accompanied him to the door. 'What you doing tomorrow?'

'Going to see someone about a wedding.'

'What? You getting hitched? You never mentioned that. Who's the unlucky girl? Wait ... don't tell me it's Nina.'

'I'm going to see the people whose wedding Tariq DJ'd at, the one that guy with the gold tooth was asking about in the pub, see if they know who he is.'

'What time you going to do that?'

'Probably late afternoon.'

'Give me a shout, I'll go with you.'

*

Zaq picked up food from the petrol station on his way to the hospital. He knew his parents would rather eat at home, so he didn't need to pick up anything for them. He parked on the street across the main road from the hospital and crossed back to the main building. He found his parents sitting beside Tariq's bed, his dad looking at his mobile phone, his mum holding Tariq's hand and stroking his head. It didn't look as if anything had changed since he'd left that morning.

'I'll stay now,' he told them. 'You both go home and get some rest.'

His dad rubbed his eyes and got to his feet, looking worn and tired. Sitting around in a hospital all day with nothing to do but wait could have that effect. Zaq's mum didn't move but continued to stroke her son's head. 'Farah, *ajaah*,' his dad said, placing a gentle hand on her shoulder. '*Chal de eh.*'

His mother moved as if she was in a trance, his dad helping her to her feet then guiding her to the door. Her face lacked emotion, her features slack, limbs weighted with lead. It was as if she'd shed herself along with her tears.

She looked at Zaq without any change in her expression, no flicker of anything. Perhaps all she saw was a ghost. The ghost of the son she used to have, the one who'd been a success, someone she'd been proud of, before he'd been found guilty of killing someone and sent to prison. The pride and joy she'd had in him and his achievements had turned to dust as the gossip spread like wildfire through Southall's tight-knit Asian community. Chinese – or in this case, Indian and Pakistani – whispers had done the rounds, getting exaggerated and embellished with each retelling, until everyone was convinced he'd always been a psychopath and it was all down to his family and his upbringing. She'd had to endure it for the five years he'd been in prison, and things hadn't got any better after his release. If anything, the rumour mill had just started up again, the gossiping aunties always needing something to snipe about, more often than not simply to distract from their own families' failings and scandals.

Although the emotional detachment he felt from his mother since he'd returned home did hurt, Zaq couldn't really blame her. He had fucked up. Even though the situation really hadn't been his fault, his reaction had resulted in a death, cost him five years of his life and, he was finding, a whole lot more besides. The weight of her disappointment was a heavy load to bear. That was one of the reasons he'd moved out, and why he avoided going home much of the time.

Left alone with Tariq, he went and sat beside the bed, put his bag of food on the seat next to him and stared at his still unconscious brother for several long minutes. The only sounds in the room came from the various machines helping to keep him alive. 'You better pull through, you fucker,' Zaq said, hoping Tariq could hear him. He didn't expect any reaction – and didn't get one. It didn't stop him hoping.

He ran his hands over his face and leaned back in the chair. At least tomorrow he'd make a start on tracking down the bastards responsible for putting Tariq in here.

Zaq got as comfortable as he could and settled in for the evening. His thoughts drifted to the fractured relationship he and his brother had, another bitter legacy of his time inside. The two of them had been close before Zaq had gone to prison. Tariq had looked up to his successful older brother. His getting sent down had changed all that. It was something that either brought families closer together or pushed them apart – in Tariq's case, the latter.

When he'd had enough of mulling over the past, his thoughts turned to Nina. Just thinking about her lightened his mood, like sunshine breaking through cloud and chasing away the shadows of his past. It'd be good to talk to her, so he sent her a message to see if she fancied a chat.

They'd been out together several times, though mostly they went out as a group, with Rita and Jags, the four of them having become good friends over the last few months. Zaq really liked Nina – she was intelligent, confident and funny, and he also found her very attractive. He thought she liked him too, but he wasn't sure where to take things from there. He was useless at reading signals and so had no idea if she saw him as anything more than just a friend. Besides, she could easily do better than an ex-con who worked at a builder's yard.

It didn't help that it had been years since Zaq was last in a relationship. He hadn't been seeing anyone for almost a year before his court case, then he'd spent five years in prison, and now he'd been out for about a year. All told, that meant he'd been single for the last seven years. That was a depressing thought. The fact that he lived and worked pretty much exclusively with guys didn't help matters.

His phone rang. He saw Nina's name on the screen and felt a jolt of excitement. 'Hey,' he answered in a low voice, 'how're you doing?'

'I'm good. How are you? How's your brother?'

'He's still the same. I'm fine. I'm at the hospital now.'

'Have the doctors said anything else?'

'No, it's still just a case of wait and see.'

'How are your parents?'

Zaq told her his mother was taking it hard, while his dad seemed to be bottling things up.

'If there's anything I can do,' Nina said. 'If you need anything . . .'

'Thanks. How's your day been?'

'It was OK. I had a lie-in, went to the gym, then just chilled out. I did some reading and was just watching TV when you messaged. I'm going to help Mum with dinner in a bit. What about you? What have you been up to?'

'Most of the day had gone by the time I woke up,' he said. 'I worked out, then went and saw Jags for a bit.' He skipped the part about going to try and recover the necklace for Jags' uncle and seeing Bongo to get a lead on Tariq's attackers.

'So, you didn't do anything to try and find the guys responsible for what happened to your brother?'

Man, she was sharp. 'Not really, but I might have a way of finding out who one of them is.'

'And if you do? What will you do then?'

'If I get a name, I'll dig a little more, find out who he is, who the rest of them are, and whether it's linked to Dutta or something else.'

'And once you find all that out, then what?'

'I don't know.'

He did. He knew exactly what he would do to them. So did Nina, probably.

'You should pass it on to the police,' she said.

'They'd need a bit more than some names to do anything about it.'

'It'd be somewhere for them to start, and you never know – while you're asking around, you might find some other things that the police could use.'

'You're right: if I find out anything that definitely ties anyone to the attack, I'll pass it on to the cops.'

'You're sure?' She didn't sound completely convinced. 'You won't try and sort things out by yourself?'

'No.' He didn't like lying to her, but he wouldn't be doing it by himself – he was pretty sure Jags would be helping.

'I know you probably want to beat up whoever did this to your brother, but don't do anything silly and get yourself into trouble. You know where revenge can lead.'

He did. 'Don't worry,' he said, 'I ain't that stupid.'

No – if he went after the guys who'd put Tariq in here, he'd make damn sure it couldn't be pinned on him.

Chapter Twenty-One

Light seeped through his eyelids, penetrating the darkness and bringing Zaq out of sleep. The closed curtains filtered much of the sunlight from outside but the room was still fairly bright. A whisper of breeze wafted in through the open windows, stirring the curtains and creating lazy waves of light on the floor. He checked the time. It was one forty-five in the afternoon. The house was quiet, his housemates all out at work. Nothing had occurred overnight so there'd been nothing to tell his parents when they'd arrived in the morning. He'd only had fleeting, unsatisfactory snatches of sleep at the hospital and had gone straight to bed when he got home, hoping for some proper shut-eye.

Now his main aim for the day was to get in touch with the couple whose wedding Tariq had DJ'd at and see what he could find out. They were most likely at work now, so he probably wouldn't be able to talk to them until later. He hoped to be able to do it before he had to go to the hospital in the evening.

But even if he managed to contact them, why would they talk to him, answer his questions? He needed a persuasive reason. He thought about various approaches and eventually hit on one he thought might work. But it'd be a lot more convincing if he had some help. He called Jags.

'I need a favour.'

'All right. What is it?'

Zaq told him.

'Seriously?'

'Yeah. Why not?'

''Cause it's a bit weird,' Jags replied. 'Look, I'll ask but I can't guarantee anything.'

'It's to help find out who attacked Tariq. I'm sure you'll be able to sort it out.'

'I'll do my best.'

'Cheers, dude. I'll come over to yours later.'

Now he was putting things in motion, Zaq felt more positive. He looked through his phone for the scan he'd taken of the booking form Bongo had shown him, and made a note of the names and phone numbers of the couple whose wedding it had been. Then he spent a few minutes composing a text message, which he sent to both of them. After that, all he could do was wait and hope they'd agree to talk to him. If they didn't, he'd have to try a less subtle approach.

As he didn't have anything to do until later, he changed into workout gear, set the timer on his phone for ten minutes and started shadow-boxing with a couple of lightweight dumbbells in his hands. As usual, he began slowly, warming up his muscles before increasing the speed and strength of the moves and combinations. He imagined attackers coming at him and blocked and parried, before counter-attacking with fists, elbows, knees and kicks. If boxing was the sweet science, then street fighting was the dirty art.

When the buzzer sounded, he put the dumbbells down and stretched. After that, he got a heavier set of dumbbells and went through a different weights routine – five whole-body exercises, three sets of each. By the time he finished, his muscles were tight from the effort and he was shiny with sweat. He finished off with longer stretches, holding each one for a count of thirty, then lay on the floor for several minutes, feeling good and relaxed. Eventually he got up, put away the dumbbells, grabbed a towel and went to shave and shower.

When he returned from the bathroom, towel around his waist, there was a message on his phone. It was from one of the wedding couple he'd contacted – the bride. She said she wasn't sure, she'd have to check with her husband. While not the response he'd been hoping for, at least it wasn't an out-and-out no. He sent a polite reply, saying what a big help it would be if she and her husband could spare just a few moments to help him. He hoped it might do the trick.

Optimistic that it would, he felt he ought to dress appropriately. He picked a new pair of lightweight navy-blue linen trousers from his wardrobe, along with a short-sleeved midnight-blue shirt to go with them, and got dressed. A new pair of navy Adidas Gazelles completed the smart-casual look he was going for. He grabbed his phone, keys, cards and cash, and went down to the kitchen where he made himself scrambled eggs on toast, which he was in the process of eating when his phone rang.

'Not still jerking off in bed, are you?' Jags asked.

'No, I ain't – and if I was, you'd have put me right off.'

'Glad to hear it . . . I think. What you doing?'

'Having something to eat.'

'You all dressed and ready?'

'I tend not to eat in the nude.'

'Good. You want me to pick you up? I'm just on my way home, not far from yours now. I can drop you back later.'

If he was going to be stuck in traffic on the way to Jags', it'd be nicer to do it in air-conditioned comfort and have some company. 'Yeah, sure.'

'I'll be there in five.'

Chapter Twenty-Two

'Blimey, you're dressed up,' Jags said when Zaq got in the car. 'Where you going?'

'I told you.'

'Oh, yeah. I forgot.' Jags pulled away from the kerb.

'You get a chance to talk to Sandy?'

Sandy was Jags' cousin Sandeep. 'Yeah, she was a bit surprised when I asked her, but she says she'll do it.'

'Great. She say what time she could make it to yours?'

'Luckily for you, she's already finished work. Got a dentist appointment this afternoon at three-thirty. Said she'd come over to mine straight after, so she should be round for about five o'clock.'

'That's perfect. We should have time to go do it before I have to head back to the hospital.'

'That's if they agree to talk to you.'

'If they don't, I'll have to think of another way to speak to them. Maybe see if Bongo can sort it out or something. Not sure how keen he'll be, though.'

Jags turned onto the Broadway and took them along the Uxbridge Road towards Hayes. 'How come you didn't ask Nina?'

'You serious?' Zaq looked at him with a raised eyebrow. 'I've only been kind of seeing her for a few months. I can't ask her to do something like this.'

'But you can ask Sandy?'

'I've known Sandy almost as long as I've known you. Ain't like I'm asking her to do anything illegal or dangerous. She's just helping me out.'

'We wouldn't normally get her involved in anything we're up to.'

'Normally it'd be shit that just involves us, and that we can handle. This is a bit different. And anyway, if I asked Nina she'd tell me not to do it, to drop the whole thing, leave it to the cops.'

'She'd have a point.'

'It's my brother, though, man. Every night I go to the hospital and see what those motherfuckers've done to him and I want to do something about it. I can't just sit around twiddling my thumbs, waiting for the cops to *maybe* get whoever did it, not when I could probably do it better and faster myself.'

Jags nodded. 'I hear what you're saying, but it could land us in trouble, you know?'

Zaq couldn't help but smile. The use of the word *us* wasn't lost on him. 'We'll have to be careful, then, won't we?'

A short time later, they pulled into the driveway outside Jags' house and Zaq asked 'What time did you say Sandy was getting here?'

Jags checked the clock on the dashboard. ''Bout half an hour or so.'

'Great. Enough time for you to make us both a cuppa.' Zaq started to get out of the car.

'Hey, don't forget these,' Jags called. Zaq ducked back into the car to find Jags shaking a set of keys at him. 'These are yours.'

They were. 'Shit, they must've slipped out of my pocket. Thanks.' Zaq slid them back into the pocket of his linen trousers.

'Lucky you got me to pick up after you.'

*

While the kettle boiled, Jags changed out of his formal work clothes into jeans and a grey T-shirt. They'd finished their tea by the time Sandy arrived just after five o'clock.

'So you want me to be your wife,' Sandy said with a smile, when she saw Zaq.

'My fiancée, actually.' He smiled back and hoped he wasn't blushing. 'But only for half an hour or so.'

'I've had stranger requests,' she said.

Jags put up his hand. 'I don't want to know.'

'Relax, it's not like I'd tell you.'

Zaq had known Sandy since they were kids. She was Jags' cousin on his mum's side, the youngest of three sisters. He hadn't known her well at first – her being six years their junior was a big difference when they were younger, but not so much the older they got. He'd see her at all the family do's Jags invited him to, the two boys being practically adopted members of each other's families. Later on, he would bump into Sandy at the same bars, pubs and parties, as their circles of friends started to intersect.

She was average height, shorter than Zaq and Jags, neither skinny nor fat, probably what you'd call athletic. Her face had a distinctly impish quality and her eyes were a striking light brown. She wore her hair long and was dressed in a black trouser suit, white blouse and heels, perfect for the role Zaq wanted her to play.

'What would you have done if I'd said no?' she asked.

Zaq shrugged. 'We would've had to think of something else.'

'How long will it take?'

'Not long. I'm just waiting to hear—' Zaq stopped as he felt his phone vibrate and pulled it out of his pocket. '*Yes*. They say we can come over about six for a quick chat.'

'What am I supposed to do when we get there?' Sandy wanted to know.

'Just pretend to be my fiancée and help me get me in the door. Once we're inside, I'll do the talking.'

'Oh, so you just want me to be your arm-candy?'

'No, that's not what I meant,' Zaq blurted defensively. 'It's just – you don't have to come up with a story or anything. I'll handle it.'

'Relax.' Sandy grinned. 'I was just teasing.'

'Cheeky cow,' Zaq said with relief. 'Anyway, you have to be good-looking to be arm-candy.'

'Bastard,' Sandy laughed. Then she said, 'Seriously though, you think they know something about what happened to your brother?'

'No, but they're sure to have heard about any trouble at the wedding and know who was involved. That's what I want to find out.'

'Where do they live?' Jags asked.

Zaq brought up the scan of the booking form and zoomed in on the address. 'Blyth Road, Hayes.'

'It's not far. Shouldn't take long to get there. You got a while. Fancy a drink, Sandy? Tea, coffee?'

'I'll have a cup of tea, please.'

'Seeing as you're offering ...' Zaq said, holding his mug out to Jags.

Chapter Twenty-Three

At about quarter to six, Jags said, 'I might as well come too. Ain't like I got anything else to do. I'll drive.' He must have seen Zaq about to say something, and added, 'Don't worry, I'll wait in the car while you two go in. Look a bit odd otherwise.'

Zaq looked at Sandy, who shrugged. 'OK,' he told Jags.

They found the place without a problem. It was a flat in one of several purpose-built low-rise blocks in an area that used to be full of large warehouses and factories, many of which had been knocked down to make way for residential properties. The area was now a weird mix of old and new, homes and businesses. They figured out which building they were after, then Jags drove on along the one-way street until he found a place to park. 'I'll wait for you here,' he said.

Zaq and Sandy got out. The block was sombre grey brick at street level, the upper five floors a patchwork of exterior cladding in varying shades of grey. Zaq couldn't help wondering if the cladding was fireproof.

'What if they start asking about our wedding plans?' Sandy asked.

'Be vague. Say we haven't decided anything yet.'

'Did you give them our names?'

'Only mine. Just mentioned you as my fiancée.'

'OK, in that case, I'm going to be Jasmine. Just think of the flower, so you don't forget.'

'Er, right.' Zaq found the right button and pressed it. 'You talk.' He nudged Sandy towards the panel of buzzers. 'It'll sound better. And remember, we're here to ask about the DJs they used.'

A crackle of static came from the speaker, then a male voice said, 'Hello.'

'Hi, this is Jasmine and Zaq. We were hoping to speak to you really quickly about the DJs you had at your wedding.'

'Oh, right. OK, come on in. We're ground floor, on the right.' Zaq pushed the door open and held it for Sandy. As they reached the flat, the door opened and a young man in a blue shirt and black trousers greeted them. He didn't look particularly happy to see them.

'Hi!' Sandy flashed a bright smile and held out her hand. 'I'm Jasmine and this is Zaq. We're *so* sorry to bother you like this but, well, you know what it's like when you're planning a wedding ... we just wanted to get an idea of what the people we're thinking of hiring are like. Honestly, we'll only be a few minutes.'

Her warmth and bubbliness seemed to dispel some of his coolness. He shook her hand and said, 'I'm Vinay.' He shook hands with Zaq too. 'Come in.' He led them along a small hall-way, then into a lounge-diner.

A young woman got up from a sofa. 'Hello, I'm Kiran,' she said, greeting them with a smile and an outstretched hand. Zaq and Sandy shook hands with her and introduced themselves. 'Can I get you a drink? Tea? Coffee?'

'No, thank you,' Sandy said. 'Honestly, we won't be staying long. Just a few questions and we'll be out of your way.'

'Have a seat,' Kiran offered, and they all sat.

'Congratulations to you both, by the way,' Sandy said.

'Thanks,' Kiran beamed. 'So you're getting married too?'

'Yes. We're just starting to plan everything.'

'We know you got to book things up well in advance,' Zaq said. 'Like venues, DJs and all that stuff. That's why we wanted to talk to you soon as we could. You used Elemental Sound System for your wedding, right?'

'Yeah,' Vinay said. 'How'd you know?'

'Someone told me. They were at your wedding. I just can't remember who it was.' Zaq made a pretence of trying to recall and then giving up. 'How were they, the DJs?'

'They were good. Knew all the tracks, new and old, to get people up. Good mix of English, Bhangra and Hindi – some pretty banging mixes too.'

'So you'd recommend them?'

'Yeah, I would.'

'This guy I talked to mentioned there'd been some trouble to do with the DJs – is that right?'

Vinay glanced at Kiran and shook his head. 'You know what Indian weddings are like,' he said, 'always some drama.'

'Did the DJs start it? Was it to do with the music or what?'

'We don't really know. We were a bit busy getting married at the time. Heard about it after, though.'

'Do you know what happened?'

'Apparently something kicked off between the DJs and some guys.'

'Guests of yours?'

'Yeah. Well, they were friends of a friend. One of your mates, wasn't it?' he said, turning to Kiran.

She rolled her eyes a little. 'Yes – Sharan. We went to school together. She's a hairdresser, did my hair for the wedding. I invited her and her boyfriend. I think one of his mates came along too. She didn't really say what it was about, but she came over and apologised afterwards.'

'My mates had to sort it out,' Vinay added. 'Separate them and keep them apart. Lucky it was towards the end of the night. I think Sharan and those guys left pretty soon after.'

Zaq nodded. 'Is she any good?' The others looked at him, confused. 'Your friend, Sharan? As a hairdresser?' It didn't lessen their confusion. They were probably looking at his close-cropped hair and wondering why he'd need a hairdresser. 'It's just, Jasmine's been on about finding a new hairdresser, and I thought . . . ' He let the sentence hang.

Fortunately, Sandy figured out what Zaq was after. 'Oh, my God, yes. My hairdresser's moved away and I've been trying to find someone decent for ages. You know how hard it is to find anyone to do your hair just the way you want it, right? Do you think Sharan would be able to do a good job for me?'

Kiran nodded. 'She's really good. Always busy. She did hair-dressing at college and got a job straight after, been doing it ever since. She's really talented.'

Sandy smiled. 'That's brilliant. I don't suppose you have her details, do you?'

'I do, as it happens. She didn't charge to do my hair for the wedding, but she did leave some cards to give out to anyone that might be interested in getting her to do theirs. I'll get you one.' She got up and left the lounge.

Zaq thought he'd better continue the charade of being inter-ested in hiring the DJs and asked Vinay some questions about price, deposit, set-up, sound quality and anything else he could think of that someone wanting to hire a DJ might ask. It turned out Tariq and his friends were making a pretty tidy sum from their part-time gig.

Kiran returned and handed Sandy a business card. 'Here you go.'

'Thank you,' Sandy said and looked at the card. 'There's only a mobile number and social media links on here,' she said. 'Does she work at a salon or anything?'

'She does, during the week. The bridal stuff is something she does privately at the weekends. I can give you the name of the salon she works at. I don't know the number but I'm sure you can look it up.'

Kiran took the card back from Sandy and wrote something on the reverse before handing it back to her. 'It's in Slough, if that's not too far for you.'

'No, I'm in Hounslow, so it should be fairly easy.' Sandy lived in Hillingdon.

They asked some more wedding-related questions, about venues, caterers, flower suppliers and things like that, most of which Sandy came up with. She seemed to know a lot about weddings, or at least what questions to ask if you were thinking of arranging one.

After a while, Zaq said, 'We've taken up enough of your time. Thanks a lot for talking to us. It's been a really big help.'

Sandy flashed a big smile and thanked them too.

'It's no problem,' Kiran said, offering a smile of her own, though Zaq could tell the couple were glad to be getting rid of them. 'I hope it's all useful.'

'Have you been on your honeymoon yet?' Sandy asked as they got to the hallway.

'Not yet,' Kiran said. 'We're waiting for September when it'll be quieter.'

'Oh. Have you got anywhere in mind?'

'We're going to Italy,' Vinay told them. 'We could've gone for something further away and more expensive but we're supposed to be moving out of this place to something a bit bigger and we want to save for that. This place was fine when it was just me on my own, but it's too small for both of us.'

'Well, I hope you have a fab time in Italy, and good luck with the move.'

When he and Sandy were outside and walking back to Jags' car, he said, 'You were brilliant in there.'

'Thanks. I always fancied being an actress.'

'Based on that performance, you should've gone for it.'

'I don't think my mum and dad would've been too happy.'

Zaq opened the door of the BMW for her and she got in the back. 'Here,' she said, holding out the hairdresser's card. 'I think this is what you wanted.'

'You might want these, too,' Jags said, handing him his keys. 'They must've slipped out your pocket again. They were on the seat.'

'Bloody pockets on these things,' Zaq said, referring to his trousers. 'Thanks.'

'Try and keep them in your pants, will you?'

'Bet you say that to all the boys.'

Sandy sniggered in the back.

Jags gave Zaq an unamused look. 'Ha, ha, very funny. How'd you get on in there?'

Zaq shoved his keys to the bottom of his pocket, to make sure they wouldn't fall out again. Then he held up the card. 'We found someone who might know the guys we're looking for.'

When they got to Jags' Zaq thanked Sandy again for her help.

'Any time,' she said with a smile. 'I hope you find whoever did that to your brother. Don't do anything stupid, though.'

She wasn't the first person to tell him that.

Traffic was heavy in Southall so it took a while to get to Zaq's place. 'I should've let you drive over to mine,' Jags grumbled when they pulled up outside. 'Remind me next time, huh?'

'I'll call you tomorrow,' Zaq said, 'once I'm awake. If you're in, I'll come over and we can figure out what to do next.'

'OK, cool.' They shook hands and Zaq got out of the car. He gave Jags a wave and the BMW sped away.

Zaq crossed the empty driveway to the front door, thinking about what he'd have to eat before heading to the hospital. As he reached the doorstep he put his hand in his pocket to get his keys ... only to find they weren't there. Shit! They must've slipped out again.

He strode quickly out to the pavement and looked down the road, hoping to catch sight of Jags but knowing he was too late. Jags would probably be on Lady Margaret Road by now. Still, he wasn't that far away. He'd call, tell him to look for the keys and drop them back if they were there.

He was vaguely aware of footsteps behind him as he reached into his other pocket for his phone, and moved to the side of the pavement to allow whoever it was to pass. He didn't realise until too late that something was wrong. The footsteps had speeded up, and there were two sets. Zaq's instincts screamed danger. He started to turn but wasn't fast enough.

The first blow struck him on the back of the head. Blinding pain flashed behind his eyes and through his skull.

He was already dazed by the first blow when the second must have landed.

Because that was when everything went black.

Chapter Twenty-Four

The first thing Zaq became aware of was pain.

A deep, throbbing pain that pulsed through his head and pushed hard against the back of his eyes. His neck was also stiff, the muscles feeling hard as clay baked in a kiln.

Next was noise and motion. He was lying on his side, in a cramped space, feeling the humps and bumps of a car driving. His hands were tied behind his back.

The last thing he became aware of was the darkness. His eyes had been shut against the pain, but when he cracked them open he couldn't see a thing. His first irrational thought was that the blows to his head had blinded him – but then he realised there was something over his head, a bag made from some rough material.

His feet weren't tied, so he stretched his legs as far as they would go, which wasn't far. It took him a little while, but he figured out he had to be in the boot of a car. What he still had no idea about was who'd grabbed him, why, and where they were taking him.

Zaq guessed they'd arrived at their destination when the car reversed, bumping over what might have been a kerb and pitching him up against the back of the rear seats. He heard the car doors open and close, followed by footsteps, then the sound of muffled voices. When the boot was opened, he was in no position to fight his way out of it, but even so he was hit several times with something heavy and hard.

'Give us any trouble,' a voice said, 'and we'll whack you over the head again.'

Zaq didn't answer. New centres of pain bloomed in his arm, side and leg, depriving him of the will to speak.

Hands grabbed him and pulled him out of the boot, painfully wrenching his shoulders and banging his knees and shins on the metal edges. As soon as he was standing, he was punched in the stomach, causing him to double up. A hand kept his head pushed down and he was dragged into a building of some sort and eventually pushed into a chair. He had to sit forward because his hands were still tied behind him. While one of the men held his arms, the other grabbed his right leg and pushed it against a chair leg. Then there was a zipping sound and Zaq felt something pulling tight just above his ankle, binding his leg to the chair. The guy did the same with his other leg. Cable ties, Zaq realised.

Next, his head was pushed towards his knees, and his arms pulled up behind him. There was a snip and his right hand came free. His arm was forced down on to the armrest of the chair. Zaq heard the zipping sound again and knew what it was even before he felt the cable tie pull and tighten around his wrist, immobilising his arm.

Even though he knew there wasn't any point, he resisted as they forced his left arm on to the other armrest. It was futile, though, and both men soon had it fastened there. Zaq let out a groan. The sound vibrating inside his skull, coupled with the effort of trying to fight them, only turned up the dial on his headache.

'Go and park the car properly, on the road,' the man who'd

spoken before said to his accomplice and Zaq heard footsteps going away.

'Not so tough now, are you?' the man said.

'Who are you?' Zaq asked. 'What d'you want?'

'You'll find out soon enough.'

Zaq sat and breathed deeply and slowly to try and lessen the pain in his head. It didn't seem to help. He heard footsteps approaching and, when the driver had rejoined his friend, the bag was suddenly whipped off Zaq's head.

He opened his eyes, squinting against the brightness he expected, but instead found the light was fairly dim, which was fortunate because anything brighter would have made his head hurt more. It took a moment to focus. He was in a large empty building with a dusty concrete floor. The two men were standing in front of him, both Asian, both scowling. He had no idea who they were. Very slowly, he stretched his neck, first from side to side, then up and down. 'I don't suppose either of you's got any paracetamol?'

They continued to stare at him. The one on the left said, 'You'll need more than paracetamol by the time we've finished with you.'

Great. The way they'd started with him was bad enough.

Zaq let his gaze roam, to get a sense of where he was. It looked like some sort of abandoned warehouse, an open space with pitted and chipped concrete pillars evenly spaced along its length and width. The place smelt of damp and disuse.

'Remember me?' the guy said.

He was about five-eight, medium build with cropped dark hair. His nose was a bit big, he had a dimple in his chin and he was dressed in jeans and a T-shirt. Nothing about him particularly stood out. 'No. Should I?'

'Yeah, you broke my fucking collarbone.'

'Did I?' Zaq tried to recall but failed. He gave a slight shrug, which only added to the discomfort in his shoulders. 'I don't remember.'

'In the car park of that pub, what was it called ... the Hare and the Tortoise?'

Now Zaq placed him. 'The Hare and Hounds.'

So they were Dutta's guys. Had they jumped Tariq too?

'You asked for it. You were trying to kidnap a girl.' Zaq wished now he'd broken the guy's arms instead.

'Yeah? Well, now I'm going to pay you back.'

Zaq didn't say anything. Maybe, given the circumstances, it'd be better not to antagonise him.

'You fucking broke my nose too,' piped up the other one. He was about the same height and build as his mate, only with slightly more hair, a wispy beard and a sharper nose. 'Hit me in the face with something, outside a park.'

Zaq remembered now – cracking a bloke in the face with the butt of a gun at the gates of Spikes Bridge Park. It had all happened very fast. He hadn't had time to look at the guy properly, so he wouldn't recognise him now. The broken nose hadn't done anything for his looks though.

'You thought we'd just forgotten about you?' the first guy said. 'Nah, mate, we don't forget shit like that.'

'You fuckers jump my brother the other day?' Neither one fitted the description Prit had given him, but they could have been part of the group that carried out the attack.

They looked at each other, then back at him. Collarbone guy said, 'Don't know what you're on about.'

Was that true, or were they just playing dumb? 'You know a guy with a gold tooth? Chunky geezer with a bit of a mohawk going on?'

'Shut up. We ain't here to answer your questions.'

'What are we here for, then?' He already knew the answer but figured talking might delay the inevitable.

'We're here to see how you like getting beaten up.'

'I can save you the trouble and tell you – I don't like it at all.'

'Think you're funny, huh? Let's see how funny you are after we finish with you. Come on,' he said to his mate, 'let's get started.'

'Hey,' Zaq said. 'This is hardly fair, me being tied to a chair like this. I don't remember either of *you* being tied up before. Why don't you let me up and we can sort this out properly, two of you against me? You'd still have the advantage.' Which they would. He just hoped fear and adrenaline would dull his pain enough that he could fight his way out of there.

'Not going to happen,' Collarbone told him. 'We been told what we need to do, and it don't include letting you out of that chair to have a fight.'

'Yeah, and who was it told you that?'

'Mahesh. You remember him?'

He did. Mahesh Dutta, who'd tried to kill him a few months ago. 'I thought he was kicking his heels inside.'

'He is, thanks to you. And he's had time to think, while he's been there—'

'Hope he didn't hurt himself.'

The guy ignored the comment. 'He reckons it was you that fitted him up, planted the gun.'

Zaq was about to shrug but remembered it would hurt. 'Don't know what you're talking about.'

'He knew that's what you'd say, but he don't see any other way it could've got there.'

'Got where, exactly?' Zaq said, though he knew exactly what the guy was referring to.

'In the car.'

'Maybe he left it there. It's got fuck all to do with me.'

'He had it on him, says you took it from him.'

'Far as I can remember, he dropped it. He probably wasn't thinking straight after I popped him. He might've picked it up and taken it to the car himself.'

For a second, the two guys looked at each other, unsure. 'Nah, he's sure it was you. He wouldn't have stuck it under the seat. Why the fuck would he have done that? Anyway, we're here to get the truth out of you and then we'll get Mahesh out of prison.'

'I can't tell you what I don't know anything about,' Zaq lied.

'Well, that's going to be tough shit for you, then, ain't it? 'Cause we're going make you talk, and while we're at it, we'll get you back for what you did to us 'n' all.'

Chapter Twenty-Five

Although Zaq was doing his best to remain calm, he could feel anxiety starting to gnaw at him. A memory flashed into his mind – the back room of a butcher's shop and the glint of a filleting knife – and fear and a sense of panic rose within him. His heart began to race; sweat prickled on his head and back. He had to calm down and think. He took a breath, then another, and cast his eyes around. He saw a sports bag with a chrome-plated metal bar sticking out of it. Maybe that was what they'd hit him with. He didn't know what else might be in there and decided he didn't want to think about it. A beating he could take – not that he was looking forward to it. It had taken him a few months to fully recover from the last one.

He'd been in fights before, in prison and out, so taking a punch would be nothing new. The best he could hope for was a good punch to the nose, which would cause a heavy nosebleed and make things messy. Maybe the sight of a lot of blood would be enough for them, make them think they'd hurt him good. He didn't see any way he could get out of the chair, so it looked as if he was just going to have to sit and take whatever they dished out.

'Start filming,' Collarbone told his friend.

Nose guy took out his mobile phone, tapped the screen and held it pointed at Zaq.

'Now ...' Collarbone said, standing to Zaq's right, just out of camera shot, 'tell us about the gun and how you stitched Mahesh up.'

'I already told you, I don't know what the fuck—'

Collarbone punched him in the face.

The blow hit Zaq in the mouth and rocked his head back. He'd been half-expecting it, but it still caught him by surprise. He felt the afterburn of the impact and a stinging sensation buzzed all around his face. He tasted blood and suspected his lip was cut.

'Shit, man,' Nose guy said, still filming, 'Mahesh said not to fuck up his face until after we got what we need.'

'Oh, yeah. My bad.' Collarbone drew back a fist and fired a solid shot straight into Zaq's midriff.

With punches to the head and face ruled out for now, Zaq had been girding himself up to take some body shots. He blew a breath out as if the air had been forced from him. It hadn't. All the fight training he'd done had taught him how to take a blow to the body, and he'd been able to tense up and absorb much of the force of the punch. He still felt it, but pretended it hurt more than it had. He let his head sag forward, to give the impression he was struggling for air, to buy some time. Time for what, though? How the hell was he going to get out of this?

A hand forced his head up. 'Not acting so hard now, are you?' Collarbone sneered. He let Zaq's head go and hit him with another punch to the body.

Zaq tensed, but the shot hit him in the lower ribs where there wasn't a lot of muscle to cushion the blow, so it hurt. He wondered if the cracks to his ribs he'd sustained before had fully healed, or whether this present punishment might break them?

'Tell us about the gun,' Collarbone said again.

If it was a toss-up between being hit in the head or the body,

Zaq would rather stick with the body, and, until they got what they wanted from him, that was what they'd concentrate on. 'Like I said before, I don't know nothing about any fuckin'—'

This time the punch caught him off-guard and slammed into his sternum, jolting the air out of him. The chair was forced back, its legs screeching against the concrete floor, making the sound he couldn't.

Zaq strained against the cable ties holding him in place, desperately trying to get some air into his lungs, but he simply couldn't. Calm ... he had to stay calm ... He took quick, shallow breaths to get at least some oxygen and was gradually able to breathe normally again. He wanted nothing more than to get free and batter the shit out of the fucker standing over him.

Collarbone must have read it in his face. 'What?' he said. 'What the fuck you going to do, huh?' He loomed over Zaq, hands balled into fists. Then he pulled his right fist back, opened it, and unleashed a stinging slap that knocked Zaq's head violently to one side. The sound cracked loudly in the open space of the warehouse.

'Hey,' Nose guy whined. 'Mahesh said—'

'Stop moaning. It was a fucking slap. Won't mark him for the camera, not so you'll notice, anyway.'

Zaq's face was burning where he'd been hit. He could still feel the imprint of the guy's hand. Slowly, he turned his head back to look at the guy. If anything, the slap had only fuelled his anger more. He stared at the guy ... and received another vicious slap for his trouble.

'I can go on like this for ages. I'm just getting warmed up,' Collarbone told him. 'You don't want to tell us about putting the gun in the car yet, that's fine by me. I'll keep on beating you till you do.'

Zaq knew that once he'd told them what they wanted to hear,

they'd go to work on his head and face, maybe a lot more as well, and who knew when they'd stop? Fuck that. The only thing he could think to do for now was drag things out for as long as possible. So it was with a sense of self-preservation rather than bravado that he said, 'Go fuck yourself.'

Unsurprisingly, Collarbone didn't like that, and went to town, hitting Zaq with shot after shot to the body, that he could do nothing to defend himself against. The only thing in Zaq's favour was that his being bound to a chair made it awkward for the guy to hit him. Not that it hurt any less. Zaq took the punches, knowing it was in his interest to act more hurt than he was. He also knew he couldn't keep it up for long. It took energy to repeatedly tense his muscles and soak up the shots. Eventually he'd tire, and then the blows would start to do real damage.

Collarbone stopped to catch his breath. Zaq took the opportunity to breathe as deeply as he could, to re-oxygenate his muscles for another stint. He let his head hang forward but his eyes looked up and out, around the warehouse, searching – for what, he didn't know.

That was when he spotted the movement way back in the shadows. What if it was another of Dutta's cronies come to join these two arseholes? Shit. And what if he'd brought along things to make Zaq confess – knife, hammer, scalpel, pliers, needles, blowtorch ...? Even lemon, chilli and salt? Things might be about to get a whole lot worse.

But the figure didn't come forward. Whoever it was seemed to be staying back, moving at an angle and sticking to the shadows. Was it some homeless person checking the place out, looking for somewhere to bed down, who'd stumbled across them? Once they saw what was happening, would they go and get help? More likely they'd want nothing to do with it and simply leave the way they'd come.

Collarbone sniffed and shook himself loose. 'OK, shit-for-brains, you ready to talk yet?'

'Yeah,' Zaq croaked, putting some pain into his voice.

'Oh.' He sounded surprised, a little disappointed too. 'All right, let's hear it, then.'

Zaq looked at the guy filming on the phone. 'I'd like to say, on record ... that I've been kidnapped by two of Mahesh Dutta's mates, who've tied me to a chair and are beating me up, trying to get me to say—'

The punch caught Zaq on the left cheekbone, jarring his head back and causing a flash of light and pain. Again the chair legs screeched on the concrete as the impact sent it along the floor. 'Fuck,' Zaq uttered, this time not having to pretend it hurt.

'Bloody hell,' the guy filming said.

'Just delete it later,' Collarbone snapped. 'Looks like I'll have to soften this fucker up some more, then we can try again when he's ready to talk.'

'It won't be no good if he looks like he's been beaten up. We won't be able to use it to get Mahesh out. He'll be well pissed off.'

'Yeah, yeah. I was just shutting him up. Don't worry – now I'll hit him where it won't show.'

During this exchange, Zaq had kept a discreet eye on the figure working its way forward, and finally got a proper glimpse of it as it moved through a shaft of light. With a shock, he realised who it was.

Chapter Twenty-Six

'Time to stop fucking around,' Collarbone said.

'Big words from a pussy beating up someone strapped to a chair,' Zaq responded, talking loudly. He knew he had to keep the two guys distracted, so the person creeping towards them could get closer without being detected. 'Let me up and we'll see who's fucking around.'

'Shut your face.'

Zaq's cheek was numb but he could feel the skin around it tightening, a sure sign that it was swelling. He ignored it. 'What's the matter? You scared?'

'I ain't fucking scared of you.'

'Let me up, then – or you worried I'll break your arms like I said I'd do if I ever saw you again?'

'You're seeing me now, ain't you, motherfucker? Don't look like you're going to be breaking any arms, does it? Fact, maybe I'll break your arms instead.'

'Going to be a bit hard with them tied to the chair like this.'

'I can smash them with that metal bar I hit you round the head with, or I can untie them, one at a time.'

'Good. One arm's all I'll need to fight you.'

Collarbone glanced at his friend. 'Get a load of this prick, will you?' Then to Zaq he said, 'You been watching too many movies, dickhead.'

'Yeah ...' Zaq saw an opening to create a major distraction and took it. 'Didn't think much of that one with your mum in it though.'

'Huh? What the fuck you talking about?'

'The one with her shagging a dog.'

There was a second of silence. Then Collarbone's eyes bulged with fury. It was like watching a kettle come to the boil. Zaq wouldn't have been surprised if steam had come out of his ears. 'You ... fucking ... *what?*' He was almost choking with rage, just as Zaq had hoped. Then, as he'd also expected, the guy bellowed like a bull and charged at him.

Zaq clamped his jaw shut, tensed the muscles in his face, and at the last second jerked his head to the left, just slipping the punch. He wasn't so lucky with the next one, a wild hook that smashed into the left side of his head. Another punch, a right, was coming at him. Fuck it. In a completely unorthodox move, Zaq threw his head forward to meet the oncoming fist, effectively head-butting it, catching the guy by surprise.

'FUCK! You bastard,' Collarbone cried, shaking his right hand.

Hopefully, he'd busted a knuckle. Seeing spots, Zaq tried to focus on what the guy would do next. He thought he saw a blur of movement near the guy with the phone, but didn't have time to be sure.

With a roar, Collarbone seized Zaq's right arm and a fistful of his hair, and kneed him hard in the chest, knocking the breath from his body. The chair teetered for a split second on its back legs, and Zaq thought he heard the sound of a mobile phone clattering to the ground. Then he jerked backwards and sent the chair crashing over on to the floor. Collarbone, still holding on to Zaq, was pulled completely off-balance. He half fell on top of Zaq, flailing around, trying to find his feet.

Zaq strained to try and turn the chair on to its side. He heard the thump of running footsteps, the meaty smack of a punch, and a grunt of pain. Then Collarbone was hauled off him, and was being punched in the face again, and again, and again. Finally, he fell to the ground beside Zaq, bleeding from mouth and nose, groaning as though he was having a bad dream. Zaq turned his head painfully and saw the guy who'd been filming also lying in a heap a few yards away.

He heard footsteps approaching and then a familiar figure was bending over to look at him.

'Need a hand up?' Jags said.

Chapter Twenty-Seven

Jags squatted down and heaved the chair upright. Then he looked at the cable ties. 'How the fuck am I meant to get these off?'

'Look in the bag over there,' Zaq told him. 'There must be some pliers or scissors in there. They used something to cut some off me before.'

Jags returned with some cutting pliers.

'I don't think I've ever been so glad to see you,' Zaq said. 'How the fuck did you know where I was?'

'Your keys must've fallen out of your pocket again. I went round a corner and they flew across the seat. I knew you wouldn't be able to get in the house without them, so I turned around and came back.'

'I was just about to call you when those two arseholes jumped me. Next thing I knew I was tied up and in the boot of a car. Where the hell are we anyway?'

'Industrial estate in Park Royal. This place was all shut up.'

With the cable ties cut, Zaq was finally able to stand up, though a little unsteadily.

'You OK?' Jags said. 'You look a right mess.'

'Thanks. I'll be fine.'

'Lucky I came back when I did. Any later and I wouldn't've seen them bundling you into the boot of their motor. As it was, I only realised it was you 'cause I spotted the stripes on your Gazelles.'

'Man, I owe you, big-time.'

Zaq took careful deep breaths, filling his lungs and slowly expanding his chest to check if there were any cracks or fractures to his ribs. When his lungs were fully inflated and he hadn't experienced any shooting pains, he was fairly sure he'd gotten away without any serious damage. His body was bruised and tender all over, but that he could live with. He was more annoyed about the cut to his lip and the swelling on his cheek. How was he going to explain those to his mum and dad?

A groan drew their attention to Collarbone, who had one arm under him to push himself up off the floor.

'Looks like he's thinking of getting up.'

Jags went over and used his foot to swipe Collarbone's arm out from under him. Across the floor, Nose guy was starting to come around too. He lifted his head and looked around, confused, blood smeared across his face.

'Stay where you are, or I'll come over there and punch your lights out,' Jags told him. 'What d'you want to do with these two?' he asked Zaq.

Good question. 'I'd like to break their fucking arms, that's what.'

'No, please ... don't,' Collarbone pleaded from the floor.

'Who are they anyway, and what the fuck did they want with you? I didn't hear what they were saying – too busy trying to be a ninja.'

'They're mates of Dutta's.'

Jags knew who that was and raised his eyebrows.

'The prick's got too much time on his hands,' Zaq said, 'so he's sitting around thinking up conspiracy theories about how he got where he is. Reckons I was behind it, that I somehow set him up.' Zaq was talking for the benefit of the two on the ground. Jags knew the truth but nodded along. 'These arseholes were going to make me confess, on camera, to planting the gun and whatever other bullshit they wanted, so they could get Dutta off.'

Talking about it had given Zaq an idea. He fell silent as he thought about it.

'You OK?' Jags asked.

'Yeah, just a sec . . . ' He could turn the situation to his advantage without having to break anyone's arms, at least for the time being. It would be brains over brawn, something even Nina might be impressed by if he ever told her about it. He told Jags, 'Get that other idiot over here.'

Jags went and hauled Nose guy over to join Collarbone on the floor.

'Empty your pockets,' Zaq ordered them both. They exchanged uncertain glances. 'Get a bloody move on!'

They emptied their pockets on to the floor – wallets, keys, loose change, a pack of chewing gum, a mobile phone. Zaq looked through the stuff and picked up Collarbone's wallet.

'Yeah, take my money,' he whined, 'just don't break my arm.'

'Shut up. I don't want your fucking money.' Zaq opened the wallet and flicked through it until he found what he wanted. He then pulled out his phone and took a photo. 'Right,' he said to Collarbone, 'I've just taken a picture of your driving licence, so I've got your name and address. I see you again, or Dutta sends anyone else after me, I'm going to come for you. And I will break *both* your arms. So it's in your interest to make sure he don't do that.' Zaq grabbed the other guy's wallet, took out the driving licence, snapped a picture of it too and dropped it on the floor. 'Same goes for you.' Then he looked inside the sports bag, and found a hammer, screwdrivers, a box cutter, duct tape and a load of thick nylon cable ties. 'You,' he told Collarbone, 'get in the chair.'

'What for?'

'Just do it, before I smack you one.'

Collarbone got up off the floor; the blood streaked across his face was starting to dry and made him look terrible. Zaq doubted he'd try anything with both him and Jags ready to lay him out. He sat in the chair. 'Arms on the rests,' Zaq ordered. He took a cable tie and secured Collarbone's wrist tight to the armrest. Then he did the other arm, and both his legs, just as they'd done to him. When Collarbone started to complain, Zaq tore off a length of duct tape and slapped it over his mouth.

There didn't seem to be another chair, so Zaq made Nose guy get up and stand in front of his friend. He stuck tape over his mouth so they wouldn't have to listen to him protest either, then cable-tied his ankles together. 'Get on your knees.' The guy just looked at him. 'On your fucking knees!' Zaq barked. Once he was down, Zaq and Jags took an arm each and dragged him to kneel opposite Collarbone. Zaq yanked one arm around Collarbone and through the gap between the backrest and the seat of the chair, and Jags did the same with the other arm, pulling Nose guy forward so he ended up with his head in Collarbone's lap. Ignoring the guys' muffled protests, Zaq got another cable tie and bound Nose guy's wrists together behind his friend's back.

'Oh, man, that just looks wrong,' Jags said, unable to stifle a laugh.

Zaq picked up a mobile phone, held it up in front of Collarbone. 'This your phone?'

Collarbone nodded.

'Insured?'

A shake of the head.

'Too bad.' Zaq flung the phone high and far across the empty warehouse. A second later they heard it shatter on the concrete.

Collarbone let out a groan from behind the tape.

Next, Zaq threw their keys as far as he could into the dark recesses of the building. Then he found Nose guy's phone, dropped when Jags had taken him down. The screen was cracked but otherwise it seemed OK. He squatted down beside the chair and waved it in front of Nose guy's face, which was turned to the side, away from his friend's crotch. 'What's the code for your phone?' he asked, and partly pulled the tape off so he could answer.

'Don't leave us like this,' Nose guy said. 'It's out of order.'

Zaq tapped him on the head with the phone. 'After what you two just did to me? You're fucking lucky I'm leaving you in one piece. Now, what's the fucking code?'

Reluctantly, the guy told him and Zaq put the tape back. He tried the code to make sure it worked. It did. Good. He stood up and said to Collarbone, 'Try not to get a hard-on, huh? I don't think your mate will appreciate it. I could be wrong, though.' Then he turned to Jags. 'Come on, let's get out of here.'

Chapter Twenty-Eight

Jags led the way through the musty, shadowy interior of the dis-used warehouse, to a fire exit at the far end of the building. The door was slightly ajar and they went out on to a narrow walkway that ran along the side of the unit. The walkway was paved, though high weeds grew between the square slabs and to either side.

They came out on to the road that ran in front of the building. Warehouses and industrial premises stretched away in either direction, and Zaq looked back at the building they'd just come from. It was all shut up, metal sheets covered the windows, and there were large 'To Let' signs fixed to the front. Parked at the kerb, directly in front of the walkway, was a Lexus saloon.

'That's their motor,' Jags said, 'that you were in the boot of. They reversed on to the pavement, right up to that alley, so no one would see them taking you in.'

Zaq walked over and snapped a picture of it.

'Souvenir?' Jags asked.

'Might come in useful. Let's get the fuck out of here. Where you parked?'

'Over there.' Jags pointed back up the one-way road. When they were in the car, Jags handed Zaq his keys. 'Here . . . try not to lose them again.'

'Losing these saved my ass. If they hadn't fallen out of my pocket, you wouldn't have come back and seen what happened.'

Jags started the car and pulled away. 'Don't make a habit of it, huh – losing your keys or getting kidnapped.'

'I'll do my best. Thanks – for coming after them and for getting me out of there.'

'You'd have done the same for me. Want me to drop you home again?'

'Yeah, please. I need to change—' Zaq's clothes were covered in muck and dirt from the warehouse '—and then get over to the hospital.'

'What about . . . ?' Jags glanced at him and waved a hand in front of his own face.

'I know, it's bad,' Zaq said, 'but ain't nothing I can do about how you look. You'll just have to live with it.'

'Bloody comedian. Maybe I should've just let them beat you up a bit more before getting you out of there.'

Jags dropped Zaq off, though this time he waited for him to get inside before he drove away. Zaq went straight to the bathroom mirror. He had a bad cut to his upper lip, so it looked like he'd got lip filler but stopped halfway through the procedure. There was a noticeable lump under his left eye, which was slightly closed, as if he was permanently wincing in discomfort. A bruise was starting to colour around the eye as well, and he had further cuts and scrapes. The back of his head hurt to touch and he could feel a lump and a crusting of what could have been dried blood. He didn't bother to clean up any of it. He wanted it to be seen.

He went to his room and put on fresh jeans and a T-shirt, then made his way downstairs. As he reached the bottom of the stairs, the front door opened and Bal came in.

'Oh, it's you,' he said. '*Kidaah?* What's wrong with your face – apart from the usual, that is?'

'It's nothing.'

'Don't look like nothing.'

'I had a run-in with a couple of guys. They wanted me to say some stuff to get their mate out of prison.'

'Anything to do with that stuff that happened before?'

'Yeah, one of those guys in prison got them to do it.'

'That's illegal, ain't it? Witness fiddling, or whatever the fuck?'

'Tampering – yeah, it is.'

'I hope you told them where to fucking go.'

'I think they got the message.'

'How you doing otherwise? How's your brother?'

Zaq held his hands out palms up, like holding a tray – the *desi* equivalent of shrugging your shoulders. 'Same as before. He's stable for now but the doctors are keeping an eye on him.'

Bal nodded. 'That's something. I hope he gets better soon. You going to be back for dinner?'

'No. I'll be staying at the hospital again.'

Zaq slipped past him and out the door, closing it behind him. He was hyper-vigilant as he went to his car, his earlier scrape with Dutta's mates making him especially wary. But there was no sign of danger or anyone waiting for him. He got into the car and drove off to the hospital.

Chapter Twenty-Nine

He stopped to pick up some food and snacks for himself, then got to the hospital as quick as he could. He parked in the same street as before, where he wouldn't have to pay to leave his car all night. Instead of going in through the main entrance, however, he went to the other side of the building, where the A&E Department and the Urgent Care Centre were. He went to the Urgent Care receptionist, who sat behind a counter with a large window and a tiny microphone.

'I'd like to see a doctor, please,' he told her.

'What seems to be the problem?'

'I was attacked by a couple of guys a little while ago and one of them hit me on the back of the head. I think I passed out for a bit. They also beat me up.' The evidence of that was all over his face.

'OK,' the woman said. She wasn't shocked or surprised – she'd probably seen and heard much worse. She took his details and told him to take a seat in the waiting area, where a nurse would call him soon. He knew the drill. The nurse would assess him and that would determine how soon the doctor saw him. The less urgent his condition, the longer the wait. Fortunately, it wasn't too busy and he figured he'd get seen fairly soon. Which was just as well, as he needed to get up to the ITU, so his mum and dad could get off home.

Despite signs that said NO MOBILE PHONES, everyone seemed to be on their phones as they waited to be seen. Not knowing how long he'd be, Zaq called his dad.

'Zaqir,' his father said, pronouncing his first name fully. 'What's the matter? Where are you?'

'I'm here, at the hospital. I'm just downstairs at the walk-in centre to see a doctor quickly, then I'll be up.' *Walk-in centre* sounded much less alarming than *Urgent Care Centre*.

'Why? What have you done?'

'Nothing much. I bumped my head and think I might have a cut. I just want to get it looked at. I won't be long. You and Mum can leave if you like and I'll head straight up as soon as I'm done here. It's not that busy so I shouldn't be too long.' He was hoping they were tired, ready to leave, and would go before he got up there. One look at his face and it'd be obvious he'd done more than just bump his head.

'If you won't be long, we will wait.'

Shit. 'OK. See you in a while.' Now he hoped the doctor would be able to patch him up so it wouldn't look too bad.

The nurse, a black woman with a slightly lilting accent, called a couple of people in before him and then it was his turn. He followed her through the doors to the treatment area and into a small consulting room.

'Mr Khan, what is the matter?' she asked him.

Zaq explained about being hit on the head, punched and kicked and how he must've been knocked unconscious for a few moments too. The nurse made notes and performed a few basic tests, then told him to go back to the waiting area and the doctor would call him soon.

This time the wait was shorter. The young doctor, who looked Middle Eastern but spoke as though he'd been brought up in one of the nicer parts of London, called him through to a different room, where Zaq explained for the third time what had happened.

The doctor started by examining the tender spot where Zaq had been struck. 'I can see a small bump with a bit of blood around it. Does this hurt?' He pressed around the bump.

'Ow! Yeah, it does.'

'And you were unconscious for a while?'

'Not sure how long. Just a couple of minutes, I think.'

'Hmm,' the doctor mused. 'We need to get you X-rayed, to make sure there isn't a fracture or anything like that.'

An X-ray would take time and Zaq was conscious of his parents waiting for him.

'Let's check your other injuries first.' He pressed around Zaq's cheek and below his eye, feeling for any shift in the bones beneath the skin. It was painful, but the doctor was satisfied there were no breaks. Then he checked Zaq's mouth and teeth, all of which, apart from the thick lip, were OK. Lastly, Zaq eased off his T-shirt so the doctor could assess his ribs. Again he pressed all around and, while it hurt in places, there wasn't the sudden sharp pain you'd associate with a fracture. 'I think you're just bruised and a bit tender in places. We'll clean up the cuts and I'll give you some paracetamol for the pain, then we'll see about the X-ray.'

'Thanks, doc. I don't suppose you could you do me a small favour?' Zaq took out his phone. 'Could you take a couple of quick pictures of my injuries before you clean them up? For the police.'

'OK, sure,' he said. And he snapped photos of Zaq's bloody lip, his cheek, the marks on his torso, and the bump and cut on his head. When he got his phone back, Zaq asked, 'Any chance I could get a write-up too?'

'I'll be typing it up on the system and can print off a copy for you.'

'That'd be great. Thanks, doctor.'

It didn't take long to clean Zaq's wounds, as there wasn't much that could be done. The cut to his head was disinfected and cleaned, as was the cut to his lip. Then the doctor gave him a couple of paracetamol tablets and some water. He printed off an X-ray form and told Zaq where to find the X-ray department, which, fortunately, was right next to A&E. 'Once you've had it done, just take a seat back in the waiting area and I'll call you as soon as I've had a look at it.'

Zaq was seen fairly soon. The X-ray didn't take long either and he was soon back in the main waiting room, which was busier now than it had been when he'd arrived. He was just wondering if he should call his dad again and tell him he wouldn't be much longer when he heard his name called. Zaq followed the doctor through to the consultation room again.

'Good news,' the doctor said. 'There are no fractures or anything else to be concerned about, just that small bump and the cut. That should heal in a couple of days, then you should be right as rain.'

That was a relief. The doctor printed off the report and handed it to Zaq, who thanked him and left to relieve his parents.

Chapter Thirty

'What's happened to you?' his dad asked when Zaq walked in.

'Oh, it's nothing. Stupid, really. I was carrying a couple of floorboards at work and one slipped out of my hands and bashed me in the face.'

His mother looked at him with concern. His dad was frowning, not with concern so much as trying to decide whether to believe him or not. 'I thought you had a few days off,' he said.

'Yeah, I have. I just popped in this afternoon to tell them I might need a few more days. You know what that Sid's like. He roped me into helping out while I was there. My own fault. Next time I'll just phone.'

His dad pursed his lips in a look of general dissatisfaction before turning to Zaq's mum. '*Ah, chaleh.*'

She bent over Tariq and planted a kiss on his forehead. When she turned to leave, Zaq saw that her eyes were wet again. As his parents passed him, his dad gave him a gruff nod but his mum reached out, grabbed his forearm and gave it a squeeze. Then they were gone.

Zaq put his bag down beside the bed, and slumped into the chair his mum had just vacated. 'How you doing, shithead?' – a fraternal term of endearment. 'If you can hear me, stop fannying around and get better, will you?' He leant forward. 'Listen, if that twat Dutta is behind what happened to you, I'm really going to fuck him up. In fact, I'll do it right here, so you can listen in. And if you can't hear, don't worry – I'll tell you all about it when you wake up.'

He gently bumped his fist against Tariq's arm, then took out his phone and scrolled through his contacts until he found the number from the card the policeman had given him the first night in the hospital. He'd added it to his phone, so he'd know if it was them calling him. Now he'd be the one calling them.

'I was told to phone in if I had any more information about my brother's assault,' he said when someone answered.

The woman at the other end took his name, his brother's name, the date of the assault and the reference number, then said, 'What information do you have?'

'I'm not sure, but it could be linked to what happened to my brother. I'm supposed to be a witness in a court case later this year, and two guys kidnapped me earlier, and tried to force me to change my story in court.'

'That's a very serious accusation.' There was a note of surprise in her voice.

'I know. I'm wondering if the attack on my brother was any-thing to do with that – a warning or something.'

'We'd like to get a statement from you if that's OK.'

'Sure.' Zaq told them where he was and that he'd be there all night.

An hour or so later, after he'd eaten one of his sandwiches and had a cup of tea, there was a knock at the door.

'Mr Khan?' a police officer said. 'Can I come in for a chat?'

'Yeah, course.' The policeman entered the room. 'Have a seat,' Zaq offered, indicating the other chair.

'How's he doing?'

'He's still in a coma. The doctors are hoping the swelling on his brain will go down by itself so they can bring him out of it. If it gets worse, they might have to operate, which is risky. That's why they're waiting. Apart from that, he's resting and healing, hopefully.'

'It's terrible. We're doing everything we can to find those responsible.'

Zaq didn't doubt it but, with their funding and numbers cut and their resources so severely stretched, just how much were they able to do? Still, reporting what had happened to him today would give the police something to go on, and would help Zaq too, by having the cops deal with Dutta.

'I was told you have some information about an attempted abduction today.'

'It wasn't just attempted,' Zaq said. 'Two guys whacked me on the back of the head, put me in the boot of their car and took me to a warehouse somewhere.'

The policeman looked surprised. He took out his notebook. 'When did this happen?'

'A few hours ago, outside where I live.'

He took down Zaq's address. 'Did you know either of them?'

'No.' That wasn't strictly true, but he wasn't about to say he'd broken one's collarbone and the other's nose before today. He seriously doubted either of those wankers would choose to mention what they'd been doing when those injuries had been inflicted on them.

'What happened then?'

'I was unconscious for a bit. When I came round, I was in the boot of a car with a bag over my head. Then they dragged me into this abandoned warehouse and cable-tied me to a chair.'

'Do you know where this warehouse was?'

'Park Royal somewhere, I think.' He gave him the road name and a description of the building.

'Do you have any idea why they abducted you? What they wanted?'

'They wanted to make me change my story in a court case to get a mate of theirs out of prison.'

'That's a very serious offence.'

'So I've been told. It's true though. They beat me up to force me to say what they wanted.'

'Is that how you sustained your injuries?'

'Yeah. They filmed it too, so they could use the video to get the charges dropped. They mostly hit me to the body, so it wouldn't show on camera, but, when I wouldn't go along with what they wanted, they lost it. I managed to grab the phone they were filming on when I got away. Here.' Zaq took Nose guy's cracked phone out of his bag and gave it to the wide-eyed policeman. 'There should be video on there of them beating me up. I don't know the code, sorry – we just got out of there as quick as we could.'

That was another fib. Zaq had looked through the phone while Jags drove him home. He'd sent a copy of the video to himself and deleted the log. He'd also seen – and left undeleted – a load of WhatsApp messages relating to what they'd done to him. When the cops saw that shit, those guys would be fucked.

'You said "we". Can I ask – how did you manage to escape?'

The best lies were those that stuck close to the truth, so Zaq explained about leaving his keys in Jags' car, how Jags had come back to give them to him, seen Zaq being bundled into the boot of the car, followed them, saw what was happening in the warehouse and then jumped the two guys and freed him.

'That's some friend you've got there,' the policeman said.

'I know. I've never been as happy to see him as I was then.'

'I can believe it. Who is this friend?'

'I'd rather not drag him into all this. I don't want those arse-holes going after him just because he helped me out.'

'I understand . . . but we need to corroborate what happened, get his side of it. We can try and keep him out of it after that.'

'Well, OK, if you can. I really don't want to drop him in it.' Zaq gave him Jags' details.

'Getting back to the actual assault, do you have other injuries?'

'Yeah. I saw a doctor when I got here, and I've got a copy of the medical report. Had to have an X-ray in case they'd cracked my skull or anything. Got the doc to take some pics on my phone before he cleaned me up.' Zaq let him have the doctor's report then got out his phone and showed him the photos.

'This is all very helpful. Would you be able to send those photos to me, for the report?' The policeman gave him a number to forward them to. 'The friend of the guys who abducted you, the one in prison, do you know his name?'

'Mahesh Dutta. He's being done for a load of stuff – assault, possession of a firearm, conspiracy to rob, all sorts. They wanted me to say the gun was either mine or belonged to the other guys he was arrested with, and some other shit about how he was framed by me or someone else.'

'Did you get the impression the men were acting of their own accord, or that they'd been put up to it?'

'They pretty much said he told them to do it. Should all be on that phone.'

'If we have evidence that he was behind this or involved in any way, it'll be a very serious matter. Witness intimidation, attempting to pervert the course of justice . . . it won't go well for him.'

'I won't be shedding any tears,' Zaq touched his swollen cheek.

'Could you give me a description of the men that took you?'

'Yeah. One's on the video, the other ain't, 'cause he was filming.' Zaq gave him a description of each man. He could have given their names and addresses too, but didn't because it would have raised questions, as would breaking their arms, which was why he hadn't done it. This way he was still able to fuck them up but wouldn't be charged with anything himself.

'Is there anything else you can tell me, any other details you remember?'

'That's about it – but I was wondering if it might've been these same blokes that jumped my brother, you know, to send a message or something.'

'We'll definitely look into it.' The policeman got to his feet. 'You've got the number. If you think of anything else concerning this or what happened to your brother, just give us a call. Same if anything else happens.'

As soon as the policeman had gone, Zaq called Jags to tell him the cops would probably contact him to get his take on what had happened earlier. 'Just stick as close to the truth as possible. You might want to play down how much you beat those two fuckers up, and don't mention how I wanted to break their arms. Maybe leave out how we photographed their driving licences too – and the way we left them. Apart from that, just tell it like it happened. They say they'll keep you out of it as much as possible. Shouldn't be a big deal.'

Jags agreed, though he didn't sound too enthusiastic about having to talk to the police.

'I'm going to send you over the pic I took of their car,' Zaq went on. 'Save it to your photos and show it to the cop.'

'Why didn't you do it?'

'Be better coming from you. Just say you followed them, parked up and took the pic. It'd seem a bit too calculated if I took it as we were leaving.'

'But you did.'

'I know, and it was calculated. This way will play better.'

'OK, fine.'

'The cops should be able to trace those two from the number plate and then hopefully tie them to the phone and to Dutta, which'll stuff them all up nicely.'

'You really think Dutta was behind what happened to Tariq?'

'I don't know. Those two pricks said they didn't know anything about it, but that don't mean anything. Dutta could've got someone else to do it, some other mates of his.'

'I'm surprised he's got that many friends. You think those two guys are still getting intimate in that warehouse?'

'Who cares? They must've worked out all they had to do was smash the chair to get free – though it would've been something to see how they managed it.'

Jags laughed. 'If you ain't sure they were the guys that jumped Tariq, what d'you want to do?'

'I reckon we find out for sure what it was about, and if it was Dutta or not. And we keep looking for the guy with the gold tooth.'

Chapter Thirty-One

After another uncomfortable night at the hospital, his various bumps and bruises doing nothing to help, Zaq returned home and went to bed. The nights were warm and sticky enough, but during the day the temperature rose and the sun lit up his room even with the curtains shut. Air-conditioning was a fantasy, and he hadn't got around to buying a fan; this was London after all, and it might be pissing down with rain next week. He made do with leaving his windows open and, stripped down to his boxer shorts, with a faint whisper of wind ruffling the curtains, it didn't take him long to drift off.

When he woke at almost two in the afternoon it was still warm, but the sun had moved to the back of the house so his room had cooled down slightly. There'd been no calls or messages from his dad since he'd left the hospital, which meant there hadn't been any change in Tariq's condition. His parents were both stuck in the limbo of waiting to see what would happen to their son. At least Zaq was keeping himself busy by trying to track down those responsible, otherwise he'd just be waiting around too.

Sitting up triggered all his aches and pains. He was aware too of the bump on the back of his head, throbbing gently, the taut skin across his swollen cheek and his thick lip. Tired as he felt, he got up. He wanted to visit the hairdresser whose details they'd got the day before, and have a chat with her. He called Jags to see what he was up to.

'Been up since seven, working,' Jags told him. 'A client fucked something up on their server and I been trying to sort it out remotely from here, else I'd have to go to Birmingham. Can't be arsed with that. How you feeling?'

'Like I been hit by a truck.'

'Nice. Any news on Tariq?'

'No. My dad ain't messaged, so I'm guessing there's been no change. So, you going to be busy the rest of the day?'

'No. Why?'

'I thought you had that server stuff to sort out?'

Jags laughed. 'I already figured out what it was an hour ago. But I don't want to make it look too easy. Want them to think it's difficult technical stuff. That's what they pay me for.'

'So, are you busy or not?'

'Why you asking?'

'I'm going to go see that hairdresser in a bit. You want to come along?'

'Yeah, it's nice out. Just give me time to run the fix on this bloody server, and eat ...'

'What you going to have?'

'I got some *chana masala* my mum made. I'm going to pimp it up, though.'

'How the hell do you pimp up *chana masala*?'

'First, I'll stir in some hummus—'

'You what?'

'It's made of chickpeas, ain't it? Same thing, only with some added flavour. Anyway, then I squeeze some lemon on it, add some fresh chilli and chopped onion, and when it's all heated up I'll grate some cheese on top.'

'Man, I hate to tell you this, but that sounds flippin' weird.'

'Tastes wicked, though, believe me, with some *naan*. Honestly, once you've tried it, you'll love it.'

'I don't know ... I could try a little bit, I suppose. There enough for both of us?'

'Yeah, my mum gave me loads. Hang on ... have you just talked me into making you lunch?'

'Nah,' Zaq said. 'I'm pretty sure *you* just convinced *me* to have some. See you in a bit.'

'See? Told you it was good, didn't I?'

'Not bad,' Zaq agreed. Jags' weird concoction was surprisingly tasty, and filling too, the hummus and cheese making it richer and heavier. Zaq mopped up the last of the sauce with a final piece of *naan*, and washed it down with some Coke Zero. 'We should get going.'

Jags grabbed his wallet and keys from the coffee table. 'You know where we're heading?'

'Yeah, it's in Slough.' Zaq took out his phone, and read out the address he'd looked up earlier.

'I know roughly where that is. Let's take my motor.'

In the car, the aircon kicked in and the interior was already nice and cool as Jags pulled out of the drive. 'What you going to say to her when we get there?'

'I'll ask her if she knows the guy with the gold tooth,' Zaq said.

'You think she'll tell you, just like that?'

'Why not? I ain't a cop or anything.'

'Yeah, but she don't know you from a hole in the ground. Why's she suddenly going to tell you?'

'She was there when it kicked off between those guys and Tariq, so she knows who they are. All I want is a name.' Sensing Jags was about to say something else, Zaq got in first. 'We'll just see what happens when we're there, OK?'

'All right, fine.' They listened to Kiss FM as they drove through Uxbridge and out towards Slough, until they reached the Five Points roundabout and the Crooked Billet where they'd had a drink with Lucky a couple of days ago.

'You heard anything from your uncle yet, about the money?' Zaq asked.

'Not yet. He's probably still trying to get it together without my aunt knowing.'

'Then we'll have to go back and get that prick to hand over the necklace.' The prick in question didn't live far from where they were.

'Yeah . . .' Jags sounded as enthusiastic as Zaq felt.

Jags' sat nav gave them the option to turn right off the dual carriageway and follow a different route to their destination. 'Let's take it,' Zaq said. He knew if they carried on they'd have to go through the heart of Slough and double back up to get to where they were going.

They found themselves on a narrow tree-lined road, with a green canopy above them, the sky barely visible through intertwining leaves and branches. To their left a small wood rushed by, while on the right a large field stretched away to more trees in the distance. With the sun shining bright and lancing its way through the tree cover to spotlight their route, and the radio playing uplifting dance anthems, Zaq almost forgot about his brother lying beaten up and close to death in hospital. Almost, but not quite.

The road narrowed to a single lane, the greenery flashing by faster as a result. Open fields could be glimpsed through fleeting gaps in the trees on both sides now. The tight section of road eventually veered left, opening out into a two-lane country road again. They followed it and soon passed Wexham Park Hospital, screened by trees, on their right.

As they went through Stoke Green, the properties became

much larger and more expensive, hidden behind high walls, thick trees and secure gates. This was the posh bit of Slough, though the residents would probably never say so. As they followed the route shown on the sat nav, they saw only greenery, sky and wealth around them. Finally, they hit the top end of Stoke Poges Lane and turned left towards Slough town centre. Eventually, the mansions gave way to 1930s semis with front gardens and driveways. The further they went, the less green and more built-up the area became, similar to a thousand other suburban neighbourhoods.

They spotted the hairdresser's, sandwiched between a betting shop and a solicitor's office in a parade of shops opposite a petrol station. Jags took a right, turned around and came back to pull into an empty parking bay outside the shops. 'Shall I come in with you? Never know, you might need my help.'

'I just want to ask her a few questions, not talk her to death.'

'Might be a good idea to have me along just to distract from the state of your face.'

Chapter Thirty-Two

The hairdressers was called Michelle's. As Zaq and Jags went into the salon, they were hit by the sweet, cloying scents of shampoos, conditioners, styling gels and sprays. A male stylist was working on a young guy's hair, and a female stylist working on a young woman's to the right.

'Hi, can I help you?' the female stylist said, smiling automatically as they entered.

She looked a little older than her hairstyle suggested and Zaq wondered if she was the Michelle the salon was named after. 'Is Sharan about?' he asked.

Her smile faltered slightly as she took in Zaq's battered appearance. 'Do you have an appointment?'

'No.'

'Just a moment,' she said, and went to the back of the salon, where she called through a half-open door. 'She'll be right out,' she said, and hurried back to her client.

A minute or two later a slim young woman appeared, dressed in skinny black jeans, a black blouse and black ankle boots, and carrying a mug. Her long, dark hair fell in thick shiny waves past her shoulders, the ends coloured sandy blonde.

'Hello, how can I help you?' she said.

'Sharan?'

Her open expression gave way to a slight frown, as she took

in Zaq's bruised face. She seemed a little pale, until Zaq realised it was because her foundation was a few shades lighter than her natural skin tone. He wondered why she felt the need to make herself up quite so much; perhaps it was expected in her line of work. Whatever – he wasn't there to talk about her make-up choices, and it was none of his business anyway.

'Can I have a quick word? About Kiran and Vinay's wedding, a couple of weeks ago . . . ' That seemed to throw her a little. 'It'll only take a minute,' Zaq assured her.

She glanced over at the older female stylist, who gave a shrug and nodded towards the front door. 'OK,' Sharan said, 'let's go outside.' She left her mug out of sight behind the reception counter and followed Zaq and Jags outside. She seemed edgy, continually glancing at cars going by.

'Kiran and Vinay's wedding, you said. What about it?'

Zaq couldn't understand why she was suddenly so snappish. Why was she so nervous? 'You were there with your boyfriend, right, and a friend of his?'

'Yeah. So?'

'They got into an argument with the DJs. You know what it was about?'

'What's that got to do with you? Who told you about it?'

Zaq kept his voice calm and neutral. 'We heard about it from a few people. What was it about?'

'I'm not being rude, but why's that any of your business? Who are you anyway?'

Zaq decided to tell her the truth. 'My brother was one of the DJs. He's in a coma in hospital right now. Got attacked and beaten up by some guys who asked him if he DJ'd at that wedding.'

Her face fell, mouth open, eyes wide, her expression one of shock – and something else.

'Your boyfriend got a gold tooth?'

'No,' she said, shaking her head, 'but his friend does . . . '

'The one with him at the wedding?'

She nodded.

'What's his name?'

Shock turned to worry and her eyes kept darting over Zaq's shoulder, constantly looking at the road behind him. 'I shouldn't be talking to you.'

'Hang on a minute – your boyfriend's mate might be responsible for almost killing my brother.' Zaq knew he had to keep calm if he wanted her help, so he focused on his breathing to try to dispel the anger he felt growing in him. How could she want to protect these guys? 'We don't even know if he's going to pull through. I just want to know what it was about – why they beat him up.'

'I thought that was all over and done with,' Sharan said, more to herself than to Zaq. 'I don't know why they'd go after your brother. I don't even know him.'

Zaq glanced at Jags, who pulled a face that said he had no idea what she meant either. 'I don't follow,' Zaq said to Sharan. 'What's it got to do with you?'

'It was all over nothing, just because I was talking to Kush.'

Zaq frowned. 'Who the hell's Kush?'

'Kushwant. He was DJing there too, with your brother, I guess.'

'You mean Bongo?'

'Ugh – ' she rolled her eyes ' – that's the stupid nickname his friends call him. I never called him that.'

'Wait – you know him?'

She hesitated. 'Yeah . . . we went out with each other back in college.'

'Hang on: you used to go out with Bongo? This whole thing was to do with you and him?'

'I don't know for sure it's got anything to do with your brother, but yes, I know Kush. The trouble at the wedding started just because we were talking to each other.'

Bongo hadn't mentioned anything about that when Zaq had talked to him. He'd have to pay him another visit and chat some more. 'How'd it start?' he asked.

Again, she cast a glance around before she spoke. 'It was stupid really. Towards the end of the reception, I was on my way back to our table from the ladies'. Kush was at the DJ booth and saw me, and came over to say hello. I was really surprised to see him; it'd been ages. We hugged, and I think he might have kissed me on the cheek, just a friendly thing, and we started chatting, catching up.'

Zaq thought he had an idea where the story was heading but let her continue.

'My boyfriend's the jealous type. He must've thought Kush was trying it on with me or something, plus he'd been drinking. He came charging over and it all seemed to blow up from there. He grabbed my wrist and just went off on one, in front of everyone. When Kush told him to leave me alone he started swearing and pushing him. That's when your brother got involved. He came down off the stage and pushed my boyfriend away from Kush. Then my boyfriend's friend joined in and it turned into a fight.'

'Why didn't you just tell your boyfriend there was nothing going on?'

'I did,' she said, defensively. 'He wouldn't listen.'

Zaq could believe it. He'd seen it enough times at various weddings and parties: guys drinking too much and then suddenly wanting to prove how tough they were. 'What happened then?'

'A load of other people stepped in to break it up, Vinay's mates and relatives. I was pulled away, to get my things and leave. I managed to go and say goodbye to Kiran and apologise, told her I was sorry there'd been some trouble, then we left.'

'You, your boyfriend and his mate?'

She nodded. 'I had to drop them off – at a pub, if you can believe it? As if they hadn't had enough to drink.'

'You remember which pub?'

'No. They told me where to go and I just dropped them. I was pissed off and embarrassed about what had happened. I just wanted to get home.'

'The whole thing was because of you and Bongo?'

'Yes, but it wasn't my fault. We weren't doing anything, just talking.'

So some drunken twat with insecurity issues had started trouble at the wedding, and the fucker with the gold tooth, maybe her boyfriend too, saw Tariq in Uxbridge and almost killed him because some guy had been talking to a girl? Was that what it was all about? It was fucking ridiculous. Did the motherfuckers seriously think they were going to get away with it? If they did, they were in for a shock.

'Who's your boyfriend?' Zaq asked. 'What's his name?' He kept his tone light and conversational – though his intentions were definitely not.

She became even more furtive, frightened even. 'I thought you were asking about the guy with the gold tooth.'

Maybe she didn't want to give her boyfriend up. OK – the other guy was the one they were after for now. 'All right, who's he?'

Her eyes flicked from the road back to him. 'I shouldn't be talking to you.'

'The guy put my brother in the hospital, over nothing. He's Bongo's mate. All he did was try and break things up, and look what it got him.'

'What're you going to do?'

That was a good question. He knew what he wanted to do and he knew what he probably ought to do. In the end, he decided to tell her what he thought she'd want to hear. 'I just want to find out who he is, so I can let the police know, let them deal with it.'

'The police?' Her voice went up a note, in alarm.

'What else? Did you think I was going to beat him up myself?'

'I don't know . . . but getting the police involved is serious. I'm not sure I want to be part of that. It could get me into trouble.'

'It won't,' Zaq told her. 'Just give me his name. I won't tell anyone how I got it. I won't even tell anyone I spoke to you. In fact, I won't mention you at all.' She was still reluctant. 'Please,' he said.

She swallowed, took a breath, and said, 'OK, his name's Satty. I've only met him a few times and that's all anyone's ever called him. I don't know what his real name is and, to be honest, I don't care.'

Zaq nodded. 'You know where he lives?'

'Slough somewhere, I think. Look, I've told you what you wanted. I have to get back to work. I shouldn't have talked to you. If anyone saw me . . . '

'So what?'

'I told you, my boyfriend's the jealous type. He wouldn't like it if he heard I was seen talking to some guys.'

'All right,' Zaq said. 'Thanks for your help, Sharan. I mean it.'

'Just don't mention where you got that name from, not to anyone.'

'I won't.'

With that, she turned and hurried back into the salon.

'We know the fucker's name,' Jags said. 'Now what? How we going to find him?'

Zaq had been wondering the same thing and had an idea. 'Fancy going for a quick drink?'

'Do bears shit in the woods?'

Chapter Thirty-Three

They drove to Old Southall and parked near the pub. Even though it wasn't quite evening, the Scotsman was already pretty busy. The crowd was a mix of older regulars, workers from the nearby industrial estates coming off early shifts, and a younger contingent who used the pub as an unofficial base of operations. The person Zaq was looking for was in the latter group.

Zaq checked the lounge and, when he didn't see who he was looking for, turned his attention to the games room. He spotted who he was after at almost the same time as the guy clocked him. He led Jags towards the group of young Asian men playing cards just past the pool tables. By the way they were throwing down their cards, it looked as though they were playing *Bhabi*.

The guy Zaq was there to see put his cards face-down on the table. He had the lean build of a super welterweight or maybe middleweight boxer, and was dressed in a tennis shirt, tracksuit bottoms and trainers. His dark hair was cropped close, and his head was nicked here and there with scars. His eyes were quick, sharp, and alive with a cunning intelligence. 'Hey, man,' he said, 'what happened to your face? Still finding trouble, huh?'

'More like trouble's finding me. How you doing, Biri?'

Biri's hard features broke into a grin, light glinting off his gold tooth. 'Same old, same old, man. Just trying to stay ahead of technology. You know how it is.' The technology he was referring to was the automotive security type, Biri being a professional car thief. 'How're things with you?'

Zaq shrugged and pulled a face that suggested things could be better.

'Oh, hey,' Biri said, 'I heard about your brother, man. That's really fucked up. You know who did it?'

'I'm trying to find out. That's actually what I wanted to see you about. Can we have a chat? You remember Jags, right?'

'Yeah, man, how you doing? Let's go get a drink.'

Biri told his friends to deal him out and the three of them went to the bar, where Zaq ordered two halves of lager for himself and Jags before Biri could order them pints, and asked, 'Pint of Stella for you, Biri?'

Biri nodded. 'What you just having halves for?'

'We both got to drive.' Zaq ordered the pint. 'I'm picking up my motor from Jags', then going to the hospital. My mum and dad are there with my brother right now. I'm taking the night shift.'

'Oh, OK,' Biri said. He led them into the lounge and they sat down at a small table, close to the open doors to the patio and garden. 'What d'you need?' He took a drink of his pint.

'I got a name, of some guy I think was behind what happened to Tariq, but I need to track him down. You and your boys get around and about – maybe one of them's heard of him, will know where I can find him.'

Biri nodded slowly. 'What's the guy's name?'

'Apparently everyone calls him Satty.'

Biri raised an eyebrow. 'He from Slough?'

'Yeah. You know him?'

'No, but I've heard the name. He's known around them ends. Shouldn't be too hard to get the lowdown on where he hangs out. I can ask around, let you know.'

'Thanks, Biri.' Zaq held his fist out and Biri bumped it with his own.

'Fancy another round?' Biri gestured at Zaq's and Jags' almost finished halves.

'Not today,' Zaq said, getting to his feet. 'Another time, though, definitely. We better get going.'

'Before you do ...' Biri said, 'Tonka's outside.' He nodded towards the patio doors.

That stopped Zaq. 'I better go say hello.'

'I'll come with you,' Jags said.

Zaq led the way round to a small beer garden at the back, basically an area of scrubby grass with some wooden picnic tables. There were pairs of guys here and there, drinking and chatting, plus a larger group of four at one of the far tables. It was the larger group that Zaq made his way to.

Tonka saw him approaching across the grass and pulled back from the conversation he'd been having with the other three. 'Well, look who it is. Long time no see.' His friends turned to look at Zaq.

'How you doing, Tonka?'

Tonka was something of a Southall legend. In his late fifties now, with steely grey hair and a medium build, he didn't look anywhere near as intimidating as his reputation led people to expect. He was considerably older than Zaq and Jags, who'd both grown up hearing stories about him. Apparently a chubby kid, he'd been nicknamed Tonka after a range of big chunky toys. He was picked on for being pudgy, so his older brothers had taught him how to stick up for himself and fight and, as everyone soon discovered, fighting was something he was very good at, and pretty soon even the older kids made sure not to get on the wrong side of him. As he grew up, he lost the fat but the nickname stuck; like the toys, he was extremely tough and, it seemed, pretty indestructible too.

By the time he was in his twenties, racism was at its height in and around Southall, and Tonka was well known in the area as a sort of Robin Hood figure, standing up not just for himself, but for anyone who was getting racist abuse. Young or old, male or female, Hindu, Sikh, Muslim or black – if he saw anyone in trouble he wouldn't hesitate to help them, though the help in question often involved bursts of extreme violence that shocked even those he was helping. The shock was usually short-lived; the gratitude much longer-lasting.

Zaq had always known who he was but had never met him properly until Wormwood Scrubs, where he'd started off his five-year sentence. He'd bumped into Tonka, quite literally, as he'd come out of his cell one day. Zaq could still remember feeling as if he'd walked into a stone pillar and had practically bounced off him. He'd started apologising before he'd realised who it was, and when he did he had frozen mid-sentence.

'Watch where you're fucking going,' Tonka had said. He was flanked by a couple of bigger Asian guys.

'Tonka . . . I'm . . . I'm really sorry, man. I didn't see you—'

'Do I know you?'

'No . . . I know who you are, though, and—'

'Where you from?'

'Southall.'

Tonka nodded. 'Yeah, I thought you looked a bit familiar. Where d'you live?'

Even though he'd been living in his own flat at the time, Zaq gave the location of his family home, where he'd grown up. 'Just off Lady Margaret Road, near Spikes Bridge Park.'

'What's your name?'

'Zaq. Zaq Khan.'

'Nah, don't ring any bells. Who d'you hang around with?'

'Jags, Soop, Harv, Sunil, Kins, that lot.'

'Oh, those wankers. You all used to drink at the Hambrough, right?'

'Sometimes, before it shut down.'

'Khan, you said? That's not very Muslim of you.'

Zaq had shrugged. 'I never been the religious type.'

'What you in for?'

Zaq didn't usually like to say but he wasn't about to blank Tonka. 'Manslaughter,' he'd mumbled. People imagined all kinds of terrible things when they heard that, and Zaq saw that Tonka was frowning too, so he hastily explained. 'I was breaking up a fight and this geezer went for me. He hit me and was going to do it again, so I knocked him down. He banged his head on the ground and died.' He didn't try to talk it up or sensationalise it.

'Must've been a hell of a punch.'

Zaq had shrugged again. 'I just knocked him down. He had a blood clot or something on the brain, that no one knew about. It burst when he hit his head. That's what killed him.'

'Sounds like self-defence to me – but you still got done?'

'Self-defence, yeah. I didn't intend to kill him. But I still punched him and that led to his death, even though it probably wasn't the actual punch that killed him. So I got manslaughter.'

'How long d'you get?'

'Five years.'

Tonka had seemed to consider for a moment, then said, 'You know anyone in here?'

'Just my cellmate, *gora* called Darren, and one or two guys he knows.'

'All right, come on. You're with us now – long as you ain't an arsehole.'

'I try not to be.'

'OK.' Tonka nodded over his shoulder. 'This is Dig and Bob,' he said, introducing his friends. 'Let's go.'

And that was how they'd met. Zaq had found out later that Tonka was awaiting trial for beating up three men who'd been racially abusing a couple of terrified young Muslim girls. No one else had done anything to help them, but Tonka had waded in and slapped the most vocal of the guys shouting abuse. When they saw he was on his own, all three had attacked him, which had resulted in Tonka knocking them all unconscious on the pavement. The police had arrived as Tonka was making sure the girls were all right, and arrested him. The three guys wanted to press charges. Tonka admitted hitting them and explained the circumstances, but their version of events was very different, and they were pushing to have him charged with more serious offences such as ABH and GBH, which Tonka disputed. So he'd ended up on remand until the case went to court.

'What sort of stuff you like to do on the outside?' Tonka asked him.

'I like to read, watch films—'

'You like to read? What sort of stuff?'

It turned out Tonka loved to read too and was pleased to find someone he could talk to about books, the rest of his prison buddies not exactly being big readers. Having been taken under Tonka's wing, Zaq's introduction to prison life had been fairly smooth, something he was immensely grateful for. He'd been introduced around as a friend of Tonka's, which meant no one gave him any shit. And then Tonka had been released, all charges against him miraculously dropped. Zaq had thanked him for all his help and Tonka had wished him the best of luck with the rest of his sentence. When Zaq was eventually transferred to Bullingdon, in Oxford, everything he'd learnt from Tonka had served him well until he completed his sentence and was released. He hadn't seen Tonka since the Scrubs. Until now.

'I'm good,' Tonka said now, extending a hand, and the two of them shook. 'What's up with your face? Still getting into fights? Thought you would've learnt your lesson.'

'Ain't no avoiding it sometimes.'

'Ain't that the fucking truth? How the hell you been? When d'you get out, anyway?'

'Been just over a year.'

Tonka did the maths. 'You did the whole five years?'

'I didn't get no time off for good behaviour. Ended up getting time added on instead, so, yeah, I wound up doing the full stretch.'

'You were a naughty boy, huh?'

'Nah, man, I tried to keep my head down. But you know how it is – some fuckers just look for trouble.'

Tonka nodded sagely. 'You can't take that shit, not inside. Anyway, you're out now. What you doing these days?'

'Driving deliveries for Brar Building Supplies.'

'Delivery driver?' Tonka raised an eyebrow. 'Smart geezer like you? Bit of a waste, innit? What'd you do before – IT, weren't it? Why don't you do that again?'

'Things've moved on in five years, man; I'm out of the loop, need to retrain, get up to date with all the latest shit, and that stuff costs money. Massive gap in my CV don't help, either. When I tell them where I been, it's usually game over.'

'That's pretty shitty.' Tonka's gaze shifted over Zaq's shoulder.

'Oh, this is my mate, Jags. I told you about him when we were in the Scrubs.'

'All right, Tonka?' Jags said.

'Safe,' Tonka nodded. 'You boys want to sit down, have a drink?'

'I'd love to but I can't. I got to get over to the hospital, see my brother. He got jumped and beaten up at the weekend.'

'Shit. I think I heard something about that. Is he OK?'

'Not really. Whoever did it fucking battered him. Doctors have put him in a coma to give him a chance to recover.'

'Fuck, man, that's bad news. You got any idea who did it?'

'All I got so far is a name, Satty, from Slough, apparently.'

'Never heard of him.' Tonka looked at his friends. 'Any of you know him?' They didn't. 'Listen, you need a hand with anything, let me know. Take my number.' He gave Zaq his mobile number, which Zaq saved on his phone.

'Thanks,' Zaq said and immediately called the number. Tonka's phone rang. 'That's me, so you've got my number too.'

Tonka saved Zaq's number, adding his name to it.

'I get anyone a drink before I go?'

'I'll have one,' Tonka said. 'Kronenbourg, cheers.'

The other three all said the same. Zaq and Jags went in to the bar. Biri was standing out on the patio, smoking a cigarette and finishing off his pint. 'You want another?' Zaq asked him. 'I'm getting a round for Tonka and his mates.'

'Wouldn't say no.'

Zaq got the drinks and Jags helped him take them back out. 'Nice one,' Tonka said, as Zaq put them on the table. 'I was serious,' he went on. 'You need a hand with anything, let me know.'

'Cheers, Tonka, I appreciate it.' They shook hands. Jags shook with Tonka too and they turned to go.

'Hey,' Tonka called, as they were leaving, 'what you been reading lately? Got any recommendations for me?'

'You ever get round to reading any Elmore Leonard?'

'That was it!' Tonka slapped the table. 'The guy you told me about. He sounded really good but I forgot his name.'

'His stuff's great. I'll text you some titles.'

They went and said goodbye to Biri, before leaving.

'All right, bruv,' Biri said, shaking hands. 'Let's have a

proper drink soon, yeah? I'll let you know if I find out anything about this Satty dickhead. You need anything else, just let me know.'

As they were driving back to Jags' place the music in the car was cut off by an incoming phone call. 'It's Lucky,' Jags said. 'Shall I answer it?'

'Yeah, why not?'

Jags hit the green button. '*Kidaah*, Uncle? All right?'

'*Haah, haah*.' Lucky's voice came through the car's high-end speakers loud and clear, so it almost sounded as though he was in the car with them. 'Listen, I got some more money together for that bastard.' Neither of them had to ask what bastard he was talking about. 'You home this evening? I'll drop it round. Then can you and Zaq can go over there and see that fucker tomorrow and get my *bhen chaud* necklace back?'

'I'm here too, Uncle,' Zaq said.

'*Arrey, kidaah*, Zaq? Hey, how's your brother?'

'The same. He ain't woken up yet.'

'Fucking hell,' Lucky said. 'But you'll still be OK to go with Jagdev tomorrow and sort this necklace business out, huh?'

'Yeah, sure.'

'Good, good. So, will you be home later, Jagdev?'

'Yeah, I'll be in.'

'I'll see you then. I hope your brother gets better soon, Zaq. *Chunga*.' The call cut off and the music resumed.

'He's got a real bug up his arse about that necklace,' Jags said.

'He's probably worried about his bollocks staying attached to his body if your aunt finds out.'

'Well, he should never have used it as a fucking marker if he didn't want to lose it.'

'That would've been the sensible thing to do.'

'Shame Lucky and sense are complete strangers, then, ain't it?'

'Yeah. Still, maybe that Shergill was just holding out for more money and he'll give it back tomorrow. Then the whole thing'll be done and dusted.'

'Let's bloody hope so.'

Chapter Thirty-Four

Zaq parked across the road from the hospital. This time he'd remembered to bring a book, as well as his phone charger, and shoved them in the bag of food he'd brought. There'd been no change in either Tariq's condition or his diagnosis. His parents both looked even more tired and drawn, as if the life-support machines keeping Tariq alive were somehow draining the life out of them. He exchanged a few words with them as they collected their things, then they were gone and Zaq was once again alone with his comatose brother.

Though Tariq looked relaxed, almost serene, lying there, the tubes and wires, the varicoloured bruises, the cuts and abrasions, and the lingering swelling all told of the violence he'd endured. Seeing him laid out like that was like thrusting a poker into the glowing embers of Zaq's rage and stoking them back into flame.

He knew the right thing to do was let the police handle it – but the right thing wasn't always the easiest or the most satisfying thing. He couldn't sit there night after night, seeing what had been done to his brother, and do nothing. He had to be doing *something*; and channelling his anger, his guilt that it might somehow have been his fault, into purpose and action was something he could certainly do.

As if she'd somehow sensed what he was thinking, Nina texted, asking if he wanted a chat. He felt as if she'd caught him doing something illicit, like looking at porn. He knew what her views on violence and typical Asian masculinity were, and normally he'd agree with her, but he simply couldn't rationalise it all away when it was so personal. He did want to talk to her, though. As long as he kept what he was planning to himself, he figured, what she didn't know wouldn't hurt her. He called her.

'Hi, how are you?' she said, when she answered.

'I been better.' She didn't know about his abduction the previous night, so he told her.

'Oh, my God. Are you all right?'

'A bit tender but I'll be OK.'

'It's so lucky Jags came back and followed them to get you out of there. I'm really glad you're not too badly hurt.'

He told her he'd informed the police so they could handle it. He hoped it might also misdirect her about his intentions towards the guys who'd beat Tariq up.

'If I'm honest, I'm surprised you didn't beat them up yourself – but I think you did the right thing. How's your brother?'

'No change yet.'

'What about your mum and dad? How are they holding up?'

'Not all that great. It's taking it out of them.'

'I'm really sorry. What time did you get to the hospital?'

'Just a little while ago.'

'What did you do during the day?'

'Slept mostly, then went over to Jags' and hung out for a bit.' He didn't mention their trip to Slough and talking to Sharan to track down Satty.

'Have you heard anything from the police? Have they found out anything about who might've attacked Tariq?'

'No,' he said.

'Would you like to maybe meet up some time this week? If you fancy a drink and a chat?'

Any other time, he would have jumped at the chance to spend time with her. 'I'd love to, I really would ... but I'm going to be here every night, at least until there's some change in how Tariq is. How about at the weekend? Maybe we could go for lunch or a coffee?'

'Sure, the weekend sounds good.'

'Thanks, Nina.'

'That's OK.' There was a pause, the kind of nervous silence Zaq wanted to fill but wasn't quite sure how to. It was Nina who broke it. 'What are you doing there now? It's too early to go to sleep.'

'I brought some sandwiches, so I'll probably have them. I picked up a book from home and might read for a bit, play a game or something on my phone, then see if I can actually get any sleep in this chair.'

'I suppose I'd better let you go. Let me know if there's anything I can do, or if there's any change with Tariq.'

'Thanks, I will. And I'll give you a call about meeting up this weekend.'

'Great. I'll speak to you soon. Take care.' And she was gone.

Zaq felt better having talked to her. Just listening to the sound of her voice seemed to lift his spirits. He felt bad about hiding things from her but knew what her reaction would be and he didn't want her disapproval. And he'd have just come across as a dick if he'd tried to argue his position with her.

He'd only just managed to navigate his way through some heavy-duty trouble a few months ago, and the last thing he needed was to get tangled up in any more. But he still couldn't let it go. He was too much a product of where he'd grown up. In Southall you learnt that you had to defend yourself, your family and your friends, the whole community – you couldn't rely on the police to do it for you.

For decades, the police had been openly racist towards the community and there'd been absolutely no faith or trust in them. It had taken a long time, but attitudes on both sides had slowly changed. Local bobbies on the beat and community policing had helped a lot. And then it had all been taken away, all the good work undone, as police numbers and resources were cut. There were no more local coppers, who knew the area and its people and who'd earned their trust. Even Southall police station was all but shut down, only the cells and some of the back offices still in use.

Now any police that came into Southall weren't from there and didn't know the place. Some brought preconceived notions and prejudices with them, which didn't go unnoticed by the people they dealt with. Faith in them had all but disappeared. When they did act, they moved slowly, being underfunded and under-resourced, constrained by the law, by procedure and by which cases the CPS thought they could win in court. Legal justice would be a long-drawn-out affair, with no guarantee of the right result. His way would be swifter, and a lot more satisfying.

Sometimes, the best form of justice was the kind that was delivered up close and personal.

Chapter Thirty-Five

Next morning, a group of doctors came into the room. They reviewed Tariq's charts and the doctor in charge asked various questions of the juniors. Zaq listened, and just as they were getting ready to leave he got up and said to the lead doctor, 'Excuse me, I didn't catch everything you said. How is he?'

The doctor, a tall slender man with receding brown hair and glasses, turned to him with a smile, though the smile became more professional than natural as he took in the cuts and bruises on Zaq's face. 'And you are . . . ?'

'Zaq Khan, Tariq's brother.'

'Well, your brother has some fairly serious injuries. For the most part, they've been treated successfully. He just needs to rest and recover. We're happy with the repair to his femur. We put in three plates to fix and strengthen the bone. Our main concern is that he has some swelling around his brain. You're aware of that?' Zaq nodded. 'Well, that's a serious issue. It's the reason we decided to put him into an induced coma, to minimise the risk of seizures and to give the swelling a chance to abate naturally. Of course, we're keeping a very close eye on him, and if the swelling develops further and increases the pressure on his brain then we'll operate straight away. It's an invasive procedure and recovery would take a lot longer than if the body can heal itself. So, it's a case of wait and see just for the moment, I'm afraid.'

'How long do you think it'll take for the swelling to go down?'

'I'm sorry, I can't give a definite answer. We have to monitor and assess day-to-day. Once the swelling has gone down, though, we'll wait another day or two for everything to settle down, and then we'll gradually bring him off the sedatives and allow him to wake.'

'But, when he does wake up, he'll be OK, right?'

The doctor paused before answering. 'The brain's a funny thing. We don't yet fully understand it. Head injuries, such as the one your brother's sustained, can affect different people in different ways. There's just no telling. We won't know how it might have impacted him until he wakes up.'

'So, what . . . ? He could have long-term brain damage?'

'It's all just speculation at this stage. Your brother could very well make a full recovery with no ill effects at all, but . . . '

'But . . . ?'

'It might be advisable to prepare for all eventualities, just in case.' The doctor gave him a consoling smile. 'If you'll excuse me . . . I need to be getting on.'

'Of course. Thanks, doctor,' Zaq said, but his mind was elsewhere.

Alone again, Zaq looked at his brother. Brain damage? Fuck. He hadn't even entertained that possibility, probably hadn't wanted to. But now the doctor had spelt it out . . . How the hell would his parents cope with that? He tried not to think about it, to stay positive, but it was lodged there like a splinter, painful no matter how much he tried to ignore it.

When his parents arrived, Zaq told them briefly what the doctor had said, focusing on the positives and omitting the worst-case scenarios. Better to give them hope. There'd be plenty of time for despair if things didn't turn out the way they all wanted.

*

When he got home, Zaq saw Manjit's Astravan still in the driveway. Inside, he could hear the rattle of plates and cutlery and went into the kitchen. *'Kidaah*, Manj?' he said when he saw his housemate seated at the dining table, polishing off some scrambled eggs on toast. 'You're running a bit late.'

The big Singh was dressed in work clothes – tan combat pants, black T-shirt, brown work boots and a black turban. 'I got to pick up some stuff on the way in. Bloke I'm getting it from don't start till ten. No point me going all the way to work then back again, so I'll just head there first. You just got back from the hospital?' Zaq nodded as he pulled out a chair and sat down opposite Manjit, who regarded him with a frown. 'What the fuck happened to you?'

'Had a run-in with some guys.'

'Who was it this time? Not the fuckers that beat up your brother?'

'No, I'm still tracking them down.' He explained about Dutta's friends and what they'd wanted.

'Shit,' Manjit said, stretching the word out and giving it additional meaning. 'I thought all that was done with.'

'So did I.'

'How is your brother, anyway?'

'Not great.' Zaq told him what the doctor had said that morning, including the part he hadn't told his parents.

'Bhen de lun,' Manjit said, managing to express shock and concern with the curse. 'I really hope he pulls through, man. You said you're still looking for the guys that did it – you manage to find out anything at all?'

'I got a nickname – Satty. I just need to track the geezer down and see if it was him.'

'And if it was?'

'What d'you think?'

'Not going to leave it to the cops?'

'Would you?'

'Hell, no.'

'There you go, then. If I thought the cops and the legal system would do a decent job of it, make the bastards that did it really pay for what they've done, I'd leave it to them, but I just ain't confident they will. The motherfuckers'll probably get off light – insufficient evidence or some shit. They won't have to suffer getting beaten half to death, having their faces smashed in and their bones broken, even though it's what they deserve. That'd be proper justice – and that's exactly what I want to get for my brother. The cops can have them after I'm done with them.'

Zaq knew that legally it would be wrong but, even though he had reservations, morally it felt right. He was too shaped by the friendships and rivalries of his youth, watching your own and each other's backs, no matter what. He'd thought he'd left all that behind, but prison had resurrected and reinforced those old attitudes. Now they were second nature to him and hard to shake off. In a dog-eat-dog world, you sometimes had to stand your ground and demonstrate who was top dog – and this was definitely one of those times.

'Remember, you need any help sorting the *bhen chauds* out ...'

'Cheers, Manj.'

'No worries. So, what you up to today?'

Zaq was about to say he intended to get some sleep when his phone rang. It was Sid from the builders' yard. 'Shit.'

'Trouble?'

'No, work.'

Chapter Thirty-Six

'*Thu kithay koh geya?*' Sid demanded, not even bothering with a greeting when Zaq answered. 'Why you not coming to work?'

'I told you the other—'

'*Haah, haah,*' Sid cut him off. 'You come in today. *Bus.*' And he hung up.

'Tosser,' Zaq muttered.

'Problem?' Manjit said.

'Just Sid at the yard being a dickhead as usual. I suppose I better go in.' He wanted to have a word with Mr Brar in any case, though he wouldn't get to the yard until about ten o'clock, so Zaq would go then. Sid could wait. 'I'm going to try a get a bit of sleep first. I'll see you later.'

Zaq went upstairs and set the alarm on his phone, in case he fell into a deep sleep. He was beginning to drift off when his phone rang. It was Sid again. Zaq ignored the call. When he called yet again, Zaq put the phone on silent. He was only going to sleep for a little while. He just hoped nothing drastic would happen at the hospital in the next ninety minutes or so.

When his alarm woke him, he felt as though he'd only shut his eyes five minutes ago. No calls from his dad. That was a relief. Several missed calls from Sid, though. He quickly brushed his teeth, splashed some water on his face and left the house.

Zaq drove to the builders' yard and parked on the service

road, round the back. In the yard, both vans had gone, which meant Shits and Ram had taken the deliveries out. He went in through the open shutter and made his way between stacks of timber and building materials to Sid's office. The door was open and he went straight in. 'What's so important?'

Sid lowered his copy of *The Sun* and looked at Zaq with a sour expression. '*Ahgeya, bhen chaud*? Where you fucking been? I calling you for ages.'

'Man, I'd just got back from the hospital. I had to get some sleep.'

'Sleep? *Theri bhen di* ... You not get paid for sleeping. You should be here working.'

'I told you I was going to be off for a few days.'

'*Haah, haah*, you had few days. This not bloody holiday camp for you.'

'Listen,' Zaq said, trying hard not to get wound up, 'my brother's still in a flippin' coma.'

'He no wake up yet?'

'He's got swelling on the fucking brain!' Zaq fired at him, causing Sid to jump back in his seat, gripping the armrests. It wasn't Sid's fault – he was just being his usual annoying self, but his attitude had knocked the weight off the pressure cooker that was barely containing Zaq's fear and emotions. 'A punctured lung and broken bones,' he continued. 'He almost fucking died. He still could. He ain't just going to jump out of bed and start doing *bhangra*, is he?'

Sid's eyes were wide, his mouth open. Although they often shouted, argued and swore at each other – as Sid seemed to do with almost everyone – Zaq had never raised his voice at him in anger before. Zaq knew it too and, getting a grip of himself, managed to speak more calmly. 'Look, sorry, Sid; it's been a rough few days. I've just come in to see Mr Brar. I need a few more days off. I've been at the hospital every night. My mum and dad are there right now. I need to sleep, then go back later. I have to be there ... for them and for my brother.'

Sid straightened in his chair, no doubt unclenching his buttocks a little. He seemed to have actually heard what Zaq had told him. He said, '*Ja, phir,*' telling Zaq to go. '*Thu ethay kee kurdah?* Brar *sahib utheh uh.*' He pointed up, in the direction of Mr Brar's office.

Zaq nodded. 'Thanks, Sid.'

'Fuck off, *hoja.*' Sid told him, but without any malice in his voice, which suggested they were OK.

Zaq made his way through the warehouse again, and climbed the bare wooden stairs to the first floor, where he knocked on Mr Brar's door.

Mr Brar was seated behind his desk as usual. It was a big desk for a big man; anything smaller would have looked out of proportion, but it made the rest of the office seem small, tight and a little claustrophobic, like being stuck in a tank with a big hungry shark that ought to be hunting prey in the open ocean.

Mr Brar frowned. 'What happened to you?' he rumbled.

'That's what I wanted to see you about. It's to do with Raj and Parm.' The mention of his sons got Mr Brar's interest. 'Mahesh Dutta sent two guys who grabbed me last night and did this.'

'What does that have to do with Raj and Parm?'

'They tied me to a chair and beat me up, 'cause they wanted me to change my story and say the gun found in Dutta's car was Raj or Parm's, and that they put it there.' That wasn't exactly what they'd wanted, but Zaq wasn't about to pass up an opportunity to spin what had happened to his advantage. 'They also wanted me to say that Raj and Parm attacked me and that Dutta and his friends were just trying to stop it, but Raj and Parm forced me to blame them. They wanted me to say it all on video, which they were probably going to give to Dutta's solicitor or something.'

Zaq could see a vein throbbing in Mr Brar's forehead and the pulsing of a muscle by his left eye. '*Ma di lun* . . . ' he muttered. 'Did you say any of those things?'

'No. That's how I wound up looking like this.'

'Then why did they let you go?'

'They didn't.' Zaq told him how Jags had seen him being bundled into the boot, followed, and managed to free him. 'I went to the hospital to get checked out, then called the police and told them everything. I thought that was the best thing to do, let them handle it. It makes Dutta look even more guilty. I thought you'd want to know. It might help Raj and Parm's case.' In truth he didn't give a shit about Raj and Parm's case, but their old man didn't know that. 'I hope that was OK?'

'*Haah, haah* . . . ' Mr Brar was frowning, distracted, no doubt by how he could use this latest development to his sons' advantage. '*Haah*. Very good. You did the right thing.'

'Might be better if you didn't mention you heard it from me, though.' Zaq being a witness in the Brar brothers' case, he wasn't supposed to discuss it with Mr Brar, who was already reaching for his phone, probably to pass on this new information to his sons' solicitors.

'Thing is,' Zaq went on, 'they did me over pretty good. I'm still a bit battered and bruised – and my brother's still in the hospital.' Mr Brar, phone in hand, impatient to make his calls, wasn't getting what Zaq was hinting at, so Zaq came right out with it. 'I was hoping I could have a few more days off.'

Mr Brar sat as motionless as a pile of bricks as he processed the request. Finally, he nodded. '*Teek*. Ram can take the deliveries for a few more days. You get better and look after your family. I hope we can use what you have told me to *dhub* that bastard

Dutta—' he pressed his thumb on to the desktop as if he were squashing a bug '—and maybe reduce the charges against Raj and Parm.'

Zaq nodded dutifully, though in reality he couldn't give a monkey's about any charges being dropped. 'Thank you,' he said, and left Mr Brar to make his calls.

'*Kee?*' Sid said when Zaq told him he wouldn't be in for the next few days. '*Theri bhen di—*'

'Yeah, he said Ram can carry on taking out the deliveries while I'm off.'

'Ram *de bond mar.*'

'What you want to do to Ram's arse is between you and him.'

'*Ah, thu duffa hoja*. You taking the bloody piss.'

'Hey, you got a problem with it, go talk to the main man.' He knew the last thing Sid would do was go whingeing to Mr Brar, questioning his decisions. 'I'll probably see you next week. Don't strain yourself reading the papers.'

He left the office to the sound of Sid still swearing, loudly and colourfully, in Punjabi.

Chapter Thirty-Seven

When Zaq's alarm woke him in the afternoon, he was still tired but at least felt a bit more rested. He was supposed to work out but decided to skip the weights in favour of something else. He packed a change of clothes into his rucksack and called Jags.

'You're awake, then?' Jags said.

'No, I'm calling in my sleep. What you doing?'

'Watching TV.'

'Hard at work, then?'

'Did all my work while you were busy sleeping.'

'We going to go see that Shergill sod about Lucky's necklace today?'

'Yeah, you coming over?'

'I am, but I want to do something at yours first, though.'

'Let me guess ... you want to have lunch?'

'Now you mention it, that's a good idea. Why don't you make something quick?'

'Why don't you f—'

'See you in a bit.' Zaq hung up.

It was another hot, sunny day and the interior of the car was like an oven. While air-con hadn't seemed worth the extra expense at the time, it did now.

He didn't fancy getting stuck in traffic on the Broadway, so headed up to the Ruislip Road and through Yeading, until he got on to the Uxbridge Road, not far from Jags'.

'What's for lunch?' he asked when Jags opened the front door.

'Don't know. Ask your mum.'

'How the fuck's my mum meant to know what you've made to eat? She's at the hospital.'

'Oh, shit.' Jags looked stricken, knowing he'd overstepped the mark. Cussing each other was automatic with them and often included family members. 'Sorry, mate. Any news on T?' Zaq told him what the doctor had said. 'Man, that's some heavy shit. If you're serious about wanting to eat, I can whip up a quick sandwich or something.'

'Course I'm serious. I ain't eaten. What you got?'

'Can do you ham, cheese and tomato.'

'Slap some mustard and a bit of mayo on it too.'

'Yes, *sahib*,' Jags said in a piss-take Indian accent while waggling his head. 'Anything else I can be doing for you?'

'Yeah, hold off making it for a while. I blew up at Sid earlier. Everything's getting to me more than I thought. I need to go to the garage, let off some steam.'

'Sure, go for it.' Jags said, and threw him the key.

The garage was a brick-built, double-sized affair at the far end of the garden. There was no rear access, so it had never been used to house any cars, and Jags had turned it into a home gym several years ago. He and Zaq had trained there together before Zaq had gone to prison. But Jags had since joined a proper gym with all the latest fitness equipment, so he didn't have to train completely alone – and also so he could eye up women. Now Zaq made the better use of it, not least because there was a punchbag there, something many regular gyms didn't have. That was what Zaq wanted now.

He let himself into the garage and went over to the racks of metal shelves that held, amongst other things, an old radio/CD player with a stack of discs. He looked through the discs until he found one full of dance tracks Jags had burned for them. Music filled the space as Zaq grabbed a set of boxing wraps from another shelf and wound them tightly around each wrist and hand, making sure his knuckles had sufficient protection.

Shaking himself loose, he warmed up on the rowing machine, pulling slowly at first, then hard for five minutes. Next he stretched, then shadow-boxed, throwing quick combinations and counters, along with blocks, knees and elbows, aimed at phantom opponents. But he wasn't able to unload with real power; for that he needed the bag, which was suspended by a thick chain from a ceiling joist. He put on a pair of bag gloves.

At first, he made light contact, finding his range and keeping his tempo fast. Then he began to increase the power of the punches, breathing hard and making primal, animal sounds. A bottled-up torrent of rage and frustration burst forth as he hammered his fists into the imagined bodies of Tariq's attackers.

Only when he'd given it everything he had did he even begin to hear the music again. He was dripping with sweat and pulling in deep lungfuls of air but he felt lighter, unburdened, the built-up anger and sense of impotence he'd felt gone for now, replaced by an inner calm. After a few more minutes of lighter bag work, he pulled off the mitts and unwound the wraps, then turned the music down and went through some more stretches, holding each for a count of thirty, until the tightness in his muscles turned into a soothing buzz.

Afterwards, he felt better than he had in days.

Chapter Thirty-Eight

'Shit, man, you're dripping sweat all over the floor!' Jags said when Zaq came into the kitchen.

'Sorry. I'm going to take a quick shower, if that's OK.'

'You better. You ain't sitting on my furniture sweating like that.'

'I won't be long. Why don't you make the sandwich to go so I can eat in the car?'

'Sure, *boss*. Anything else I can do for you while I'm at it?'

'You could grab me something to drink as well. Cheers.'

'I look like your fucking servant?'

'Actually, I think you—'

'Fuck you,' Jags said, giving him a middle finger salute.

'You think he'll be home?' Jags said as he locked the French doors to the garden.

'We'll find out. He ain't there, maybe we can find out where he is or when he'll be back.'

'Here's your sandwich.' Jags handed Zaq a package wrapped in foil along with a bottle of water.

'Mate, you're a star.'

Jags nodded in agreement.

'You got the cash?' Zaq asked.

'Yeah, Lucky dropped it off yesterday. He wanted to come

with us but I was like, what the hell are you going to do there? We're the ones that'll be going in to get it. Plus, I'm taking my motor this time, so he'd have to stand by the road like an over-the-hill rent boy.'

'Can you imagine if someone actually stopped to pick him up?'

'Damn, man, that's my uncle; I don't need to be thinking about shit like that. Let me just grab the money and then let's go.'

Jags went upstairs and returned with a padded envelope.

In the car, Zaq put the envelope between his thighs while he ate the sandwich. 'How much is there this time?' he asked.

'Twenty grand.'

'That's double what he owes.'

'Yeah, I know. Just hope it's enough for that greedy bastard.'

The air-con cooled Jags' BMW quickly, so that it was soon bearable going on pleasant. It didn't take them long to get to Uxbridge, then head out into the leafy greenery waiting just beyond the western fringes of London. There was other traffic, but it wasn't rush hour and they made good time.

'There it is,' Jags said, slowing, then turning off the road and easing up to the gates of the Shergill property. He got out to press the button on the intercom beside the gates, and spoke into the microphone.

'They say anything?'

'No. I just said we were here to see Shergill.' He drove between the opening gates and along the drive between the lawns and trees, and stopped next to the other cars parked in front of the imposing house.

The front door opened as Zaq and Jags got out of the car. The same man-mountain who'd greeted them before watched them approach, his eyes taking in the injuries to Zaq's face, and let them enter before telling them to stop, as he closed the door behind them. A lump of rock would have had more personality than this guy, Zaq thought. The guy with the moustache, who they'd seen last time, was waiting in the hall.

The big guy gestured at them to raise their arms. They reluctantly did so, and were patted down with paddle-sized hands. Then he pointed at the package. 'What's in there?'

'Money,' Jags said, taking the envelope from Zaq and unfolding it to show the cash inside. 'For your boss.'

The big guy grunted and said, 'This way.' This time he led them to a broad set of double doors on the left side of the main hall. He knocked and opened one of the doors, going in and holding it open for Zaq and Jags. 'These two again,' he said, as they entered.

The room was done up in white, cream and gold, a study, office and lounge combined. Behind a solid oak desk the size of a dining table sat Mr Shergill, his cuff links catching the light from the large windows that looked out on to the drive. In the middle of the room, a pair of sumptuous cappuccino-coloured leather sofas flanked a heavy glass coffee table. The walls were taken up by shelves full of books, magazines, knick-knacks and plenty of photographs, many of which seemed to feature Shergill with various people. Zaq felt a weird sense of *déjà vu*, as if he were in Mr Brar's office back at the builders' yard – or rather, the sort of office Mr Brar probably dreamed of.

Moustache guy closed the door, and he and the big guy took up station there, blocking the exit. Shergill continued annotating some papers for a few minutes, before he finally deigned to look up. 'What do you two want now?'

'We've come about the necklace again,' Jags said.

Shergill sat back in his chair, looking for all the world like a *desi* Bond villain – all he needed was a cat in his lap. 'I thought I already told you about that. What part of *I'm keeping it* did you two idiots not understand?'

'We've brought more money. My uncle's doubled what he owes you.'

'Really?' He gestured to the package in Jags' hand. 'That's what you're holding there? Taj . . . '

Moustache guy took the folded envelope from Jags and handed it to his boss. Then he took up position to Shergill's right, hands clasped in front of him, staring at Zaq and Jags with cold snake-like eyes.

Shergill took out four bundles of cash and flicked through one of them. Zaq could tell by their colour that the notes were all twenties. 'I already told you my decision about this,' Shergill said to Jags, 'but here you are again, bothering me at home, disturbing me while I'm working. What do I have to do for you to finally get the message?'

'Give the necklace back and we won't bother you any more.'

Shergill's face clouded and he sat back again, fingers steepled, a thoughtful expression creeping onto his face. It was something of a surprise when he said, 'OK,' and nodded as if agreeing with himself. He pushed himself up out of his chair. 'Wait here,' he said, and strode over to the door, which the giant held open for him, and left the room.

The big guy resumed his position in front of the closed door, while Moustache guy – Taj – remained beside the desk staring at them. Zaq couldn't imagine he had many friends – he didn't seem the warm happy-go-lucky type.

'Sod this,' Zaq said. 'Don't know how long he's going to be; might as well be comfortable.' And he sat on the sofa. Jags joined him.

The seating was firm, and the leather was soft, and cooler to the touch than expected. Shergill's guys stood watching them. Well, they were being paid to stand there. Zaq wasn't.

He took the time to look at the photographs around the

room. He recognised some of the people in them with Shergill – Bollywood actors and Indian cricketers; the rest were probably family members. There were some nice pieces of Indian art too, not the tat you picked up in a bazaar but tasteful quality sculptures, carvings and some miniature paintings.

The door opened and Shergill came back into the room, carrying a square, red velvet-covered jewellery case, big enough to hold a dinner plate. He handed it to the big guy. '*Deh, enu,*' he said, nodding at Jags. He never seemed to do anything himself, ordering his henchmen to do everything instead. Zaq wondered if one of them had to wipe his arse for him too?

The big guy dropped the case into Jags' lap rather than handing it to him, and stayed looming over them. Shergill resumed his seat behind the desk. Jags opened the case. Zaq wanted to take a look to see what all the fuss had been about, but instinct told him to keep his eyes on what was going on around them. He heard the case snap shut, and Jags said, 'OK, thanks. We'll be on our way then.' He stood up. Zaq did likewise, though he remained wary. It all seemed a little too easy. Maybe Shergill *had* just been holding out for more money. But something just didn't feel right to Zaq . . .

'*Enah nu bhar dekaah de,*' Shergill instructed one, or both, of his minders. Taj reached the door before either Zaq or Jags, and held it open. The big guy was behind them, which put Zaq on edge.

Out into the hall, Zaq grabbed Jags' arm, pulled him to the side and gestured for the other guys to lead the way. Shergill's men must've decided there was no point arguing about it and headed to the front door. They watched with dour looks as Zaq and Jags left the cool of the hallway and went outside, where the late afternoon heat hit them like a brick wall.

Chapter Thirty-Nine

Once they were in the car, with the AC cranked high, Zaq opened the case. Displayed on white silk was an intricately worked Indian gold necklace. He could tell it was Indian gold by its colour, a richer, deeper hue that came from a higher gold content, most probably twenty-four-carat. The necklace itself was formed of gold petals set with a multitude of small, brightly sparkling diamonds. The centrepiece was a large emerald, surrounded by more tiny diamonds, with another emerald hanging below it, also surrounded by diamonds. On either side of the two central emeralds was a delicate gold trellis, with a diamond at each juncture.

'Wow, it's some necklace. Lucky must've been crazy to use this as a marker.'

'Tell me about it. I better call him once we get out of here and tell him we got it. He's probably shitting bricks, waiting.'

As they started towards the gates, another car was already coming in. Zaq recognised it as the same gunmetal-grey BMW Z4 they'd seen the last time they were here, only this time it had the roof down. The driver was youngish, in his mid-twenties, with precision-styled hair and a neatly manicured beard. He was frowning at them with disdain. Zaq might have been wrong but he had the distinct impression the guy was the worst kind of spoilt bastard.

'He seems nice,' Jags said, heavy with sarcasm.

As Jags drove towards the gates, they closed. 'Wonder if they're going to make us wait while they open them?' The answer was, no. They started to open again, so Jags was able to drive straight through. 'Maybe there's a sensor or something.'

'Or they're watching us on a camera.' Zaq said.

As Jags turned left on to the main road, Zaq felt his phone vibrate in his pocket. 'Hey, Biri, what's going on?'

'The usual, man. How you doing? How's your brother?'

'He's the same, for now. Nothing we can do but wait.'

'That's rough. Listen, I'm calling about that guy, the one you was asking about?'

'What about him?'

'Some of the guys I spoke to know who he is, they've seen him around and that. They say he's a bit of a prick.'

'That don't surprise me. You find out anything else?'

'Yeah, he hangs out at a pub called the Lemon Tree in Slough. In there quite a lot. Runs with a bit of a crew, though, so if you're thinking of doing anything you might want to be a bit careful.'

'Careful's my middle name.'

'Not what I heard.'

'Thanks for the info, mate. I appreciate it.'

'No worries, man. Any time.'

Zaq ended the call just as they were approaching the roundabout and the Crooked Billet pub. 'Can you hold off calling Lucky for a bit and swing a left towards Slough?'

Jags glanced at him. 'How come?'

'I got a lead on this Satty motherfucker. Pub in Slough. We ain't far away; thought we might check it out quickly.'

'What you going to do if he's there?'

'Beyond smashing the guy's face in? I don't know.' Now that they were getting closer to finding him, Zaq realised he probably needed a better strategy than going straight in and attacking the fucker. Last thing he wanted was to get done for GBH. A lot of people might see the justice in it if he beat seven shades of shit out of the guy, but the law wouldn't, and with his record he'd end up straight back inside. And then there was what Nina would say. 'Let's just go see what happens,' he told Jags. 'Anyway, it's a pub and it's hot . . . I'll buy you a quick half.'

'Now you're talking.'

Zaq looked up the pub on his phone and how to get there. 'It's not far. Wexham Road. If we can turn right a bit further down, it'll be easy to get to.'

They could turn right, and did, at some traffic lights, then simply drove to the end of the road, turned right again and carried straight on until they saw the pub, just after a petrol station. It stood on a corner plot, set back from the busy Wexham Road. They checked out the pub as they went by.

'Nice,' Jags said, though it was clear from his tone he meant exactly the opposite.

Zaq had to agree. One thing you couldn't accuse the Lemon Tree of was having any airs and graces. Squat and boxy, the place was more functional than fancy. It looked like it had been built in the 1970s, with other bits added later.

Jags took a left at a mini-roundabout. 'Flippin' hell, check out the name of the road – Shaggy Calf Lane. You can tell we're out in the sticks.'

The pub didn't look any better from that side either. Much of it was obscured by boards put up like a fence, one advertising Sharky's Restaurant which was part of the pub, another a DJ night, and another informing them that the pub had a shisha lounge.

'Park there.' Zaq pointed towards a line of empty spaces on the right, where a couple of trees screened the car park from the house next door. 'Probably better to park facing out, in case we need to make a quick exit.'

'What're you planning to do?'

'Don't know. What should I do with this?' He held up the necklace case.

'Stick it in the glove compartment. It'll be safe enough.'

Zaq put the case there and Jags locked it. They got out of the car and he set the alarm.

Inside the pub was a lot better than the outside had led them to expect; light and bright, with white-painted walls and a solid-wood floor that looked new. Zaq cast his eye around the small groups of customers, mainly guys, but didn't see anyone who fitted Satty's description. They ordered two halves of Kronenbourg and went and sat at a table by a window, so Jags could keep an eye on his car.

'Cheers,' Zaq said, and they clinked glasses. There was nothing quite like a cold beer on a hot day and they both gulped down most of theirs in one hit.

'Oh, man, that hit the spot,' Jags sighed.

'It hardly touched the sides. You want another?'

'OK, one more won't hurt.'

It was late afternoon; the place would probably get busy soon, as people started to finish work. Zaq surveyed those already there. A group of three Asian lads sat at a table towards the front of the pub, and there was another group of three older Asian men, a couple of white guys together and another two on their own. Zaq turned his attention to the three lads, trying not to make it obvious. They were drinking beer and chatting loudly, though Zaq couldn't make out what they were talking about. Did they know Satty? Probably, if they were regulars, though he couldn't exactly go and ask them.

He went to the bar to get another couple of halves. This time they could nurse their drinks, see if they could overhear anything or otherwise pick up some information. He had to wait a few minutes to get served, not because the bar was busy but because the barman had disappeared somewhere. He eventually got the beers and was just heading back to their table when the door opened and a guy strode into the pub. He was of average height but solidly built in a gym-pumped way, dressed in track-suit bottoms, white trainers and a short-sleeved shirt that clung to the contours of his chest and abs. His hair was gelled up on his head, dark but with the odd glint of a lighter, coppery shade, and he had a gold hoop in each ear. He glanced at Zaq on his way over to the group of three lads, walking with a cocky strut that was close to arrogant. He didn't open his mouth, but Zaq was certain that, if he did, he'd have a gold tooth.

Chapter Forty

As Zaq put the drinks down on the table, Jags' eyebrows were raised in an unspoken question – *is that him?* Noisy greetings welcomed the newcomer and he went to the bar to get a round in. He and the barman seemed to know each other, the barman pulling pints while chatting to the guy.

Zaq was certain this was Satty. He fitted Prit's description of the guy who'd approached them in Uxbridge. And this piece of shit – strutting around, laughing and joking, having beers with his mates – was the fucker responsible for Tariq being in a hospital bed, hooked up to a load of machines, comatose, battered and bruised. Zaq felt anger heating his core like some sort of radioactive material, and his heart beat like a drum. Good job he'd vented on the punchbag before they left Jags' place, otherwise he would've gone straight over and decked the bastard.

Doing anything in here would be no good. The guy's friends would jump in, and there were too many witnesses. He didn't want to get done for another serious violent offence. That would also mean the end of everything with Nina – to her, he'd be just another Southall rudeboy whose answer to everything was violence.

'What you want to do?' Jags asked.

'I want to cause that fucker some pain,' Zaq said, keeping his voice low, 'like he did to Tariq.'

'I'll back you up, whatever you do.'

'Thanks. We got to be smart, though. Can't do it in here – too many witnesses and cameras. Let's have these,' he indicated their drinks, 'and see if I can think of anything.'

Laughter erupted, and raised voices traded insults in Punjabi and English, Satty braying like a donkey.

Zaq wanted to punish him – break his bones, damage his organs and spill his blood. He realised his jaw was clenched and he was grinding his teeth. He forced himself to relax and take some deep breaths. He couldn't let anger blind him and make him do something he'd regret. He had to think, find a way to get the guy without being seen as the aggressor.

'You OK?' Jags asked.

'It's just . . . that fucker's right there. I just want to go over and smash a chair over his head, but I know I can't.'

'Maybe we should just leave it for now. We know where to find him. We can come back another time and sort him out.'

It was probably the sensible thing to do . . . but Zaq couldn't do it. It wasn't in him to walk away. If it was, of course, he might never have gone to prison. They couldn't sit there much longer, though; they'd almost finished their beers, and neither of them could drink any more as they both needed to drive.

Jags said, 'At least we got the necklace sorted for Lucky. It's one less thing to worry about.'

'Yeah,' Zaq agreed, though his attention was still focused on the other table. What he needed was to get the guy on his own somehow . . . As he watched, Satty said something to his mates, drained his pint, got up and headed for the door. 'He's leaving.'

Satty had come in through the same door as Zaq and Jags, but he left through the other door, the one that faced the main Wexham Road. Through the window, Zaq could see him walking away. Maybe that was it for today, their chance gone? One of the others got up and went to the bar.

'We might as well finish these and go,' Zaq said, unable to keep the frustration from his voice.

Satty's mate returned to the table with two pints of lager, then went back to ferry over two more, placing one where Satty had been sitting.

Zaq put down his glass. 'They've got him another drink. He must be coming back. Let's wait a bit.'

He could feel the tension ramping up again, knotting his stomach as he slowly sipped his beer to make it last, and watched through the window. Some minutes later, the guy came walking back towards the pub, and Zaq saw him open a new pack of cigarettes. He must have gone to the petrol station next door to get them. He'd have to smoke outside, which meant he'd be alone out there ...

Zaq downed what little remained of his beer. 'Go and wait for me in the car – and be ready to leave in a hurry.'

'What the fuck are you going to do?'

'I'm going to go and have a word with that prick.'

'You sure that's a good idea?'

'No, but I ain't got a better one.'

'You're not going to do anything stupid?'

'Do I ever?'

'All the fucking time.'

'Just be ready to go, OK?'

They got up and left through the nearest door, straight into a vertical wave of heat. Jags headed to the car, while Zaq veered right, towards the front of the pub.

He saw Satty near the entrance, smoking and looking at his phone. He also saw that a security camera covered the area. He would have to improvise and play it just right. So he took out his own phone and pretended to be busy on it as he approached. He felt Satty look his way, possibly sizing him up, but Zaq concentrated on his phone and the guy went back to whatever he'd been doing. When Zaq got close enough he said, 'You got a spare cigarette, mate?' even though he didn't smoke.

'Nah, it's my last one.'

That was funny – Zaq had just seen him open a fresh pack. Tight bastard. 'Are you Satty?'

The guy frowned, suspicion clouding his face as he clocked the marks on Zaq's face. 'Who's asking?'

Zaq saw a flash of gold in his mouth. It just confirmed what he already knew. 'Me, obviously.'

'What's it to you?'

'You a mate of Mahesh Dutta's?' Zaq put his phone away, adrenaline fizzing through his system, his limbs tingling in readiness. He forced his facial muscles into an unnatural smile. It was hard, but he thought he managed it.

'Who? Nah. You got the wrong person.'

'You're Satty, though, right? You fit the description.'

'What description?'

'Of a guy looks exactly like you, jumped someone in Uxbridge on Friday night, put him in hospital.'

'Don't know what the fuck you're talking about.'

'I think you do. It was you that jumped him, you and a bunch of your arsehole friends.' Zaq kept smiling as he spoke, his words at odds with the affable expression on his face.

'So what if it was? What the fuck you going to do about it?'

'The guy you jumped – he's in a fucking coma, you dumb shit.' He grinned. 'You made a big mistake and I'm going to make sure you pay for it.'

It took a moment for Satty to unpick the meaning of the words from the pleasant manner in which they were delivered. When he did, his expression darkened. He flicked his cigarette away and shoved his phone in a pocket. 'Fuck off, you crazy cunt.'

Zaq backed away, laughing, but raising his hands in a conciliatory manner. 'Why?' he said. 'You shitting yourself? You should be.'

Emboldened by Zaq backing away, Satty came towards him. 'Who the fuck d'you think you are?'

'Your dad.'

'The fuck you on about?'

Zaq grinned wider. 'I was a bit desperate the other night ... so I fucked your mum.'

Everything went still for a second. Then Satty erupted and charged at Zaq, his features twisted with rage, just the reaction Zaq had been goading towards. Cussing his mum was always going to have that effect; it had worked with Dutta's mates and he'd been sure it would work now too.

Satty's right arm was pulled back as though he was going to lob a brick. Zaq's expression altered from a grin to a look of shock and he shuffled back a few paces. Satty aimed a meaty fist at Zaq's face with all his weight behind it. Zaq leant back and threw his hands up as if cowering in a panic. He managed to block the punch and retreated another couple of steps, still acting completely shocked. 'That all you got?' he goaded, though with a look on his face that said *please don't hit me*.

With an animal snarl, Satty brought his left fist around in a scything hook, trying to take Zaq's head off. Zaq stepped neatly out of range and slapped Satty's arm away as it flew past. 'Fuck me, you're useless.'

'I'll fucking kill you.'

'You reckon?'

Satty lunged for Zaq, trying to grab him. Zaq brought his arms up, deflecting Satty's hands wide, then stepped in with a short sharp punch. Satty walked right on to it, and Zaq felt the satisfying crack of bone and the pop of cartilage as he smashed Satty's nose, leaving him stunned. Then Zaq allowed his anger to explode in him like a supernova, not so much a red mist as a red storm. He channelled all his rage and fury, and unleashed a real wrecking ball of a punch with the sole aim of demolishing the piece of shit in front of him. He was prepared for the impact – Satty wasn't. The punch slammed into his face just under his left eye. The connection was bone-jarring and its force sent Satty crashing to the ground a few feet away in a heap. Instinctively, Zaq moved in to press the attack, propelled by a burning desire to stamp on the fucker and break his bones, damage him like he'd damaged Tariq . . . but he managed to restrain himself, just.

'Oi! What the fuck?' Satty's friends came rushing out of the pub.

Zaq leaned over Satty's prone form. 'This ain't over,' he said, only loud enough for Satty to hear. 'You ain't getting off that easy.' Then he backed away, hands raised. 'Hey, he started it,' he said. 'I was just defending myself.'

'Satty . . . ? You all right?' One of them knelt down beside his friend. Blood and snot from his busted nose were smeared across his face. He looked a mess.

'You fucking prick!' one of the others yelled at Zaq.

'We'll fucking have you!' another shouted, all brave and macho, seeing as they were in a group.

Not one of them actually came towards him, though, no doubt deterred by the fact he'd put down the biggest of their number. Zaq kept his hands up in a placatory gesture and continued to move away.

'If any of you three were with him on Friday night, you better watch out too,' he said.

No one said anything, the three of them probably trying to

work out where they'd been on Friday night. Zaq continued backing away until he got to the corner, then he turned and ran to the car. Jags already had the engine running, and put his foot down before Zaq could even close the door.

Chapter Forty-One

'What the fuck happened?' Jags asked as they sped away from the pub along Shaggy Calf Lane.

'You know where we're going?'

'Yeah, we should be able to get back round to the main road from here and head home.'

Zaq told him about the exchange of words and the brief fight with Satty.

'*I'm your dad?*' Jags was shaking his head. '*I fucked your mum?* No wonder he went for you.'

'That was the point.'

'I thought you might do him over. Didn't think you were going to cuss his family too.'

'There were security cameras covering the entrance.'

'So? They'll still have you decking him.'

'Yeah, but it'll look like he started on me and I was just defending myself. I made sure I was laughing and smiling as I talked to him.'

'Even when you were saying all that stuff? Telling him you fucked his mum?'

'Yeah, and I let him take a couple of swings at me first before I hit back and floored him. After that, all they'll have on camera is me checking he's OK and backing off when his mates come out. If anyone does go to the cops, it'll look as if I didn't do anything until he attacked me and forced me to. I doubt they will, though. He won't want to shout about getting decked right outside his local, and if they check the video themselves they'll see it shows him going for me. He won't take that to the Old Bill.'

'I'm surprised you only hit him twice.'

'It weren't the right time or place. But it'll do for now. We know who he is and where to find him. That was just the deposit on the battering I'm going to give him.'

'You want to go back for him? Wasn't that enough?'

'You're joking, right? After what him and his mates did to Tariq? No way that was enough.'

'We know who he is now, so why don't we just pass his name on to the cops, let them deal with it?'

'Not yet. I ain't done with that motherfucker. I got to pay him back in full, not let him off with just a slap. *Then* we give him to the cops.'

'What'll Nina say about it all?'

'She don't need to know anything about it, nor does Rita.'

'OK, I ain't going to tell them. She might find out some other way, though, if it all goes pear-shaped.'

'We'll just have to try and make sure that don't happen.'

'Whatever you say.'

They turned on to the main road through Slough, passing the station and the big Tesco store until, further along, they took a left on to the road that would take them back to Uxbridge and then home.

'I might as well call Lucky,' Jags said, 'tell him we got the necklace. He'll be over the moon.' He turned the music down and used voice commands to make the call. 'Hey, Uncle,' he said when Lucky answered. 'We got the necklace. Just on our way home with it now.'

'Fucking brilliant. I love you, boys. How long will you be?'

'Be home in about half an hour.'

'I need to head off to the hospital soon,' Zaq said when they were back at Jags' place. It was evening, even though it was still light outside and the sun was shining low in the sky. 'I'll stick around for a bit, though, see Lucky before I go.'

Jags opened up the windows and the French doors, allowing the slight breeze to stir the air, then filled the kettle and turned it on. Zaq, hungry following his exertions at the pub, sat down, wondering what he'd have for dinner. He'd already got Jags to make him lunch and didn't want to take the piss by asking him. Looked like it'd be sandwiches from the petrol station again.

Jags brought their teas over. 'You want a biscuit? I got chocolate digestives. Dark ones.'

'Why you even asking? Bring them over.'

Jags brought the pack. Zaq munched one, enjoying the dark chocolate, and was washing it down with some hot tea when the doorbell rang.

'That'll be Lucky.' Jags got up and went to let his uncle in.

Lucky followed Jags into the lounge. 'Well done, boys, well done. You don't know how relieved I am. Come on, Jagdev, get us something to drink.'

'We're having tea.'

Lucky looked aghast at the mugs on the coffee table. 'Tea? Fucking hell, get me a proper drink. I'm celebrating.'

'Whisky?'

'Well, seeing as you're offering ... just a little peg.' He used his thumb and forefinger to give a rough idea of the amount. They were about two inches apart. 'OK, where is it?' he said, rubbing his hands.

'Give me a chance. I haven't even got the bottle out yet.'

'No, no, the necklace. Where's the necklace?'

'Oh, it's there, on the dining table.'

Lucky went to the table, a big grin plastered across his face. He had every reason to be pleased – his problem had been sorted out without his wife finding out, and he had a drink coming. He frowned slightly at the case but picked it up and opened the lid. His reaction wasn't what Zaq was expecting. The grin faded from his face as he stared at the contents. After a moment, he looked first at Zaq and then over at Jags. 'What the fuck's this?'

'It's the necklace, the one we got back for you,' Jags said.

'It's a *bhen chaud* necklace, all right, but it's not *my* fucking necklace. You got the wrong one!'

Chapter Forty-Two

Zaq got up and joined Lucky at the dining table. Jags hurried over with a tumbler of whisky in his hand. Lucky dropped the jewellery case on to the table, took the glass from him and knocked back the contents. He wasn't celebrating.

'You sure that ain't it?' Jags asked.

''Course I'm fucking sure. I know what my own necklace looks like.'

'That's the one he gave us.'

'Don't *you* know what your auntie's necklace looks like? You've seen it enough times.'

'She's got more than one. Ain't like I memorise them.'

'That bastard's taken my money and given you this rubbish instead!' Lucky shoved the case away from him, across the table. 'I bet that isn't worth anywhere near twenty grand, either. Probably just some cheap crap he had lying around his house. I bet he's sitting over there on his fat arse right now, laughing at us.'

Jags leaned forward to look at the necklace glinting and sparkling in its case. 'It's got diamonds – at least I think they're real diamonds – and emeralds, like you said.'

'This one's got two small emeralds. Your auntie's has got three big ones.'

'You didn't think to mention that before? Can't you just give this to her? Tell her you bought her a new one?'

Lucky looked at Jags as though he had a screw loose. 'The stones in this thing are tiny. The whole thing's probably worth just a few grand at most. Even if I did buy her something new, she knows I'd never get rid of the other one. It's a family heirloom, been passed down from one generation to the next for almost two hundred years.'

'Wow, that long?' Zaq said.

'Yes.' Lucky looked at Zaq's face for the first time, and his eyes narrowed. 'What happened to you?'

'It's nothing.'

Lucky sniffed and carried on. 'My wife only wears it on special occasions. Next time there's one of those, and it isn't there, I'm dead. And if anyone else in the family finds out what happened to it, it won't be just your auntie that kills me.' He put his hands to his face and rubbed hard. 'Shit, shit, shit.'

'I'm not sure what more we can do,' Zaq said. 'He don't want to give it back, and he's being an arsehole about it. Maybe you should just go to the police.'

Lucky took his hands from his face, his eyes wide. 'I told you before, no police.'

Zaq glanced at Jags, who raised his eyebrows and shrugged. 'Why not?' Zaq asked.

'It's ... family stuff, that's all.'

'What sort of family stuff means you can't go to the police?'

'Nothing I've heard about,' Jags said.

'We don't really talk about it. If you needed to know, you'd have been told.'

'Well, if you ain't going to the cops,' Zaq said, 'what *are* you going to do about getting it back?'

'We'll have to think of something else, some other way.' There was an edge of panic in Lucky's voice.

'We ... ?'

'You boys have got to help me.'

'If you want us to help you, then you got to tell us everything. Why can't you go to the police? We need to know exactly what the score is.'

Lucky bit his lip, then closed his eyes and shook his head as he contemplated what to do. Finally, he let out a sigh and opened his eyes. He picked up his glass from the table and waved it at Jags. 'Get me another, and let's sit down.'

Jags brought another big shot of whisky, placed it on the coffee table in front of his uncle then sat down opposite him next to Zaq. Lucky picked up the glass and sipped the whisky. He was silent for a while, Zaq and Jags waiting for him to say something.

Eventually, he took a deep breath, and said, 'All right, I'm going to tell you the story I was told by my grandfather and my dad. Only the immediate family know it, and then only those that are trusted with looking after the necklace and keeping it safe.'

'Like you?' Jags said, which earned him a dirty look from his uncle. Zaq nudged him to shut him up.

'Everyone else is just told a very basic version of the story,' Lucky continued. 'It's from India, it's old and it's been in the family for a long time, passed down from grandfather to father to son, on and on.' He took another sip of whisky. So far, he hadn't told them anything they didn't already know. 'The reason I can't go to the police about it, though . . . ' He swallowed.

Zaq and Jags waited.

' . . . is because it's stolen.'

'*What?*' Zaq and Jags exclaimed together.

'What d'you mean, it's stolen?' Jags demanded. 'Are you saying my great-great-grandad, or whoever, was a thief?'

'Not exactly.'

'Not exactly? What does that mean?'

Lucky rubbed his chin as he looked around the room, searching for the right words. 'Let me tell you the whole story, how *my* grandfather – your *great-grandfather* – told it to me, and how my dad did too. Then maybe you'll understand.'

Chapter Forty-Three

'How much do you know about Indian history?'

'I know Partition was in 1947,' Jags said.

Zaq nodded. 'Me too.'

'No, I mean before that – older history.'

Zaq and Jags shrugged.

'Don't you boys read any books?'

''Course we do,' Jags answered. 'Just not history books.'

'Maybe it's good I'm telling you about this, then. You might learn something.' Lucky sat forward on the sofa. 'So, about two hundred years ago, Punjab was the most powerful kingdom in the whole of India.' He spoke with pride. 'At first, it was made up of lots of little states which were all united by the great Maharaja Ranjit Singh. The Lion of the Punjab, they called him, even the British. Punjab was the home of the Sikhs for hundreds of years, until the British carved it up and gave most of it to the bloody Muslims for Pakistan.' He glanced quickly at Zaq. 'No offence.'

'None taken,' Zaq said. Lucky knew Zaq's family well. Even though they were from Pakistan, they were from Punjab too and spoke Punjabi just like Jags' family. Both families were very friendly – but history was still history. 'It was the British who drew the border, though,' Zaq added.

Lucky's lip lifted in a sneer. 'And what a bloody mess they made of it. Overnight, they split Punjab in two, stranding people in different countries, on both sides of a new border. The Sikhs on the Pakistani side were suddenly a minority under Muslim rule with a border between them and Amritsar, the spiritual home of Sikhism. Who would want to have to cross a border to go to their own holy place, which the day before they were perfectly free to visit? No one, that's who. So the Sikhs caught on that side of the border packed their things, or were forced to, and left their land and their homes behind, to get across into India.'

'It was the same for the Muslims on the other side,' Zaq pointed out.

Lucky nodded. 'True. The Muslims were a minority in India as it was, and those left there were suddenly an even smaller minority, while there was a brand new Muslim nation just across the border. They feared what would happen to them under majority Hindu rule, so they packed whatever they could carry too, left everything else, and went the other way across the border.'

'And that's when the killing started.'

Lucky became solemn. 'That's right. The Sikhs were angry that their homeland, the kingdom that Ranjit Singh had created, was being split, with the majority of it going to Pakistan. Muslims there were throwing Sikhs out of their homes, taking their money and their land, saying it didn't belong to them any more, that they had no place in Pakistan. Anyone who argued was killed.'

'The same happened the other way too, didn't it?'

'*Haah*. The Muslims on the Indian side who didn't flee were thrown out of their homes, others killed. There's nothing to be proud of on either side – people who'd been living together peacefully for years, suddenly turning on each other. It could all have been avoided if the British had told people in advance where the border was going to be – that's what they originally planned to do – so people would have had a year, or several months at least, to sort everything out and cross the border in an orderly way. But they announced it the day before the border actually came into effect and started a panic.'

Zaq knew some of this. There'd been a whole load of TV programmes a while back, marking the seventieth anniversary of Partition. It had brought back memories for a lot of people who'd either lived through it or been directly affected by it, many of whom had never spoken about their experiences before.

Lucky went on, 'As word spread of whole communities, of one religion or the other, being butchered, the violence spread like wildfire. Reprisal killings happened all over.' He shook his head. 'Around a million people died. It wasn't even a war. It was an act of government – the British bloody government – who simply stood by and watched as men, women and children were slaughtered. Then they just packed up and left, leaving behind the mess they'd created.'

They were silent for a moment, before Jags asked, 'What does all of that have to do with the necklace?'

'*Haah, haah,*' Lucky put up his hand, acknowledging that he'd digressed somewhat. 'OK, where was I?'

'You started off telling us about Ranjit Singh, then got on to Partition.'

'Ah, yes. So . . . Ranjit Singh, the Lion of Punjab, loved jewels. In Lahore – that was the capital of Punjab then; now it's in Pakistan – he had a treasury full of them. Everything you could imagine – diamonds, rubies, emeralds, pearls and mountains of gold and silver. He even owned the Koh-i-Noor, the most famous diamond in the world, which he got from Shuja Shah of Afghanistan.'

'Are you saying one of our ancestors stole the necklace from Ranjit Singh?' Jags asked.

'No,' Lucky barked. 'No one would steal from Ranjit Singh. Not in our family, anyway.'

'But I thought you said it was stolen?'

'If you bloody listen . . . When Ranjit Singh died,' Lucky continued, 'there was all kinds of trouble about who would take his place. He had eight sons, and they all fought over who should become the next ruler of Punjab. For the next few years, the various princes were poisoned, beaten or shot to death – it was like that bloody *Game of Thrones* everybody watches – until the only one left was little Duleep Singh. He was only five years old when he became Maharaja of Punjab.

'Those who were already in positions of power liked the idea of the boy being Maharaja because they thought they could get him to do what they wanted. No one expected what actually happened . . . the boy's mother, Rani Jindan, said she would rule in her son's name until he was old enough to govern for himself. Many in the court didn't like that at all.

'Now, the British had always wanted to take over Punjab. They didn't dare try while Ranjit Singh was alive. But after all the fighting over the throne, and with a woman in charge, they saw a chance. They offered to support Rani Jindan and the young Maharaja, while at the same time bribing her enemies at court, playing each side against the other. Then they brought troops right to the border of Punjab, knowing that would provoke a response. When the Sikh army rode out to push them back, it was just what the British had been hoping for. They accused the Sikhs of waging war on them and used it as an excuse to bring whole armies to the Punjab.'

'That's all very interesting,' Jags cut in, 'but what about the necklace?'

'I'm getting to it. Don't you young people have any patience? That was the first Anglo-Sikh war and the British only managed to win with the help of some powerful Sikhs they'd bribed with promises of titles, land and wealth. But, even as they marched into Lahore, the British knew they were still greatly outnumbered by the Sikhs in Punjab, so they did a deal. They said they would simply *help* the Maharaja govern the kingdom, then, when he was sixteen, and old enough to govern by himself, they would leave on good terms. It was all bullshit. They made Duleep – he was only about eight at the time – sign a treaty. All those in power thought it was fine, as they got to keep their positions and their wealth.

'The only person who saw through it all was the Maharaja's mother, Rani Jindan. She warned everyone not to trust the British but they ignored her. So with the help of some of her closest and most trusted supporters she began secretly taking treasure out of Lahore, so the British wouldn't get their hands on it. She would have taken the Koh-i-Noor as well but it was too heavily guarded. One of our ancestors was among those who helped Jindan smuggle out the treasure, to keep it safe until it could be returned to Lahore and the Maharaja.'

'So it wasn't stolen?' Jags said. 'Whoever took it was helping this Rani Jindan take it out of the city.'

'That's right. But that's not how the British saw it. After they got Duleep to sign the treaty, they kept making changes to it without consulting anyone. First they took over all the fortresses in Punjab to secure their position, then they took control of the treasuries, and finally they broke up the armies. When they took over the treasuries, they got hold of the . . . what do you call it – a list of everything?'

'An inventory?' Zaq offered.

'*Haah, haah*, the inventory. They had an Englishman go through everything. The first thing they checked on was the Koh-i-Noor, which was still there, but they found that quite a lot of the most valuable other pieces were missing. They had been smuggled out and the British had no way of finding them. Jindan's servants claimed not to know how the items had gone missing, even after they were beaten and tortured. It didn't take the British long to realise that Jindan had appropriated the missing jewels, and that she'd use them to raise an army against the British occupiers.'

'Did she?' Jags asked.

'She didn't get the chance. The British made up a list of charges against her and had her thrown in prison, first in Lahore, then in a fortress miles away from the city. Those who were looking after the jewels waited patiently for her to be released, so the treasure could be used to get rid of the British. But after a year or so she was moved hundreds of miles away, to a fort in the mountains. She never set foot in Punjab again.'

'What happened to the necklace and the other jewels?' Zaq said.

'Nothing,' Lucky replied. 'What could they do with them? If they took them back, they would have been arrested by the British and executed or imprisoned. With all the spies and agents working for the British, they didn't know who to trust, and they couldn't mention the treasure to anyone else, either, in case they were killed for it.'

'So what did they do?'

'They kept it, waiting for the Maharaja to come of age, when he could use the treasure himself to raise an army. But it never happened. The British had already separated him from his mother; now they sent the boy far away from Punjab, and had him brought up by a British family. Then, after a few years, news came that he'd been sent to England. Those faithful to him and his mother prayed for their return and kept the treasure safe, hoping the boy would come back a man and drive the British out of their kingdom for good. But, just like his mother, he never set foot in Punjab again. He was the last Maharaja of Punjab.'

'Shit,' Jags said.

'The people who'd been entrusted with looking after the treasures then got stuck with them. Over time, some of the pieces may have been hidden and lost, others maybe broken down and sold off bit by bit, but our family was very loyal to the Maharaja and the kingdom, and the necklace was passed down secretly, generation to generation, until we could give it back to its rightful owners. Unfortunately, that never happened. Duleep Singh died in England and so our family kept hold of the necklace, hoping it might go to one of his children.

'Through two world wars the Sikhs fought for the British, hoping that they might once again reclaim the state of Punjab for their services. After the Second World War, as rumours of independence spread, we Sikhs finally thought we'd be granted what we'd been wishing for. But when Partition came, the Hindus got Hindustan – India as you know it – the Muslims got Pakistan, and the Sikhs ... we got bugger all. *Bhen chaud*, we were left as a minority in both countries, our ancestral homeland split down the middle and given away to others.

'Who could we give the necklace back to? Duleep Singh's children were all brought up as British and there was no homeland for them to reclaim, even if they'd wanted to. India was ruled by a majority Hindu government, and Pakistan was Muslim. We had no choice but to keep hold of it in the family. It was the safest place for it.'

Until you decided to use it as collateral in a card game, Zaq thought. He could see Jags was thinking the same, though neither of them said it out loud.

'So, now you know the history of the necklace and how we come to have it.'

They were quiet for a moment, letting the story sink in. Then Zaq asked, 'How did you manage to get it over here, to England?'

Lucky gave a snort of laughter. 'That was easy. My mum, Jags' *dhadi*, just wore it. Walked right through customs, no questions asked. That was in the early '60s. Back then, none of the *gorai* thought we had anything valuable, apart from maybe some gold wedding sets. It helps that it doesn't look that flash and my mum made sure she wore an outfit that it matched, so it didn't look out of place or attract any suspicion.'

Zaq smiled. It was brazen and clever. 'Why can't you go to the police about it now? All of that stuff about it being taken was so long ago, and in India.'

'Because it was the British government that declared it stolen back then, and as far as they're concerned it's probably still officially stolen property that belongs to them. What do you think will happen if I go to the police? I'll tell you – as soon as I give them a description of it, they'll put it on the computer and a big notice will flash up saying it's been stolen or looted, or some bullshit like that. Then they'll be knocking down my door as well as that *bhen chaud* Shergill's.'

He paused, took a sip of whisky, and said, 'It's not just the British police and government I'm worried about though.'

'Why? Who else is there?' Zaq said.

'What do you think the reaction will be from our community, here and in India, if someone is arrested for possessing missing treasure that belonged to the Maharaja of Punjab? Even though we didn't actually steal it, our whole family, here and in India, will instantly be seen as thieves. We will be branded the worst sort of criminals, the lowest of the low, stealing from our own Maharaja, our own country. Everyone will disown us. We'll lose jobs, business, friends, everything – and that's if we're lucky enough not be beaten or killed as traitors. Even here people will treat us differently . . . ' He gave Jags a hard look. 'All of us. We'll be shamed and humiliated in front of everyone.'

'But you could say what really happened,' Jags said. 'How it was taken to keep it safe from the British.'

'Who would I tell? Who would be willing to listen?'

'The police. The newspapers. Everyone.'

'You think they will listen to me? If the British government say it was stolen from them, that's all anyone will believe. *That's* the story that will be on the news and in all the papers. And even if the Indian government argues that it should be returned to them, that it's rightfully theirs, they will also say it was stolen, *from them.* Our family will be thieves in the eyes of both the British and Indian governments – in the eyes of the whole world.

'The only way to avoid all of that is to get it back. That Shergill bugger doesn't even know what he's got, but if he takes it to a jeweller and has it valued – or, worse, tries to sell it – questions will be asked. And if it leads the police to him he'll tell them he got it from me – and how – and then we really will be fucked.' He drained the rest of his drink.

Zaq finally understood why Lucky was so desperate to get the necklace back.

'Knowing all that, why the hell did you gamble with it?' Jags said.

'I didn't think I was going to lose it, did I?' Lucky snapped. 'I was so sure I had a winning hand. How was I supposed to know that bastard had the only set of cards that could beat it?'

Chapter Forty-Four

'Well, Shergill's got the necklace,' Zaq said, 'so I guess we have to go back there and be a bit more forceful. No more trying to be polite or taking no for an answer.'

'What about those two jokers?' Jags said. 'His minders or whatever?'

'I guess we might have to put them down, show him we mean business.'

'I'll take the fucker with the 'tache.'

Which meant Zaq would have to deal with the giant. 'That figures. Uncle, maybe you better give us a proper description of the necklace, so we get the right one.'

'Give me a pen and paper,' Lucky said.

Jags grabbed a pen and notepad from a small table in the corner and handed them to him. Then Zaq and Jags watched as Lucky drew a large circle. 'This is the necklace, made of solid gold.' Under that, he drew three fairly large ovals, with a similar-sized teardrop shape below each one. 'These are the diamonds and—'

'Wait – what . . . ?' Jags interrupted. 'I know which necklace you're on about now – but those aren't diamonds, are they? They don't look like diamonds. They're massive. I thought they were just crystal, or glass, or something.'

'No, they're diamonds,' Lucky said. 'Indian diamonds. Back

in Mughal times they valued them for their size and didn't cut them. That's why they're flat and don't sparkle like you'd expect them to. Cutting them to make them sparkle is a Western thing, probably so smaller stones seem more dazzling and can sell for more money.'

Jags traced one of the ovals with a finger. 'One diamond that size must be worth a bit, let alone three of them.'

'Probably,' Lucky agreed.

'Probably? Don't you know?'

'Er – it's not something you can just take and get valued.'

'The diamonds aren't really that big, are they?' Zaq asked. He didn't know much about gems, but he knew they were usually a lot smaller than the ones in the drawing. The only ones he'd seen that big before were in the Tower of London.

'Nah,' Jags said, 'they're bigger. The drawing ain't to scale.'

'And what are those?' Zaq pointed to the teardrop shapes under the diamonds.

'Those are the emeralds,' Lucky said.

'And they're bigger than that too?'

'Yeah. There's the gold as well,' Lucky added. 'Each of the diamonds is set in solid gold, and the emeralds are attached with gold.'

'That's some serious necklace,' Zaq said. 'And you really don't know what it's worth?' He couldn't even begin to guess at its value.

'No, but forget that for now,' Lucky said dismissively. 'No matter what it's worth, we have to get it back.'

'You think Shergill knows?'

Lucky thought about it. 'I doubt it. He won't know its history. He'll know it's valuable, though. I'm counting on him not knowing the big stones are actually diamonds. He probably wants it for the emeralds. They're bound to be worth a fair bit, though not as much as the diamonds. The gold will be worth something too.'

'If he doesn't know what it's worth, he'll get it valued, won't he?' Zaq pointed out.

'*Bhen chaud*, then the shit'll really hit the fan! We have to get it back before he does that.' Desperation was written all over Lucky's face.

But how exactly were they supposed to do that? 'OK, I suppose me and Jags'll have to go and see him again. But what if he still won't give it back?'

'Break his legs or something. Just get me in there and I'll do it.'

Zaq wasn't sure that'd be such a good idea. 'We can threaten to get the cops involved.'

'I already told you, no police.'

'Relax, we ain't actually going to call them. We'll say you didn't do it before 'cause you didn't want anyone to know you'd bet the necklace in a card game, but now he's taking the piss you got no choice but to have him done for theft.'

'Look, say whatever you want, as long as you don't get the cops involved and you manage to get the bloody necklace back.'

'All right. Tomorrow we'll go pay Shergill another visit.'

Chapter Forty-Five

After another night at the hospital, Zaq went home and slept until the early afternoon. Then he called Jags.

'I'll come over so we can go see Shergill about the necklace.'

'Yeah, let's get it over and done with.'

When Zaq arrived at his house, Jags opened the door with just a towel wrapped around his waist.

'I hope you ain't planning on going like that,' Zaq said. 'Though you could try dropping the towel to distract them, while I find the necklace.'

'Just give me a few minutes, then we can get going.'

'Any news on Tariq?' Jags asked, as they got into the car.

'Not really. He had another CT scan yesterday. The swelling's still there and they're still waiting to see what happens. If it gets bigger, they'll have to operate. If it gets smaller, they can think about bringing him out of the coma and seeing how he is.'

'We just got to hope for the best, mate.'

But be ready for the worst, Zaq thought to himself. The possibility that his brother might have suffered some sort of long-term brain injury made him feel sick. All of a sudden, the broken nose, loose teeth and couple of black eyes he'd probably inflicted on that Satty motherfucker seemed like small change compared to what he'd done to Tariq. But it wasn't over; there was still a debt to settle.

Trouble was, Satty would be on his guard and was sure to recognise Zaq next time. Zaq realised he might've made a mistake. Maybe he shouldn't have gone for Satty yesterday, with cameras all around and his friends there. He hadn't thought it through properly; he'd let his anger get the better of him. He'd make sure it didn't happen again.

Satty would have to wait for another day, though. Right now, Zaq told himself, he had to concentrate on helping Jags get Lucky's necklace back.

The journey didn't seem to take long. This was the third time they were making the trip so it was starting to get familiar. It was a nice day and a pleasant drive: the sun shone, music played and they were in air-conditioned comfort. Jags steered the conversation on to films, TV shows and books to lighten the mood. As they got closer to the Shergill house, though, the subject changed.

'If he's still being a dick about it, we'll take Little and Large out in front of him, show we mean business, and then make him hand over the necklace.'

'Make him how?' Zaq said.

'I don't know ... might've been a while since someone punched him in the mouth. Maybe that'll impress the seriousness of the situation on him.'

'Just slap him. It'll still shake him up but won't leave any lasting marks, in case we need to deny it later. Course, we have to take care of those two goons first.'

'I got dibs on the one with the 'tache, remember?'

'How could I forget? I get the Incredible Hulk.'

'Didn't you train for that sort of thing while you were inside?'

'Only against normal-sized human beings.'

'Don't worry, mate, once I take care of Tweedledum I'll help you out with Tweedledee.'

'Tweedle Tree, more like, size of the fucker. Just make sure Shergill don't call the cops. Grab his mobile first, rip out the landline, then help me, if I need it.'

'Whatever you say.'

At the Shergill property, Jags got out, went to the intercom, and pressed the button. He had to wait a minute for anyone to answer, then Zaq saw him speaking briefly into the microphone. Then he shrugged in Zaq's direction.

Zaq leant across and lowered the driver's window. 'What's going on?'

'I think it was that big sod I just spoke to. He said to wait. Probably gone to chat to the big kahuna.'

This time the wait was longer. Eventually, the intercom crackled to life and Zaq heard the voice say, 'Mr Shergill's not in.'

Jags was pissed off. 'If he ain't in, why'd you go and ask him? You could've just said so.'

'He's not in to you,' the guy said. 'He doesn't want to see you, says your business is all done. So you need to leave and don't come back.'

'What the f—?' But the guy had already hung up. 'They ain't going to let us in.'

'We'll see about that.' Zaq got out of the car, went over and pressed the intercom button himself.

This time it was answered quickly, but before Zaq could say anything the voice snapped, 'I just told you – leave.'

'We ain't going anywhere,' Zaq said. 'Your boss has got something that don't belong to him, we're here to get it back, and we ain't going anywhere till we get it. You tell him that.'

'You got what you came for last time. You wanted a necklace, you got one. That's what you paid for. Now get lost.'

'It wasn't the one we came for, and your boss fucking knows it. We've brought his with us and he can have it back, do whatever the fuck he wants with it. But we're getting what belongs to us.'

'You ain't doing jack shit. Now fuck off, before I come out there and make you.'

'You can f—' But the guy had already hung up. 'Fucking tosser.' Zaq tried the intercom again, but there was no answer.

Swearing, Jags jabbed the button with his thumb and kept it there ...

Until Zaq nudged him. 'Look.' He nodded towards the house. Jags followed his gaze and finally let go of the intercom. The giant and Moustache guy had come out of the main door. Despite the heat, they were both dressed in black as before.

'Bloody hell,' Jags said, 'I forgot how big that fucker is. You sure you can take him?'

'I guess we'll find out. Once they open the gates, you do the talking, I'll keep an eye on them. The second either of them makes a move, I'll go for the big one and try to put him down.' He just hoped he'd be able to.

'What're they waiting for?' Jags grumbled.

Both men still stood by the front door, like a mismatched pair of statues. Even at that distance, it was plain they were scowling.

Then Zaq said, 'Who the fuck's that?'

A third figure had come out and joined the other two, and the three of them started down the drive towards the gates. It wasn't Shergill though – it was the young guy they'd seen driving the BMW Z4 when they'd left last time. Zaq felt he had to be Shergill's son. He looked completely at home, dressed in a red athletic vest and a pair of silky shorts, flip-flops on his feet. He was carrying something black and tubular with a large curved container on the top.

'What's that he's carrying?' Jags said. 'You think he's got the necklace in there?'

'Can't tell at this distance. But somehow I don't think so.' As the trio drew closer, something clicked in Zaq's memory. 'It's a fucking paintball gun!'

'A what ...?'

Before Zaq could elaborate, the trio stopped on the other side of the gates, about three metres away. The young guy was slenderly built but gym-toned, hair perfectly gelled, eyebrows salon-shaped. He had a smarmy grin on his face.

'You jokers were here the other day,' he said. It was obvious he hadn't picked up his accent at any state school. 'And now you're back again, making a lot of noise, bothering my dad and disturbing everyone else.'

'We're here to get back something that belongs to us,' Jags told him.

'I heard you got what you came for last time.'

'Well, you heard wrong then. We were palmed off with the wrong thing.'

'So why did you take it?'

'We didn't know at the time. Your dad did though, and he tricked us.'

'That doesn't seem like it'd be hard to do. As far as my dad's concerned, the matter's closed. You asked for a necklace, and he gave you one. You even checked it before you left, I believe, so any fault is your own. Now get back in your car and leave.'

'No way,' Jags said. 'We ain't going anywhere till we get our necklace. We brought the other one back. Your dad can hand over the right one, then we'll leave.'

'As I've already told you, the matter is closed. So you need to get in your car and leave, and this time don't come back.'

'And, as I just told you—'

The guy swung the paintball gun at Jags. There was a sound like the top of a fizzy drink can being opened, then something struck one of the gate's iron railings and Jags was hit with a spatter of orange paint. 'Fuck!' he yelled. 'You—'

This time the paintball hit Jags in the body, splattering in a burst of bright orange. 'Ow! Motherfucker!'

Zaq had been paintballing once and remembered how painful it was being hit by a ball at close range, even through heavy overalls with a sweatshirt underneath. Jags was just wearing a lightweight polo shirt. A hit like that would raise a circular welt on his skin.

'Hey—!' Zaq didn't get the chance to finish. Shergill's son turned the gun his way and fired twice.

Zaq instinctively raised a hand in front of his face and was hit in the chest and stomach. The impacts made him wince, and for a split second his brain confused the wet exploding paint with blood. He felt his heart rate rocket and the familiar, queasy feeling as adrenaline flooded his body.

The compressed-air sound of the gun firing came again, along with laughter. Zaq tensed ... but this time it was Jags who was hit again.

'Ow! You fucking—' Another shot cut him off.

'Let's get out of here,' Zaq called, but Jags was already going for the cover of the car.

Shergill's son continued firing, still laughing, and hit each of them a few more times. Even once they were in the car, orange paintballs thudded on the bodywork and exploded on the windscreen.

'I'm going to kill that fucking arsehole,' Jags raged. He put the wipers on, which only smeared the paint across the windscreen. Then he sprayed water and turned the wipers up to full, which managed to clear the screen just enough to see through. He reversed fast back to the main road, as paint-balls continued to hit the car. Then he put his foot down and sped away.

'Motherfucker,' he said bitterly.

Chapter Forty-Six

About fifty metres up the road, Jags turned sharply right onto a gravel road and then right again, parallel to the main road. He went on for a bumpy few metres before skidding to a halt, screened from the road by thick hedges. He sat breathing hard, staring at his hands gripping the steering wheel.

'What are we doing here?' Zaq asked after a few moments.

'I need to calm down so I can fucking drive properly.' Jags turned off the engine. 'And I want to check the car over. I swear I'm going to kill that little prick.'

'I hear you.' Zaq could feel a stinging sensation wherever he'd been hit. 'He's got it coming, big-time.'

'Fuck, you've got paint on you – and on the seats.'

'Shit, sorry. So have you.'

'Fuck's sake. Pass me the baby wipes from the glove compartment.' Jags kept a pack in the car for cleaning his hands at the petrol station. He took them, got out of the car, and used a wipe to clean the paint from the leather seat. It smeared a little but overall did a good job. 'Thank fuck for that.'

'Pass me one.' Zaq had mostly been hit on his clothes, so not a lot had transferred on to the seat. 'It's helping a bit,' he said, 'but we really need to wash all our stuff.'

Orange paint was splattered all over the windscreen, bonnet, grille and lights, with splodges on the windows and all along the bodywork on Zaq's side too. Swearing, Jags pulled another wipe and ran it over the bonnet, making a clean line through the paint. 'Least it comes off.'

Working together, they spent quarter of an hour getting off as much paint as they could, until the car looked more or less presentable. 'I'll still need to take it for a proper wash,' Jags said, 'and hope this shit don't dry too solid.' He got a carrier bag from the boot and they put the used wipes in it, to throw away later. 'Shit, those fucking paintballs hurt.' He lifted his paint-soaked polo shirt to check himself over. There were angry red welts all over his torso, each larger than a £2 coin.

'Damn, they look pretty nasty,' Zaq said, lifting his own T-shirt to inspect where he'd been hit. He too had several stinging welts that had risen like monstrous insect bites.

'That little fucker. I'd like to take that gun off him and shove it up his arse, paint his insides with it.'

'You and me both,' Zaq agreed.

'And we still ain't got the necklace. Shergill's still got it, probably still in the house somewhere. We need to get in there and make him give it to us.'

'Water's wet and fire's hot. Tell me something I don't already know.'

'This is serious, man.' For once, Jags didn't seem in the mood for jokes.

'All right, but we ain't getting in the front way, so we need to find another way in.'

'Like what?'

'If I knew, I'd be telling you right now. We have to think of something.' Zaq looked along the stretch of gravel they were on. It led to what looked like a salvage yard, and was screened from the road that ran past Shergill's house by a wall of foliage. 'Come on,' he said to Jags, and set off.

'Where we going?'

'Just up ahead ... we should be able to see the house from there.'

He heard the car alarm beep as Jags followed him. Fifty metres further on, he found a spot that afforded them a good view of Shergill's property through the bushes and crouched down there. Jags joined him.

'Now what?'

'We watch the place, and maybe see something that'll help us. In the meanwhile, get your phone out and pull up a map of this place.'

'What for? We know how we got here.'

'Just get the map up.'

'How come I got to do it? What's wrong with your phone?'

'Yours has got a bigger screen, so we can see it better,' Zaq explained.

Jags took out his phone and brought up a map of the area but the gravel road and the salvage yard weren't on it.

'Go to the satellite image,' Zaq said, pointing at a little menu icon. The map switched to a highly detailed aerial view of the area.

'Bloody hell, you can see everything.' It certainly showed much more than the map view. Roads, paths, trees, hedges, all were visible in full colour.

'Zoom in on where we are.'

Jags used his thumb and forefinger to enlarge the image.

'All right,' Zaq said, 'this is the turn we took. The car's about there, so we're here.' He moved his finger left. 'Which means this is Shergill's place, right there. See, that's the turn-off that leads to the gates, and there's the driveway going up to the house. Move the picture so we can see the back of the house.'

'Is that a swimming pool?' Jags zoomed in on a rectangle of blue in the back garden.

'Looks like it, and that's a big patio around it. The building next to it might be a pool house. Keep going.'

Jags scrolled further, to the end of the garden, and Zaq used his fingers to zoom out a little. Both Shergill's and his neighbour's gardens seemed to end halfway towards a field, and the space in between looked like a small park or landscaped garden.

'Maybe that bit belongs to both of them?' Zaq said. 'There might be a wall or something, but we could probably get over it and maybe find a way into the house.'

'What about his guys and that fuckwit son of his?'

'Hopefully we'll surprise them, take them out, and tie them up with cable ties like those fuckers used on me the other day. Then we can focus on Shergill and the necklace. First time we were there, those bi-fold doors were all wide open. It's still hot. We go late evening, there's a good chance they'll be open again and we can go straight in.'

'I'm going to find that bloody paintball gun and shoot that little shit in the dick.'

Zaq was still looking at the satellite image. 'What's this?' he said. 'It looks like a path or road on the other side of his neighbour's place.' It was hard to make out through the tree cover in the aerial shot. 'Go to Streetview.'

Jags hit the little square that changed the image to a driver's eye view. He used a finger to turn the image around so it was facing the front of Shergill's property.

'Move past the neighbour's place.' Jags double-tapped the screen and the image moved a few metres along the road. 'That's still the neighbour's. Go a bit further ... ' Jags double-tapped again. 'There.' Zaq pointed at what looked like tyre ruts leading off the road.

It took Jags a little bit of back and forth to hit on an image that allowed them to see the side road properly, not that there was much to see. It was overhung with bushes and trees, grass growing high between the tyre ruts. 'Don't look like it's used much,' he said.

'Zoom in a bit ... That looks like a gate there.' Jags zoomed in a bit more and they could make out a low, finely wrought iron gate across the track. 'Don't look like it's used at all – which is perfect for us. We can hop over the gate and get to the back of the house.' Zaq tapped the screen to go back to the satellite image. 'We can go down there and cut across this bit of open ground here, or go right to the end and see if we can come in through the trees there. That might be best – we'd have cover until we get close to the house.'

'What if there's cameras and sensors, or an alarm?'

'They'd only put the alarm on at night or if they're all out. We're aiming to go in when they're there, so chances are we might not have to worry about that stuff. We'll need to have a getaway set up, though.' He followed the gated-off track beside the neighbour's property to its end. 'Look, it joins up with this road going by these other houses.' He moved the image on the screen to follow the new road, which led to another road that ran parallel to the disused track before running up to join the main road a few hundred metres south of Shergill's house. 'Man, this is even better. We can take this road, come up around the back of Shergill's place, or close enough, and we can leave the car there to make our getaway.'

'That sounds like a good—'

'Wait, what's going on?' A flash of light from the Shergill property had caught Zaq's attention. Looking up from the phone screen, he pulled back a bit of foliage to get a better view. 'Someone's leaving.' A Jaguar SUV with a brash electric-blue paint job was approaching the gates, which were already opening. It drove through the gates and paused briefly before turning and going right past Zaq and Jags' position. 'It's Shergill.'

'And his two dickhead minders with him.'

'Come on,' Zaq said, moving away from the bushes, 'let's get after them. If we follow them, we might get a chance to grab Shergill, ditch his two numpties, and bring him back here to get the necklace. It'd give us two less people to worry about and save us having to try and break in.'

'It's worth a shot. Let's go.' Jags sprinted ahead of Zaq to unlock the car, they jumped in, and Jags made a quick three-point turn, got them to the road and pulled out to follow Shergill's car.

Chapter Forty-Seven

Keeping one or two cars between them, they followed Shergill through familiar territory back towards Uxbridge.

'Good job we cleaned the paint off the car,' Jags said. 'That bright orange crap would've been visible a mile off.'

'Yeah. With any luck, they'll have thought we pissed off and didn't hang around, so they won't be looking out for us behind them.'

Jags managed to keep the Jaguar in sight all the way through Uxbridge, into Hillingdon and then Hayes. 'If we weren't following them, I could just turn off here and go home, get changed out of this messed-up gear.'

'Stick with them for now. You can change later.'

They carried on through Hayes. 'Southall up ahead,' Jags said. 'You think that's where he's heading?'

'Maybe.' They crossed the bridge over the Grand Union Canal into Southall proper. Something about being on home turf made Zaq more positive about their chances of getting the necklace back, like the home ground advantage in a football match, even though the outcome was far from guaranteed.

They hit the Broadway, with its kaleidoscopic array of fabric shops, jewellers, restaurants and supermarkets. This was no sedate small-town high street. The colours, smells and noise combined in an exuberant cacophony unique to the place. There was nothing subdued about the bright, bold colours of the outfits in the boutiques and clothing shops either, and the air was filled with the aromas of freshly ground spices, *jalebi*, *tandoori* grills and frying *samosas*. The community had made the area its own and put its stamp on the place, loud and unashamedly proud. No matter how much it might piss you off if you lived and worked there, like the girl in the movie said: there really was no place like home.

Two-thirds of the way along the Broadway, the Jaguar's indicator light signalled right, and it swung over and pulled into a loading bay outside some shops on the far side of the road. Jags slowed down, so they could see what was happening. Shergill got out from behind the wheel and his towering minder got out the other side and handed him a package. The guy with the moustache, Taj, got out of the back and into the driver's seat, pulled out into the traffic again, and took the next right on to a side street while Shergill and his minder walked over to a jeweller's shop and went inside.

'I'm going to jump out here,' Zaq said, already opening his door. 'Try and park somewhere, and I'll call you when they come out.'

The shopfront was simple and well-maintained, painted a tasteful light grey with white trim. Above the display windows the name KANG was spelt out in solid silver letters, along with the word JEWELLERS. Higher up, hanging from the first floor, was a sign with a pictogram of a cut diamond. Altogether, the place had a high-end look and feel. Zaq had passed it countless times but never set foot inside.

Almost exactly opposite the jeweller's, on the other side of the road, was a bus stop which would have afforded Zaq a good view into the premises. The only trouble was, it was right outside another jeweller, and it had cameras. The staff would no doubt be on the lookout for any dodgy geezers acting suspiciously, which was exactly what Zaq would be doing. The next shop along, however, was a small Indian café that sold *samosas*, *pakoras* and *jalebi*. It was a perfect spot to sit and watch from. Zaq made for it and checked out Kang's as he did so. The display windows either side of the entrance were full of elaborate gem-set necklaces and earrings worked in dazzling Indian gold. The twenty-four-carat gold favoured by Indians was a deeper, richer hue than the nine-carat stuff you got in high street stores, or even the more pricey eighteen-carat material used by more upmarket western jewellers.

There was an outer and an inner security door, both undoubtedly made of toughened glass, which created an airlock. One door had to be closed before the other would open, making it difficult for anyone to rob the place. Through the glass Zaq could see Shergill, with his freak of a minder at his shoulder, at the rear counter, talking to a man in a grey suit. It looked to Zaq as though they knew each other, the other guy all laughs and smiles. Then he gestured with a hand and Shergill joined him behind the counter. The other guy – was he the owner or the manager? – entered what must have been a code into a keypad and opened a door that led to the back of the shop. Zaq saw Shergill signal his minder to wait, and go through the door with the other man.

Zaq ducked into the café, keeping an eye on Kang's as he decided what to order. He wasn't a big a fan of *jalebi* or other Indian sweets but he was partial to *samosas* and *pakoras*. So he ordered four *samosas* – two meat, two veg – and a cup of *chai*. 'I'm going to have them here,' he told the guy behind the counter, who was clearly taking in the orange stains on Zaq's clothing. 'Can you put them in takeaway containers, though, in case I have to leave in a hurry?'

The place was quiet and Zaq picked a table near the front, where he had a good view across to the jeweller's. A minute later, the guy brought over two brown paper bags with the *samosas*, a takeaway cup of *chai*, a paper plate, napkin and two small Styrofoam containers, one of green chutney, the other with *imli*, a tamarind dipping sauce. Zaq took a sip of the tea. It was scalding hot, spiced and sweet. Keeping his eyes on the jeweller's, he took the lids off the sauce containers, then took out a *samosa* and was just about to take a bite when his phone rang.

It was Jags. 'What's going on?'

'I was just about to have a *samosa*.'

'You what? I thought you were watching Shergill.'

'I am. Couldn't stand out on the street like a lemon, though, could I? I'm in a café opposite. Had to buy something. Where are you?'

'The geezer with the 'tache went down Beachcroft Avenue and parked up there. I didn't want to drive past him so I carried on down to St George's Avenue.' It was only three streets away.

'OK, stay there, and I'll let you know when they're leaving.'

'What you think he's doing in there?'

Zaq kept his voice low. 'Well, he didn't go in for a massage. He went in the back with some guy, the manager or the owner, I think. They looked pretty pally, obviously know each other. I reckon maybe Shergill's trying to find out what the necklace is worth.'

'Shit. If the jeweller susses those are diamonds on it, there's no way that greedy fucker's going to give it back.'

'The guy's a jeweller; he's bound to suss what they are, else he's in the wrong bloody job. You're right though – once Shergill finds out those big rocks are diamonds, he definitely won't want to give it up.'

'What d'you think it could be worth?'

'How the hell should I know? Stones that size? Bound to be a lot, that's for sure.'

'Erm – you think we should try and take the necklace off him when he comes out?'

'Are you crazy? Here, on the Broadway, in the middle of the afternoon, people and cameras everywhere? That'd be risky, and dumb. Nah, we'd be better off doing it nearer his place. We'd still have to deal with his two guard dogs, though, and we don't know what they're packing. I'd rather not get shot if I can help it.'

'What are we going to do then?'

'Let's wait and see what happens. An opportunity might just present itself.'

'Fine,' Jags said. 'Enjoy your *samosas* ... greedy bastard.'

'I got two for you as well, but if that's how you feel ...'

'I didn't mean it. You know I love you really.'

'I'll call you in a bit. Might have to eat your *samosas*, though ...'

Chapter Forty-Eight

For what seemed like ages, nothing happened at the jeweller's. Shergill's hulking minder stood with his hands clasped in front of him, and a shop assistant moved around behind the display counters, but there were no other customers.

Zaq dipped a *samosa* into the green chutney and took a bite. The tea had cooled down enough for him to sip and went well with the spicy minced lamb filling. He ate slowly, taking his time, not knowing how long he might have to sit there. When he'd finished the first *samosa*, he started on a vegetable one. It was good too, with soft potato filling mixed with onion, peas and spices. He could easily have eaten the other two and told Jags he'd had to, to remain in the café.

His phone vibrated in his pocket. He saw a message from Jags: Anything?

No, he responded, then added, Samosas are really good, just to wind him up. A single emoji came back, a hand giving him the middle finger.

Zaq finished his tea but kept hold of the cup, as if there might still be something in it.

About half an hour after they'd gone in, the Jaguar was back to pick up Shergill and his minder. It partly blocked Zaq's view of the shop, but he could still see Shergill emerge from the back room.

He was already on his phone to Jags. 'Get over here quick. They're just leaving, heading back towards Hayes. I'll cross the road; pick me up outside the jeweller's.'

The minder moved ahead of his boss and got the doors for him. With a wave to the guy in the suit, Shergill left the premises, carrying the package he'd taken in. Taj waited beside the car, eyes scanning the street, until Shergill had got in. Then he climbed in the back. The man-mountain took the front passenger seat.

Zaq got up, grabbed the bags with the remaining *samosas*, and left the shop. He crossed the road, slipping between moving cars and waited on the opposite kerb. A moment later Jags stopped in the road for a second so Zaq could get in, and they were off.

'Got your *samosas* here,' Zaq said, holding up the bags of food. 'I won't drop them in your lap, though. I'll keep hold of them for you.'

'Thanks. There they are,' Jags said, nodding ahead of them. The big SUV was an easy car to follow, visible over the tops of normal-sized cars, and the electric-blue colour did nothing to help it blend in. 'Where d'you think he's going now?'

Zaq shrugged. 'Ain't got a clue, mate. Depends what that bloke back at the jeweller's told him. We need to know whether he takes it back to his place, or somewhere else.'

As it turned out, they trailed him back the way they'd come, until Shergill turned in at the gates to his house. Jags turned on to the gravel road they'd taken earlier and pulled over. They got out and walked to the spot from where they'd watched the house before, Jags tucking into his *samosas* as they did so. Zaq pulled some small branches aside, so they could both see the blue Jaguar parked near the house and three men walking to the front door.

'What now?' Jags said, around a mouthful of food.

'Well, he's back home, but did the package he brought out have the necklace in it?'

'I doubt that greedy sod would've left it there – especially if the guy told him those big stones were fucking diamonds.'

'Either way,' Zaq said, 'we need to go have a word with the jeweller.'

The drive back to Southall took longer as they hit the early evening rush. Parking was a real pain in the arse now that almost everywhere was for permit-holders only. The pay-and-display bays on Saxon Road, just off the Broadway, were all full, but Zaq and Jags knew there were more spaces further along; they looked like permit-holder places but were in fact pay-and-display, though you'd only know that if you spotted the tiny sign that told you where they ended. Jags found a free space, bought a ticket, and they walked up to the Broadway, crossed over at a traffic island and went to the jeweller's.

'I should've stopped at home on the way and got changed.' Jags said. Their orange-splattered clothes were drawing some strange looks. 'The bloody paint's dried hard, too.'

'Sod it, we're here now. Let's see if we can talk to the guy. I just hope they let us in looking like this.'

When he heard the security lock buzz and disengage, Zaq pulled the door open. There was a slightly longer hesitation before they were buzzed through the sturdier inner door into the shop.

'How can I help you?' asked the man in the grey suit, his tone suggesting he wasn't particularly eager to. His smile oozed salesman charm, even though his eyes didn't. He looked them up and down, noting the paint on their clothes and the bruising on Zaq's face.

'We just want a quick word, Mr Kang,' Zaq said, giving the man a cool smile. 'You are Mr Kang?'

'*Haah.*' The man nodded.

'About a necklace.'

'Oh?' Kang's eyebrows went up. 'Which necklace would that be?' he asked, gesturing at the display cases.

'The one Mr Shergill brought in a little while ago.'

Kang's eyes met Zaq's and the fake warmth left his face, replaced by a scowl. 'I cannot discuss my customers' business with you or anyone else,' he said with a dismissive flick of the wrist.

Zaq approached the counter and lowered his voice. 'Maybe you'd rather discuss it with the police?'

The jeweller's eyes flicked over to his assistant, who was watching what was going on from behind the counter on the right. Zaq glanced his way too. The guy was young, maybe early twenties, with a wispy beard and a neat black turban. A son or a nephew perhaps, learning the family business, though, judging by the look on Kang's face, maybe not learning everything about it.

'He brought it in to show you, right?' Zaq asked. Kang didn't respond. 'Course he did. Maybe he wanted you to give him a valuation. Surely you must've wondered where the hell he got something like that from?'

Standing next to Zaq, Jags said, 'It ain't his. It belongs to my uncle, been in our family for almost two hundred years, and that arsehole Shergill's taken it. We want it back.'

'What d'you think the police would say if we told them you were knowingly handling stolen goods?'

'I don't know anything about it being stolen,' Kang said in a low, urgent voice.

'You do now,' Zaq said. 'I doubt it'd do your reputation any good. And who knows – the police might well want to look over everything else you've got here. Maybe even the tax office, if we were to call them.' That was a threat guaranteed to tighten the sphincter muscles of many an Asian businessman.

'There'd be government interest as well,' Jags added. 'And not just the British government. The Indian government would have an interest in it too. That piece is originally from the Punjab. Everyone would want to know what you were doing with it.'

'Ooh, I wouldn't want all that shit raining down on me,' Zaq said.

Kang swallowed and put his hands up in a calming gesture. 'Listen, I know nothing about any of that. Mr Shergill is a customer of mine. He brought in a necklace and asked me to have a look at it. That's all I did.' He flicked another nervous glance at his assistant, who was doing a very poor job of trying to look busy. 'Anyway, how do I know what you're saying is true? That it really belongs to you?'

'You got a pen and paper?' Jags said.

Zaq was as puzzled as Kang by the request. What was Jags going to do?

He swiftly replicated the sketch of the necklace Lucky had done for them the day before and pushed it across the counter to Kang. 'This is what it looks like.' He used the pen to point out the main features. 'It's twenty-four-carat Indian gold. The three big stones here are diamonds and the ones below are emeralds. Like I said, it's been in my family for almost two hundred years. But it's older than that, could date back to the Mughals.'

Perspiration glistened on Kang's forehead. Their considerable knowledge of the necklace was obviously making him uncomfortable.

'Maybe we should talk back there?' Zaq nodded at the door behind Kang. 'Like you did with Shergill earlier.'

He was clearly surprised Zaq knew about that, but recovered himself and nodded. 'If you're going to try and rob me, you won't get far. Everything's on CCTV, and the jewellery is all invisibly marked.'

'Relax – we ain't here to rob you. We're the ones who've been robbed. We just want to get back what's ours.'

Chapter Forty-Nine

Kang cleared his throat and beckoned them around behind the counter. '*Ravi, enah nu ahneh de,*' he told his assistant, who opened a gate and allowed Zaq and Jags through. Kang had already opened the door to the backroom and ushered them in. '*Ethay dekhee,*' he said, telling Ravi to keep an eye on things in the shop.

The back room was an office and workspace combined. One desk held a computer and trays overflowing with paperwork; a second had various tools and cloths strewn across it. There were a couple of work lamps and a large magnifying glass on an adjustable arm. On the wall was a line of small-drawer filing cabinets and shelves crammed with jewellery boxes in varying sizes. At the far end of the room was a workbench, cluttered with hand and machine tools.

Kang leaned against the desk with the computer. Zaq and Jags took up positions facing him.

'What did Shergill want?' Zaq asked. 'I'd say he wanted you to look at the necklace and tell him what it's worth.'

Beads of sweat on Kang's forehead caught the light. He nodded.

'And ...? What did you tell him?'

'It wasn't as simple as just looking at it and giving a valuation,' the jeweller said cautiously. 'It is a very unusual piece, not like anything I've handled before. At first I didn't think it was anything special, but, as I examined it, I realised I might be mistaken and did some tests to be sure. I knew it was Indian and old but Mr Shergill didn't say where it had come from and he doesn't have any paperwork for it. How did it come to be in your family?'

'What's that got to do with anything?' Jags said, but then must have realised that sharing his knowledge would help bolster his claim to the necklace, because he went on, 'It belonged to Ranjit Singh, Maharaja of Punjab, then to his son Duleep Singh, the last Maharaja. One of my ancestors was part of the royal court in Lahore. When the British took over Punjab, the Maharaja's mother Jind Kaur – Rani Jindan – gave the necklace to my ancestor to keep safe, so the British wouldn't get it. It's been in our family ever since.'

Kang was nodding. '*Haah, haah* ... that sounds believable. You know much more about it than Mr Shergill.'

'That's because it belongs to my family, like I said. All *he* knows is that it might be worth something.'

Kang gave a nervous laugh. 'Oh, it certainly is. I couldn't believe it when I tested it; neither could Mr Shergill.'

'Couldn't believe what?' Zaq asked.

'The value of the thing. At first I didn't even pay attention to the stones, because of their size. I thought the white stones were just crystals, and the green ones probably paste or semi-precious. I was sure it was just a waste of my time, but decided it would be quicker and easier to take a look, give a rough estimate and send him on his way, so I examined it.

'To start with, I concentrated on the gold. When I saw it was very pure, high quality, I looked more closely at the workmanship. It's not a style you see these days and I realised it was an antique piece. Then I thought, if the gold is such good quality, it follows that the gems might also be high quality. So, I checked the green ones first, thinking there was a slim chance they could be real emeralds.'

'And they were.' Zaq wasn't asking a question.

'They were indeed, and big too, roughly ten to twelve carats each, and of the most exceptional quality.' Kang was getting excited, warming to the subject.

The most Zaq knew about emeralds was that they were green. Carats and quality didn't mean much to him. 'And then you checked the other stones – the diamonds?'

Kang nodded. 'Of course. Even then I was thinking they couldn't possibly be diamonds, not that size. But when I tested them, I was amazed. They are the biggest diamonds I have ever appraised. Mr Shergill was very pleased to hear that.'

'I bet he was,' Jags muttered.

'He obviously wanted to know what it was worth,' said Zaq. 'What did you tell him?'

'Without being able to take the stones out and look at them properly, I could only give a rough estimate ...'

'Which was what?'

'Surely *you* know its value. You already know so much about it.'

'Pretend we don't.'

Kang looked from Zaq to Jags. 'While I was trying to work it out, I remembered I had once seen something similar, only I couldn't remember where. So I looked on the computer.'

'And ...?'

Kang sat down at the computer and tapped the keyboard to bring it to life. 'Can't you just tell us?' Jags demanded.

'Mr Shergill was impatient, just like you, but he changed his mind when he saw what I am about to show you.' Kang logged in and brought up a web browser. 'The necklace looked fairly old, so I typed in *antique*, and it was also Indian in style, so I typed *Indian . . .*' He typed the words into Google.

Zaq looked at Jags, who rolled his eyes. The jeweller gave them a running commentary as he typed in various search terms, probably trying to show what a computer whizz he was. Once he'd typed in *antique Indian diamond emerald necklace*, he finally hit the search key. A fraction of a second later the results were displayed. He moved the cursor and clicked on *Images*. The results switched to a page of photographs that matched the search terms. 'There,' Kang said, sitting back in his seat, sounding satisfied with himself.

Zaq didn't see the point of all this, but leaned forward and started scanning the images from left to right. Yeah, there were some beautiful-looking necklaces, but what the hell was he—?

And then he saw it. Third row down, towards the middle.

'Shit,' Jags said. He'd spotted it too.

They were looking at a photograph of a necklace, almost identical to Jags' drawing, the only difference being that the one on-screen had five diamonds and five emeralds, whereas theirs had three of each.

'It looks like the same design,' Jags said.

'It is, except for the number of stones.' Kang said. 'I would guess that they were made together, originally part of a set. Mr Shergill's necklace—'

'*Our* necklace, you mean!'

'Yes, of course,' Kang allowed. '*Your* necklace is the lesser one. I would say the one in the picture was created for one of the Mughal shahs and yours probably for a favourite wife or son.'

The caption below the image read *Splendours of Mughal India*.

'Can you bring up a larger image?' Zaq asked.

Kang opened a drop-down section with a larger version of the photo. The necklace was laid out in a specially designed case that displayed it to best effect. To the right of the main image were several different photos of the same necklace.

'How about those?' Zaq pointed to the other images.

'Exactly,' Kang said.

Zaq didn't know what that was supposed to mean but watched as the jeweller enlarged the next image. The new photo showed the necklace in the same case but a head-on view. Two white-gloved hands were holding the case to the camera. 'Holy fuck,' Zaq said, without thinking.

'Oh, shit,' Jags said.

'*Haah*,' Kang nodded. 'You see what it says, heh?'

Zaq didn't respond; nor did Jags. They were staring at the caption in disbelief. It was from the website of an international auction house.

RARE MUGHAL NECKLACE
SELLS FOR $20 MILLION.

A unique Indian 17th-century Mughal Golconda mirror diamond necklace, featuring some of the world's oldest and largest diamonds, was sold yesterday at auction in New York for an astonishing US$20 million . . .

'Of course,' Kang said, 'the necklace Mr Shergill showed me won't be worth quite as much as that, as it's a slightly smaller piece.'

'How much are we talking about?' Jags croaked.

'As I told Mr Shergill, it's hard to give an exact figure, but based on this— ' he gestured at the screen '—I would guess maybe fifteen million dollars. That would be roughly—' he did a calculation in his head '—eleven to twelve million pounds.'

'Bloody hell', Zaq said..

'Of course,' Kang continued, 'the other necklace was sold about seven years ago, so Mr Shergill's, or *yours*, or whosever it is—'

'It's ours,' Jags stated.

'—could be worth more now, possibly thirteen or fourteen million, maybe as much as fifteen.'

Zaq looked at Jags and saw his own astonishment mirrored in his friend's face.

Kang saw it too and frowned. 'You didn't know what it was worth?'

'It hasn't been valued in a while,' Jags said.

'If I might ask . . . if it belongs to you and your family, why does Mr Shergill have it?'

Why indeed? If Lucky had known what the necklace was worth, he'd have been better off putting down his car as a marker, or even his house.

'He was just supposed to be holding it for a while, but now he won't give it back,' Jags explained.

Knowing how much it was worth, Shergill was now even less likely to return it. 'Did he say what he might do with it?' Zaq asked Kang.

The jeweller nodded. 'He asked me about the possibility of selling it, but a piece like that, especially with this other one—' he gestured at the screen '—going for so much, would be very difficult to sell. The lack of paperwork would also be a big problem. Questions would be asked about where it came from and how he comes to have it. And if, as you say, it once belonged to the Maharaja of Punjab, and if the Indian and British governments were to get involved, it could be very complicated. Unless . . .'

Zaq and Jags waited. 'Unless, what?' Jags said eventually.

'Well, unless he wanted to sell it privately, without any fuss, though he would most likely have to settle for a lot less than it could fetch at auction.' Kang frowned. 'There is also the possibility of breaking the piece up and selling the gems individually. Depending on the quality, each of the diamonds could sell for three or four million pounds. The emeralds could be worth up to a couple of hundred thousand pounds each, and the gold could be sold by weight. It would be a shame to destroy something so beautiful, but it could be done.'

'It ain't his to destroy,' Jags pointed out.

Kang just shrugged. 'I can't stop him from doing what he wants with it.'

'No, but we can,' Zaq said. 'If he wants to sell it, will he come to you?'

'I don't know. Perhaps.'

'Well, if he does, or if you hear anything else about what he's going to do with it, let us know.'

'I'm not sure that would be a good idea,' Kang said. 'You obviously don't know Mr Shergill very well. He certainly wouldn't like it if he found out I helped you.'

'Don't worry, we won't tell him. But if we find out you helped him sell it, we'll definitely let the police know and you can explain to them how you handled a stolen antique and helped arrange its illegal sale. We'd rather avoid that, so just let us know what he's up to and we'll keep your name out of it. How's that sound?'

From the look on Kang's face, it didn't sound too good. He was stuck between the proverbial rock and a hard place. 'I don't see what good it will do you.'

'It won't do us any harm either. Just a call to let us know what he's going to do with it so we can try and get it back for its rightful owner and keep you from getting in trouble with the authorities.'

Kang let out a breath, his shoulders sagging 'Just a call – that's it. I'll tell you whatever he tells me, and that's all. I can't do anything more.'

Chapter Fifty

Only when they were sitting inside the car did Jags say, 'Fucking hell – fifteen million!'

'I know. Lucky'll shit a brick when he finds out.'

'And Shergill knows how much it's worth, too. Ain't no way he'll give it back now.'

'Not willingly, anyway,' Zaq said. 'We'll have to take it off him.'

'You think Kang will help us?'

'For all we know he's on the phone to Shergill right now, telling him we were just there. Looks like we either grab Shergill somewhere and force him to give it to us, or we break into his place and grab it ourselves.'

'What if he tries to sell it before we get a chance to do either?'

'If we know about any sale we can disrupt it, maybe even get hold of the necklace then.'

'Neither of those options sound that great.'

Zaq had to agree. Their only choices were kidnapping, burglary or robbery, any of which could land him back in prison. 'Only thing in our favour right now is that he won't be able to sell it straight away. Any deal for that sort of money will take a while to set up, which gives us a bit of time.'

'What if he don't want to sell it?'

Zaq thought about that. 'Then we got a bit more time to work something out ... but I don't see him keeping it. He only kept it 'cause he thought it might be worth something, and now he knows it is – and a bloody fortune too! – I doubt he'll pass up all that money just to sit and admire the thing.'

'You're probably right.'

'Plus, he knows it's got history and might be hot. First it was just Lucky who knew about it, then you and me, now Kang. The more people who know about it, the more word'll spread and then others'll be after it too. And, as far as Shergill knows, there's also a chance that if Lucky gets desperate he might go to the cops. I doubt he'll just wait for that to happen. I was him, I'd want to sell it fast then sit back and count the money.'

'You're right.' Jags started the car and the air-conditioning kicked in, quickly cooling the interior. 'We need to hurry up and think of a plan to get it back.'

'Let's see what we can come up with.'

'What d'you want to do now?'

Zaq was about to say 'Go home and get changed' but then remembered something. 'Let's go over to Woodlands Road. I want a word with Bongo.'

It wasn't far from where they were. A couple of minutes later they turned off the Broadway and down the one-way street. Zaq directed Jags to the house and had him park nearby. 'Wait for me, yeah? I won't be long.' Sure enough, he wasn't long at all. 'He weren't there. Sod it. Can you swing past my place so I can get changed quickly?'

They continued to the end of the street and turned left on to Beaconsfield Road. They were about halfway to South Road when Zaq suddenly said, 'Stop. Pull over. There he is.' He'd spotted Bongo walking along the pavement, probably heading home from the station. 'Wait for me.' Zaq jumped out and jogged back, calling out Bongo's name.

It took Bongo a second to recognise him. 'Oh, hey,' he said, as Zaq reached him. 'How's it going? How's T doing?'

'He's the same as he was before. Listen, I've got a bone to pick with you.' Zaq jabbed a finger in his direction. Bongo's face fell, but he didn't seem shocked or surprised. 'You told me you couldn't think of anything that happened at that wedding you and Tariq were at, any trouble – but that was bullshit, weren't it?' Bongo didn't deny it. He didn't say anything. 'There was a fight, and it was because of you and some girl.'

Bongo looked decidedly uncomfortable. 'It wasn't like that. We weren't doing anything. Those two arseholes just kicked off.'

'Why didn't you fucking *tell* me?'

'Shit, man, I . . . I know who you are. I know your rep. I wasn't sure how you'd take it, how you'd react if I told you it might've been because of that.'

'How d'you think I'm going to react now?' The pavement was busy, and people seeing and hearing their heated discussion were giving them a wide berth.

'Look, I'm sorry, man.'

'Fuckin' idiot. You could've saved me a load of time and effort if you'd just been upfront with me. I had to track down your ex, Sharan, and she told me what happened.' Zaq drew his fist back, making Bongo flinch. 'I ought to smack you one.' But he didn't. Instead, he let his hand drop. 'Now, tell me what you know, all of it – and don't leave anything out this time.'

'OK . . .' Bongo said, breathing a bit easier. 'Me and Sharan used to go out in college, East Berks, in Langley. I was there for two years and we were pretty serious. We just kind of drifted apart afterwards though. She was working in Slough and I got a job in the City, so it was difficult to keep seeing each other. We were still friends, though, you know, on Facebook and everything. I knew she was seeing someone. Anyway, me and T were playing that wedding in Slough and I had no idea she was going to be there, so it was a complete surprise. I said hi, and we were just chatting – catching up, being friendly, you know? It was harmless.'

Zaq wondered if it really had been all that harmless? Guys were guys, after all, especially where girls were concerned.

'Anyway,' Bongo continued, 'then this guy comes up, all flippin' attitude, and she didn't look happy to see him. Turned out it was her boyfriend. He was well pissed, being loud and a bit of an arsehole really.'

'What did he look like?'

Bongo shrugged. 'Wearing a suit, same as every other guy there. About my height, shortish hair, bit of a beard, kind of similar to most other Asian guys. I see so many people at weddings and gigs, I don't know if I'd even recognise him again.'

'All right, then what happened?'

'He grabbed Sharan, pretty rough, and tried to pull her away. I thought he was out of order and told him to leave her alone. He told me to fuck off and twisted her arm. I didn't even think, I just grabbed him to make him let go of her. By that time, T had seen what was going on. He stuck a track on the deck and jumped down from the stage to try and break things up. That's when the other dude rocked up.'

'The stocky guy with the gold tooth?' Zaq said. Bongo nodded. 'The one I asked you about before, and you said you didn't know anything?'

'Shit, man. I'm really sorry about that. I'm telling you everything now though.'

'Go on, then.'

'I'd let go of the boyfriend and backed off, and T was trying to calm things down when the other guy bowled in and shoved T, told him to fuck off. T told him to go fuck himself and it all blew up. Geezer went for T, there were a few punches thrown, and everyone jumped in to stop it. T and the gold-tooth guy were pulled apart, there was a bit of shouting, and both those other guys were bundled off. Didn't look like anyone else knew them but they could see they were both pissed, and just got them out of there.'

'Anything happen after that?'

'By the time all the hoo-ha died down, Sharan and her boyfriend were gone. I didn't see her again. I made sure T was OK and we just got on with what we were doing. Shit like that happens now and again, man, any gig where guys are drinking. Occupational hazard, I guess. We usually manage to avoid it. I tried calling her afterwards, to make sure she was all right, but I didn't get to talk to her.'

'You know this second guy? Seen him around anywhere?'

Bongo shook his head. 'I think he's from Slough, though.'

'The name Satty mean anything to you?'

'No.'

'Well, according to Prit, he's the guy that jumped T and put him in hospital, him and his mates. I don't know if the boyfriend was involved, but he might well have been. You can make yourself useful by asking around about them. Maybe one of your mates from college will know them. I want to find the motherfuckers and get them for what they did to Tariq.'

Bongo swallowed. 'OK, sure.'

'Call me soon as you find anything out.'

Chapter Fifty-One

Jags drove Zaq home so he could wash and change, then they both went back to Jags' house, where Zaq picked up his car and went to the hospital. He'd been so busy running around the last few days, he'd hardly had time for a proper dinner, and once again he had to stop on the way for convenience food to see him through the night.

'There's been a slight change in Tariq's condition,' his father said at once when he arrived. 'The doctors say it looks as though the swelling to his brain is starting to go down. They'll keep monitoring him and, if it continues to reduce, they say they'll take him off the medication and allow him to wake up. He won't be out of the woods, though – they'll still need to do a full assessment to see if the injury will have any long-term effect.'

After his parents left, Zaq ate and then read for a while. He thought about calling Nina but decided to do it the next day so they could work out what to do at the weekend. Eventually, he settled down for another night of not sleeping very well in a hospital armchair.

In the morning, the doctor doing the morning rounds gave Zaq the same news he'd heard from his dad. 'It may not look like it yet,' he said, 'but things are moving in the right direction.'

Zaq conveyed this to his parents when they arrived, then went home to bed.

Daytime sleeping wasn't something that came easy to him. He never managed to sleep as well as he did at night, so he woke several hours later not feeling as rested as he would have liked. He checked his phone and saw a bunch of missed calls from Tariq's mate Prit and a couple of WhatsApp messages from Jags. The only reason Prit would be calling would be something to do with Tariq so, after a quick visit to the bathroom, Zaq called him first.

'What the hell did you do?' Prit demanded.

'What're you talking about?'

'I gave you Bongo's number so you could go talk to him – not this.'

'What the fuck are you on about?'

'You didn't have to do that to him, man.'

'Do what?'

'You know what – beat him up. That's exactly how he thought you'd react; that's why he didn't tell you straight off. What happened to T wasn't his fault. How was he meant to know they'd go after him?'

'I ain't got a clue what you're going on about.'

'I gave you his number the other day and you went round and saw him . . . '

'Yeah, so?'

'When you found out T might've been jumped because of Bongo and some girl, you went and saw him again and blamed him.'

'I didn't blame him. But he should've just told me . . . '

'Then you beat him up.'

'Hang on a sec, I never touched him.'

'You saw him yesterday, though, innit? People saw you arguing with him on the street.'

'Yeah, I was pissed off at him for making me waste my time.

If he'd told me everything at the start, I wouldn't have had to go tracking down the bride and groom from the wedding, or his ex-girlfriend. That's what I was having a go at him about. Then I asked him to find out whatever he could about the guys that started on them at the wedding. I gave him a name to go on and then I left him.'

'Then how come he's in hospital, battered even worse than T was? They don't know if he's going to pull through.' Prit sounded properly upset, maybe even close to tears.

'What the fuck . . . ? I keep telling you, I don't know anything about it,' Zaq said. 'It's got nothing to do with me. All I did was talk to him, and he was fine when I left him. What d'you know about what happened?'

'Just what I heard. You were seen arguing with him and then he got a call last night, said he was going to see someone about a booking or something, but didn't come back. A dog-walker found him unconscious in Brookside Park and called an ambulance. Apparently his heart stopped beating and he had to have CPR till the ambulance got there.'

'What time was that?'

'He was found about eleven.'

'What time did he go out?'

'I don't know, about nine-thirty, ten o'clock.'

'I was at the hospital then, with T. Got there about seven, seven-thirty, so my parents could go home. I was there all night. Nurses will have seen me there. Whatever happened to Bongo, it was nothing to do with me.'

That calmed Prit down. 'Then who was it?'

'I don't know.' But even as he said the words, Zaq suspected he did know. 'It could've been the same guys that jumped Tariq. The bust-up at the wedding involved both of them. They already got Tariq. Maybe they came after Bongo too.'

Prit was silent for a moment, then said, 'Shit.'

'I already know who one of the guys is and I'm working to find out about the other one. Then I'm going to get them both for what they've done.'

'Oh, man ... if it wasn't you, I'm really sorry for accusing you like that.'

'All I did was have words with him, that's all.'

'People saw you arguing ... your name's been mentioned by more than one person.'

That meant his name would probably get to the cops, and they'd want to talk to him too. 'Forget it – I'd have thought the same thing. If the cops come and ask me about it, I can tell them where I was.' He was pretty sure that the overnight nurses could vouch for him, as well as hospital CCTV if it came to that.

'You don't get it. Ain't the Old Bill you need to worry about. Bongo's family, all his cousins and mates and that, they'll have heard the same thing. They think it was you, and they're going to come after you.'

'Fuck.'

Prit was right. If they heard Zaq had been arguing with Bongo shortly before he'd been beaten senseless in the park, they'd draw their own conclusions, no doubt largely based on Zaq's reputation. They wouldn't wait for the police to act; they'd come after him themselves with violent intent. That was definitely something he could do without.

'I need to talk to them. You know any of his family?'

'I know Bongo's cousin, Gugs, pretty well. Listen, I'll call him and tell him what you've told me and that you didn't have anything to do with it. He can tell the others.'

'OK, you do that.'

'I don't know how long it'll take for the word to get around, though. So you probably want to watch your back for a bit.'

'I'll do that. Make sure you tell them I was at the hospital with Tariq last night,' Zaq said.

'I will.'

'What hospital's Bongo at?'

'Hillingdon.'

'Same as T. I'll be there again tonight. If Gugs or anyone wants to talk to me, they can find me in his room in the Intensive Treatment Unit.'

Zaq ended the call, dropped his phone in his lap and rubbed his face. What a shitty start to the day.

Chapter Fifty-Two

Maybe Jags had some better news for him.

'You just wake up?' Jags asked.

'Pretty much.'

'You ain't seen the news, then?' Zaq hadn't. 'Get your laptop,' Jags told him. 'There's something you need to see. I'll wait.'

Zaq opened up his laptop. 'Go to the *BBC News* website,' Jags directed him. 'Now click the *Local News* tab, and type in *Southall*. See it?'

He saw it all right. His stomach went queasy as he processed the headline: **SOUTHALL JEWELLER MURDERED LEAVING SHOP.**

'It ain't . . . ?'

'Read the story,' Jags told him.

> A prominent Southall jeweller was attacked and robbed as he left his business premises on the Broadway, in Southall, west London, yesterday evening. The attack took place at around 8.00 pm on Beachcroft Avenue, as the jeweller approached his car, just yards from the busy main shopping area. An eyewitness said, 'I saw two masked men rush the victim and beat him to the ground. They were punching and kicking him. It was just horrible.' The men made off with the victim's briefcase,

which reportedly contained items of jewellery, leaving him unconscious and with multiple injuries. Passers-by came to his aid and the police and ambulance service were called, but the victim suffered a cardiac arrest and died at the scene. Police have launched a murder inquiry and are appealing for witnesses who may have seen the attack, or the two robbers who fled on foot. Anyone with information is asked to call police on 101 or Crimestoppers anonymously on 0800 555 111.

'Shit,' Zaq said. 'It doesn't mention his name. Maybe it ain't—'

'It is. I checked. It was Kang, the bloke we spoke to yesterday.'

'Shit,' Zaq said again. 'I don't believe it. I just talked to Tariq's mate, Prit. Bongo was jumped last night too. He's in the same hospital as Tariq.'

'Bloody hell, two separate incidents in one night. That's some bad luck.'

'It was for them two – both guys we talked to.'

'Yeah. Listen, I don't know about the Bongo thing, but maybe we should go to the cops about what happened to Kang. We'll be on the CCTV in the shop. There's two of us . . . and two guys jumped him.'

Jags was right. 'Bollocks. But the timing'll prove it couldn't have been me. I was at the hospital about the time Kang was attacked. I should be on camera there, going in and up to Tariq's room. What did you do after you dropped me off?'

'Went home, got changed, and then gave the car a quick wash to get that bloody paint off.'

'Anyone see you?'

'The neighbours, people on the street.'

'OK. Did you talk to anyone on the phone?'

'No, but I texted Rita. She called a bit later.'

'All right, that's good. If the Old Bill check your phone signal it'll place you at home, so we're both covered. They'll want to know why we were at the jeweller's, talking to Kang. We'll have to tell them something – just not about Shergill and Lucky's necklace.'

'What, then?' Jags said.

Zaq thought for a moment. 'We can't say we were looking at stuff to buy. The security tape'll show we didn't look at anything. Plus, Kang's assistant was there and he'll probably have told the cops we were there about something else.' He considered it some more, then had an idea. 'Has Lucky still got that other necklace, the one Shergill palmed off on us?'

'I guess. Why?'

'Get it off him. We'll say we were there to get it valued.' He worked the story out as he talked. 'If the assistant said anything about us mentioning a necklace, it'll fit, and explain why we went in the back. We can say he asked us to come through so he could examine it properly.'

'What if they ask where we got it from?'

'We'll tell them it's Lucky's. He asked us to take it to Kang. Make sure to tell Lucky as well, so he backs us up, in case they check with him. And if they ask where he got it he can say it's from India, passed down through the family, so he don't have a receipt for it. We've got pretty decent alibis for when the attack happened, so hopefully the cops won't bother digging any further.'

'It might work,' Jags said. 'Should I tell Lucky what we found out from Kang yesterday?'

'No. Let's keep that to ourselves for now. We don't know how he'll react when he finds out how much it's worth. Probably better to tell him once we've got it back.'

'OK.' There was a moment of silence, then Jags asked, 'Who do you think did it?'

'Could've been anybody, a random mugging, someone wanting to knock off a jeweller ...'

'You really believe that?'

'No, I don't. It feels like too big a coincidence, so soon after he told Shergill about the necklace and how much it's worth.'

'He told us too.'

'That kind of proves my point. Maybe the greedy bastard didn't appreciate Kang telling us, and didn't want him talking to anyone else. Or maybe we really shit Kang up with all that talk about the cops and the government, and Shergill didn't trust him not to blab.'

'If it was Shergill, you think they really meant to kill him?'

'I don't know. If they just wanted to scare him they went a bit too far.' Zaq closed the laptop.

'There's more,' Jags said, 'and it gets worse.'

'How the hell can it get any worse?'

'The cops might not be the only ones we need to worry about.'

'What're you talking about?'

'When I was phoning around to find out if it was Kang that got robbed, I called Jaspal to see if he'd heard anything.' Jaspal was a mate of theirs who lived in the street adjacent to Beachcroft Avenue, where the robbery had happened.

'Yeah, and ...?'

'He'd heard all right – it's all everyone's talking about. He's the one confirmed it was Kang that was killed. Anyway, he mentioned something else, something I didn't know, and I ain't sure you do either.'

'What's that then?'

'Kang was married.'

'So what? Big deal.'

'To Tonka's sister.'

The name hit Zaq like a slap in the face. Shit. That was bad. Real bad. If Tonka thought for one second they'd had anything to do with his brother-in-law's death, they were in serious trouble – the sort that could prove fatal.

Chapter Fifty-Three

'I'll have to go see Tonka,' Zaq said. 'Tell him we were there talking to his brother-in-law before it happened.'

'You sure that's a good idea?'

'Better I go and tell him than he hears it from someone else and comes looking for us. Shit, it don't look good, the two of us being there, then he's jumped by two blokes. You don't need to be Einstein to work out that in this case two and two equals us fucked.'

'If his maths is anything like yours, you sure you'll leave in one piece?'

'We might have to prove it wasn't us. We both reckon Shergill was behind it, right?'

'Yeah – like you said, it's too much of a coincidence it happened the same day. First Shergill went to see him, then us.'

'We need to go see Shergill again and rattle his cage, see how he reacts, before I talk to Tonka.'

'What good will that do? Ain't like he'll just hold his hands up and say it was him.'

'We'll push his buttons, wind him up, see if he lets anything slip that we can use and take to Tonka. Might also give us some leverage to make Shergill hand the necklace back —it's that or we go to the cops, about the necklace and his motive for killing Kang.'

'We go to the cops, we'll lose the necklace for good.'

'It's just a threat, for now anyway. We need to get the necklace back, but after that he's got to pay for what he's done. They all do.'

'If he gets nicked, he'll spill everything about the necklace.'

'I was thinking about that. We've still got the other one, right, the one he gave us? We'll just say that's the one he's on about and he's talking shit. Ain't no way that's worth fifteen million quid.'

'OK', said Jags, 'so when d'you think we should go see the fucker?'

'No time like the present. Let me get ready and I'll come over to yours. In the meantime, why don't you go to the police station and tell them you were at the jeweller's yesterday to get that necklace valued. I'll stop on my way to yours and do the same. Better that, than them nicking us 'cause they want to talk to us about it.'

Zaq had wanted to work out but was now too keyed up to concentrate properly. His stomach felt light and he knew he had to move to burn up the adrenaline that was making him queasy. He got up, put his laptop on the desk, then grabbed his towel and shower stuff and went to get ready.

After eating a bowl of cereal he left the house. As he was getting into his car, he received a message from Jags. Just been to the cops. Told them we were there to get valuation. They asked me how much he valued it at. Didn't have a clue. Said £7k, in case they ask you too.

Cool, Zaq texted back. He drove to Hayes Police Station and went in to speak to someone. When it was his turn to be seen, he told the woman behind the counter the same story Jags would have – that they'd gone to see Kang to get a necklace valued for Jags' uncle. Kang had taken them in the back to give the necklace a quick examination, told them it was worth about seven grand and they'd left. 'I would've gone to the Southall police station but it's closed now, innit.' He said he'd come forward because he'd seen the report of the murder on the news. He didn't remember seeing anyone suspicious hanging about outside. He explained that at the time of the attack he'd been at Hillingdon Hospital at his brother's bedside. He left his contact details in case they needed to talk to him further.

The woman printed off two copies of his statement, had him read and sign one and gave him the other to keep. It was all easy enough for now, but once they learnt he had previous for a violent offence, and if they couldn't find anything on the real attackers, they might well decide to see if there was anything they could pin on him.

He didn't mention anything about Bongo. It didn't have anything to do with Kang's murder and, in any case, the fact he was at the hospital covered Zaq for that attack too.

'How'd it go?' Jags asked when Zaq got to his.

'OK. It'll do for now. Should keep the cops off our backs until we get the necklace sorted, and then we can drop Shergill and the rest of his lot in it.'

'You still think we should go and see him?'

'Unless you got any other ideas?'

'Nah, man. Can't even think straight, with the murder and everything.'

'Let me have a glass of water and we'll go.'

Zaq offered to drive. 'If Shergill's son wants to fire paintballs at us again, my old motor getting shot up ain't as serious as your BMW.'

'It's OK,' Jags said. 'I'll park away from the gate. But if that little fucker shoots at us again, I swear I'm going to get over that gate and wrap that little pop gun round his neck.'

Zaq believed him – though it meant he'd have to go over the

gate with him to hold off Little and Large, while Jags took care of Shergill junior.

It was another hot, sunny day and the drive to Iver was a pleasant one, but the reason for their visit made it a sombre journey. Jags put some music on and they didn't talk much. Zaq looked out of the window, imagining the various ways things might go when they got there. He was pretty sure Jags was thinking the same.

When they arrived, Jags drove past the house, then turned back, pulling off the road on to the grass a little way before the entrance to the Shergill property. 'Let's see if they'll let us in this time.'

They walked to the gates, where Zaq pressed the button on the intercom.

'Yes?' a voice crackled through the speaker.

'We're here to see Mr Shergill,' Zaq said. 'And before you tell us to get lost, go and tell him we're here to talk about Mr Kang. He either talks to us, or he can talk to the police about it. We'll wait.'

The speaker went dead. 'Guess he's gone to check.'

Jags was looking through the gate at the main doors of the house. 'I don't see that little twat with his gun yet.'

Nothing happened for a couple of minutes. Then there was a buzz and a click, and the gates began to open. 'All right,' Jags said, starting towards the car. 'Let's go.'

They got in and drove through the open gates, up the drive to the house. The other cars were there, except the Mercedes. Jags parked and they got out and went to the front door. It opened before they reached it, and Shergill's two minders came out. Taj with the moustache hung back by the door, while the man-mountain came forward to meet them. He put up a hand to stop them, then gestured with both hands that they should raise their arms to be searched.

Zaq knew the drill, theatrical though it seemed, and raised his arms and let himself be patted down, the guy's big hands moving over him like carpet-beaters. Jags did likewise. Satisfied they weren't carrying any weapons, the minder held a hand out and said, 'Phones.'

'You what?'

'Mr Shergill said so,' the guy told him, in his rumbling bass voice. 'You want to talk to him, you hand over your phones.'

Zaq realised Shergill was making sure they couldn't record the conversation. That kind of precaution only made him more convinced that Shergill had been behind the attack on Kang. He nodded to Jags and they handed over their phones.

'I better get it back when we leave,' Jags said.

The guy didn't seem to give a shit. He led them inside, Taj holding the door open and closing it once they were in. The big guy dropped their phones into a bowl on a table beside the door, then gestured for them to follow him. He led them across the hall, to the office they'd been to last time. Taj stayed close behind them.

A thought struck Zaq: if they had killed Kang, what was to stop them trying to do the same to him and Jags, right there and then? Suddenly wary, they continued to Shergill's office. The lead guy knocked on the door, opened it and they went in.

Chapter Fifty-Four

Shergill sat behind his desk, like before. What was it with Asian men and their big desks? He was wearing a royal-blue shirt with white cuffs and collar, chunky cufflinks and the top couple of buttons undone. He regarded them as they entered the room and came to stand in front of the desk.

'What the hell do you two want now?' The disdain in his voice was matched by the look on his face.

'Same as before,' Zaq said. 'The necklace.'

Shergill sat back in his chair. 'I already gave you a necklace.'

Zaq heard the door open and glanced behind him. Taj had stepped aside to allow Shergill's son into the room. When he saw Zaq and Jags, his lip curled in a faint smile and he moved over to lean against the sideboard. 'What're these two idiots doing back here?' he said, acting tough because his father's minders were there to look after him.

Zaq sensed Jags tense up next to him and hoped he wouldn't do anything stupid. If they were anywhere else it would be a different story, but they were here for the necklace. Jags didn't say anything, though he was staring daggers at the cocky little shit. 'Relax yourself and let the grown-ups talk,' Zaq told the boy, so they could get back to the reason they were there, and he turned back to face Shergill senior. 'You gave us a necklace, all right,' Zaq said, 'just the wrong one.'

'I gave it to you, you checked it, you accepted it and you took it. As far as I'm concerned the matter's closed. It's not my bloody fault you didn't know what you came here for.'

'Well, we know now, so why don't you just hand it over and we'll be on our way.'

Shergill's face clouded. 'Who the hell do you think you are,' he demanded, 'coming in here and trying to tell me what to do? You're nothing and nobody. I should have you beaten and thrown out.'

Talk about delusions of grandeur. Who the fuck did the guy think he was? A lord of the manor? A *nawab* in India?

'You could try.'

Shergill seemed to seriously consider it.

'You know what? Let's just cut the shit,' Zaq said.

'Hey!' Shergill's son called out. 'Don't talk to my dad like that.'

Zaq ignored him. 'You've got our necklace and we want it back. Hand it over and that'll be the end of it. If you don't, you'll leave us no choice but to go to the police and tell them about you, the necklace and Kang.'

'You fucking threatening my dad?'

'Donny, *chuup kar*,' Shergill snapped, silencing his son. His eyes didn't leave Zaq. 'You don't have any proof,' he said.

'You'll be on the security video – that'll put you there yesterday. When we tell the cops about the necklace and how much it's worth, I think they'll be able to figure out your motive easily enough.'

A calculating smile crept across Shergill's face. 'Kang phoned and told me you'd been there to see him. All your talk of stolen goods, police and governments had him panicking. Who knows who else he might have told about it? And, if you did send the police his way, he would've told them anything to keep himself out of trouble.'

'So you had him killed?'

'Me? No, I had nothing to do with it.' The words were a denial but the gloating tone and manner suggested the complete opposite. 'Apparently he was attacked by two men, just like the two of you.'

Had the bastard been trying to set them up? Now he thought about it, Zaq wouldn't put it past him. 'It wasn't us, though,' he said. 'And we were both elsewhere when the attack happened and we got witnesses to prove it. We've already been to the police and told them we were at the shop yesterday and what we were there for.' Shergill's smug look dissolved. 'Don't worry, we haven't mentioned the necklace, not yet anyway. Like I said, you give it to us and we'll walk away, forget everything else. You don't, and I'm sure the police'll be very interested in what we've got to say.'

'If you do that, you won't get the necklace back either.'

'If you don't give it to us, why would we care who gets it? Just as long as it ain't you. Museum, British government, Indian government, the state of Punjab, some private collector, won't matter. It'll be all the same to us.'

Shergill didn't like that. His brow creased into a frown. No one spoke for a moment until, eventually, he said, 'Do you know how many millionaires and billionaires there are in India?'

Zaq shrugged. 'What's that got to do with anything?'

'There are more than almost anywhere else in the world. I could take the necklace over there and sell it to one of them.'

Zaq had heard of crocodile tears but right now he was getting a crocodile smile.

'They'd be happy to pay for a historical treasure like that, maybe even more than Kang said it could be worth. They have the money for it.'

'It ain't yours to sell, though.'

'I could cut you in for a share. We would all make money and do very well out of it.'

A share? What the hell was he talking about? What would that even be? Five per cent? Ten, if they were lucky? Zaq trusted him about as far as he could throw him. Actually, even less. 'Like I said, it ain't yours to sell.'

'Well, I have it and I will do as I please with it. Possession is nine-tenths of the law.'

'All right then. You can have all ten-tenths of the law up your arse, for theft, handling stolen goods and conspiracy to murder at the very least. People have killed for a lot less.' Zaq stared at him, maintaining a poker face while Shergill tried to work out if he was bluffing. 'Today's Friday. I'll give you till Sunday to think it over and come to a decision – give the necklace back or risk going down for murder. I'll leave you my number. Let me know what you decide.' He reached for the notepad and pen he could see on the desk and wrote down his number. 'Sunday,' he reiterated, then turned to Jags. 'Let's go.'

Chapter Fifty-Five

Neither Zaq nor Jags spoke until Jags had started the engine and they were rolling towards the gates, which started to open as they approached.

'We really going to the cops if he don't give it back?' Jags asked while they waited for the gates to open enough to drive through.

'I don't know. I just said it. I wanted him to believe it, though.'

'If we do go to the cops, Lucky'll likely lose the necklace for good, the whole story'll come out and he'll be in deep doo-doo with my aunt. He won't like that. And if the story gets into the papers, and everyone finds out where the necklace came from, the shit'll really hit the fan.'

'Things work out the way we want, that idiot back there'll hand the necklace over and we won't have to mention it to the cops.'

'What about Kang? As far as I can tell, that wanker had him killed so he wouldn't talk to anyone else. We just going to keep quiet about that?' Jags drove through the gates towards the road.

'No. Once we get the necklace back, we won't *go* to the cops ... but there's nothing stopping us from calling Crime-stoppers anonymously and telling them to look at Shergill for the murder.'

'He'll know it was us.'

'So what? If we've already got the necklace back, it won't matter.'

'What about proof? If we get the necklace back, we can't tell the cops that was his motive for killing Kang, not unless we tell them all about the necklace too, and Lucky won't want that.' Jags turned left, taking them back the way they'd come.

'We'll leave all that for the cops to sort out. We'll have done our bit.'

'Will it be enough, though? If no one else gets done for it, it could put us back in the frame and Tonka will want some answers.'

'Shit, you're right. I'd better talk to him, explain it weren't us.'

'Suppose Shergill still don't agree to give it back? Then what do we do?'

'We got till Sunday to work something out. We'll have to go with either getting into the house and taking it, or grabbing Shergill somewhere and making him hand it over. If we can't do either of those and can't think of anything else, we'll have to sit down with Lucky and have a serious talk about going to the cops for real and telling them everything.'

'He won't want to do that.'

'It's either that or he lets Shergill just have the necklace. Which d'you think he'd prefer?'

'Neither.'

'Then we better get it back, by hook or by fucking crook.'

Something else had been bothering Zaq but he'd pushed it aside while they'd focused on Shergill. Now that was done, it was on his mind again.

'What happened to Bongo . . . it must've been the same guys that jumped Tariq, that Satty fucker and his mates.'

'What makes you think that?'

'Bongo was done over the same way Tariq was, beaten up

and pretty much left for dead. And just before I smacked Satty up the other day I told him he'd got the wrong person – that Tariq never even went out with Sharan. I didn't mention Bongo by name or anything, but they could've found out and gone after him.'

'How would they have found out?'

'Maybe they asked Sharan.'

'You think she'd have given Bongo up like that?'

'I don't know . . . but maybe we should go and ask her.'

The hairdressers where Sharan worked wasn't far and it didn't take them long to get there. Jags parked near the shop and waited while Zaq went in. The older woman he'd thought was the owner last time was there, along with the male hairdresser, both busy with clients. When they heard the door, they both looked over. The guy looked quickly away, back to his client. The woman's professional smile disappeared as though it had been jet-hosed off her face. 'Can I help you?' she asked, trying to sound friendly but not managing it.

'Is Sharan here?'

The hairdresser excused herself from her client for a moment and came over. She dropped her voice but her tone was sharp. 'No, she isn't. She doesn't work here any more. She phoned and quit, yesterday, just like that. She's left me right in the lurch. She was jumpy ever since you came in the other day. What the hell did you say to her?'

'Nothing.'

'Well, it must've been something – and now she's gone.'

'Do you know where?'

'No,' she snapped, eyes flashing. 'First, it's that boyfriend of hers and now you, whoever you are, turning up and causing trouble for her – and for me.'

'I . . . I—' Zaq didn't know what to say.

'Now, unless you actually want a haircut, I think you'd better leave.' She gave him a hard look and turned back to her client. 'Sorry, my love . . .'

Zaq left the shop and went back to the car.

'That was quick,' Jags said. 'What did she say?'

'Nothing – she wasn't there.' He told him about the conversation with the owner.

'That's weird. What do you think happened?'

'Don't know.'

'What d'you want to do now?'

Then Zaq remembered something. 'Hang on.' He dug around in his pocket and pulled out the business card they'd got from Kiran, the bride whose wedding the trouble had kicked off at. 'I thought so . . . her mobile number's on here.' He took out his phone, keyed in her number and waited. The phone rang at the other end but no one answered. He tried again. This time, after several rings, it was picked up. 'Sharan?'

'Who's that?'

'It's Zaq. We spoke the other day, at the hairdresser's.'

'Oh . . . Look, I've got nothing more to say to you, OK? So just leave me alone.'

'It's about Bongo – er, I mean Kush.'

There was a pause, then she said, 'What about him?'

Was that worry in her voice? 'He was attacked last night and beaten up real bad.' He heard her gasp. 'He's in the hospital.'

'Oh, my God.'

'Did anyone ask you about him, want his details, anything like that? Your boyfriend, maybe, or his mate Satty?'

When she spoke, her voice was trembling. 'Yeah, they asked me about him – about you too.'

'What?'

'You beat Satty up outside a pub, didn't you?' She didn't wait for an answer. She already knew it must have been him. 'They asked me if I knew who you were and if I'd talked to you?'

'What did you tell them?'

'I lied. If I'd told them the truth, it would've been even worse.'

'What would have?'

'Nothing. It doesn't matter. I said I didn't know who you were or what they were talking about. Then they starting going on about Kush. I told them it was all over nothing, that we'd been at college together, we'd only been chatting. I don't know if it's jealousy or insecurity or what, but they wouldn't let it go. Need to prove what big men they are. They kept asking and asking, made me tell them.'

'Look, whatever's happened, it ain't your fault. You didn't know what they'd do.'

'Yes, I did,' she said. Zaq didn't need to see her to know she was weeping. 'You already told me what they did to your brother, so I knew exactly what they'd do to Kush – and I still told them. I was going to call Kush today and warn him. I didn't think they'd do it so soon, though. Now I'm too late, and he's hurt because of me.'

'It's not your fault, it's theirs: Satty and your boyfriend. It's all on them. Look, can I come and see you, just for a few minutes, to chat about what's happened?'

'What is there to talk about?'

'What's happened to Kush – and my brother too. He's still in a coma. Satty and your boyfriend are well out of order. What else are they going to do? Who else are they going to hurt?'

'What can I do about that?'

'Help me stop them.' Sharan was silent. 'Or d'you think they should just get away with what they've done to people we care about?'

'No, of course not – and it's not fair of you to say that.'

'I'm sorry, but please help me. Kush didn't deserve what they've done to him and neither did my brother.'

'And what are you going to do? The same as they've done to Kush and your brother?'

He wasn't sure that was what she wanted to hear, so he said, 'I don't know. If I can prove it was them, I can go to the police.'

'And if you can't?'

'Then I'll think of something else.' He didn't elaborate. He probably didn't need to. 'Either way, they'll pay for what they've done. Will you help me? Just a quick chat, that's all I'm asking.'

She took a moment to think about it. Finally she said, 'OK, just a few minutes.' She gave him her address. 'Hurry up, if you're coming. I won't be here long.'

'On my way.'

Chapter Fifty-Six

The address was for a flat in the Chalvey area of Slough. On the way, Zaq filled Jags in on the details of the conversation he hadn't been able to overhear. It took about ten minutes to drive there and another couple to find somewhere to park. The flat was in one of two blocks, connected in a T-shape.

'I'd better go in alone,' Zaq said. 'She seemed a bit upset. Might be best not to crowd her.'

'Fine. I'll wait here in the car – *again.*'

Zaq got out and found the right door with the buzzer for the flat number Sharan had given him. He pressed and after a moment the intercom crackled. 'Hello.'

'Hi, Sharan? It's Zaq. We spoke—'

'I know.' The door lock clicked open. Zaq went up the stairs to the first floor. She must have heard him, as the door opened before he reached it. She looked out briefly then moved back behind the door. 'Come in.'

She closed the door behind him, and led the way to a small lounge. It was modestly furnished but neat and tidy – apart from all the bags, packed and piled on the sofa. 'You going somewhere?' Zaq asked, nodding towards the bags.

'Yeah.' She didn't offer any more than that.

'Looks like you're going for quite a while.'

'What did you want to talk about? Can you make it quick? I need to get all this stuff in the car before it gets late.'

As she spoke, Zaq noted that she looked different from the last time he'd seen her. Her hair was brushed forward over her forehead and inward on either side of her face. She was a bit agitated, which he put down to her being eager to load her car and get going – until he studied her more closely and realised that what he'd thought were shadows on her face were bruises. 'Hey,' he said, holding his hands up in a placating gesture and backing off to give her some space. 'What happened?' He gestured to her face.

She stopped trying to avoid his gaze and looked directly at him. 'I knew it was a bad idea to let you come here.'

'Did Satty do that to you?' Zaq felt his anger go from a simmer to a boil.

'No ... it was my boyfriend. Satty watched, though. If he'd been told to do it, he would have.'

'What the hell ...?' Who the fuck were these guys, attacking and assaulting people at will, acting like they were untouchable?

'I told you,' Sharan said, 'I didn't want to tell them anything about Kush. I said they should just forget about it but ... when I wouldn't tell them what they wanted, they made me.'

'By hitting you?'

'He's always been a bit ... rough, but he's never done anything like this before.'

'You mean your boyfriend?'

She gave a harsh laugh. 'Not any more, he's not. I've put up with his shit long enough. Underneath all the talk and the attitude, he could be really nice, and he was most of the time. That's why I stayed with him. I thought we had something special. Maybe I was hoping I could change him or calm him down, bring out his better side. But he's got a mean streak. I've seen it a few times but never directed at me ... not until the other night, anyway.'

'What happened?' Zaq asked, with genuine concern.

She took a moment before answering. 'He called me at work the day before yesterday, said he wanted to see me.' She spoke about it in a detached way, without emotion. 'I told him to come over after I finished work. When he turned up, he was with Satty and straight away they started asking me about you and then the guy I was talking to at Kiran's wedding, Kush. I thought that was all over and done with. I told him it was nothing, that he should just forget about it. He exploded, started shouting, calling me all sorts of things. I said he needed to either calm down or leave. That's when he grabbed me and pinned me against the wall. I told him to let go of me, and he just slapped me. I was shocked. I don't even know what he said after that, but when I didn't answer him he slapped me some more, and then the slaps turned into punches.'

Zaq's jaw was set tight as he listened, his hands balled into fists. Even though the rational part of him knew that his desire to mete out violence of his own was probably the wrong way to react, another part of him wanted nothing more than to give the fuckers a taste of their own bloody medicine.

'I couldn't believe it was happening,' Sharan said. 'He was telling me it was my fault, that I was making him do it by not telling him what he wanted. I knew right then it was over between us, that whatever I'd thought or hoped we could have together was just wishful bloody thinking. But I was scared and I wanted him to go, both of them, so I ... I told them what they wanted to know.' She hung her head, her long hair shrouding her face.

Zaq thought she was crying. 'It doesn't sound like you had much choice.'

She looked up. Her eyes were wet but there were no tears now. 'How bad is he hurt?' she said. 'Kush, I mean?'

'Pretty bad, from what I heard. I don't know all the details. He's at the same hospital as my brother, so I might find out later when I'm there.'

'Can . . . can you let me know how he is? I want to make sure he'll be OK.'

'Sure, I'll message you.' Zaq looked at her packed bags. 'Where are you planning to go?' he asked.

'I'd rather not say.'

'I just meant, you've got a place to stay, right?'

'Yes, I have.'

'Good. Look, seeing as you're leaving and you've broken things off with your boyfriend – sorry, ex-boyfriend – will you help me?'

'I just want to get out of here. I don't want anything to do with any of this.'

'It won't have anything to do with you, I promise. It'll be between me, your ex and Satty, for what they did to my brother and Kush, and – even though you don't want any part of it – for what they did to you too.'

'Will you really go to the police?'

'If I can get some proper proof that the police will act on, then yeah.' Though he didn't say *when* he'd take anything like that to them.

'OK, I'll tell you what I can. Not for me though – I'm out of here. I'll help you for Kush and for your brother. What do you want to know?'

'Who are they and where can I find them?'

She took a deep breath and said, 'I already told you what I know about Satty; there's not much more I can tell. His name's short for Satpal or Satvinder, something like that. He lives in

Slough, over towards Wexham somewhere, I think, and he drinks in a pub called the Lemon Tree or at another place called the Three Tuns. That's about it.'

Well, at least he knew she was telling him the truth. 'What about your boyfriend, sorry, your ex . . . will you tell me who he is now?'

'OK,' she said in a resigned tone. 'His name's Daljit, but everyone calls him Donny – Donny Shergill.'

Chapter Fifty-Seven

'Donny Shergill . . . ' Zaq repeated.

Sharan frowned. 'Do you know him?'

'No, I don't – but I think I know *who* he is.' He wanted to be sure. 'Have you got a picture of him?'

Sharan picked up her phone from the coffee table and went through it until she found what she was looking for, then turned the screen to Zaq. There, posing for the camera with a haughty smile that was more like a sneer, was Shergill's son Donny, whom Zaq had seen just a little while ago in his dad's office.

What the hell? He tried to get it all straight. Satty and Donny Shergill were best friends; the two of them had been at the wedding together and Donny had started the fight with Bongo and then Tariq, which Satty had weighed into. Maybe both of them had attacked Tariq in Uxbridge and Bongo in Southall. He'd been looking for Donny Shergill all along, without ever realising that the stroppy little shit in front of him at the Shergill house – the same arsehole who'd shot paintballs at them – was also the perpetrator of the attacks on Tariq and Bongo. A proper chip off the old motherfucking block.

'Are you OK?' Sharan asked.

'Yeah, I'm fine.'

Finding them both shouldn't be that much of a problem now. He knew where Donny lived, and Donny would surely lead them to Satty. The only worry was, now that he knew Donny was behind what happened to his brother, would he be able to restrain himself long enough to get Lucky's necklace back before fucking them up?

'Thanks,' Zaq said. 'You've been a big help. I'm sorry about what happened to Kush, and what Donny did to you.'

'He's an arsehole. I should have realised it sooner.'

Zaq wasn't about to disagree with her. 'If your stuff's ready to go, I can give you a hand taking it down to the car.'

She thought about it, then said, 'OK. It'll save me a couple of trips. Thanks.'

Most of what she was taking was packed into two large suit-cases. Zaq took them, while Sharan brought along a big make-up case and a few canvas shopping bags of other things. Down in the car park, she unlocked a white Ford Focus hatchback and Zaq put the cases in the boot and managed to squeeze the make-up case in with them. The other bags went on the floor in the back. She locked the car and they went back to get the rest of her stuff.

Zaq saw Jags raise his hands in a *what-the-hell?* gesture. He just gave him a nod and carried on back up to the flat with Sharan. He slung a large sports bag over his shoulder and picked up two packed cardboard boxes. Sharan put on a rucksack, picked up a laptop bag, her handbag and the last couple of shopping bags. 'That it?' Zaq asked.

'All the important stuff. I'll get someone else to come and get the rest.' They left, Sharan locking the flat after them.

Outside, Zaq put the boxes and the sports bag on the back seat. Sharan put the rucksack and bags on the floor next to the others. Her handbag and the laptop case went on the front passenger seat. Zaq said, 'That's everything. You all set to go?'

She nodded. 'Thanks for your help.'

'No problem. Thanks for helping me with the info. I hope you'll be—'

'Shit.' Sharan was looking past him, towards the road.

'What's the matter?' he asked, turning to look.

A black Mercedes sedan was creeping past the small car park where they were standing, windows down, and the driver and passenger, both Asian males, staring right at them.

'Donny's mates,' Sharan said.

Zaq watched as the car slowed, then stopped in the middle of the road for a couple of seconds before driving on. Parked cars were in the way but he was still able to see the roof of the Merc as it drove on a little further and pulled over. He waited to see if the guys got out but neither did.

'They've stopped over there,' he told Sharan. 'You think they're waiting for you, or me?'

'I don't know. They're probably phoning Donny to tell him they've seen me talking to a guy.' She didn't sound happy about it.

'Can you drive off the other way?' Zaq pointed in the opposite direction to the one the Mercedes was facing.

'No, it's a dead end. They'll just wait for me. I don't want them to know I'm leaving, or for them to follow me and let Donny know where I'm going.'

Zaq thought fast. 'OK, listen. My mate's parked over there in the black BMW. Let me get in the car with him, then you come out. We'll pull out behind you, and, if they follow, we'll hold them up so you can get away. How's that sound?'

'Yeah, OK.' She was a bit panicked. 'Can we just do it quick? If they're on the phone to him, he could get here soon and then I don't know what'll happen.'

'All right. Just give me a few seconds. Thanks again for your help, and good luck.'

She hurried over to her car, while Zaq jumped in next to Jags.

'Those two arseholes in the Merc were giving you well dirty looks,' Jags told him.

'I know. I saw them. They might be phoning her boyfriend – shit, you'll never guess who he is.' He couldn't, so Zaq told him. 'Shergill's son.'

'You're fucking kidding!' Jags said, in disbelief.

'No, I ain't. Here she comes. Start the car and get right after her. We're going to hold those dickheads up if they try and follow her.'

Jags pulled out immediately behind Sharan's Ford Focus and the guys in the Mercedes pulled out straight after them. Jags followed Sharan, not going particularly fast but fast enough that the Mercedes couldn't overtake them. Up ahead the road curved to the left and split into a filter lane to turn right; Sharan was in it, signalling to go right. Jags did the same and so did their tail. When there was a gap in the oncoming traffic, Sharan took the turn, quickly followed by Jags and the Mercedes.

'This is better,' Jags said. The road they were on was one-way and only single lane, so there was no way the Mercedes could get past them. 'Now we can properly hold them up.' Jags slowed down and they watched Sharan's car pull further and further ahead. The road wasn't very long, though, and they saw Sharan signal to turn right again. The two behind them would certainly have seen it too.

'We'll have to carry on after her,' Zaq said, 'and slow them down as long as we can.'

They reached the end of the road where Sharan had turned and went right too, under a railway bridge, then had to take another right as the road ahead had a *No Entry* sign.

'Sorted,' Jags said. 'This road's even better than the last one.'

It was. They were on another one-way road, again with only a single lane, though this one was even tighter than before, which meant Jags could slow down and let Sharan put real distance between herself and them. Pretty soon she was out of sight, and there was no way for the Mercedes to get past and pursue her.

'Where's she going?' Jags asked. 'I saw all the stuff going in her motor.'

'She didn't say. Somewhere away from this Donny Shergill piece of shit. He beat her up, you know, to make her tell him about Bongo. And it was him and that Satty fucker that beat up Tariq. We been chasing our tails trying to find out who he is, and he was right in front of us the whole time.'

'Firing fucking paintballs at us, too.'

'Yeah, and that.'

'Motherfucker.'

They cruised along, in no hurry at all, the Mercedes stuck behind them. Jags, probably for the first time ever, was happy to stick to the twenty miles per hour limit painted on the road. There was no sign of Sharan in front. It was a long road. When they eventually reached the far end, it widened to two lanes for a short stretch, so vehicles could turn in to get to a McDonald's on the left and a big hall on the right, and it ended at a junction with a main road. A set of traffic lights helpfully turned red as they got to them. They had no idea which way Sharan had gone or how far away she was.

'What now?' Jags said.

'Head home, and try to work out what we do next.'

Chapter Fifty-Eight

When the lights turned green, Jags went left, taking them back towards Slough.

'They're still behind us,' he said, looking in his rear-view mirror.

Zaq shrugged. 'So, let them follow. We can take a scenic route home, waste their time till they figure out we ain't meeting up with Sharan and piss off.'

Jags turned the music up and followed the road north through the heart of Slough, around a one-way system and past the railway station which was in the middle of being upgraded for the arrival of Crossrail. The Mercedes stayed with them all the way.

Further on, as they left the new part of town behind, the road narrowed to just two lanes. Beyond Slough, the muted colours of brick, cement and concrete gave way to more and more greenery. The houses became larger and more spread out, and then stopped altogether, the road carrying straight on through a wall of trees and foliage. They went from urban to rural in the blink of an eye.

'They given up yet?' Zaq asked.

'Nope, still behind us.'

The road snaked on. Under normal circumstances it would have been pleasant driving through trees and greenery, with the early evening sun casting a golden glow and long shadows, but Zaq's mind was turning over what he'd learnt from Sharan, trying to think of a way to get Donny Shergill and Satty while still securing Lucky's necklace. A good deal further on, Jags turned left at a roundabout, taking them past a hospital, and glanced in his mirror.

'I think the passenger's on his phone. They must be wondering where we're going.'

'Do *you* know where we're going?'

'I know Uxbridge is over there somewhere.' Jags jerked his thumb to his right. 'The sat nav's on. I'll just keep going this way for now and it'll tell us how to get back home.'

Soon everything became more rural again; trees, shrubs and fields all around them. They went through a little village, all very middle England, a world away from the streets of Southall. Just after a pub, Jags said, 'We can take this right, here. It goes past Black Park and then back down to the Crooked Billet, a nice big circle for those two idiots behind us and it'll be easy for us to shoot home from there.'

'Good,' Zaq said. 'I need to get back and head to the hospital.'

Jags made the turn and drove them through woodland as trees and hedges crowded in on either side of the road, casting the way ahead into dusky shadow. The odd turn-off here and there afforded quick glimpses of driveways that were barred by gates or disappeared into the greenery. The only other car was the black Mercedes behind them. The road made an S and then opened into a long straight. They finally saw another car coming in the opposite direction.

'What the fuck's he doing?' Jags said, looking in his mirror. 'Is he trying to overtake us?'

Zaq looked back and saw the Mercedes had pulled out behind them but wasn't accelerating to overtake. Instead the driver was flashing his headlights. Zaq turned to see the car coming the other way flashing its lights too, the glare of full beams blinding them. Jags instinctively took his foot off the accelerator and they slowed slightly. The lights in front snapped off and the vehicle skewed sharply across the road, blocking their way. Jags stamped on the brakes and the BMW skidded off the road on to the grass verge. The Mercedes pulled up right behind them, cutting off any retreat.

The vehicle in front, Zaq now saw, was a Range Rover. The doors opened and four men got out.

'What the fuck . . . ?' Jags said.

Zaq threw a glance over his shoulder. The two guys in the Mercedes were also getting out. Too late, he realised what had happened. 'It's a fucking trap.'

Chapter Fifty-Nine

'Get out,' Zaq said.

'What?' Jags was astonished. 'Are you fucking crazy?'

'We stay in here, we're sitting ducks. They'll just smash the windows and drag us out. We got a better chance outside, taking them on.'

'They touch my car, I'll fucking kill them.'

'That's the attitude.'

'But there's six of them.'

'Best not waste any time, then. Let's go for the two behind first. That'll just leave four. Come on.' Zaq was already out of the car, and then running towards the Mercedes. Jags followed his lead.

The guy at the passenger side of the Mercedes stepped out with his hands raised to stop Zaq. 'You ain't going any—'

Zaq punched him hard in the gut, and followed with an uppercut and a straight right that dropped the guy to the ground. He heard the driver cry out as Jags laid into him, and something thudding against the car before hitting the tarmac. Zaq had to make sure his guy stayed down, so he stamped on his nuts. The guy groaned and curled up like a dying flower, hands cupping his damaged balls. He wouldn't be getting up in a hurry.

Putting both guys down had taken mere seconds. Zaq and

Jags spun round to face the four coming from the Range Rover. Trusting Jags to do the same, Zaq started towards them. They stood their ground but he sensed their confidence wasn't what it had been a few seconds before – the swift takedown of their friends had thrown them and made them hesitate. Zaq had trained for encounters like this in the prison gym. Now he'd put that training to good use and keep them on the back foot.

'It's him,' one of them said. 'The cunt I told you about, from the pub.'

It was Satty. And there was another face Zaq recognised – Donny fucking Shergill.

'There's still four of us,' Donny told his friends. 'We can take them.'

'We'll see,' Zaq said.

Donny and another guy came around the front of the BMW towards Zaq, while Satty and the remaining guy went for Jags.

'What were you doing talking to my girlfriend?' Donny said, taking from his pocket something that looked like a short bar.

Zaq didn't bother to answer. He wasn't going to let the arse-hole distract him. Suddenly Donny flicked his wrist and the bar shot out another two feet. Shit! It was an extendable metal baton, the type used by the police.

Donny was grinning, more confident now he was armed. He was bouncing with energy, keyed up and ready to strike. Even his mate seemed boosted, knowing they had the advantage. 'She doesn't know anything about the necklace, so what were you doing with her?'

Zaq concentrated on the baton. It was something that could cause him real damage, and he needed to neutralise it straight away. 'She ain't your girlfriend any more,' he told Donny.

'What the fuck does that mean?'

Zaq didn't elaborate. Let it distract him, he thought.

Donny's face clouded with anger. 'I'll just beat the answer out of you.'

Zaq had learnt how to deal with a stick attack – which was basically what this was – but hadn't practised recently. He replayed the technique in his head and hoped he could still execute the moves. He had to be closer, though, so he shifted into a fighting stance, left side on, hands up, and edged forward. He could hear Jags exchanging insults with the other two but couldn't risk looking to see what was going on. He just hoped he'd be OK.

'Come on, then,' Donny barked, and the baton swung whistling through the air in a savage arc.

Zaq was just out of range but took a slight step back all the same. As soon as Donny started to pull his arm back for another swing, Zaq sprang forward, arms out in front as if he were diving in for a hug. His hands went over Donny's shoulders either side of his head, and then down, pinning Donny's moving arm against his body, preventing it from swinging any further, and rendering the baton useless. With his right hand he pulled Donny's head forward, head-butting him in the face. Then Zaq rammed a knee into Donny's groin and felt him sag.

At this point Donny's partner, who'd stayed off to one side, not wanting to get hit by mistake, rushed at them; Zaq grabbed Donny's shirt and swung him around to knock his friend off balance. Then Zaq brought his left hand up on the inside, keeping Donny's right hand trapped under his armpit and exerting pressure on his wrist. With his right hand he delivered an open-palm strike to Donny's forearm, smashing it away – minus the baton, which was still held under Zaq's left arm. Zaq took hold of it. Now he was the one who was armed, and he knew better how to use the weapon effectively.

Donny's partner hadn't seen the move and, still thinking he

had a good chance, came rushing back at him. Zaq stepped back, again assuming a fighting stance, left hand up in front, right hand up close to his face. But the guy didn't see that Zaq was holding the baton in his right hand, hidden over his shoulder. As he came in, Zaq spun from the waist, bringing the baton round in a vicious downward arc straight on to the inside of the guy's right thigh. The thwack of steel on flesh was instantly drowned out by a scream of pain.

The guy grabbed his thigh with both hands, and Zaq struck again, this time hitting him on the upper left arm. Another scream. The guy let go of his thigh with one hand to grab his arm, his eyes screwed shut, teeth gritted. Zaq brought the baton over in a tight overhand swipe that connected with the top of the guy's left shoulder, catching the fingers of his right hand too. His yell of agony was cut off as Zaq fired a side-kick into his chest that launched him into the bushes at the side of the road.

Something whizzed past the back of his head and Zaq spun round to see Donny, whose punch had just missed him. Zaq hit him in the side with the baton. Donny shouted in agony, arms coming down to protect his body, and Zaq swung again, putting all his weight into it, and whacked Donny's upper arm with such force that it knocked him sideways. His scream echoed under the trees. Zaq stepped towards him with the baton drawn back, but Donny, face twisted in anger and pain, turned and ran for the Range Rover.

'Come back here, you little shit!' Zaq shouted. He saw that Jags was still holding his own against Satty and the other remaining member of the little gang of fuckwits. He wanted to help his friend, but he didn't want to let Donny get away. His hesitation allowed Donny to make it to the car and get behind the wheel. Fuck that. As the engine roared to life and the headlights came on Zaq rushed over to the car and swung the baton, smashing out the driver's side headlight. The sound was like a gunshot. He took another swing, this time at the windscreen, but the baton bounced off, leaving a big chip and a crack. He drew back the baton for another strike, this time at the wing mirror or perhaps the driver's side window, but Donny, his face panicked, shoved the car into reverse and backed away at speed. Then he spun the car around and roared off, abandoning his friends.

Fuck him. Zaq went to help Jags, but the smashing glass and the urgent sound of the car backing away at speed had stopped everyone else in their tracks. Seeing Zaq, baton held low, running towards them grim-faced and fiery-eyed, and realising it was now two against two, Satty and his accomplice backed away towards the Mercedes. The two guys Zaq and Jags had put down first were back on their feet but in no mood to join in. The passenger was leaning on the car roof for support, still wincing and holding his balls.

Zaq kept walking determinedly after Satty.

'Let's go!' Satty yelled. His friends by the car didn't need telling twice; they got straight in, and the driver started the engine. Satty and his friend ran for the Mercedes, both heading for the nearest rear door. Satty thrust his friend away, forcing him around to the other side. 'This ain't fucking over,' he shouted at Zaq, and then hastily got into the car. The driver didn't hang about; he shot backwards before either of the back doors was shut, then turned and – like Donny Shergill – roared off. Zaq stood in the road, holding the baton at his side like a lightsaber, and watched them go.

He looked at Jags. 'How you doing?'

His friend was bleeding from his mouth and nose, and looked a little roughed-up. 'I'm OK,' he mumbled. 'Could've been worse, but I managed to block some of their punches with my face.'

'So I see.'

'I gave them some solid shots, too. That Satty's a dirty fucker, though.' Jags nodded at the baton. 'Where'd you get that?'

'Donny pulled it out on me.'

'Right dirty bastards, the lot of them. That must be pretty lethal, from the screams I heard and the way you smashed his light with it.'

'It is. I gave them some pretty solid whacks.'

As Zaq said this, he and Jags heard rustling off to the side of the road and a figure appeared, limping slightly.

It was Donny's mate, the one Zaq had hit with the baton and kicked into the bushes. In their rush to get away, they'd left him behind.

Chapter Sixty

Zaq pointed at him with the baton. 'I want to talk to you.'

The guy searched left and right for his friends' cars, which had been there a few moments before, maybe even thinking of running. But he must have realised that, even if he hadn't been hurt, he wouldn't get far. His shoulders sagged, and he seemed to resign himself to having no choice but to talk to them. Zaq strode over, and the guy put his hands up in surrender. 'OK, OK . . . just don't hit me again.'

'Straighten up the car at the side of the road,' Zaq instructed Jags over his shoulder. 'Then come find us.' He prodded the guy with the end of the baton. 'Move,' he said, and pointed away from the road, into the trees. The guy just looked at him dumbly. Zaq drew the baton back. That got him moving.

They pushed through the bushes and shrubs that bordered the road and on between the trees, which stretched away as far as they could see into the deepening gloom. Zaq could hear Jags moving the BMW, followed by silence when he cut the engine, then the thud of the car door being closed and the bleep of the alarm being set. Some distance from the road, Zaq told the guy, 'OK, stop, turn around and face me.'

He waited till Jags caught up with them, then said to their captive, 'What was all that about? I mean, forcing us off the road and coming at us. What the fuck did you think you were doing?'

The guy swallowed. 'It was Donny and Satty's idea. You should be talking to them.'

'They ain't here though, are they? You are. Might've been their idea, but you were part of it. What was the plan?'

The guy didn't say anything, just looked at them with a mixture of fear and defiance.

'Don't want to talk?' Zaq took a step forward. 'I'll happily beat it out of you one word at a time if I have to.'

'Donny got us together to go out and find you, both of you,' the guy said hastily. 'But then he got a phone call saying some guy was talking to his girlfriend. He didn't like that. Told the guys on the phone to follow you, so we could come and get you. When they described you and the car, Donny knew right away who you were. He couldn't believe it. Saved us the trouble of having to find you.'

'Why'd he want to find us? What was the plan? To beat us up like you did that DJ last night?'

The guy clammed up again. Zaq raised the baton, ready to strike, glad for an excuse to whack the fucker. 'Need me to jog your memory?'

The guy held his hands up again. 'Listen, man, it wasn't my idea. Satty called us up, said Donny was going to pay us to help him sort some business for his dad.'

'What kind of business? And sort how, exactly?'

The guy hesitated again. Zaq started to swing the baton. 'Take care of some people,' he blurted.

'*Take care?*' Zaq said. 'You mean like you took care of that guy last night? That's attempted murder, you fucking prick.'

'That's down to Donny, man,' the guy protested. 'He lost it, got carried away. He said we were just going to teach him a lesson, give him a bit of a kicking. So that's what we did. Then Donny just flipped, lost it big-time, went proper psycho. We had to drag him off the guy.'

'How did you get the guy to go to that park?'

'Donny called and gave him some shit about wanting to book a DJ, gave him the address of a house by the park and told him to come over. When he turned up and got out of his car, we grabbed him and dragged him into the park.'

'And that's when you did him over?'

'We were just supposed to warn him off Donny's girlfriend. But then Donny flipped out, Satty too. I didn't sign up for that.'

'But here you are again today.' Zaq's grip on the baton tightened, his muscles taut, wanting to smack the guy up, but managing to restrain himself ... just. 'Hoping for more easy targets, huh? Bet we're not what you chickenshit motherfuckers expected. You just left that guy in the park last night. He almost fucking died.'

The guy swallowed again. 'I told you, man, that was Donny and Satty. Once they were done with him, we just got out of there in case anyone had called the cops.'

'And you'd have done the same to us today?'

'We were supposed to beat you up, scare you off some business with his dad.'

'Scare us off!' Zaq said, unable to keep his voice reasonable. He clenched his jaw and took a breath to regain his composure. 'What the fuck you think he brought this along for?' He waved the steel baton in front of the guy's face. 'To tickle us with? He was going to crack our fucking heads open with it. You'd have been party to an actual fucking murder. Two.' And then he remembered Kang. 'If you ain't already.'

'What?' the guy said, but not as though he didn't know what Zaq was talking about. More like he'd just been caught shitting on someone's doorstep.

'Where were you yesterday, before you jumped that DJ?'

'Nowhere ...'

'You were somewhere. Like in Southall maybe, when that jeweller was robbed and murdered.'

'I don't know nothing about that.' The words came out too fast, too defensive. The motherfucker was sweating guilt.

'Yeah, you do. You were there.'

'I wasn't, I swear. I was just waiting in the car. I didn't know what they were going to do. Donny and Satty said they had to go and do something and we had to wait for them. They were gone for about half an hour, and when they came back they had a briefcase.'

Zaq glanced at Jags. 'What time was that?' he asked the guy.

He shrugged. 'About eight, I guess, maybe a bit after.'

'What was in the briefcase?' Jags said.

'I don't know. I didn't see. They didn't open it. They just put it in the boot and then we left.'

Zaq was sure Jags was thinking the same as him – the briefcase would tie Donny and Satty to Kang's murder. But what had they done with it?

'They had it with them today,' the guy said helpfully.

'What?'

'It was still in the Range Rover.'

Why did they still have it? If they'd wanted to make it look like a robbery, they'd done that. Why keep hold of it and drive around with it? Zaq couldn't figure it out. If the cops found it in the car, Donny and his mates would be in real deep shit ... 'Where would they have gone now?' Zaq asked.

'How should I know?'

'What were you going to do after you sorted us out?'

'We ...' the guy hesitated. Zaq waited. 'We were supposed to go and get someone else.'

'What d'you mean, *get*? Pick them up, or what?'

'No, *get*, like we were supposed to *get* you ... fuck them up and that.'

What was it with these guys? They seemed to think they could drive around and attack whoever they wanted, with no comeback at all. Well, they were in for a huge shock when he and Jags caught up with them. 'Who?' Zaq demanded. 'Who're they going to get next?'

'I don't know. Some old dude Donny's old man wants out the way of some business he's got going on.'

'The old dude got a name?'

'Probably, but Donny and Satty never mentioned his full name, just a first name or a nickname.'

'Yeah, well, what was it?'

The guy thought for a second and said, 'Lucky.'

Chapter Sixty-One

'Fuck,' Jags said.

'Phone and warn him,' Zaq told him.

The guy knew something was up. 'What?'

'Never you mind,' Zaq said, as Jags took out his phone and called Lucky. 'Empty your pockets,' Zaq ordered, waving his hand for him be quick about it.

'What for?'

'Because I said so.'

The guy's face curdled into a sour expression but, looking from Zaq to the baton and back again, he must have decided he'd be better off doing as he was told. He took out a phone, a wallet and a set of keys, and handed them over.

Zaq stuck the baton under his arm, took the phone in his right hand and turned it off. Then he threw it as far as he could into the trees.

'Hey . . .'

'Shut up,' Zaq said. He slung the keys in a different direction.

'Fuck's sake,' the guy grumbled.

Watching in case he tried anything, Zaq opened the wallet, went through it and pulled out the guy's driving licence.

'I've tried twice but I can't get through,' Jags said, rejoining them. 'What we going to do?'

They could call the cops, but Zaq quickly discounted the

idea. It would raise too many questions – *How do you know these men are going to attack him, and why?* And Lucky wouldn't like the cops turning up on his doorstep. Jags' aunt would be full of questions too, and she'd know better than the cops if her husband was lying. Anyway, if Donny and his mates saw the cops, they'd just drive past, try again another time. Besides, the plan was to get the necklace back first, then turn them all in to the cops. But they had to do something . . .

Zaq had an idea. 'Here,' he said, and handed Jags the driver's licence. 'Take a picture of this on your phone.' He chucked the wallet far into the undergrowth.

'Shit,' the guy muttered.

Jags' flash went off as he snapped the pic. Then he handed the licence back to Zaq, who flicked it away like a playing card, and gave Jags the baton. 'Watch him. If he moves, hit him.'

'Can I hit him anyway?'

'Up to you.'

'What about Lucky?'

'I'm going to make a call.' Zaq took out his phone and moved away from them. He called a number, willing it to be answered. It was.

'*Kidaah?*' a male voice said.

'Manj, you at home?'

'It's Friday, man. We're getting a takeaway and some booze in as usual, innit. How's your brother doing?'

'A bit better, thanks. The others there with you?'

'Yeah. You coming?'

'Not tonight. Listen, I need a really big favour. I need you and the boys to get round to Jags' uncle's place, right now. Some guys are on their way over there to do him over. Me and Jags would go but we're too far away and won't get there in time.'

'No problem. I'll go. Bal will definitely be up for it. I'll grab the others too. What's the address?'

Zaq checked the exact address with Jags, and relayed it to Manjit.

'How many of them are there?'

'Four,' Zaq told him, 'unless they picked up more on the way.'

'What do you want us to do when we get there?'

'If there's nothing happening, just wait. Me and Jags are on our way. If there's any *punga* going on, pile in and sort the motherfuckers out. Try and keep hold of them till we get there, if you can.'

'All right, man. *Ficker na kar*, we're on it.'

'Cheers, Manj. I owe you guys.'

He heard Manjit calling out to Bal and the others before he hung up. 'It's sorted,' he told Jags. 'Manj and the boys are going over to Lucky's now. If Donny's posse turn up and run into that lot, they won't know what's hit them. We need to get over there though.'

'OK,' Jags handed the baton back to Zaq. 'What about him?'

Zaq looked at the guy. 'All right, I'm giving you a choice,' he said. 'We beat the shit out of you, so you can't walk out of here, or you give us all your clothes. Pick.'

'What?' the guy said disbelievingly.

'Why don't we just tie him to a tree or something?' Jags suggested. 'Enough of them around.'

'We do that, who knows how long he might be stuck out here? He can't get free, or no one finds him, he could die. At least the other way he'd be able to walk out of here after a while.'

'Good point.'

'That what you want?' Zaq asked the guy. 'Get tied to a tree, maybe get eaten by foxes or squirrels, or whatever the fuck else lives in these woods?'

'I'd rather beat the shit out of him,' Jags said, 'than have to see him naked.'

'Me too.'

'You guys are mad,' the guy said.

'You're lucky you're getting any choice at all. Now choose, before we go ahead and beat you so hard your relatives in India will feel it. I'm going to count to five. One ... two ... three ... four ...'

'OK, OK,' the guy said. 'Fuck it, I'll take my clothes off.'

'Hurry up, then.'

The guy took off his T-shirt, trainers and jeans, and dropped them on the ground. 'And the rest,' Zaq told him, referring to his boxer shorts and socks.

'Oh, come on ...' he protested.

'Everything. All off.'

The guy peeled off his socks, and lastly, with one hand covering his much-diminished manhood, his boxers.

'Grab his stuff and take it to the car,' Zaq said to Jags, who didn't look overly keen at having to pick up the guy's things. But he did, and tramped off through the undergrowth to the car.

'You ain't going to leave me here like this?' the guy whined.

'That's exactly what we're going to do,' Zaq said. 'And remember, we got a picture of your driving licence with your name and address. You come anywhere near us again, we'll know exactly where to find you.' He whacked the baton into the ground several times for added emphasis, but also to collapse it down so he was better able to throw it far into the trees. The guy stood, drawn and huddled, eyes wide. He backed off as Zaq took a step towards him. 'One more thing,' Zaq said. 'Were you in Southall last Friday night?'

'No,' he said, shaking his head.

'You sure about that? I could've sworn I saw you there.' Zaq had never seen the poor fucker before in his life.

'Nah, it weren't me. I was in Uxbridge that night.'

'Is that right?' Almost as an afterthought, he asked, 'Who with?'

'Donny, Satty and a few others.' The guy frowned, maybe realising there might be some significance to the information. 'Why?'

'I thought you might've been.' Zaq stepped forward and hit the guy with a quick four-punch combination, left-right-left-right, the first three merely precursors to the power and venom he put into the last one, which caught him smack on the jaw and spun him round to crash face-first to the earth, lights out, goodnight.

Zaq looked down at the bare form lying unmoving on the ground. 'That was for Tariq, you piece of shit.'

Chapter Sixty-Two

The shadows were gathering and thickening under the trees as they raced along the narrow country road, even though the sky above was still light. They were cutting through Black Park towards the main road that would take them back to the Crooked Billet. From there it was a single road to Uxbridge, and another to Southall.

'Man, this road's a lot longer than I thought,' Zaq said. 'That fucker wakes up, he's going to have a long walk in the nod like that.'

'What d'you mean, when he *wakes up*?'

'I asked him where he was on Friday night, and he admitted to being in Uxbridge with Donny and Satty. So I punched his lights out.'

'I'd say he got off light, then,' Jags said.

'Yeah. We got bigger things to worry about right now.'

They saw the main road up ahead, brightness at the end of the tunnel of trees they were speeding through. 'This'll do,' Zaq said, grabbing the guy's clothes from the back seat and lowering his window.

'For what?'

They reached the junction and Jags slowed to take the left turn that filtered into the main road. 'This,' Zaq said, and shoved the clothes out of the window. They landed all strewn out along the roadside verge.

The route back might have been straightforward, but it still took time to get to Uxbridge and go through Hillingdon and Hayes. Zaq tried calling Manjit, but got no answer. Jags tried Lucky with the same result. All they could do was drive, and hope everything was OK.

'Those fuckers weren't after Sharan earlier, were they?' Jags said, after a while.

'No, they were following us.'

'Why'd they come after us?'

'Obvious, ain't it? They already killed Kang. Why not do the same to us? There's only you, me and Lucky who know about the necklace now. Once we're out the way, Shergill can pretty much sit back and count his fifteen million quid.'

'That's what I figured ... the bastard. What about Tariq and Bongo, though?'

'They got nothing to do with this. That's just something Donny and Satty got going on. I doubt they even know we're anything to do with Tariq and Bongo ... ' His voice trailed off, as the wisp of an idea came to him and got him thinking.

Jags knew him well enough to know something was up. 'What?' he said.

'Nothing ... or maybe something. I need to think about it. Right now, we need to get to Lucky.'

Jags drove as fast as he could get away with. They hit Southall and he took them along the Broadway, all the way to the police station, where he turned off then took a right and went to Burns Avenue, where Lucky's house stood on a corner. Even before they reached it, they saw the blue lights of police cars, and people milling about. It was obvious something had happened.

Jags parked as close as he could and they got out and hurried over. Outside the house was a police car with a cop standing by the open rear door. Bal was sitting on the back seat, his feet on the pavement, talking to the cop, who was taking notes. Bal saw Zaq, but made no sign that he knew him.

Zaq spotted Manjit at the corner, the big Singh standing taller than everyone else around him, including the cops. Dips and Lax were with him. He saw Zaq and nodded away from all the commotion, signalling they should talk in private. He said something to Dips and Lax and walked away, crossing the road to the opposite corner.

'I'm going to chat to Manj,' Zaq told Jags, 'and find out what happened.'

'I'm going in to check on Lucky, see how he is.'

'Cool. I'll meet you back out here.'

Zaq nodded to Dips and Lax and went over to join Manjit. They shook hands, Manjit's rough builder's paw exerting a powerful grip. 'What happened?' Zaq asked.

'Just what you said. Good job you called when you did. We got here just in time – those *bhen chauds* were beating up Jags' uncle and trying to drag him to a car.'

'What did you do?'

'What d'you think? We jumped out and piled into the fuckers. Easy for them when it was four against an old man – different story when we showed up. Bal and me gave them proper lick shots. Dips and Lax got stuck in too, once they saw those guys weren't going to stay and fight.'

'So after you laid into them . . . ?'

'They shit themselves and ran to their cars, down there,' he pointed to the road where Jags had parked, 'and drove off.'

'Two cars? A Merc and a Range Rover?'

'Yeah, that's right.'

Killing Kang, trying to get him and Jags, and now Lucky – it was all connected to the necklace. Shergill was targeting anyone who might mess up his chances of disposing of it and making a pile of money. Fifteen million pounds was a big incentive. People had killed for a lot less, as Zaq was well aware. The fact they thought they could get away with it showed just how arrogant or else seriously fucking deluded they were, maybe even both.

'Listen, man, thanks for grabbing everyone and getting over here. We really owe you.'

'Don't worry about it. *Ghar de gul eh.* You'd do the same for one of us, innit? We all would.'

Zak knew it was true. Argue and bicker though they might, he and his housemates were a brotherhood of sorts, and helped each other out any way they could. The fact that four of them had dropped everything and driven straight over, into potential trouble, because Zaq had asked for their help was a perfect example of that. 'Who called the cops?' he asked.

Manjit shrugged. 'His wife, one of the neighbours, anyone. There was a lot of shouting and noise, even before we turned up, I think.'

'How come the cops are talking to Bal?'

'They talked to all of us.'

'What d'you tell them?'

'We all said we were on our way to the offy, innit, to get some beers and a couple of bottles, it being Friday an' all, and we were driving by and saw some guys beating on someone and we jumped out to help. That's it. Bal's telling them the same thing now.'

'You mention the cars they were driving?'

Manjit gave him a knowing look. 'Nah. Seems to me like you know what's going on and will want to handle it yourself. We just said they ran off, we didn't see no cars.'

'Safe, man.' Zaq put up his fist and Manjit bumped it with his own. 'You leave Pali at home?'

'You know he ain't the fighting type, so we sent him to the restaurant to pick up the food.'

'Safe,' Zaq said with a laugh. 'What you going to do now?'

'We really do need to go to the offy and get some drinks.'

'Well . . .' Zaq fished out his wallet and pulled out two twenties, which he folded and handed to Manjit. 'Here, drinks are on me, for helping out.'

'You don't need to do that.'

'I know, but I want to. Come on, man, take it.'

Manjit reluctantly took the cash. 'I'll tell the others. You going to be back to eat and have a shot?'

'I'd love to, but I got to get over to the hospital.'

'How is your brother?'

'He's on the mend, I think, slowly. Won't know for sure until he wakes up, and that might be another couple of days.'

'Really hope he pulls through OK, man.'

'You and me both.' Zaq spotted Jags coming out of Lucky's house and looking around. 'I better go. Thanks again, man. I really appreciate it.' They shook hands. 'Tell the others too.'

Zaq started across the road and nodded his thanks to Dips and Lax who were waiting for Bal and Manjit. There were still police around, both inside and outside the house. He caught Jags' attention and could see the anger blazing in his eyes.

'Those fucking bastards . . .' Jags growled. He looked like he wanted to kill someone.

'Is Lucky OK?'

'Yeah, no thanks to that Donny motherfucker and his mates though. He's pretty shaken up; so's my aunt. I owe Manj, Bal and that lot.'

'All right, come on, let's get out of here. I got to get over to the hospital anyway. Tell me what Lucky said on the way to yours.'

Chapter Sixty-Three

Bal was just finishing up telling the cop his version of events. Zaq caught his eye again and nodded his thanks. Bal looked back at the cop and nodded too, seemingly agreeing with whatever the cop was saying but really telling Zaq it was cool. Zaq would thank him properly next time he saw him.

They got in the car and Jags drove them up past the house, towards Lady Margaret Road and then the Broadway. He was fuming, Zaq could tell.

'You get a chance to talk to Lucky properly, find out what happened?'

Jags hit the steering wheel. 'Man, if we hadn't found out where those fuckers were going and called Manj and the guys in time, who knows what they would've done to him.' He was breathing hard, trying to keep a grip. 'He said he'd just got home, washed, changed and cracked open a beer when the doorbell rang. He answered it and there was four geezers there, young. He didn't know them – he's never seen that Donny prick before – and they just laid into him, grabbed him, punched him, kicked him, dragged him out of the house. My aunt heard the noise and came out, and tried to help. One of the motherfuckers hit her, knocked her down. So she ran back inside and called the cops.'

Zaq could sense Jags' anger increasing as he told the story.

'Lucky said he tried to fight, but there were too many of

them. He weren't going without a struggle, though, and tried not to let them take him. They'd got him out the gate into the road when my aunt came out again, screaming at them to let him go. They were all making a hell of a racket, so maybe some of the neighbours called the cops too. Lucky said just when he thought he couldn't hold them off any more and they were going to drag him to their motor, another group showed up – "a big Singh, a stocky fucker, and a couple of others".'

'Manj, Bal and them.'

'Yeah, I know. Anyway, they piled into those wankers, and the tossers shit themselves. Soon as Manj and Bal started hammering them, they let him go and legged it off down Kingsley Avenue. He didn't clock if they had motors or anything.'

'Manj did – said they were in a Range Rover and a Merc.'

'Definitely Shergill and his mates, then.'

'Yeah. Then what?'

'The cops turned up and started giving Manj and the guys a hard time, till my uncle told them they'd helped him.'

'Did you tell Lucky who it was attacked him?'

'I was going to ... but I wasn't sure how he'd take it. You know how he is sometimes, flying off the handle, shooting his mouth off. Didn't think I should risk it in front of my aunt and with the Old Bill there. Better to tell him once he's got over the shock.'

'Probably right. He going to be all OK?'

'Took a bit of a battering, got some cuts and bruises – but yeah, he'll be fine. My aunt's pretty scared, though. I rang Jas and told him to grab a couple of my other cousins and get over there, stay a couple of nights, in case the arseholes come back and try again.'

'Good idea.' They'd left Southall and were driving through Hayes. 'We need to sort this whole mess out, and soon,' Zaq said. 'Those motherfuckers have got a lot to answer for.'

'Damn fucking right.'

'I got to head to the hospital; I'm late as it is. But let's try and decide which option we're going to go with to get that bloody necklace back for Lucky, and then work out how we deal with those fucking pricks, good and proper.'

Jags nodded, his hands still tight on the steering wheel. 'What if we don't manage to get the necklace?'

'Then we'll have to see if Lucky'd be willing to give it up and go to the cops.'

'What with? We ain't got no proof to tie them to the shit they done.'

'They've got the necklace, and they've still got Kang's case. That'll give them motive and tie them to his murder.'

'Why don't we just go to the cops right now, then?'

'I'd be all for it but we should probably check with Lucky first. Plus, I don't trust those slippy fuckers.'

'You talking about the cops or Shergill's lot?' asked Jags.

'Both. We were at the jewellers yesterday, so we'll be on the security video; and Kang was attacked by two blokes. All it'd take is for Shergill and that lot to say we gave them the case and we'd be right in the frame for it.'

'You were at the hospital when it happened though, remember?'

'I've also got a criminal record. Two of us, at the scene, it's a definite link. If the cops ain't got anything better to go on, they might try and make something stick. That's bad enough on its own, but I'm even more worried about Tonka thinking we might've killed his brother-in-law.'

'Fuck, I'd forgotten about that.'

'I ain't saying we don't go to the cops. All I'm saying is, we got to have something solid to prove it was those guys, beyond any doubt.'

They were quiet for the remainder of the journey. Zaq tried

to figure a way to get the necklace back that would see Shergill's mob face justice, and not implicate themselves, but it seemed as if everything was stacked against them. If they took the necklace by force, Shergill would try to frame them for Kang's murder; the same would happen if they went to the police. And it wasn't just the cops they needed to worry about. They needed some leverage over Shergill. But what?

When they reached Jags' place, Zaq said, 'I'll come over tomorrow and we can try and work out what we're going to do.' Jags agreed and they shook hands. 'Laters.'

Zaq made a quick stop on the way to buy some food and snacks, then parked across the road from the hospital in the usual place. He walked fast through the building, to the Intensive Treatment Unit and his brother's room.

His dad frowned. 'What time do you call this? You're late.'

'I know. I'm really sorry,' Zaq said. 'I got held up doing something. How is he?'

'The doctors say there's been some more improvement, though it's slow. They might take him off the medication in a day or two and allow him to wake. Only then will we know how he really is.'

His mum was gathering her things together.

'Hi, Mum.'

Her eyes glistened, though her face seemed dry. She probably had no more tears left to cry. She looked empty, a husk of her usual self, hollowed out by grief and worry. Zaq wished there were something he could do to put everything right, to somehow take away the pain and put the joy back into her life.

'I'll keep an eye on him now,' was all he could manage.

His mother couldn't quite manage a smile, just a slight twitch at the edges of her mouth, but she gave him a nod. Then she and his dad left.

Zaq looked at his brother lying battered, broken, fifty shades of bruise, and was hit by a wave of sadness. How had his little brother ended up in this state? Flashes of younger, happier times came to him, when they'd been as close as brothers could be: playing games around the house; pretending the staircase was a mountain and crawling up it; playing football in the park and their back garden; watching movies and TV together and discussing them afterwards. That was back when they saw each other every day and talked all the time. Happy memories of better days. Things were very different now. They'd grown apart and hardly saw or talked to each other any more. Maybe, with time, they could fix the cracks in their relationship and become close again – except now there was a very real chance that might never happen.

He knew who was responsible – not just that Satty prick but Donny fucking Shergill too. This was all their fault. His heart thumped in his chest like a war drum and his breathing grew faster and shallower as his body tensed with the desire for retribution. It only compounded his rage to know he'd seen the guy three times before but hadn't known he was the fucker he'd been looking for all week until today, when Sharan had finally given up his name. If he had known, he might've beaten him to a bloody pulp and stopped him in his tracks. But because he hadn't known and done anything about it, a man was dead, and another was in the hospital fighting for his life. And if things had gone differently that evening there might've been three more to add to that tally.

Zaq realised being angry now wasn't going to solve anything. Better to store it and keep it for when he could use it. What he needed to do now was calm down and get a grip. So he breathed deeply, long, slow breaths to clear his mind, as he compressed all his rage down into a single dense point that he locked away deep inside himself until required. And when that time came, he'd go absolutely fucking supernova.

'I'm going to get those bastards,' he told his unconscious brother. 'Donny, his old man, Satty, the whole fucking lot of them. We'll get that bloody necklace back from them too. I just got to think of a way for us to do it.'

Chapter Sixty-Four

Zaq rummaged in the bag of stuff he'd bought from the petrol station, and opted for a chicken and avocado sandwich first, along with a pack of salt and vinegar crisps and a bottle of Coke Zero. He had another sandwich and a chocolate bar for later. After he'd finished eating, his phone vibrated in his pocket. Nina was calling him. He remembered they were supposed to arrange to meet up tomorrow. Damn – with everything that had been going on, it had totally slipped his mind. He didn't think he'd be a fun date in any case.

Nina asked after his brother, and Zaq told her the latest.

'That's good news,' she said, 'that the swelling's starting to go down.'

'Yeah, it is.'

'Is everything OK? You sound a bit down ...'

'I'm all right. It's just ... there's a lot going on at the moment.'

'Anything you want to talk about?'

He paused, wondering how much he should tell her. 'I know who beat up Tariq.'

'Oh ...' She sounded hesitant. 'What are you going to do about it?'

'I don't know. It's a bit complicated.'

'What's complicated about it? Surely you just go to the police, tell them and let them handle it.'

'The guys that did it, they're mixed up in something else me and Jags are trying to sort out. If I go the cops, it'll wreck that and probably land us in trouble too.'

'What sort of trouble?'

'The serious kind.'

'What are you and Jags up to?'

'Like I said, it's complicated, a family thing to do with Jags. Not really my place to say. You can ask him. He'd have to be the one to tell you.'

'Is it anything illegal?'

'No, not really. They've got something that don't belong to them and we're trying to get it back but, if we get the cops involved, there's a good chance they'll stitch us up for something bad that we didn't do – but they did.'

'You're right; it does sound complicated.'

'Me and Jags are trying to think of a way to get what we want from them that won't leave us in the shit.'

'If you manage to do that and get back whatever it is you're after, will you go to the police then?'

'If we can prove what they've done, we will.'

'And if you can't?'

'Be no point going to the cops without proof.'

'I know you, though. If you don't go to the police, you won't just let them off the hook for Tariq. Or for whatever else they've done.'

'If there's enough evidence for the police to handle it, then great. If there ain't . . . '

'You really think that will be the answer?'

'If the only other option is to let them walk, then yeah, I'm afraid I do.'

Nina was silent for a moment. He was expecting her to argue, but her voice was calm. 'In that case just be careful. Don't do anything silly and get yourself into trouble.'

'I won't, not if I can help it.'

'I wouldn't want anything bad to happen to you.'

'You wouldn't?'

'Of course not.'

Zaq had become so used to being angry and frustrated the past few days that he was surprised by the swirl of warmth he felt radiating from the centre of his chest, like the welcome glow of a candle in the dark. He even felt himself smile. 'Really?'

'Yes, really,' she told him.

And just like that, the conversation shifted. He asked how she'd been, what she'd been doing since they'd last talked. She told him about work, Rita, friends, TV shows, music – all the real-life stuff he'd been missing out on because he'd been so wrapped up in everything to do with Tariq and Lucky and all the others. It made him realise what a fucked-up week he'd had and how much he wanted things to get back to normal. It was easy to chat to her and he found he was able to put his worries out of his mind for a while.

'What do you want to do about tomorrow?' she asked, as the call seemed to be drawing to a natural conclusion.

Zaq wasn't sure what to say. He didn't want to brush her off but he also didn't want to inflict a date on her where he might be preoccupied with other things. He wanted to be able to give her his full attention. He'd also have to come to the hospital, so it might all seem a bit rushed.

Nina must have sensed what he was thinking, and said, 'You've got a lot going on at the moment, I understand that. Why don't we do it another time? Maybe mid-week, or next weekend?'

'You sure that's OK?'

'It's fine. Just don't do anything stupid or get yourself hurt before you can take me out.'

'It's a deal,' he said, chuckling, and hoping he could deliver on it.

After Zaq ended the call, he sat in the hospital chair feeling lighter than he had all week, the warm glow inside continuing to keep the shadows at bay.

He purposely hadn't told Nina about Kang's murder. It would have taken things to a whole different level, and he was sure she would've told him to go straight to the police, or even wanted to go herself, no matter what he said to get her to wait. He hadn't exactly lied to her, just omitted certain details.

Thinking about the murder again caused the warm glow he'd been feeling to wane slightly.

It was snuffed out completely a few minutes later when a man he didn't know came into Tariq's room.

Chapter Sixty-Five

'You Zaq?'

The man was about five-eight or five-nine, with an average build under his loose-fitting black jeans and T-shirt, though his thickly corded forearms told a different story. He seemed slightly rough around the edges, unshaven, with a thick growth of dark stubble and black hair that was cropped but overgrown, like a lawn in need of a trim. His features were angular, his skin tawny brown, his eyes hard.

'Yeah,' Zaq said.

'I'm Gugs. Bongo's cousin. Prit said I'd find you here.'

'Right,' Zaq said, remembering the conversation he'd had with Prit earlier ... had it only been that morning? So much seemed to have happened since then. He got up and extended his hand, which Gugs seemed to consider for a moment before he came forward and shook it. 'Prit told me what happened to Bongo. I'm really sorry. It's fucking out of order.'

Gugs gave him a stark look. 'Yeah, well, people saw you with him yesterday, you know? Said you were arguing with him, laying into him on the street, and next thing you know he's been done over and is in here.'

Zaq met his gaze. 'I had words with him, yeah – about Tariq.' He nodded towards his brother. 'Bongo knew more about what happened and why my brother was attacked than he let on. I found out he'd been holding stuff back and was asking him why he didn't just tell me, 'stead of making me run around and find out myself. He could've saved me a whole lot of time and hassle finding who fucking did this. I was annoyed, yeah, and I told him so, but that was it. He ain't the one put my brother in here. All I'm interested in is getting those fuckers back.'

Gugs looked at Tariq. 'How's he doing?'

'Not great. He's been in a coma since he got jumped last Friday. Doctors can't say for sure how he'll be when he wakes up.' Just talking about it revived Zaq's anger.

Gugs shook his head. 'Shit.'

'How's Bongo?'

'Properly fucked up, in an even worse state than your bro.'

'I'm sorry, man. What've the doctors said?'

'Not much. He's hurt bad. They don't seem that hopeful.'

'Shit. If he'd just told me straight off what happened at the wedding maybe I could've—'

'What wedding?'

Zaq told him about the wedding Tariq and Bongo had DJ'd at and the trouble that had occurred there. 'I found out about it anyway and managed to track down his ex, who told me about it. That's all I was pissed off about. I told him that, then asked him to try and get me some info on the guys that did it from anyone he knew in Slough. He said he would. That's how we left things.'

'Fucking *ma chauds* that done all this are from Slough?' Gugs growled.

'Yeah. I figured Bongo would have more luck by talking to people he used to go college with. He was helping me, so I had no reason to do him over. I don't know if he found out anything before he got jumped.'

'You know who the fucking guys are?'

'Matter of fact I do,' Zaq said. Gugs' eyes narrowed. 'The

same lot came after me and my mate today, but for a different reason. They got no idea I'm connected to Tariq and Bongo. I only just found out they were the ones responsible for all this.'

'Who the fuck are they? Tell me and I'll go sort them out.'

Zaq put up his hands to placate him. 'Hold on a sec. Like I said, I got some other stuff going on with these guys I need to deal with first.'

'Fuck that – this is family!' Gugs said, almost aggressively.

'You think I don't know that? That's my brother lying here. This other stuff's family too,' Zaq said, Jags being like a brother to him. 'I got to get the other shit sorted and then ...' Zaq's voice trailed off as a vague idea started to form in his mind. 'Maybe we can help each other out.'

'Help each other how? I ain't interested in nothing except beating those guys into dog food.'

'The guys that did this have got something I need to get back from them. If you help me get what I want, I'll help you get the guys who did Bongo over.'

'What kind of help you talking about?'

'I ain't worked it all out yet, but maybe something like this ...' Zaq gave him a rough idea of what he was thinking about. It wasn't a proper plan yet, more a combination of ideas that had been swimming around in his head for a while and had finally begun to coalesce into the vague outline of something that might work.

Gugs listened, thought about it for a moment. 'When you want to do it?'

It was a good question. 'I might be able to set it up for the day after tomorrow.'

'And you're sure they're the guys that fucked Bongo up, and your brother?'

'I'm absolutely positive.'

'All right, I'm in. That means me and all of Bongo's family and mates too. Let's fucking do it.'

'You're sure?' Zaq said. 'And you'll wait until my other business is taken care of?'

'Yeah, we got a deal.' Gugs held out his hand and they shook on it. 'Just as long as I get those fuckers.'

'You will. Let's swap numbers.'

'Cool.'

Numbers exchanged, Zaq said, 'I'll come and see Bongo a bit later.'

Gugs shook his head. 'I don't think that'd be a good idea, not at the moment. Best let me talk to the others first, tell them what you've told me, then maybe they'll change their attitude towards you.' He started to leave, then turned back. 'It's lucky for you Prit called and told me you didn't have nothing to do with what happened to Bongo. Enough people saw the two of you arguing and – well, everyone knows your rep.'

'I'd probably have thought the same if I was you.'

'But then Prit explained what happened to your brother and how it's linked to what happened to Bongo, so I thought I better come and talk to you, and find out for myself.'

'And . . . ?'

Gugs ran a hand over his stubbly jaw. 'Looks like we're both after the same fuckers. Plus, you don't strike me as a bullshitter.'

'Thanks,' Zaq said. 'And in a couple of days you'll know for a fact I ain't.'

Chapter Sixty-Six

Zaq spent the next few hours sitting by his brother's bed, trying to come up with a plan. He pictured the outcome he wanted to achieve and tried working back from that to figure out what he'd have to do to make it happen. He went through a slow-breathing routine, hoping it would help clear his mind so he could think, but, with so much whirling around in it, that was easier said than done. Yeah, he'd had a moment of inspiration, a vague idea for a plan, that he'd convinced Gugs to be part of. But now he had to work out the actual details.

It all boiled down to two things that had to happen. One was getting the necklace back. That was part of the 'what?'. He still had to figure out the 'where?' and the 'how?'.

Fortunately, the hospital was relatively quiet and he had all night to go over and over how things might work out, to imagine all the different scenarios, and try to factor in all the variables. In the end, he got tired thinking about it. Maybe he needed to sleep on it and run through it all again when his mind was fresher. He pulled out his phone and distracted himself with some games and social media, until he grew tired of that too.

Later on, he had his other sandwich and the chocolate bar with a mug of tea he made in the kitchenette. Then he settled in the chair and tried to get some sleep. He dozed fitfully, aware of the nurse moving around the room every hour when she came in to check on Tariq. By the time his parents arrived, he was looking forward to getting home and crawling into his own bed for some real rest. His dad's mood had greatly improved after a proper dinner and a comfortable night at home. He was no longer annoyed at Zaq.

There wasn't much for Zaq to report. The doctors were late on their rounds, so he hadn't received the latest update that morning. He decided not to wait around; if there were any developments he should know about, his dad would call. His mum had already taken the seat Zaq had just vacated. He told his parents he was going home and would see them later.

The roads weren't very busy early on a Saturday morning, so it didn't take long to get back to Southall. It helped that a lot of the Asian businesses didn't open until about ten or eleven – Indian timing, everyone joked. But the familiar high-street names observed more usual business hours and opened around nine, and people were already heading to work.

He wondered if any of his housemates would still be at home. It might be Saturday but it was still a working day for all of them. If Zaq hadn't got the time off, he would have been out driving deliveries that day too.

He got out of his car, locked it and started towards the house. Two men in their fifties, dressed in T-shirts and tracksuit bottoms, earrings glinting in their ears, were coming along the pavement towards him. Past incidents had made Zaq wary, but these guys were older than anyone he'd had trouble with; also they looked familiar, though he couldn't place where from – maybe they lived on the street. They seemed like a couple of proper old-school Southall geezers. They didn't look at all out of place.

Zaq was still on his guard as they walked by and turned his head to watch them go. But, as he did so, a meaty arm snaked around his throat and pulled him backwards, off-balance. The nearest guy had got behind him and taken him in a chokehold. As the air to his brain was cut off, Zaq felt his legs being picked up. He was powerless to fight back and was only able to put up a weak struggle. He heard the sound of a car and felt himself floating toward it. His vision blurred, like looking through gauze. He tapped frantically at the arm around his throat, like an MMA fighter signalling submission. Then everything went dark.

When he came round, his neck and throat hurt and his head was buzzing. He was in the back seat of a moving car, wedged between the two goons who'd taken him off the street. Immediately a meaty hand grabbed the back of his neck and thrust it forward and down, so he was looking at the floor. Both his wrists were grabbed and his arms pulled back and held, effectively immobilising him. He tried to struggle, but there was nothing he could do.

'Relax,' the bloke on his right told him. 'Someone wants to talk to you, innit.'

'What's wrong with a fucking phone?' Zaq croaked.

With no other option, he did what the guy had said and relaxed his muscles. Best save his energy for when they got to their destination and tried to get him out of the car. All he could do for the moment was listen to the Punjabi music playing on the stereo and wonder where they were going and who the hell wanted to talk to him.

With his head down, Zaq had no idea where they were heading. The car stopped and started repeatedly for traffic lights, and to make turns, but he had already lost any sense of what direction they were travelling in. The two men didn't talk, so there were no clues from them either.

Then they stopped, and Zaq heard the driver lower his

window and speak to someone. There was the sound of a gate being opened and they started moving again. They drove on, turned a corner and eventually came to a stop. The guy on Zaq's left opened his door and started to drag him out by his wrist. The guy on Zaq's right, who still had hold of his neck and other wrist, pushed him across the seat and out of the open door. They kept his head down and his arms twisted up high, and made him walk like that so all he could see was the ground immediately in front of him. He sensed other people around them, as they passed from bright daylight into the dim stillness of a building interior. He was marched across a concrete floor, the sounds of their footsteps echoing slightly, which suggested a big open space. Then there was the sound of other voices. They came to a halt, and finally the hands holding him shoved him forward and let him go.

He stumbled a couple of steps, then slowly straightened up, not knowing what to expect – Donny, Satty and those shitheads, or more of Dutta's mates, wanting him to talk on camera.

What he saw was six hard-looking men in front of him and, taking a glance over his shoulder, another five behind, including the two who'd bundled him into the car and probably the driver too. Whatever was going on, it was bad. He was seriously out-numbered, with nowhere to run. He heard footsteps, and the men in front of him parted to allow someone through.

When he saw who it was, Zaq wasn't sure whether to be relieved or scared.

Chapter Sixty-Seven

'Tonka.' Zaq said. 'I was going to come and see you.'

Tonka regarded him dispassionately. 'Is that right?'

'Yeah, soon as I heard about what happened to your brother-in-law.'

'Soon as you heard, huh? It happened Thursday evening. Today's Saturday. What you been doing?'

'I been trying to sort out that shit with my brother, the guys that put him in the hospital. Got sidetracked with that.'

'Anyone might think you were trying to avoid me.'

'No,' Zaq said. 'Why would I do that? I got no reason to avoid you. In fact, I wanted to come and talk to you.'

'Yeah? What about?'

Zaq swallowed. His palms were sweating and he wasn't sure how this was all going to go. 'I saw your brother-in-law on Thursday afternoon. I was at his shop.'

'I know,' Tonka said. 'I got copies of the security video. You and your mate were there. Then a few hours later he's jumped in the street, robbed and beaten to death by two blokes who match your descriptions. Funny that, huh?'

'It ain't funny at all.'

'You got that right. Now, what am I supposed to think?'

'I know how it might look, but it wasn't us; we had nothing to do with it.'

'You would say that, though, wouldn't you? Even if you did do it.'

'I've never robbed anyone in my whole life. If I was going to start now, why the hell would I do it in Southall, where everyone knows me?'

Tonka shrugged. 'People do stupid things all the time.'

'I wasn't even in Southall when it happened. I was in Hillingdon, at the hospital, sitting next to my brother. First I heard about it was yesterday morning, and I went straight to the cops, 'cause I knew I'd be on the video. They're probably checking with the hospital right now, which'll prove that's where I was.'

Tonka didn't look convinced. The guys standing around looked equally sceptical. 'If you and your mate didn't do it, then what the fuck were you doing there?'

'You said you got the CCTV from the shop, right?'

'Yeah, so? You're the only two in it who fit the description of the guys that attacked him.'

'All right, but an hour or so before we were there, a bloke went in to see him, older geezer, had a minder with him, big fucker, I'm talking seven-foot or something. The minder waited in the shop while the guy went in the back with your brother-in-law.'

Tonka was frowning. 'How d'you know all that?'

''Cause I was following that guy.'

'What the fuck you talking about?'

'Me and Jags followed him there,' Zaq said. 'I was in the *desi* café over the road, watching. If you check the video from the cameras at the front of the shop, they might've caught me.'

'Why the fuck were you following him?'

''Cause the fucker's got a necklace that belongs to Jags' uncle, and we're trying to get it back off him. He took it there.'

'What you saying? You jumped my brother-in-law 'cause you thought he had it in his case?'

'No,' Zaq said. 'The guy didn't leave it there; he took it away with him.'

'How d'you know that?'

'We followed him from the shop to his house, then we came back to talk to your brother-in-law.'

'Who's the guy?'

'Some rich fucker with an attitude, who don't like to return gambling markers.'

'That's what the necklace business is about, huh?'

'Yeah. Jags' uncle was in a poker game with the guy and used the necklace to cover a bet.'

'That was a pretty stupid thing to do,' Tonka said.

'That's what we told him.'

'How big was the bet?'

'About ten grand, but the geezer's being a total arsehole about it. Jags' uncle went to pay what he owed but the bloke wouldn't hand it over. So he paid double to get it back, 'cause it's his wife's and she'll kill him if she finds out.' That got a laugh from the guys standing around. 'The wanker took the money but gave us the wrong necklace, some cheap knockoff. Now he ain't giving the necklace or the money back.'

'That's all very interesting, but it still don't explain what the guy has to do with my brother-in-law getting robbed and killed.'

'I was just getting to that. When we went back to talk to your brother-in-law, we told him the necklace was stolen, and that if we didn't get it back we'd have no choice but to go to the cops. He got real worked up about it, said he didn't want the cops coming around.'

'You trying to say my brother-in-law was a bit dodgy?'

'No, but this other guy definitely is. He don't seem the type who got rich legally. Your brother-in-law said they did business together. Maybe he just helped him out now and again, you

know, selling stuff under the counter, certifying hooky diamonds, giving bumped-up insurance valuations, I don't know.'

'We all bend the rules a bit, cut a few corners here and there.
He was a good bloke, though – and even more than that, he was
family. My sister and her kids are in fucking pieces, and so is
everyone else.'

'I can imagine,' Zaq said. 'The guy felt comfortable enough to
bring the necklace to your brother-in-law, though, and have him
look at it, no questions asked. Maybe Kang was worried what the
cops might find if they started digging around?'

'All you're giving me is a load of hot air, unless you got something to back it up.'

'I know your brother-in-law called the guy right after we left
him, and a few hours later he was killed as he left the shop. The
guys that attacked him took the briefcase to make it look like a
street robbery rather than a targeted killing, which is what it was.'

'That could still have been you and your mate.'

'It wasn't. Next day, when we heard what happened, we knew
that rich prick had to be behind it, so we went and confronted
him. He as good as admitted it. He knew all about us talking
to Kang because your brother-in-law had called and told him.
There must be a record of the call somewhere, maybe from
his mobile or the shop's landline. We thought we could get the
necklace in exchange for keeping quiet about his involvement
with your brother-in-law's murder.'

'So you were just going to keep your mouths shut about what
he'd done?'

'No fucking way. We don't owe that shitbag anything. Soon
as we got the necklace, I'd have come and told you.'

'That was yesterday. You didn't come and see me, and you're
only in front of me now 'cause I had you brought here.'

'The guy didn't give us the necklace. I gave him till Sunday to change his mind. I was going to come and see you before then, but we never figured on him sending the same guys after us that killed your brother-in-law.'

'You what?'

'Me and Jags were lucky to escape. They wanted to silence us, just like they did your brother-in-law. Went after Jags' uncle too, so he wouldn't go to the cops if anything happened to us. You can check it out. There was a big ruck outside his house on Burns Avenue last night. Cops were there and everything. The whole street will be talking about it.'

'What happened to your mate's uncle?'

'He's pretty shaken up. They started beating him and tried to drag him to a car but I'd called some mates nearby, who got there just in time to fight the fuckers off.'

'Who the fuck is this guy? I should go and talk to him.'

'He won't admit to anything. It'll just be our word against his.'

'And maybe you're just feeding me a load of bullshit,' Tonka said. 'All I'm getting is words, nothing solid.'

Just then, Zaq had a lightbulb moment as another piece of the mental puzzle he'd been working on fell into place. 'What if I can get you proof?'

'Of what?'

'That this guy's responsible for your brother-in-law's death, that it was all his doing?'

'If you can prove it, so I know for sure you didn't have anything to do with it, then you get to walk away in one piece. You said he won't admit to it, though, so how you going get the proof?'

'I'll need a bit of help – from you,' Zaq said.

'From me?' Tonka's eyebrows were raised. 'What sort of help?'

'There's something else I got to tell you first.'

Tonka waited.

'The guys that killed your brother-in-law . . . they're the same fuckers that beat up my brother and put him in a coma. I just found that out yesterday.'

'What the fuck?' Tonka said. 'Proper bunch of *bhen chauds*.'

'They are. And they put Tariq's best friend in the hospital as well, same night they killed your brother-in-law. So I got my own reason for getting these bastards too.' Zaq looked Tonka in the eye. 'I'll get you proof they killed your brother-in-law – but there's two things I want before you fuck them up.'

'You ain't in a position to be making fucking demands of me.' Tonka gave him a hard stare. 'You got some balls, though. What d'you want?'

Zaq told him.

Tonka weighed it up, and after a moment he said, 'OK, that seems fair enough.'

'We got a deal, then?'

'Yeah, we got a deal,' he nodded. 'Now, what sort of help d'you need from me?'

Zaq explained what Tonka would need to do.

'Is that it?' Tonka said when he was finished. 'That's all you want?'

'I think so, for now. If there's anything else, I'll call you.'

'Fine. Just one thing, though . . . What if they kill you first?'

Fuck! Zaq hadn't thought of that. 'Take it as an admission of their guilt, I guess.'

Tonka laughed. 'You're fucking crazy,' he said. 'That's probably why I like you.'

'I'll need to get in earlier though, to set up some stuff beforehand.'

Tonka waved one of his guys over and asked for something, which the guy took out of a pocket and handed over. Tonka tossed the item to Zaq – a bunch of keys. 'Anything else?'

'Not right now. And you're cool with what we agreed on? We got a deal, yeah?'

'Sure. You get me what I want, you get what you want. Fair's fair.' He extended his hand and, as the two of them shook on it, Tonka's grip tightened, exerting a crushing pressure on the bones in Zaq's hand. 'But you better convince me you didn't have anything to do with it, 'cause if I think you're fucking me about I'll put you in the ground. You get me?'

Zaq looked him in the eye. 'I get you.'

Tonka released his hand.

Zaq winced as he opened and closed his fingers, trying to work out the pain, and said, 'Don't suppose there's any chance of a lift home?'

Chapter Sixty-Eight

Zaq got a lift home from the same three guys who'd brought him to see Tonka. They were a lot more jovial this time around. Only one of them sat in the back with him on the return trip, which meant more room and a more comfortable ride. The other sat next to the driver. 'No hard feelings, heh?' the one next to him said, slapping him on the back.

'Nah, it's cool,' Zaq replied, without much conviction. What else was he going to say? It had come to him where he'd seen them before – earlier in the week, with Tonka at the Scotsman.

As they drove away from the boarded-up warehouse, Zaq realised they were in Hayes. Inside, he'd asked Tonka about the place, and Tonka had told him he'd bought up all four warehouses on the site and had finally received planning permission to knock them down and build flats instead. It was going to be a right money-spinner.

It was still fairly early morning by the time they dropped Zaq back at the house, but by then all his housemates had already gone and the place was nice and quiet. He let himself in, had a quick bowl of cereal in the kitchen then went upstairs to try to sleep. He opened the windows, pulled the curtains closed, then stripped to his boxers and fell on to the bed. He turned off the vibrate function on his phone and set the ringtone to its very lowest level. If he was in a deep sleep he probably wouldn't hear it, but if he was half-awake he would.

He lay with his eyes closed, not sure if he'd be able to sleep because of all the thoughts swirling around in his head. He concentrated on taking deep breaths in, holding them and then exhaling, counting for each step four-seven-eight. It slowed everything down and helped to clear his mind. Then he tried to arrange his thoughts into some kind of order. He didn't get very far before he fell fast asleep.

It must have been a deep sleep, because when his phone's ringtone eventually woke him it had reached the end of its forty-second sequence and stopped, just as he reached for it. It was just after one in the afternoon. He'd slept for about four hours. There were two missed calls, one from Bongo's cousin Gugs, and one just now from Prit. Zaq stretched, rubbed his face, then sat up and called Prit back.

'Hey, Zaq, where you been?'

'Asleep. I was at the hospital all night. What's up?'

'Sorry, didn't mean to wake you. You won't have heard, then ...'

'Heard what?

'Gugs has been trying to get in touch with you. Bongo died this morning.'

'Shit.' It hit Zaq harder than he expected, harder than when he'd learned about Kang, and that had been bad enough. Another life needlessly ended, over nothing, and this one a lot closer to home: Tariq's mate, the same age as him, a life cut short, never to be fully realised. Zaq was knotted by conflicting emotions: sorrow for Bongo and his family; relief that Tariq was still alive although no one knew what sort of state he'd be in when he woke; and hatred for those responsible, not just for his brother's condition but for two murders as well.

'I'll ring Gugs now.' Zaq ended the call with Prit and tried Gugs. 'I just heard about Bongo,' he said when Gugs answered. 'I'm really sorry.'

'Yeah,' Gugs said brusquely. 'Who're the fucking guys that beat him up? Give me their names. We're ready to go and fuck them up, right now.'

Zaq understood how Gugs felt but he had his own shit to worry about. He wanted to get Shergill, Donny, Satty and the whole bunch of shit-wipes every bit as much as Gugs did, but he also had to get proof for Tonka that he and Jags had nothing to do with Kang's murder, not to mention getting Lucky's necklace back. 'I thought we had a deal.'

'We did, but that was before Bongo ... when he was still here.'

'I told you, there's stuff I got to sort out first before anything happens to them. Either you're on board with that and going to wait until tomorrow like we agreed, or you'll have to wait till afterwards and I can't promise you anything then.'

'What's that supposed to mean?'

'There are other people involved now, who've also got beef with these fuckers.'

'Like who?' Gugs demanded.

'You know Tonka?'

The silence that followed spoke volumes. Finally Gugs said, 'How's he involved?'

'Ain't my place to go discussing Tonka's business, man. You want to know, you can ask him.' Everyone in Southall, and probably beyond, knew full well that unless you were tight with Tonka you never ever went up and asked about his private business. He might politely refuse to answer in public but he'd come and find you later and hammer the refusal home so you'd know never to make the same mistake again. 'He agreed to the same deal, just like you did. You don't want to be part of it any more, that's fine. But if you're thinking of doing anything that screws up what we're doing, I'll have to tell Tonka.'

Zaq gave Gugs time to absorb it.

'So Tonka's involved, and he's going along with everything you want?'

'Yeah. He wants those guys too but he agreed to let me do things my way, like I explained to you.'

'So, me and Tonka will be working together?'

'Yeah, that's right.' It wasn't as if Tonka needed Gugs' help, but if it made Gugs feel better about things, there was no harm letting him think it.

'OK,' Gugs agreed, though Zaq detected a hint of reluctance. The prospect of going up against Tonka had certainly made him rethink. 'We'll do things your way.'

'I'll be in touch.'

Zaq ended the call, went to the bathroom and returned to his room. Before he did anything else, he had to write down the outline of his plan and work out the details. He sat back in bed with a clipboard he used to hold his weight-training logs, and began making notes. First he made three lists, of the people now involved: Tonka and Gugs on one side; the Shergills, Satty and that lot on the other; himself, Jags and Lucky in the middle. He now had a location for what he was going to do and wrote that down. He'd need to scope the place out properly later. Right now, he needed to figure out *how* to do what he wanted. He let his mind wander, hoping it might light upon a solution if he didn't push too hard. Whenever he seemed to be flying off in some completely random direction, he would reel his thoughts back in and start again. He doodled on the paper and drew lines of connection to help him.

When it did come, it seemed so simple he didn't know why it had taken him so long to think of it. He scribbled down some notes, then began working out the details, including things they'd need to get and do to make it work. It was mostly logical thinking – deciding exactly what he wanted to do and figuring out what he'd need to do it. He ran through various scenarios, trying to work out the variables and factor them into his scheme. It took some time, but when he'd finished he thought he'd worked it all out. Then he made a list of items they'd need. He did a quick online search for some of them, to make sure it'd be possible to get them. One thing was a little trickier to get than the others, but it still ought to be possible.

He put the laptop aside, called Jags and told him about Bongo and his meeting with Tonka.

'Fuck,' Jags said. 'That's two people dead 'cause of those crazy arseholes. Would be more if they'd managed to do us and Lucky over too.'

'Yeah, they need to be sorted out good and proper, and I think I've figured out a way to do it.'

'Great, but what about the necklace?'

'We get that back too.'

'OK, I'm listening.'

Zaq explained the plan to him. It didn't take long. When he finished, Jags said, 'Is that it?'

'Yeah. Best to keep it simple. Less things to go wrong that way.'

'It's simple, all right, like that other plan you came up with a few months back to take care of Dutta and the Brars.'

'It worked, didn't it?'

'Yeah – don't ask me how, though.'

'Planning and bit of luck.'

'We'll need luck this time too. There's more people involved. You sure Tonka and this Gugs will stick to their side of it?'

'I told them both what we want, and they agreed. Tonka shook on it and I don't see him going back on that. Besides, he still gets what he wants out of it – they both do – and he'll keep Gugs in line.'

'You really think it'll work?'

'Don't know for sure. But why not? If it goes the way I hope, we're out of the shit with Tonka and everybody's happy.'

'Everybody except the Shergills and that lot.'

'You really worried about them?'

'Nah, fuck them. Let's do it.'

Chapter Sixty-Nine

Zaq had divided the list of things they needed into those he'd pick up and those he needed Jags to get. He read out the things Jags would be getting. 'Two pay-as-you-go SIM cards with a big data allowance. Two shirts – they got to be good material, nothing thin and flimsy, and they got to have at least one chest pocket each. Get different colours if you can; if we're dressed the same it might look a bit weird. We'll also need a sheet or two of thick card, from an art shop or somewhere, and a scalpel.'

'This reminds me of the last time you had me go out and get all the stuff we needed.'

'Least this time you don't have to pick up any ladies' underwear.'

'Oh, yeah – shit, that was well embarrassing.'

'Anyway, I'm getting some of the stuff this time too. Last thing you need to find is some small wireless mics that'll work with an Android phone.'

'Why? We ain't got Android phones.'

'I know. I'm going to get us some later. Get two of the mics; I'll send you a link to the sort of thing I mean. I don't know how easy they'll be to find, so you might want to look them up online and get them first.'

'OK. Anything else?'

'No, that's it for you. I'll pick up the rest of the stuff. Make sure you get it all today, and pay for everything in cash.'

'All right, keep your hair on. I will.'

'Let me know when you've got everything, and I'll come over to yours so we can make sure it all works.'

'What you going to do now?'

'I'm going to go check the place out. Then I'll pick up the bits and pieces I need to get.'

'OK, see you later.'

Zaq used his phone's web browser to find the type of wireless microphones he wanted. He copied and pasted the link into WhatsApp and sent it to Jags. That done, he went through his plan one more time. He had a nagging feeling he'd missed something . . . then realised what it was.

He searched the things on his bedside table until he found the card he was looking for then typed a message into his phone:

> Hi, it's Zaq from yesterday. You need to call
> me. It's urgent.

He sent it to the number on the card and wondered how long it'd be before he got a response. Or if he'd get any response at all.

It would take Jags a while to track down the wireless mics and get the other stuff. The things Zaq had to do shouldn't take long, which meant he probably had time to squeeze in a quick workout. He warmed up with some shadow-boxing, then stretched, and was halfway through his weights routine when his phone rang. He put down the dumbbells, and recognised the last four digits of the caller's number as the one he'd sent the message to.

He answered. 'Hey, thanks for calling me back.'

'I almost didn't,' Sharan said. 'I'm getting rid of this SIM today and getting a new number. I've had enough threatening messages from Donny and Satty. I'm so over that guy. I don't know what I ever saw in him. He might have money but he's got no class. I see that, now I'm away from it all. So what do you want? You said it was urgent.'

Zaq wasn't looking forward to telling her but she'd find out sooner or later, and it might encourage her to help him now. 'Bongo – I mean, Kush ... he died this morning.'

There was a moment of silence as the news sank in. 'What?' Shock was evident in her voice.

'I thought you'd want to know. He never woke up after what Donny and his mates did to him.'

'Oh, no,' she managed. 'No, no, no ...'

'I'm sorry.' He listened as she tried to contain her distress. 'He didn't deserve what they did to him.'

'No, he didn't.' There was a hard edge of anger in her voice.

Zaq hoped that meant she'd be prepared to help him. 'Can you let me have Donny's phone number?'

'Huh?' The request seemed to catch her by surprise.

'I want to talk to him, and so do some of Kush's family. Give me the number and I won't bother you again.'

'You won't be able to bother me again anyway,' she pointed out. 'Not once I get rid of this SIM.'

'You're right. So, one last favour, then.'

She thought about it.

'Do it for Kush,' Zaq added. 'All I want is Donny's number.'

'So you can talk to him?'

'Yeah.'

'And what happens after you've talked to him?' She was no fool. She knew talking wasn't going to settle a goddam thing.

'What happens after happens, innit? It won't have anything to do with you.'

She hesitated a moment longer, then said, 'OK, I'll text it to you.'

'Thanks, I appreciate it.'

'Don't mention it. I mean that. Don't mention it to anyone.'

'I won't.'

'But they should pay for what they did to Kush.'

Zaq didn't say anything else. He didn't need to.

'Bye, then,' she said and hung up.

Zaq finished off his workout, while he thought about what to say when he called Donny. Weights done, he stretched again, for longer this time, pushing and holding each stretch so he could feel the bunched muscle fibres being pulled apart, the initial pain giving way to a pleasurable buzz. Afterwards, he stood by the windows, taking long, deep breaths, and allowed himself to cool down in the slight breeze. He took off his T-shirt and used it to wipe the sweat from his face and brow, as he looked out at the sun-drenched and shadow-dappled street.

Feeling calm and collected, he picked up his phone and made sure to withhold his number before calling Donny Shergill.

'Yeah? Who's that?' the cocky little shit answered.

'That guy you and your motherfuckin' mates beat up the other night ... he died in hospital this morning.'

'Who is this?'

'So, along with the jeweller, that's two murders you're responsible for. And you also attacked someone in Southall last night, which the cops know all about.'

'Who the fuck are you?'

'And you fuckwits coming at us yesterday means you got no more chances.'

'Oh, it's you.'

'Yeah, shit-for-brains, it's me. Now you hand over that necklace or we'll make sure you go down for both those murders and an attempted murder too. You'll be looking at a real long time behind bars, and I doubt your little buddies will be there to help you out.'

'Fuck—'

'Shut up. Tell your old man to call me today, otherwise we go to the cops and tell them everything – fuck the necklace and fuck you all too.'

'Listen, you—'

'I didn't call to listen to you. Just tell your old man – I don't hear from him today, it's game over.'

Chapter Seventy

After showering, Zaq saw a missed call from a number he didn't recognise. His gut told him it was probably Shergill senior. He decided the guy could stew for a while and carried on dressing. Then the same number called again. This time he answered.

'Who am I talking to?' Shergill demanded, in his usual bullish manner.

'You know who it is. *You're* calling *me*, on the number I gave you yesterday.'

'Who else is listening?'

'No one.'

'How can I be sure of that?'

'You'll just have to trust me.'

Shergill barked out a laugh. 'What do you want?'

'I'm sure Donny told you.'

'I don't like people making threats.'

'And I don't like people trying to kill me. I gave you time to think things over. Instead you sent your boy after us. That was stupid. Now give us back the real necklace and that'll be the end of it. Otherwise we tell the cops everything.'

'Tell them what? You can't prove anything.'

'The police'll find all the proof they need after we've told them what we know. You'd be surprised how much evidence they can get from mobile phones these days. I bet Donny had his phone on him when he and his mate did Kang over. All the cops have to do is track his mobile signal and they'll see he was right there when the murder happened, at exactly the right time. They'll also see he was there for the other attack, which is now also a murder.'

'What other attack? What murder?'

'Oh, that's right – you probably only told him to take care of Kang.'

'I don't know what you're talking about.'

'Donny had a personal beef with someone and decided to take care of it while he was in the area. The guy died this morning. So that makes two murders.'

Zaq could sense the tension at the other end of the line as he listened to Shergill's heavy breathing.

'There's also the attack on Lucky last night. What d'you reckon – GBH, or attempted murder? Too much of a coincidence for Donny to be in all three places, just at the right time. You don't want to give the necklace back? Fine; we'll just tell the cops all about it, and your link to Kang. Once they see the connection there, you can bet they'll look a lot harder at everything else we tell them. Then you'll be waving bye-bye to that big fancy house of yours and swapping it for a prison cell.'

Shergill was silent for a moment, then he said, 'Not that any of this shit is true, but what do you want?'

'I've told you what I want.'

'Maybe we can come to some sort of arrangement?'

'There's only one arrangement left. You fucked up any chance of anything else when you sent your little wannabe gangster son after us yesterday. I should be talking to the cops right now. Only reason I'm talking to you is 'cause we want the necklace back. That thing ain't even mine, though, so personally I'll be more than happy to go to the cops and have you, your boy and the rest of your dumb fucks nicked.'

Shergill was snorting like an angry bull. 'All right. If that's all that's going to satisfy you, then I'll give you what you're asking for.'

'You'll just be returning what's ours in the first place.'

'And once you have it, how do I know that will be the end of the matter, that you won't go to the police anyway?'

'You got my word – we get the necklace back, we won't go to the cops.'

'Your word?' Shergill laughed. 'Is that all?'

'It's worth more than yours.'

'And I'm just supposed to believe you? It's not much of a guarantee.'

'Take it or leave it. It's the only guarantee you're going to get. So, what's it going to be?'

Shergill took a moment to think it over. 'OK, fine,' he said. 'I'll just have to believe that you will keep your side of the bargain.'

'Yeah, you will.'

'How am I supposed to give it to you? Will you come here to the house to get it?'

'We're not that stupid,' Zaq said. 'I'll call you on this number tomorrow evening and tell you where to bring it and when.'

'Tomorrow evening? But I have plans to—'

'Change them.' And Zaq hung up.

Now what he needed was some cash for the things he had to get. He dragged the foot of his bed away from the wall. Then he peeled back the carpet and lifted out a loose floorboard. In the space underneath were several carrier bags containing the cash that Jags had given him a few months ago. He counted out four hundred pounds, then put everything else back. Leaving one small window open, he locked the rest, grabbed his keys, cards, phone and notes, went and had a bowl of cereal in the kitchen, then left the house.

Chapter Seventy-One

Zaq's first stop was the warehouse he'd been inside earlier that day. This time he wanted a proper look around. He parked well away from the small industrial site and walked the rest of the way. The warehouse sat behind a spiked, metal-slatted perimeter fence, the only entry via a locked double gate. Zaq took out the keys Tonka had given him and unlocked the gates. The site was home to four warehouses: three blocky brick structures on the right, and a long, narrower building on the left. The one Zaq wanted was the first on the right.

The building itself was two storeys of tan-coloured brick, with a corrugated metal roof. All the ground-floor windows were closed up with perforated metal grilles, the entrance door shuttered. There were hardly any other windows. At the near corner of the building, there was a full-height metal roller shutter and a small fire door next to it. High up, there was a patch of wall that was noticeably lighter than the rest, suggesting that a sign had recently been taken down.

At the main entrance Zaq tried a few more of Tonka's keys until he found the right ones for the heavy-duty padlocks securing the shutter. Then he let himself in through the door, locked it behind him and headed towards the main part of the building. He passed some stairs that probably led up to the offices on the upper floor, and went through a set of double doors, past a small kitchen and some toilets, and into the warehouse proper, a large, wide-open space thick with shadows. A row of small windows ran the length of the rear wall just under the roof, but even so there was little daylight to illuminate the gloomy interior. Zaq searched for light switches and three rows of fluorescent lights eventually strobed to life. What they showed him was a big, empty shell, with nothing to show what sort of business might have been there before.

It was perfect.

Zaq explored the rest of the building. There was another fire door in the rear wall, the type that opened by pushing the bar down to release the deadbolts. He studied it and came up with an idea to make it open from the outside that he hoped would work. As he carried on walking, he noted two rows of thick steel pillars evenly spaced across the main floor. Zaq went over and examined one; it was made up of three seven-foot sections, bolted and possibly welded together. A small shelf was formed where the sections joined. Just what he wanted. There was a similar row of pillars against the front wall and also at the rear. He nodded to himself. The area between the front wall and the pillar nearest to him was where he wanted them, which meant he'd have to orchestrate things so that that was where they'd actually be.

Then Zaq went over to the smaller fire door at the front, beside the big shutter. He tried it from the inside and it swung open, no problem. Good. He'd use it to let Shergill in. He walked around a bit more, getting a feel for the place, then went back to the light switches. The switch panel on the wall had twelve switches, only nine of which controlled the lights. Zaq played with them to figure out which lots of lights it would be best to have on when the time came. He settled on the middle section, between the front wall and the first line of pillars and the central section adjacent to that.

The last thing he did was look for the fuse box. Tonka had told him it was over in the corner near the main entrance. Zaq eventually located it, and when he opened it up was pleased to find that each fuse switch was labelled. He selected the one for the outdoor security lights, and turned it off. Better to be safe. Although it would be Sunday tomorrow and the area would be quiet at night, there was no point lighting the place up like a beacon.

That done, he turned off all the lights, left the building, locking up behind him, and went shopping.

Chapter Seventy-Two

'Hey, man, where you at?' Zaq could hear through the phone that Jags was driving.

'On my way home,' Jags said. 'Had to go all the way over by Brent Cross to get the mics, so I went to the shopping centre there to get the other stuff. I got it all.'

'And you paid for everything in cash?' Zaq asked.

'Yeah, I did. What you doing?'

'I checked the place out, and I got the phones and the other stuff we need.'

'You remember to pay for everything with cash?'

'Ha, ha. I did, as a matter of fact. How far you from home?'

'I'm on the A40 now, coming up to the Target roundabout.'

'I'm in Yeading. I'll head to yours and meet you there.'

Zaq hadn't been waiting long before Jags pulled into the drive-way. They carried their shopping bags inside and dumped them on the dining table.

'First thing we got to do is make sure these fit,' Zaq said, grabbing one of the wireless mics Jags had got and one of the smartphones he'd bought.

'They better, 'cause I sure as hell ain't driving all the way back over there to return them,' Jags grumbled.

Zaq unboxed the items, carefully in case they had to return

either one. After a quick look at the instructions, he pushed the wireless receiver into the headphone jack with no problem. 'Brilliant. It should work. Let's get them all charged up, then we can test them properly.'

Jags plugged both bits of equipment into power sockets in the lounge. Zaq unboxed the second phone and mic, and Jags took them through to the kitchen and plugged them in to charge. Next, Zaq checked out the shirts Jags had got. One was black, the other charcoal-grey, each with two breast pockets. The material was lightweight cotton but good quality.

'Which colour d'you want?' Zaq asked.

'I'll take the grey.'

Zaq threw it to him. 'Try it on. Make sure it fits OK.' He tried on the black one. It was a bit tight across the chest and shoulders but that was better than it being loose. Jags' seemed to fit him well too. Zaq took his off and draped it over the back of a dining chair. 'I'll sort them out tomorrow.'

'What d'you mean, sort them out?'

'So everything fits properly.'

'How d'you mean?'

'The stuff we bought – it's got to stay in place, can't move around. And the phones won't fit with the mic receivers attached.'

'Whatever, man, long as you know what you're doing.'

'I do, I think. I'm kind of making it up as I go along.'

'That really fills me with confidence.' Jags' tone made it clear it did nothing of the sort. 'What's the rest of this stuff for?'

'I'll show you tomorrow,' Zaq said. 'In the meantime, I need to get over to the hospital. Don't suppose you got anything to eat?'

'I got *rajma* and rice, and some *matar paneer* too.'

'How long's it been in your fridge?'

'I just picked it up from my mum's this morning on the way home from the gym.'

Having survived mostly on cereal, sandwiches and junk snacks for the past week, Zaq was all for it, and pretty soon they were eating spicy kidney beans along with the cubed Indian cheese and pea curry, poured over mounds of fragrant and flavourful pilau rice. Jags had even chopped up a little red onion and chilli and doused it in lemon juice, to sprinkle on for added zing. The offer of a nice cold beer was extremely tempting but Zaq opted for Coke instead. He'd still pick up some snacks on the way, to eat during the night, but at least they wouldn't have to serve as dinner.

When he got to the hospital, Zaq found his mum and dad sitting in Tariq's room, much as they had all week. They looked worn, and concern had deepened the lines in their faces.

'How is he?' Zaq asked.

'Same,' his dad said. 'He hasn't woken up yet but the doctor says he is doing OK, getting better slowly.'

It sounded like good news but his dad was frowning. Zaq knew why: it was because no one could say how Tariq would be when he woke up – whether he would make a full recovery or be left disabled and brain-damaged for life. He and his dad both knew it, but neither wanted to talk about it in front of Zaq's mum.

'All right. You guys go on home now.'

His father put his hands gently on his wife's shoulders. *'Ah, chalay,'* he said, and helped her up. They gathered their things and got ready to leave.

His mum looked at Zaq for the first time since he'd arrived, taking in the smudged bruises slowly fading from his face. 'How are you?' she asked. 'Are you OK?'

It was the first time she'd asked him about himself all week. 'I'm fine,' he told her, doing his best to smile. She touched him lightly on the arm then moved towards the door.

His dad gave him a gruff nod as he left. 'See you in the morning,' he said. 'And let us know if there's any change.'

Once they'd gone, Zaq turned the chair his mum had been sitting on so he could see both Tariq and the door. 'Come on, you div,' he said to his brother, 'you been asleep long enough. When you going to wake up and start being an annoying tit again?' He waited in the vain hope that his words might reach Tariq and provoke some sort of reaction ... but there was nothing. He continued to gaze at his brother and mentally told him: *I found the fuckers that did this to you and I'm going to get them.* He willed Tariq to receive the message and draw strength from it, no matter how unlikely that was.

Then he took the sheet of notes out of his pocket, and began to go over every detail, in preparation for what they were going to do next day.

Chapter Seventy-Three

Zaq dozed fitfully, not that he would have slept much in the hospital chair anyway. His mind was in overdrive throughout the night, constantly turning over possibilities. Eventually, the hushed sounds of night-time on the ITU ward gave way to the noise of the new day as the shifts changed and brought a rush of activity. By then Zaq was longing for his own bed and a few hours' proper sleep.

The day shift nurse came in and checked Tariq over, making notes on his chart. A little later the doctor came on his morning rounds, followed by a gaggle of junior doctors. It was the same doctor Zaq had spoken to last time.

'He's doing a lot better, physically speaking,' he told Zaq. 'We've been gradually reducing the meds that have been keeping him asleep. And now he's out of danger we've stopped them completely, so we just have to wait till he's ready to wake. His vital functions are all normal, the swelling to the brain – which was our main concern – has gone, and there's good activity. But we won't know exactly how he might have been affected by it – whether there's any cognitive impairment – until he wakes up and we can run some further tests.'

It was promising and worrying at the same time. 'So he could wake up soon?'

'When he's ready to, he'll come out of it. Then we can see how things are and what, if any, further action needs to be taken.'

'Thanks, doctor. I appreciate everything you're doing for him.'

'That's what we're here for,' the doctor said. He had a tired, kind face. He gave Zaq an encouraging smile and left to see the next patient.

So Tariq might wake soon – but what sort of condition would he be in when he did? That was the question hanging over all of them, the unspoken fear they all had. Zaq being sent to prison had been a major shock for the family but he was out now and they were all doing their best to forget about it. This was something else, something that could have a very real and permanent effect on all their lives. No amount of payback could make up for what Zaq stood to lose . . . but he was too far down that road now, and Donny, Satty and the others deserved to face the consequences of what they'd done. In that respect, it was a simple decision, to carry on and see things through.

His parents arrived a little later and Zaq told them what the doctor had said. He tried to spin it as positively as he could but there was no getting away from the fact Tariq might never be the same again. They all knew it, and hoped and feared in equal measure.

'I'll come back early today,' Zaq told his dad, 'so you can go home and get some more rest. Thing is, though, I really need to pop out for a couple of hours this evening. Could you come back then, just for a bit?'

'Why?'

'I just need to help Jags with something. Won't take long, and then I'll be straight back here.' That was what he hoped, at least.

His dad gave him a suspicious frown, a look Zaq knew well from his teenage years. Jags, though, was just as much a part of his family as he was of Jags'. To Zaq's mum and dad Jags was like an extra son. The two boys had gone through school and college together, remained close through university and gone on to land good jobs in the City. His parents had always viewed Jags as a good influence – something they were even more grateful for since Zaq had got out of prison – so there was never any issue with the two of them hanging out together. Mentioning that he was helping Jags, therefore, meant his dad grudgingly agreed to his request.

Sunday morning meant that his housemates were likely to be at home. It was still early when he got in and he could hear the snores from behind the doors of their rooms. They'd probably been drinking the night before and were sleeping it off, so he might be able to get some sleep before they woke up and started making a racket.

It was a little after nine o'clock, and he set alarms on his phone for one-thirty and two o'clock. He couldn't afford to sleep for any longer: he had things to do.

It might have been mental exhaustion, or simply the comfort of being in his own bed, or maybe some combination of the two, but, whatever the reason, he almost immediately fell into a deep sleep.

Zaq cracked open an eyelid, grabbed his phone and stopped the alarm. It was one forty-five and the alarm had been sounding, on and off, for a quarter of an hour. It felt as though he'd only just gone to sleep; his eyelids felt weighted, wanting to close of their own accord. He was tempted to turn off the second alarm and go back to sleep but then railed at himself – there were things to sort out. He could sleep later.

He forced himself out of bed and grabbed his towel. He could hear his housemates laughing and talking downstairs as he crossed the landing to the bathroom. The shower refreshed and revived him. He got dressed, then called Jags. 'I just got ready,' he told him.

'What d'you want, a medal?'

'I was thinking,' Zaq said, ignoring him, 'if I come over and eat at yours, we can get started on everything, otherwise I'll be a bit longer getting there.'

'I ain't your personal chef, you know.'

'OK, don't worry about it. I'll grab something here, then head over.'

Jags sighed. 'Nah, I can make something by the time you get here – and you're right, it'll save time. What d'you want? *Tutti* on toast OK?'

'I was thinking more like eggs.'

Jags sighed again. 'All right, cool.' And he rang off.

On his way out Zaq ducked into the communal kitchen/ lounge/diner where the guys were sitting around watching a cricket match and chatting. 'Listen, you lot,' he said, 'thanks for the other night. I mean it – you really might've saved Jags' uncle's life.'

'Man, them pussy clarts were nothing,' Bal declared. 'They ran soon as me and Manj started weighing in to them, didn't even put up a decent fight. I would've given them some proper licks, innit, five-to-one against an old *uncleji* like that. Fuckin' little shits. What's happening with them anyway? You know who they are?'

'Yeah, don't worry, I'm planning to sort them out.'

'Hope you manage it better than last time you had trouble. Seemed like you were getting your arse kicked every other day then.' He squinted and studied Zaq's face. 'Don't look like you're doing much better now.'

'Don't worry, it's all safe.'

Bal pulled a disbelieving face. 'If you say so. You need some proper back-up, just let us know, yeah?'

'I will; thanks, Bal.' Bal meant well, but involving him would be like taking a sledgehammer to a nut, an extreme solution to a more delicate problem. Manjit just nodded, letting him know everything was cool. When Bal was up on his high horse, giving it the bigun, the others knew to just let him talk. It was a lot easier that way. 'I got to get going,' Zaq said. 'But listen, I owe you all a drink.' That got a good response. 'So next weekend, yeah? I'll get the drinks in for all of us.'

Chapter Seventy-Four

'Here,' Jags said, putting a plate down in front of Zaq. On it was a thick slice of toast cut diagonally, and on each half a thick slice of ham with a fried egg, and cheddar cheese grated on top. 'You want ketchup or chilli sauce with it?'

'Man, this is great. Cheers, Jags. Chilli sauce.'

Jags brought over a bottle of Encona then went back to the kitchen. 'I'm just making tea.'

'Is all the stuff charged?' Zaq asked, around a mouthful of food.

'Yeah, it is.'

'OK, we'll go give it a quick test soon as I've eaten.' The eggs on toast were good and Zaq made short work of them. He'd almost finished by the time Jags brought over their tea and sat down. Zaq finished the last of his food then pushed his plate forward and sat back to take a sip of his hot, strong tea.

A frown was knitting Jags' brows.

'What's up?' Zaq asked.

Jags shrugged. 'Just . . . you really think this is going to work?'

'Can't say for sure, but why not?'

'It just seems a bit too simple.'

'Keeping it simple means there's less to go wrong.'

'But if anything does, we could both be in deep shit.'

'That's why we're going to test the stuff, make sure it all works, so there's less likelihood of any fuck-ups.'

'We're still relying on those guys to react the way we want. How d'you know they will?'

Zaq pulled out the piece of paper with his notes and laid it on the table. 'Let's go over it again. But this time, put yourself in their shoes.'

They went through it all, with Zaq asking Jags at each stage what he would do if he were in their position. It turned out he'd do pretty much the same thing they were hoping Shergill and the others would do. It seemed to reassure Jags and boost his confidence. They finished their tea and Zaq said, 'Right, I'll wash these dishes, then we need to head to the park.'

'The park? What we going to the park for?'

Zaq took the dishes to the sink. 'We got these phones so they can't be traced to us. Be a bit stupid if, first time we turn them on, it's right here in the house.'

The park in question was only a few minutes' walk from Jags' house. They went in through the open gate, and continued across the sun-bleached grass towards the far side. Zaq figured that if they were over by the busy Uxbridge Road it might make tracking the phone's signal more difficult.

They found a space away from other people and sat down. Zaq had a quick read of the wireless mic instructions, which were simple and straightforward. They took a phone each, stripped off the back, inserted a SIM card and closed them up again. They then turned on the phones and downloaded the software apps they'd need, before adding each phone's number to the other's contacts list. After that, they paired each mic with its transmitter and tested them with the phones, getting up and walking around to check the sound and signal quality. Both were better than Zaq had thought they'd be.

Back at the house, Zaq took out the shirts Jags had bought the day before and put the black one on. 'OK, you put on the grey one,' he told Jags.

'What for?'

'To figure out which side you want the phone on.'

Both opted for the left, then took the shirts off again. Zaq slipped one of the phones into the pocket of his shirt, with the screen facing inwards. The pocket was deep enough, but too wide for the phone to sit without moving around. 'It's got to stay in place,' he muttered. 'Where's the card you got yesterday? And the scalpel?'

Jags handed him the roll of thin card and the scalpel he'd bought. Zaq placed the phone on the card, so the top centimetre or two was off the edge of it. 'Can you get me a ruler and a pen as well?'

'Anything else the *sahib* might be wanting?'

Zaq shot Jags a dirty look. Jags went upstairs and returned with a plastic ruler and a pen. Zaq used them to measure and mark the card and then draw lines across it. He cut along the lines and ended up with a length of card slightly shorter than the phone but three or four times its width. He folded the card around the phone, so that one part was the same width as the shirt pocket, while the other part was a lot longer. He marked both the edge of the phone and width of the pocket on the longer section then folded the excess card back and forth on itself, to fill the gap, so that when he slid the phone and the sleeve into the pocket, it was just the right width for the pocket and the folds of card on the side held the phone firmly in place and stopped it moving.

'You should be on *Blue Peter*,' Jags said.

'Is that still on TV? Pass me the duct tape, will you?'

Jags handed it to him. Zaq cut off a short length of tape and wrapped it around the cardboard sleeve to reinforce the construction. Then he slipped it back into the shirt pocket, stood up and put the shirt on. The phone was held tight in place, no movement left or right. 'How's it look?' he said.

'I can hardly see it.'

'Brilliant. OK, let's do the other one.'

When he'd repeated the whole procedure with the other phone and shirt, he located where the headphone socket was in relation to the pocket of each shirt, and used the scalpel to make a careful incision at the rear of each pocket. He pushed the connector jack of the mic receiver through the little cut, and plugged it into the phone, so that the phone was hidden snugly in the pocket, and the receiver was hidden inside the shirt.

The last thing he had to do was find where the outward-facing camera lens was and use the scalpel again, to carefully cut a small circle out of the pocket directly in front of the lens to give an unobstructed view. From a distance, and in shadow, it should be unnoticeable.

Zaq tried the shirt on again. 'How about now?'

Jags took a step back and looked it over. 'Man, that's good – you can't see a thing. You sure it'll work?'

'Only one way to find out.'

When Zaq had finished the other shirt, they headed to the park once more, wearing the shirts and carrying the actual microphones with the small transmitter units in their other pockets. At the far side of the park, they took the phones out of the improvised holders and turned them on. Zaq opened the app and called the phone Jags was holding. Jags answered, so they were both connected. Zaq slipped the phone back into the card sleeve in his pocket, turned on the receiver and plugged it into the phone from inside his shirt. Then he turned on the microphone and walked away from Jags, talking as he went. About twenty metres away he stopped. Jags gave him a thumbs-up signal.

Zaq turned off his mic, unplugged the receiver, and took his phone out so he could check Jags' transmission. Both picture and sound were sharp and clear. He gave Jags a thumbs-up too. They turned everything off and went back to the house.

Chapter Seventy-Five

Nerves were starting to get to Zaq. It felt as if he had a swarm of butterflies fluttering around in his stomach. The day was getting away from them and it would soon be evening when, for better or worse, they would put his plan into action. They had to get what they wanted and deliver what he'd promised, otherwise things could go very badly for him and Jags. They couldn't afford any screw-ups. There'd be no second chances. That was why he'd got two of everything, so they had a back-up in case anything went wrong. There were still some things to sort out, but now Zaq needed to calm himself down, get his head straight and focus.

'I should've brought some workout gear,' he said, 'so I could do a couple of rounds on the bag.'

'There's some of your stuff upstairs,' Jags said. 'You left it here. It's all washed.'

'Nice one. All right if I go and use the bag?'

'Knock yourself out ... not literally.'

Zaq changed into shorts and a workout top, grabbed the key, went through the French doors and down the garden to the garage. Inside he put a mix CD on the old boom-box. As he had done many times, he warmed up – this time on the rowing machine – stretched, then wound a set of wraps around his wrists and knuckles, before pulling on a pair of bag gloves. He started slow, circling left and then right around the heavy bag, jabs followed up with quick combinations. The punches got faster and harder the more into it he got. Before long, he was adding forearm and elbow strikes, knees and the occasional kick.

He always imagined the bag as an opponent; this time he pictured Donny Shergill and Satty, and what he'd do to them. Concentrating on it helped clear his mind. It wasn't the violence of it so much as the mental focus on getting the moves and the techniques just right, and the sheer physical exertion. Soon he was throwing rapid flurries of punches, along with other strikes, attacks and counters, sweat flying off him. He managed to vent the anger and frustration that had been choking him, and when he finally stopped, spent, he felt calm and clear-headed, somehow lighter, as if all the worries that had been weighing him down had been lifted from him. The main thing now was what would happen later, and there was no point stressing about that unnecessarily. All he could do was see it through and hope everything worked out. And on the subject of what was going to happen later ...

He picked up his phone and made two calls. Each time, he ran through the plan and what he expected to happen. After each call he received a text message with a phone number he didn't know. With that taken care of, Zaq stretched, then picked up the sweaty wraps, locked the garage and went back to the house.

'Feel better?' Jags asked.

'Yeah, much.' Zaq threw the wraps in the washing machine. 'I called the others, let them know what's going to happen.'

'They all good with it?'

'Yep.' That didn't seem to wholly convince Jags, and Zaq wondered if he was feeling as nervous as he had earlier.

'Maybe you should go work out on the bag too. It'd help calm your nerves.'

'Nerves? Why would there be anything up with my nerves? It's not like we're going to try and do a deal with a bunch of rich prick psychos who've already killed a couple of people and want us out of the picture too. No, wait ... that's exactly what we're going to do, innit? It's going to take more than hitting a bag to calm my nerves. How the hell do I let you talk me into these things? I must need my head examining.'

'Mate, I been telling you that for years.'

Zaq showered and dressed. He thought about asking Jags for something else to eat before he headed to the hospital, but decided he didn't want to take the piss, especially not with Jags already so keyed up. 'Right, I'm going to make a move, let my mum and dad get off early so my dad can come back later and cover for me while we go do what we're going to do.'

'He OK with that?'

Zaq shrugged. 'Not exactly, but I told him I was helping you with something and wouldn't be too long. You know he likes you, for some reason?'

'It's 'cause he's a great judge of character.'

'Either that or he's losing his marbles.'

'Ha, ha. What time you coming back?'

'I reckon nine-thirty's a good time to do it, so we should probably get there about eight-thirty to set things up. I'll ask my dad to come and sit with Tariq from seven-thirty, so I can get here for eight. Double-check everything's fully charged so we can head straight out.'

'All right, cool. I'll have everything ready.'

'Make sure you call Lucky and get him here for eight too ... and just tell him what we agreed.'

'OK, will do.'

They shook hands and pulled each other into a hug. 'Go hit the bag or something,' Zaq said. 'Wouldn't hurt to be warmed up and ready, just in case. See you later.'

His parents were surprised to see him so early. His dad had clearly forgotten their conversation the previous evening, and Zaq's mother checked her watch with a confused look.

'I told Dad I was going to come early today,' Zaq explained, 'so you can both go. You've been here all week.'

Zaq's dad told her in Punjabi that it was true; he hadn't mentioned it because it'd slipped his mind. She turned back to Tariq, lying motionless as a carved effigy, just as he had been for the past eight and a half days. She seemed emotionally, physically and spiritually drained. Even her tears seemed to have dried up.

'*Chal phir, hum chaldeh huh,*' his dad said to her, and started gathering his things together. After a moment, she began to do the same.

Zaq said to his dad in a low voice, 'Can you come back for seven-thirty? Just for a while, so I can pop out and help Jags with that thing?'

His dad looked at him with a put-upon frown. But Zaq had been there every night for over a week and didn't think he was asking too much. After a moment his dad gave a nod.

'Thanks, Dad.'

Zaq positioned the chair the way he preferred, then settled down for the next few hours until his dad returned. It was still early, and he was too keyed up to feel tired. He'd made his usual pit-stop at the petrol station and picked up a couple of sandwiches, snacks and a drink. He figured he'd better eat now, give his food a chance to settle, so he wouldn't feel sick later when the nerves and adrenaline really kicked in.

He gazed at his brother as he ate, only half-seeing him, his attention elsewhere as he tried to work out if there was anything he might have overlooked.

Some time later, he focused intently on Tariq. 'Tonight's the night, mate,' he told him. 'Time for some payback.'

Chapter Seventy-Six

By seven-thirty, Zaq's dad still hadn't arrived, and Zaq was on edge. His right leg was bouncing and he didn't know what to do with his hands. Waiting was only making him more anxious.

It was almost a quarter to eight when his dad finally sauntered in. Zaq couldn't say anything as he was doing him a favour by coming at all.

'What's that?' Zaq said, pointing to the packet of biscuits his dad had in one hand. In the other he was carrying a book.

'Chocolate digestives,' his dad said.

'You didn't bring those from home.' They both knew Zaq's mum didn't allow him any biscuits. He was supposed to be on a diet, doctor's orders. Chocolate digestives were his favourites.

'I stopped on the way and got them. Seeing as I'll be here on my own, I'll make myself a nice mug of tea, have some of these, and read while I wait for you to come back.' He seemed quite pleased with himself.

'You ain't going to eat all of those?'

'I'll eat however many I eat, and give the rest to the nurses,' he said, grinning.

'All right, whatever. I got to go.' Zaq started for the door. Good job he'd allowed extra time.

'Don't say anything to your mum about this, OK?' his dad called after him.

Once in his car, Zaq called Jags. 'My dad got here late. I'm just leaving now. Did you call Lucky?'

'Yeah, told him to be here for eight, like you said.'

'Cool. I should get there about the same time. The stuff all charged and ready to go?'

'Yeah, it's all good.'

'Right, stick everything in a rucksack, the other bits too. We should leave as soon as we can. See you in a bit.'

Zaq didn't see Lucky's car when he pulled up outside Jags' house. 'Lucky not here yet?' he asked when Jags let him in.

'I told him to get here for eight, so he must be on his way.'

It was ten minutes past. 'Bloody hell, if everyone's going on Indian timing we'll be at this all night. Good job we ain't working to a strict timetable. You got a pen and some paper?'

In the lounge Zaq took out his phone, found the two messages he'd received earlier in the afternoon, and wrote down the phone numbers he'd been sent. He added another number from his call log, then put the paper in his pocket. 'Where shall I put this?' he said, holding up his own phone.

'Drawer in the kitchen, last one on the right.'

'OK. We might as well put the shirts on before Lucky gets here.'

They each put their shirt on over a T-shirt and buttoned it up. Zaq checked everything else was in the rucksack and zipped it shut.

A few minutes later, Lucky finally arrived. '*Kidaah*, boys?' he greeted them.

'Hey, Uncle.' Zaq said, putting his phone into the drawer. He'd left it turned on, even though he wouldn't be using it for the next couple of hours. Jags came and put his phone in the drawer next to Zaq's.

'You really think that *bhen chaud* will give the necklace back?' Lucky said as he and Zaq shook hands.

'I don't know,' Zaq replied. 'That's why you're coming along: in case anything goes wrong.' That didn't do much for Lucky's confidence. 'Come on, we better get going so we can get set up before we get them there.'

They took Lucky's car, Zaq directing them until they arrived at the warehouse in Hayes. Zaq jumped out, unlocked the padlock and swung the gates open. Lucky drove in and stopped.

'Go round the back of this warehouse and wait out of sight,' Zaq told him. 'I'll go in the main entrance. There's a fire exit at the back; I'll come out that way in a bit.' He watched Lucky drive along the side of the warehouse and disappear from view behind it. Zaq walked along the front of the building, noting with satisfaction that none of the security lights came on, and went to the shuttered main door. Just as he had that morning, he opened the two padlocks, threw the shutter up and unlocked the entrance. Once through the door, he pulled the shutter back down and locked the door from the inside.

There was just enough street light coming through the windows to allow him to pick his way along the corridor and into the warehouse proper. He found the panel of light switches and tried them until he'd turned on the two sections of lights he'd decided on earlier: just the middle sections at the front and centre of the big space. The rest of the place remained in shadow and darkness. Then Zaq went to the fire exit at the rear, pushed the bar down and went out, making sure the door stayed open, and walked over to Lucky's Mercedes to grab the rucksack. 'I'll need your help,' he said to Jags, 'to sort out some stuff inside.'

'What about me?' Lucky said. 'Shall I come in with you?'

'No, just wait here. We won't be long, then we'll come back out.'

Lucky didn't seem too thrilled about that, but Zaq ignored it and he and Jags went back inside.

Chapter Seventy-Seven

Zaq left the fire exit open to reassure Lucky. In the warehouse, the lights he'd turned on threw the shadows of the steel pillars across the concrete towards them. Zaq stopped between the front wall and the first line of pillars, at the edge of the lighted section.

'This should be about right.' He opened the rucksack and took out the burner phones, handing one to Jags. Then he took the piece of paper from his pocket. 'OK, let's add these numbers to our contacts.' He read out two of the phone numbers, and they saved both into their phones. Only Zaq typed in the third number and saved it.

Next, Zaq got out the mics, transmitters and the little receiver units that would connect to their phones. 'Let's just plug these in for now.' Then they switched on the mic units and paired them to the receivers. Once they were synced, Zaq looked around. 'We'll want those guys to be in the light so ... we'll be here ... You be them for a minute, and go over there.'

Jags moved into the light. They wouldn't want to shout at each other but they wouldn't want to be too close either. Zaq gauged a suitable distance of roughly three metres apart. But he realised he'd moved into the light himself. 'Let's move a bit,' he said, and they moved in unison, with him backing towards the shadows. 'Let me know when there ain't so much light hitting me.'

They took several paces then Jags said, 'That's fine. I can see you but the light's a lot dimmer.'

Zaq slipped his phone into his pocket. 'Can you see the phone?'

'Yeah, I can see the receiver sticking up.'

'Don't worry, that'll be hidden once we do it properly. I'm talking about the phone itself.'

'Nah, not really. Can sort of see the shape of it, but I know what I'm looking for.'

Zaq kicked a scrap of wood over to where he'd been standing to mark his position.

Jags looked around, found a length of blue nylon box strapping, and laid it on the floor where he'd been.

'OK, stay there, I'm going to call you.' Zaq turned on the mic transmitter and went over to the nearest steel supporting pillar. Stretching up, he could just reach the first shelf-like join. He placed the transmitter right up against the pillar, its coiled wire hidden beneath it. He manoeuvred the mic to the edge of the shelf, facing Jags.

Then he took out his phone from his pocket and went back to his original position, opened the app and called Jags, then put the phone back in his shirt pocket. He could hear a crackling sound as Jags answered. They'd have to turn down the volume on both phones when they were done with this.

'Wow, I'm really clear!' Jags exclaimed.

'How's the sound?'

'A bit weird. I can hear you speaking out loud and through the phone.'

'Go right over to that corner. You'll be able to tell better from there.' Jags walked towards the main shutter, and stopped. Zaq spoke as if Jags was still standing where the blue strap lay on the floor. 'If you could be anywhere else right now, where would you be?'

'In bed with Rita,' Jags called out.

'Fat chance of that ever happening.'

'I heard that too, you cheeky sod.'

'All right, come back over.' He waited for Jags to join him. 'It works, then? You wouldn't have been able to hear what I said otherwise.'

'It was really clear. Even though you were all the way over here, it sounded like you were right in front of me.'

'Great. Let me try now. I'll go that way.' Zaq jerked his thumb over his shoulder. 'Keep talking to me like I'm still just here.'

Jags tried to keep his voice at a steady volume. The further away Zaq moved from him, the fainter his actual voice got, yet the sound from the phone remained clear and constant. Jags was right, it was a bit strange.

They went through the same procedure with Jags' mic. Zaq placed the transmitter on another side of the same pillar but trailed the mic around so it too was facing towards Jags' mark. The wire was thin, the mic itself tiny. 'Can you see it from where you are?' Zaq asked.

'Not at all.'

'Cool. I'll turn the mics off for now, save their batteries.' Then Zaq and Jags turned off the receivers plugged into their phones and disconnected them for the time being.

'I'll make sure everything else is set,' Zaq said. He sent a message to each of the numbers he'd received earlier, and got two responses almost straight away. 'We're good to go,' he said to Jags. 'Time to invite that prick here.'

Chapter Seventy-Eight

The third and last number Zaq had saved into his burner phone was Shergill's. He rang it now.

'Hello?' Shergill answered. He wouldn't have recognised the number calling him.

'You got a pen and paper? I'll give you the address of where to come.'

'What sort of time do you call this? I've been waiting all—'

'I'm calling you now. It's up to you – the necklace, or the cops kicking down your door and dragging you and your son off to prison. You want the address or not?'

Shergill muttered to himself, then said, 'Give me the bloody address.'

Zaq gave him the address of the warehouse. 'It's the first one, facing the street. There's a fire door next to the shutter. It'll be open. Come alone and bring the necklace, or the deal's off. We'll be waiting.'

'Who's *we*?'

'Just me and my friend.'

'Two of you, and me on my own?'

'What the fuck're we going to do to you? Ain't like we're here to rob you. You just give us the necklace and we all walk away. Now get a move on.' Zaq didn't wait for him to whinge about anything else and hung up. 'Right,' he said to

Jags, picking up the rucksack, 'I doubt it'll take him long to get here. We better talk to Lucky, then sort out the last couple of bits.'

On the way to the fire exit, Zaq took out the roll of duct tape and put it on the floor, behind the next steel pillar along from where they'd set up the mics.

Lucky was a bag of nerves when they got to the car. 'What's going on?' he said, his words tumbling out in a rush.

'Shergill's on his way,' Zaq said. 'I told him to bring the necklace. He should be here soon.'

'You trust that fucker? I bloody don't.'

'That's why you're here. Anything goes wrong, you call the cops straight away.'

'What about the necklace?'

'These fuckers have killed two people already. I don't want me and Jags to be three and four. If we get the necklace, great; but if things go pear-shaped you call the bloody cops ... OK?'

'OK, fine,' Lucky said, like a man who'd just discovered his whisky had been switched for apple juice.

Jags scowled. 'You could at least *sound* like you care about us more than that flippin' necklace.'

Lucky just grunted.

'Jags'll have a message all ready to go, on his phone. If the shit hits the fan in there, he just has to press Send and you'll receive it straight away. Soon as you do, ring 999 and get the *mammai* here fast as you can. *Only* call them if you get Jags' message, though, not for any other reason, otherwise you'll mess everything up. You got that? *Only* when you get Jags' message.'

'*Haah, haah*, I got it.'

'Stay right here. Don't go wandering off. We don't want them to see you. And keep your phone handy.'

'*Oh, mehnu putha.*'

'Right, we better get back inside. We got a few last-minute things to do before he gets here.'

When they got to the open fire exit, Zaq rummaged for the nylon luggage strap he'd bought. He put it around the bar that opened the door from the inside and pulled until there was a tight loop around the bar and a long trailing end, which he fed under the door. 'I'll shut the door, you pull that end straight up, see if it opens it from the outside.'

He pulled the door closed. When Jags pulled on the strap outside, it pulled the bar down and the door swung open. 'Leave the end of the strap out there on the ground.' Jags did so and came in, Zaq shutting the door after him.

'What now?' Jags said.

'Let's go and turn the mics on.'

They returned to the marked places. Zaq reached up the steel pillar, and switched on both mics. Then he pulled out the improvised phone holders he'd made and they slipped them into their shirt pockets. Using his burner phone, Zaq made a group call to Jags and the two other numbers. Jags answered, and, once the other two numbers were logged into the call, he plugged the mic receiver in and turned it on to check the sound. Jags did the same. Everything worked OK. They turned down the speaker volume on their phones – they wouldn't need to hear anything – then unplugged the receivers, pushed the phones into the cardboard holders in their pockets and plugged the mic receivers back into the phones through the small, specially cut holes.

'How's it look?' Zaq asked.

'Can't tell you've got anything in there. Me?'

'Same. It doesn't show at all. I did a good job with the card.'

'You're a real art ninja.'

'Just one last thing to do.' Zaq went to the smaller fire door at the front of the building, pushed down on the bar to swing it open part-way and left it ajar. Then he came back and kicked the wood marker away into the shadows.

'What now?' Jags said.

'We wait.'

Chapter Seventy-Nine

'I think I need to take a dump,' Jags said. 'Either that, or I'm going to be sick.'

'It's just nerves, 'cause we're standing around waiting. Once he gets here, you'll forget all about it. Shouldn't be long now.'

Jags wasn't the only one feeling nervous. Zaq's stomach was tying itself into knots as well. A line of sweat trickled down his back, and it wasn't just the stuffy heat inside the warehouse causing it. A lot was riding on what would happen in the next hour or two, and he had no idea whether his plan would work. It was enough to make a polar bear at the North Pole sweat.

They talked to distract themselves, each trying to allay the other's fears and bolster their confidence. They kept their voices low, so nothing was picked up by the microphones.

They could hear traffic going by on the road outside, a lot lighter than it had been earlier. Eventually they heard a vehicle turning into the industrial site, and saw a flash of headlights through the open fire door as they swept across the front of the building. Zaq thought he heard more vehicles, but couldn't be certain, because of the roar of the powerful engine out front.

The two friends stood tall and prepared themselves.

The engine shut off and they heard more than one car door open and close, followed by approaching footsteps. The fire door was pulled open with a screech of metal on stone. One, two, three figures came in. Zaq hadn't turned on the lights in that far corner of the warehouse, but he had no problem identifying the first person through the door. The guy had to duck to get in; he stood over a foot taller than the other two and was built like the proverbial brick shithouse. After him came Shergill. Taj, the small guy with the moustache and the attitude, was last.

Zaq and Jags stayed put and let the trio come to them. As they moved into the light they could see that Shergill was wearing a flower-patterned summer shirt, cream chinos and loafers. The other two were dressed all in black as usual, so they looked like a pair of *desi* henchmen from a knockoff Bond movie.

Zaq knew where the piece of strapping was on the floor, marking where he wanted them. He'd estimated the distance well. They stopped just short of it, not close enough to be grabbed suddenly, but not so far away that they'd need to shout. If trust could be measured by physical proximity, it was clear neither side trusted the other. They would, however, have to speak louder than normal, which was perfect for the mics to pick up.

'I told you to come alone,' Zaq said.

'You brought your friend, so I brought a couple of people too.'

'All right, let's get this over with. Give us back the necklace and we can all go home.'

Shergill barked a laugh. 'That's it, huh? After everything you've threatened me with? I'm just supposed to accept that'll be the end of it – that you'll just walk away and keep quiet; that you won't try to use it against me later?'

Zaq had expected this reaction – in fact, he'd counted on it. 'We just want the necklace,' he said. 'That other stuff's got nothing to do with us. Give us what we want and we'll forget all about it.'

'Ha! You really think I'm dumb enough to believe that?

Why the hell would I trust you? Once you have what you want, there's nothing to stop you going to the police, especially to clear yourselves. That's not a risk I'm willing to take. I have a better solution.'

'And what's that?'

Shergill gave an evil grin. 'We finish what we started.'

'Meaning what?'

'Simple – I don't let either of you walk out of here. Problem solved.'

Shergill nodded to Taj and the giant. They pulled up their T-shirts, exposing what looked like knife handles shoved into the waistbands of their tracksuit bottoms, and pulled the blades out. Only they weren't knives ... they were machetes.

'You two must be really stupid, to think you can tell me what to do and just walk away.'

'And you were worried about trusting us?' Zaq said. 'You're right, though ... after all the shit you've pulled, we would've been stupid to trust you. That's why we didn't. You make a move towards us, we've got a message all ready to send to Lucky.' Jags put his hand in the pocket of his jeans. It was a bluff, though; his pocket was empty. 'Soon as he gets it, he'll call 999 and have the cops here, before you can scratch your arse. He knows everything too, and if he don't hear from us in twenty minutes he'll go straight to the cops and tell them all about you, your son, and the murders.'

Shergill's eyes narrowed. 'I was wondering why he wasn't here. Where is he? At home? While we finish with you, I'll send someone straight over to his place to take care of him before he goes to the police.'

At that moment, scuffling sounds came from outside the fire door Shergill had entered through. The door screeched open and a group of six men barged in dragging someone between them, who was struggling to break free. The last one pulled the fire door partly closed.

Zaq recognised the captive being brought towards them. It was Lucky.

Chapter Eighty

Two guys threw Lucky sprawling to the ground in front of Zaq and Jags. Jags knelt and helped his uncle to his feet.

'I ... I'm sorry, boys,' Lucky said, his voice shaky. 'I didn't see them. I thought I saw a car go by – then all of a sudden these *ma chauds* were dragging me out of my car, punching me, kicking me ...'

'Don't worry about it, Uncle.'

Shergill's eyes gleamed and a grin scythed across his face. 'Well, well,' he said. 'Looks like Lucky's not so lucky after all, huh? Not at home, where he might have had a chance to get to the police before we got him, but right outside. Of all the places he could have been! You three really are stupid.'

Donny and Satty pushed their way forward and stood like a pair of puffed-up cockerels, staring malevolently at Zaq and Jags.

'We got a fucking bone to pick with you two,' Donny announced. 'And you, old man,' he sneered at Lucky.

'Not you on your own, though, right?' Zaq said. ''Cause you'd shit your pants. Only tough now there's nine of you.'

'We'll see who's shitting themselves in a minute.'

'I owe you for what you did outside the pub too,' Satty chimed in

Another man pushed his way to the front. 'Remember me, you fucking arseholes?'

'You managed to find some clothes, then?' Zaq said. It was the guy they'd stranded naked in the woods near Black Park.

'Yeah, no thanks to you two fuckers. When I heard we were going to get you today, I went out and got this specially.' He pulled a small metal rod from his back pocket and extended the steel baton with a hard flick of his wrist.

'Donny,' Shergill said, 'make sure there's no one else here, huh?'

Donny delegated the task to another of the guys, who went to take a look around the rest of the warehouse, then disappeared to check the offices and other rooms.

'There's no one here,' Zaq told Shergill.

'I'd rather make sure.'

'Why? So there are no witnesses to what you're going to do to us?'

Shergill grinned like a shark. 'Exactly.'

'So, rather than accept the money that's owed to you, plus interest, and return something that don't belong to you, you'd rather kill us, is that it?'

'You understand perfectly,' he said, with a typically Indian twist of the hand to emphasise the point. 'You're a bloody annoyance, buzzing around like flies that won't go away. So I'll do to you just what I'd do to a fly ...' He clapped his hands together, the sound echoing like a gunshot in the empty space, then brushed his hands, as if cleaning something off them. 'Then you won't be bothering me any more.'

Zaq heard footsteps from behind as the guy who'd gone to check out the rest of the place came back. 'There's no one else here,' he confirmed.

'What about Kang?' Zaq asked, sensing his time was limited. 'Why kill him?'

Shergill still grinned, clearly enjoying having the upper hand.

'Are you thinking of filming or recording all this?' He chuckled to himself. 'It doesn't matter if you do, you know that, right? You're not going anywhere, and once we're done with you we will take your phones or any cameras and destroy them. No one will ever see or hear anything that happens here tonight. So you can ask away. It won't make any difference.'

'What if the cops are listening?'

Shergill's gang visibly tensed, and even Shergill was disconcerted for a moment. But then the grin crept back. 'He's bluffing,' he told his men. 'If the police were here, why was that idiot sitting outside in the car? And if they'd been to the police already we'd be under arrest by now, not standing here listening to this rubbish. What would he have told them, anyway? A fairy story with no proof? Certainly not enough to get them to put on a big operation to watch this place. And talking of proof . . . ' Shergill's grin grew wider. 'They may not have any, but we do. Donny . . . where's the briefcase?'

Chapter Eighty-One

'It's in the boot of the car,' Donny said.

'Perfect.' Shergill raised his voice almost theatrically, like an actor hamming to the crowd, demonstrating his own cleverness. 'When we're done with these fools, we'll leave the case, and what's in it, here with them.'

Zaq realised what he meant. 'You mean Kang's case, the one that was taken when he was killed? When you killed him?'

'Taking the case made it look more like a robbery. If we'd left it, the police would have been looking for some other reason for what happened.'

'Why the fuck did you have to kill him?'

'I couldn't trust him any more. He was scared. You saying you'd go to the police made him panic. People talk, especially in our community, and he didn't want the police poking into his business, damaging his reputation. And he was babbling some rubbish about the government too. The *bhen chaud* told me to give the necklace to you to avoid any trouble. He should have kept his mouth shut and not talked to you. I didn't know who else he might blab to. And if the police did turn up at his door he would have told them everything. I couldn't have that, so I had him taken care of.'

'By sending your boy and his friend to murder him?'

'I ain't a fucking boy,' Donny snarled.

'No,' Shergill said, 'just to put him in the hospital, actually, so he would get the message not to talk. But he had a heart attack.' He shrugged dismissively. 'These things happen. He should have taken better care of himself. But now you've presented us with the perfect way to tie the matter up to our advantage. We'll leave the case here with you, so it will look as if you were the ones who robbed Kang and then you fought over the jewellery – a disagreement among thieves – and each died from your injuries.'

'Aw, theri ma di phudi,' Lucky swore at Shergill.

'No one's going to believe that,' Zaq said.

'Who cares?' Shergill replied. 'As long as it diverts attention away from us.'

'It ain't just Kang's murder you're all linked to.'

'That was Donny's business,' Shergill said. 'I didn't know about that at the time.'

'I know all about his business ... ganging up on people and beating the shit out of them when they ain't expecting it.'

'What other murder? What the fuck you talking about?' Donny demanded.

'Ain't you heard?' Zaq said. 'The guy you attacked in Brookside Park – Kush – he died in hospital yesterday.'

'I don't know what you're on about.'

'Yeah, you do. You and that piece of shit ...' Zaq nodded at Satty.

'Fuck you,' Satty responded.

' ... went and beat Sharan up, got Kush's name and number from her.'

'She fucking talked to you?' Donny's eyes flashed. 'Wait till I see that mouthy bitch; I'll teach her a fucking lesson she won't forget.'

'It'll be some wait. She's gone – and I don't think she's coming back. Turns out she don't like being beaten up by a little prick who thinks he's a big man.'

Donny was visibly seething. 'I'm really going to enjoy smashing your fucking face in.'

'Like you did with Kush, huh?'

'Fuck that cunt. He had it coming.'

'Why? 'Cause he talked to your girlfriend – sorry, *ex*-girlfriend? You thought he was competition?'

'Competition? He was no competition to me, just a shitty DJ working at some crappy wedding we went to, trying it on with my girl.'

'And that's why you started a fight with him?'

'He's the one that started it.'

'By trying to stop you roughing Sharan up.'

'Fuck him. He should've kept his fucking nose out of it.'

'So it all kicked off, and you were the ones that got thrown out.'

'We were going anyway. It was a shit do.'

'But you were still pissed off about it, and then you saw the other DJ in Uxbridge, Kush's mate, the one that stepped in to break things up. You jumped him when he left the pub, beat him up so bad you put him in a coma.'

Donny frowned. 'I don't know what you're talking about.'

'Yeah, you do. You and your mates jumped him last Friday night.'

'What makes you think it was us?'

''Cause I been looking for the fuckers that did it all week and it's led me straight to you two.'

'Why we chatting to these arseholes?' Satty said, bumping his fists together. 'Let's just fuck them up.'

'Why're you so interested in that, anyway?' Donny asked. 'What the fuck's it got to do with you?'

'That guy you beat up last week, the other DJ – he's my brother.'

Realisation dawned on Donny's face and Satty's. 'I thought you were just after the necklace.'

'Yeah, that too. I was helping my mate and his uncle out. It's just a coincidence that it was your old man happened to take the necklace. I was coming after you anyway, I just didn't know there was a connection at first.'

'And here we are,' Donny said, spreading his hands wide. 'You've got me at last, or should I say – I've got you?'

'Like you got Kush, huh? You beat up your girlfriend to get his details, and then what? You called him out to Brookside Road with some bullshit story?'

'That's right. I phoned him, said I wanted to talk about hiring him for a big party. When he got out of his car, we grabbed him and dragged him into the park . . . and yeah, we did him over. So what? What the fuck you going to do about it now?'

'If someone hadn't found him, he would've died right there where you left him. Doctors couldn't save him, though. He's dead 'cause of you.'

'Boo fucking hoo. Cocky motherfucker got what was coming to him. He was begging us to stop . . . but I showed him what happens when you fuck with me.'

'Yeah, you're real tough when there's a whole bunch of you against one person.'

'Well, you're going to find out, aren't you?'

Zaq thought he'd got enough. '*JALEBI, JALEBI, JALEBI!*' he yelled.

Everyone stared at him as if he'd gone mad.

Chapter Eighty-Two

'He's lost the fucking plot,' Satty jeered.

'Shitting himself, 'cause he knows what's going to happen,' Donny added.

'Oh, I know what's going to happen, all right,' Zaq said. He backed up a step, causing Jags and Lucky to do the same.

'Enough of this *bakwas*,' Shergill barked. 'Just take care of them and let's get out of here. I've got better things to do than stand around in this *bhen chaud* warehouse all night.'

'Come on, then,' Donny ordered his little posse.

Shergill nodded to Taj and the giant. 'Help them.'

The group started to spread out and approach Zaq, Jags and Lucky, who were backing away.

'There ain't no getting out of here,' Donny told them. 'If you run, you won't make it outside.'

'Who said we're going to run?'

Donny frowned, not understanding. The others continued to advance, the guy they'd left in the woods scraping the end of his steel baton along the floor and eyeing Zaq with bad intentions.

Just when Zaq thought the posse might lose patience and rush them, he heard what he'd been listening out for – the loud scrape of metal on concrete, followed by footsteps. 'Oi!' someone shouted.

Shergill's gang spun around as a group of about fifteen men

came in through the fire door behind them. Unlike Donny's gang of young thugs, these men were older, bigger and better armed. They were tooled up with baseball bats, pickaxe handles, swords, pistols and even a shotgun.

The last guy in slammed the fire door shut and they all advanced in a loose line. There was another crash from the rear corner behind Zaq and Jags as someone pulled on the luggage strap and opened that fire door. Through it came another large group, who shut the door behind them. There were another fifteen, but younger, closer in age to Donny's little band. They too were armed, with metal bars, bats, knives and chains. The two groups surrounded Shergill's smaller group and Zaq, Jags and Lucky.

'What the hell's going on?' Shergill demanded uncertainly. 'Who are you?'

'Shut up,' someone told him and whipped a pistol up, hitting him on the side of the head. Shergill cried out, stumbled sideways and fell to his knees. Blood ran down the side of his face.

'HEY!' Donny shouted. Two other guys immediately levelled guns at him.

The guy standing over Shergill grabbed him by the collar, dragged him towards Donny's group, and threw him on the ground. 'You fuckers better drop what you're holding,' he said calmly.

Taj and Shergill's big minder glanced at each other, then placed their machetes on the ground. The guy with the baton put it down as though it had suddenly become red hot.

'Was it enough?' Zaq asked the man with the pistol.

'Yeah, it was enough,' the gunman said.

Donny had helped his dad up. 'What the fucking hell is going on?' Shergill demanded, touching his face and looking at the blood on his fingers.

Zaq answered. 'You were right,' he said, 'we really would've been stupid to trust you. So good job we didn't. When you caught Lucky outside, you thought you'd totally fucked our back-up plan ... that's what we wanted you to think. Grabbing Lucky out there made you all big-headed, thinking you'd out-smarted us and that was it.'

'So what was I doing out there?' Lucky said indignantly.

'Sorry, Uncle,' Jags apologised. 'It was part of the plan.'

'*Bhen chaud*, what plan?'

Zaq explained. 'With Lucky caught and in here with us, you thought you had us all. You didn't give a shit if we were trying to record or video you, 'cause you knew we weren't going to leave here alive. Like you said, you'd take our phones and find any other cameras afterwards, so you weren't worried about that. Except ...'

There was total silence, everyone listening to Zaq.

' ... we weren't recording you or making a video, at least not like you thought, to take to the cops. If we'd been doing that, we really would've been fucked. No, what we *were* doing was live-streaming everything to a Skype group video call. Not to the police, though. Me and Jags here were both filming you, mainly for the benefit of two others who were watching and listening to everything. I should probably introduce them.'

The guy with the pistol pushed his way through Donny's group and came to join Zaq.

'This is Tonka ... who just happens to be Mr Kang's brother-in-law.' He let that sink in for a moment. Another man came to join them and Zaq said, 'And this is Gugs, Kush's cousin. He's here with some of Kush's friends and family.' Zaq paused again. 'And they both just heard you confess to their murders.'

Chapter Eighty-Three

When trying to come up with a plan, Zaq had kept the acronym K.I.S.S. – Keep It Simple, Stupid – very much in mind. The more complicated it was, the more could go wrong. The plan he'd managed to devise had certainly been simple, but also effective.

He'd intended all along to use Lucky as a decoy to make Shergill think he'd got everyone involved, and so encourage him to talk. Zaq had been careful to steer things away from mentioning the value of the necklace. Sure, for Tonka and Gugs this was all about family honour, but fifteen million pounds could easily complicate things. Even now, he'd have to make sure Shergill didn't try and use the necklace to bargain his way out.

Tonka's and Gugs' groups had been waiting in cars, not too close to the warehouse, but near enough that they could be there in a matter of minutes. The good thing about using the mobile phone network was that they didn't have to be close by; they could be anywhere with a decent phone signal and still be able to see and hear everything perfectly. With the phones hidden in their pockets, though, Zaq and Jags wouldn't have been able to pick up Shergill's gang's voices well enough, so they'd needed the wireless mics to make sure Tonka and Gugs heard exactly what was said.

The video call had been live-streaming even before Shergill

and his men got there and the plan had been for Tonka and Gugs to start recording it and drive closer as soon as they saw Shergill arrive. When Zaq gave the signal, shouting *jalebi* three times, they'd left the cars and approached on foot, Gugs' lot going around the back while Tonka and his guys came in through the front fire door.

'You remember our deal?' Zaq asked Tonka and Gugs. They both nodded.

'You better hurry up, though,' Tonka told him. 'I ain't going to wait all night for you.'

'Don't worry, I shouldn't take long.' Zaq walked up to Shergill, who was still bleeding. 'Where's the necklace?'

Shergill gave him a hard stare, anger and defiance now over-riding any fear he might have felt. 'I didn't bring it.'

'That's no surprise. Let's go and get it. You and me, right now. We drive to your place, pick it up and come back. Everyone else waits here. Try anything funny and you'll never see your son again.'

'Fuck off,' Donny said.

Shergill seemed to be calculating. He said, 'Let me and Donny go, and I'll give you the necklace in exchange.'

There was a clamour as the others realised what Shergill was proposing – and that it didn't include any of them.

'Shut up,' Tonka ordered. They did.

'In case you hadn't noticed, you ain't in any position to negotiate,' Zaq told Shergill. 'Now let's go and get what don't belong to you.'

Shergill's eyes flicked around, searching for some way out. It was only a matter of time before he'd try to buy his way out by offering the necklace to Tonka and Gugs. If he did, it could make things a lot more difficult for Zaq, Jags and Lucky. Zaq knew he had to prevent Shergill blabbing and get him out of there. He strode towards Shergill. 'Come on. Quit wasting time and let's go.'

Shergill started to say something but Zaq walked right up to him and punched him in the gut – not really to hurt him, as much as to stop him mentioning the necklace's fifteen-million-pound price tag. The big man wasn't expecting it and doubled over, gasping for air.

'Hey, you motherfucker,' Donny yelled.

Zaq was about to push Shergill towards the exit when Tonka growled, 'Enough of this shit,' went over to Shergill's man-mountain of a minder and raised his gun, pointing it right between the bigger man's eyes. Everyone froze. 'You fuckers are trying my patience,' Tonka said. Then he dropped his arm and shot the minder in the foot.

The gunshot made everyone jump, the sound reverberating around them. The giant let out a scream and fell to the floor. Tonka pointed the gun at Donny, and said to Shergill, 'Now get a fucking move on or the next bullet's for him.'

'OK, OK,' Shergill wheezed, hands up in a placatory gesture.

Donny didn't say a word or move a muscle, not with Tonka's gun still on him.

'Jesus, Tonka,' Zaq said.

'What? It won't kill him.'

Zaq swallowed, his mouth suddenly dry. Shooting people hadn't been part of the deal. 'OK, look, take Donny's phone. I'll call you on it from his old man's. You don't hear from me, you know what to do.' He hoped Tonka knew that meant to rough the captives up as he saw fit and then to hand the recorded confessions over to the police – and not actually shoot Donny or anyone else. Even though it hadn't been part of the plan, Zaq had to admit it'd done the trick.

'Phone,' Tonka said to Donny. He didn't need to be told twice.

Zaq disconnected the mic receiver and took the phone and cardboard out of his pocket. He ended the video call and shut off the phone, before handing it to Jags. 'Sort this out for me.' What he meant was, take it apart and remove both the battery and the SIM card. None of the phones used for the Skype call would ever be used again. They would all be destroyed. 'Get these guys together,' he said to Jags. 'Grab all their phones, and tape their mouths up so you don't have to listen to them. I left some duct tape over there. And see if you can find them something to tie around his foot.' He pointed to the big minder, lying on the floor with blood seeping from his wound.

'Right, get your phones out,' Jags ordered the group as he moved away.

'You too,' Zaq said to Shergill, who had recovered from the punch. 'Give me your phone.' Shergill gave him a dirty look but handed over his phone. 'Car keys too.' Zaq held out his hand for them and Shergill dropped them in his palm.

'It ain't far,' Zaq told Tonka. 'Only in Iver. Won't be busy this time on a Sunday, so I shouldn't be too long. I'll call in about ten minutes.'

'We'll be waiting.'

Zaq shoved Shergill towards the fire door. 'Let's go for a drive.'

Chapter Eighty-Four

Zaq pressed the key fob to unlock the Jaguar SUV parked in front of the warehouse. 'You drive,' he told Shergill, and got in the passenger side. 'You got any tissues or wipes in here?'

'In there,' Shergill grunted, indicating the glove compartment.

Zaq looked inside, took out a pack of tissues, opened it and handed them over. 'Get that blood off your face as best you can. Last thing we want is the cops to stop us. That wouldn't be good for Donny at all.'

Shergill's jaw was set and he was breathing heavily through his nose. His top lip twitched as if he wanted to sneer, but he kept his mouth shut. He took the tissues and pulled down the sun visor mirror so he could see what he was doing. He dabbed away the fresh blood but had to rub harder at the dried stuff.

'Shove the used tissues in the door pocket,' said Zaq, putting on his seatbelt. He handed Shergill the keys. 'Let's go.'

Shergill reversed then drove out of the industrial site on to the main road. Nearly all the shops were closed, which meant the roads were fairly quiet. Zaq knew the area well from all his deliveries in this part of west London and he directed Shergill, looking at the Jaguar's sat nav screen now and again just to make sure he was right. He took them through Hayes and Botwell, into Hillingdon where they passed the hospital where Tariq and his dad were at that very moment. That knowledge hardened Zaq's resolve to see things through.

Instead of carrying on through Uxbridge, he told Shergill to skirt the Brunel University campus and go through Cowley, turning on to a B-road that would take them to Iver. The houses thinned out gradually until there were long stretches with no houses, and no streetlights either. Traffic was sparse.

They hardly spoke, but, after they'd crossed a bridge over the M25 motorway, Zaq asked, 'Who'll be at home?'

Shergill didn't answer, holding the steering wheel tight and grimly looking straight ahead.

'All right, what's the code for your phone?'

Shergill maintained his stubborn silence.

'Fine,' Zaq said. 'Suit yourself. But, if they don't hear from me, they'll think something's happened, and they might put a bullet in Donny. I'd say they've waited long enough to be getting a little edgy.'

'One-nine-nine-six,' Shergill said though gritted teeth. 'If anything's happened to him ...'

'What're you going to do?' Zaq snapped. 'You had every chance to give the necklace back. Lucky even gave you twice what he owed you, but that wasn't enough. You want to blame someone for what's happening now, look in the fucking mirror.'

They came to a mini-roundabout and turned on to Iver High Street. Zaq entered the code to unlock the phone, found Donny's name in the contacts and called the number. The phone rang for some time before someone answered. 'Tonka?'

'Zaq?'

'How's it going over there?'

'OK. We're just waiting on you. A deal's a deal, right. What's happening your end?'

Zaq kept his eyes on Shergill as he talked, in case he decided to try anything. 'We're almost at the house but the guy's in a strop and won't answer my questions. I was hoping you could help convince him. I'll put you on speaker.'

Shergill threw Zaq a glance as the speaker crackled to life.

'Right,' came Tonka's voice, 'I got his boy here. You want me to rough him up?'

'If that's what it takes.'

'Wait ...' Shergill said, as they heard a ripping sound and a yelp.

'That was just the tape, you pussy,' Tonka said.

'Dad—' Donny's voice was cut off by the dull smack of a punch.

'All right, stop!' Shergill yelled. 'I'll give you what you want. Just leave him alone.'

'He gives you any more hassle,' Tonka said, 'let me know. Maybe we'll cut off a finger next ...'

It looked to Zaq as though Shergill had got the message. 'Thanks, I will. Can you pass the phone to Jags?' A moment later, Jags came on and Zaq took it off speaker. 'Listen, I'll be at the house soon. I'll call you when I'm there, again when I've got the necklace, and then when we're on our way back. Anything happens and you don't hear from me, tell Tonka. He'll know what to do.' Zaq ended the call. 'Now,' he said to Shergill, 'who's at home?'

'No one,' came the surly answer.

'Where's your wife?'

'I told you we had plans tonight. We were going to a dinner party. I told her I had some business to take care of, so she went on her own.'

'What time's she coming back?'

'I don't know. Late.'

'Good.' Hopefully, they'd be in and out well before she returned. 'And there's no one else there?'

'No.'

Zaq believed him. Each time he'd been there, he hadn't seen anyone else apart from the people that were now accounted for.

The road bent sharply to the left, then right, and a little further on they left Iver behind. The small houses gave way to trees and the dark expanse of open fields on either side. They passed a tyre place and came to a T junction, with a mini-roundabout in the middle and a pub diagonally across from them. Shergill was already indicating and in the lane to turn right.

There were no streetlights on the road they turned on to, and darkness pressed in around them. Thick hedges and trees hemmed them in on either side, with sometimes a wall flashing by that belonged to one of the hidden properties set back from the road. The route was dead straight, and a few minutes later Shergill signalled, slowed down and turned off the road at his house.

Chapter Eighty-Five

The gates began to open automatically as the Jaguar rolled up. They drove through and continued up to the house. Security lights came on, illuminating the broad parking area. Zaq noted the security cameras mounted on the front of the house.

Shergill stopped the car and turned off the engine.

'Hang on,' Zaq told him. He unlocked the phone and called Donny's number again. Jags answered. 'I just got to the house. We're going in. I'll call you when I've got the necklace.' He hung up. 'Remember, don't try anything funny. They don't hear from me in a few minutes, you know what'll happen to Donny. Right, let's go.'

Shergill grunted, and they got out of the car. He opened the front door and switched on the hallway lights. The alarm system's warning tone sounded repeatedly and Zaq watched closely as Shergill entered the code to turn it off. He had to trust that the guy was sufficiently worried about his son that he wouldn't enter a distress code to alert someone.

With the alarm silenced, the house was still and quiet. Zaq waited for any sign that someone else might be present, but none came.

'OK, where's the necklace?'

'Upstairs.'

'Lead the way.'

'It's in my bedroom. That's private.'

Was he fucking kidding? 'Suit yourself.' Zaq started to make a call.

'OK, OK.' Shergill flapped his hands, urging Zaq to stop.

He led the way across the hall, up the stairs and towards the rear of the house. He opened a door on the left, went in and turned on the lights. Zaq followed him into a huge bedroom. Against the far wall was a king-size bed, nightstands and lamps on either side. At the foot of the bed was a low, heavy-looking storage unit, on top of which, facing the bed, sat a big flatscreen TV. The right wall was made up of floor-to-ceiling windows, with a glass door that opened on to a terrace overlooking the now-dark garden. The lighting was from recessed spots in the ceiling that shone down on to a soft, thick-pile cream carpet.

There was a door in each corner, either side of the bed. Through the one on the right, Zaq could see an en-suite bathroom. Shergill crossed the room to the other door and went through it, with Zaq close behind him. It turned out to be a large walk-in dressing room. Through an identical door on the far side, slightly ajar, Zaq could see another bedroom. Half the dressing room was filled with men's clothing, shoes and accessories, the other half with women's. Zaq guessed the other bedroom had to be Mrs Shergill's.

Shergill went to one of the full-height fitted wall units and said, 'Look the other way.'

'You must be joking. I ain't turning my back on you. I'm only here for the necklace. I don't give a shit about anything else you've got.'

With a sullen expression, Shergill slid his hand inside the wall unit and there was a loud click. Zaq's heart leapt in his chest, the unexpected sound pushing a surge of adrenaline through him. He was ready to pounce at the slightest hint of Shergill bringing a weapon out. Instead Shergill pulled the central section of the wall unit towards him and swung it to the side on some sort of special mechanism.

Zaq craned forward and saw the door of a wall safe, roughly half a metre square, with an electronic keypad.

'At least let me open this with some privacy.'

'Not a chance. Hurry up.'

Shergill covered the keypad with one hand as he tapped in the code. Zaq heard four beeps followed by a longer one, and then the sound of the electronically controlled bolts being drawn back. Shergill pulled the safe door open to reveal piles of cash, jewels and various papers and files. Zaq watched intently as he reached in and pulled out a dark blue velvet bag.

'Here,' Shergill grunted, thrusting the bag at Zaq. 'Here's what you wanted.'

'Open it,' Zaq told him, 'and show it to me.'

Shergill huffed like a schoolboy with the hump, but opened the top of the bag and shook the necklace out into his hand.

Zaq saw straight away that it really was the necklace Lucky had drawn, and strikingly similar to the picture Kang had shown them in his shop. 'OK, put it back in the bag and give it to me.'

Shergill did as he was told and handed it over. It felt lighter than Zaq had expected. The necklace and the stones felt solid enough, but he didn't feel as though he was holding something worth fifteen million pounds in his hand.

Shergill was about to close the safe when Zaq said, 'Hang on a minute. Lucky only owed you ten grand, but you took another ten off him and didn't even give back the right necklace. I think you need to give that extra ten back.'

'*Theri bhen di . . .*' Shergill cursed.

'What are you moaning about? You've got the ten he actually

owed you from the card game, so everything's square. Ain't like you're losing out, so stop being such a greedy bastard and get it.'

Shergill reached into the safe again and pulled out a brown envelope. It looked a lot like the one Zaq and Jags had brought with them the second time they'd come to see him.

'Take out the money and count it.'

'I thought we needed to get—'

'Just do it.'

Shergill cursed again, sat down on a padded bench in the middle of the room, and pulled out a handful of fifty-pound notes. 'Fifty .... a hundred ... one-fifty ... two hundred ... two-fifty ...'

Once he got to a thousand Zaq could see there was roughly nine times that amount remaining, and said, 'OK, that looks like ten grand. Stick it back in the envelope and let's go.'

Shergill stuffed the notes into the envelope and gave it to Zaq, who shoved it in the back pocket of his jeans. He let Shergill shut the safe and swing the section of wall unit back in front of it. When it was done, there was no way to tell there was anything was behind it.

Zaq let Shergill go ahead of him into the bedroom. Halfway to the door Zaq told him to stop. He took out Shergill's phone and called Donny's number.

When Jags answered, he said, 'I've got it. We're just leaving to come back now.'

Chapter Eighty-Six

At the top of the stairs, Zaq remembered the security cameras outside. 'Where's the CCTV saved?' These days there'd be no tapes or DVDs; the footage would be on a hard drive or a digital video recorder somewhere in the house.

'Huh? Oh ... they're just dummy cameras,' Shergill shrugged.

'Bullshit.' You didn't shell out for a place like this, fill it with expensive gear and then skimp on the security. Shergill even had two minders on his payroll. He had to be lying about the cameras. Zaq took out the phone again. 'We can ask Donny instead, maybe break a finger or two so we know he'll tell the truth. Then, if he says the cameras are dummies, I'll believe it.'

Shergill gave him a baleful stare. Zaq gave him a couple of seconds, then began entering the security code.

'All right, I'll show you! Just put the phone down.'

Zaq looked up, but kept a finger hovering over the phone as if deciding whether to go ahead anyway. This time he was the one giving the baleful stare, hoping to make it clear he didn't appreciate being messed around. 'Get going, then,' he said.

Shergill led the way downstairs and across the hall to his office. He turned on the lights and headed to his desk with Zaq right behind. One of the two computer monitors was still on. Then Zaq saw that it wasn't a monitor at all, but a live feed from the security cameras around the property. The screen was divided into six sections, each covering a different part of the house, one showing the hall they'd just walked across.

'Where's it all saved?' Zaq said.

Shergill pointed to the right side of the desk, where Zaq saw purpose-built sections that housed a computer and other equipment. He looked under the top of the desk and found a rectangular box with small green flashing lights. 'That it?'

'*Haah.*'

'Turn it off and unplug it, then take it to the car. We're taking it with us.'

Zaq watched Shergill switch off the monitor and the DVR box, then unplug it and pull out all the connecting wires from the back. He slid it off the shelf using both hands.

'Time to go,' Zaq said, nodding toward the door.

They went back into the hall and to the front door, where Shergill said, 'Can you get that?' He held up the DVR box to show his hands were full.

Zaq had been careful not to touch anything since they'd arrived. He wasn't about to start now. 'It ain't heavy. You can manage one-handed.'

Shergill grumbled but shifted the box under his arm and opened the door. 'At least let me set the alarm.'

'Go ahead.' It would probably look better if the alarm were set, to show no one had broken in. 'Now turn off the lights and shut the door behind us.' Outside, they went to the car and Zaq had Shergill put the DVR box in the boot before they got in the front. Zaq put on his seatbelt and called Jags again. 'We're in the car. Be there soon.'

They took the same route back and the drive was just as un-eventful. Zaq sent Jags a couple of quick text messages en route, to keep him updated on their progress. When they arrived, Zaq had Shergill drive around behind the building, out of sight of the road. They got out, and Shergill was about to open the back to retrieve the DVR box until Zaq said, 'It's fine, leave it there. I'll take the keys.'

'Why?'

'Because I said so.' He held out his hand.

Shergill handed them over, though he gave Zaq a look that could've curdled milk.

Zaq nodded towards the fire door. 'That way.'

Shergill went first. When they got to the door he stopped, not seeing any way to open it.

'Pick up that strap,' directed Zaq, 'and pull it up hard.'

Shergill wasn't used to being ordered about and clearly didn't like it, but Zaq was fine with that. The big man bent down, lifted the strap and heaved it up. There was a loud clang and the door swung open. Zaq shoved him through the opening and followed him inside.

Chapter Eighty-Seven

Donny, Satty and their band were all sitting on the floor, mouths taped, eyes full of fear, hands cable-tied behind them, surrounded by armed and angry men. The big guy who'd been shot was still lying on the ground. Someone had tied a T-shirt around his foot to try and staunch the bleeding. He was obviously in pain but didn't look too bad otherwise.

Zaq shut the fire door and pushed Shergill forward. Without being asked, Jags tore off a strip of duct tape and slapped it over Shergill's mouth. Shergill tried to rip it off. 'Leave it alone,' Jags told him. Then he dragged Shergill through the cordon, pushed him to the ground beside his son and used a cable tie to bind his hands behind him.

'You get what you wanted?' Tonka asked Zaq.

'Yeah, thanks. We still good for the other thing?'

'Yeah, it'll be entertaining, innit?'

Gugs nodded too.

Lucky, standing nearby, looked decidedly uncomfortable and out of place. He'd known nothing of what was going to happen, so had been just as shocked as Shergill and his mob when Tonka and Gugs' groups had burst in armed with guns and other weapons.

'Here,' Zaq said, holding out the velvet bag containing the necklace. 'Take this, get in your car and go straight home. Don't go anywhere or do anything else on the way, got it?'

Lucky took the bag and nodded.

'Then first thing tomorrow morning, before you go to work, take this bloody thing straight to the bank, put it back in your safety deposit box and leave it there.'

Lucky continued nodding, like a toy dog in the back of a car.

'And don't talk to anyone about anything that's happened tonight – *not anyone.*'

He was still nodding. Zaq just hoped the words had got through to him. 'Go on, get going. Jags, see him out.'

'Come on, Uncle, let's get you out of here.'

They'd only gone a few steps when Tonka said, 'Hang on a minute.'

What was this? Zaq swallowed and tried to remain out-wardly calm. They just needed to get Lucky out of there with the necklace.

'Let's have a look at this necklace, then, seeing as it's caused so much aggro.'

Zaq nodded to Jags that he should go ahead and do it. Refusing would be unwise. Jags eased the bag from Lucky's hand and took out the necklace. Zaq could feel his heart thumping. He was surprised no one else could hear it. His insides felt as if they were having a rave.

Tonka studied the necklace for a long moment. 'Hmm,' he said finally. 'It don't look like much.'

'It's mostly sentimental value,' Jags explained. 'Been in the family for ages.'

'Well, fuck it, you wanted it, you got it. Now let's get on with things.'

Jags returned the necklace to the bag, and hurried Lucky away.

Zaq nodded towards the group sitting dejectedly on the floor. 'You take all their phones and keys and stuff?' he asked Tonka.

'It's all in a bag over there.' Tonka waved in the direction of a heavy-duty bin liner over by one of the pillars. 'Right, which two was it?'

'Them, there.' Zaq pointed at Donny and Satty, who were both staring at Zaq with hate-filled eyes.

'Get them up,' Tonka ordered, and Donny and Satty were hauled to their feet.

Shergill, sitting on the floor with his hands bound behind his back like the others, tried to shout from behind the tape over his mouth and attempted to get up. But another of Tonka's guys gave him a hefty kick in the side that stopped him and made him stay put.

'Cut them loose,' Tonka said, referring to Donny and Satty.

They flinched when a guy came forward with a wicked-looking hunting knife and brandished it for them to see. He moved behind them and cut the ties securing their wrists. Another guy ripped the tape viciously from their mouths, making them both cry out.

As Jags came back from seeing Lucky off, Donny was rubbing his wrists, giving Zaq an evil look. 'About time you let us up,' he said. 'You got what you wanted, now you better let us go.'

Satty was trying to look defiant now too, sticking his chest out and jutting his jaw forward.

'You're forgetting something.'

'What's that?'

'My brother.'

'What about him?'

'You put him in the fucking hospital. You don't just get to walk away from that.'

Donny frowned. 'You got the necklace back.'

'The necklace was nothing to do with me. That was a favour for my friend. Now I get what I want, which is payback.'

'What d'you mean, payback?'

'You like beating people up – so now try me.'

'What the fuck are you talking about?'

'You want me to let you walk out of here, you got to fight me first.'

Chapter Eighty-Eight

Donny looked Zaq up and down, no doubt trying to work out if he thought he could take him in a fight. 'Bullshit,' he said.

That was a no, then. 'What's the matter – you chicken? Oh, wait, I forgot – you don't like fighting people on your own, do you? You got to be in a gang so you outnumber them. Tell you what, then, seeing as I want to fight both of you anyway, I'll fight you together, the two of you against me. You like that better, or you still scared?'

'I ain't scared of you,' Donny said.

'Me neither,' Satty chipped in.

'What about them?' Donny indicated Tonka, Gugs and their men.

'They'll just watch. The deal is, you fight me and, win or lose, I'll let you all walk out of here.'

'Win or lose?'

'Yeah . . . you don't even have to beat me.'

'Oh, we'll fucking beat you,' Satty assured him.

'And that'll be it – we can all leave?'

Zaq nodded. 'Far as I'm concerned, I'll have got what I wanted and you can all piss off.'

Satty whispered to Donny and Donny said, 'OK, then, fine. The two of us against you . . . and no one else here joins in.'

'They won't. This is just between us.'

'Come on, then,' Satty said. 'Let's do it.'

'Good. Give us some room,' Zaq said to everyone else.

As Tonka and Gugs' men widened the circle, Zaq felt something in his back pocket. He realised it was the envelope with Lucky's ten grand in it. He'd forgotten all about it. He held it out to Jags. 'Hold on to this, will you?'

'What is it?'

'Some of Lucky's cash. I forgot to give it to him.'

Jags took it and stuffed it in his pocket.

Donny and Satty were shaking themselves out, preparing to fight. Zaq still felt loose from his workout on the bag earlier. He just had to stay calm and treat this like one of the many sparring sessions he'd had in the prison gym – defend himself, neutralise their attacks, counter, and take down or take out his opponents. In prison and out on the street, you didn't always find yourself in a one-on-one situation. More often than not you'd be up against multiple attackers, so it was worth the extra bruises to train for such scenarios.

Of course, training against guys who knew how to fight was harder than going up against your average dickhead, and more often than not Zaq had found himself taking a bit of a beating. But on a few occasions he'd successfully managed to defeat two or three people, which gave him some confidence now.

Zaq sized them up, and decided Satty was the one to watch. He was bigger and more heavily built than Donny, and seemed more inclined to fight. Also he wanted to get Zaq back for knocking him on his arse outside the pub. In contrast, Donny was slimmer, and gym-toned for looks rather than functional strength. He'd shit himself and run when they'd fought that evening on the road near Black Park, but seemed more full of himself and confident with Satty at his side.

Wondering if Satty had whispered some kind of plan to

Donny, Zaq tried to think what he'd do in their position. Probably get Donny to attack as a diversion, so Satty could come at him from behind, land a couple of knockout shots or get him in a choke, then they'd both finish him off. Or they might both charge him at once, in which case he'd have to back off, retreating and defending, until he saw an opening. However it played out, Satty was the main danger.

Zaq twisted from the hips, loosening up his back, and stretched his neck and shoulders. He was close to his two opponents now, maybe two metres separating them. He took up a fighting stance, left side forward, hands up, light on his feet. Donny and Satty split up, Satty moving to Zaq's left, Donny going to the right. For now, Zaq didn't look at either one specifically, but at the ground between them. That way they were both in his peripheral vision and he'd see any move either made. If they moved further apart, though, that would make things a lot harder.

For the moment he waited, hoping to draw them in to attack by just standing there, not even looking at them, apparently an easy target for them to pick off. His heart and mind raced, and adrenaline flowed through him like an illicit drug, forcing beads of sweat to pop out of his skin. There were murmurs and comments from the guys around them, urging them on, impatient for a show. But Zaq ignored them and focused on Donny and Satty.

Movement on the left ... Satty came in and threw a jab. Zaq flinched out of reflex, adrenaline spiking as he moved to block it, but Satty wasn't within range so his punch fell short anyway. Now Donny darted forward from the other side and threw a punch. This one came closer, and Zaq pulled his head back so it passed just shy of his face. Donny had gone for a big right and his momentum carried him forward, off-balance.

Zaq shoved him on the shoulder and sent him staggering on a couple of paces.

Zaq had only twisted from the waist and, as his upper body twisted back, he was just in time to meet Satty, who was rushing at him from that side. Zaq's right hand was already in motion from twisting; all he had to do was let the punch go and put some weight behind it. He wasn't set up quite right for it, so it didn't have as much force as it might have, but his fist still smacked into Satty's face. A murmur rippled through the spectators.

Something crashed into the back of Zaq's head. Donny had regained his balance and come at him from behind. As a second punch landed, catching the back of his ear, Zaq turned, raising his right arm to block Donny's next big right with his forearm. Zaq's feet were positioned all wrong, right foot in front, and he wasn't used to throwing a straight left. Instead, he twisted his hips and used the torque to drive his left arm straight in front of him. The martial-arts-style palm strike caught Donny by surprise, ramming into his mouth and rattling his teeth. Zaq pressed his advantage, stepping forward and pushing Donny back with the hand that was still in his face. This move brought him back into the orthodox stance he was used to and he launched his own big right, putting his full weight behind it. The punch slammed into Donny's left cheek and sent him flying, feet leaving the ground, to land on his back in an explosion of dust. Hoots and cheers went up around them.

Then something big hit Zaq in the back and threw him to the ground. He barely managed to get his arms up to stop his head hitting the concrete. His arms smacked straight on to it, though, sending pain lancing through his bones. Ignoring the pain, Zaq rolled on to his back just as Satty launched a kick at his head. Instinct took over and Zaq threw his arms up, crossed, in front of him. The kick added to the pain, but his head was safe. He grabbed Satty's tracksuit leg and yanked hard, pulling him off balance, so Satty was forced to take a big step forward, arms flailing to try and stay upright. His upper body bent forward over Zaq, who brought his right knee up to his chest and kicked straight upwards, catching Satty just below the sternum and launching him off and away. More shouts and cheers.

But, as he turned to get up, Donny's foot slammed into his ribs. Donny kicked him again, before Zaq dodged a third kick and scrambled to his feet. Fortunately Donny had been kicking like a footballer taking a penalty rather than stamping down with his heel, which would have done more damage. Now they were both on their feet, Donny didn't seem quite so keen to engage him. Zaq saw that Donny's lip was split, blood dribbling down his chin, and his left cheek was starting to swell from the punch he'd taken.

Zaq got both opponents back in view. He reckoned they must've figured out they couldn't take him one-on-one, so they might decide to attack together. Zaq just about saw Satty move out of view, circling behind him, as Donny diverted his attention by bouncing on his feet and coming forward. Had Satty signalled him to do it? Was this their plan? Zaq decided to take a calculated risk and play along with it.

Suddenly Donny leapt at him with a feral cry, in an all-out attack, fists flying, his face a mask of hate and rage. The ferocity of it was a surprise, as was the fact that he had the balls to do it. With all the noise, it had to be a diversionary tactic. Zaq put his hands up, tucking his elbows in, to protect his head and body as best he could and let the punches batter his arms. But, while he allowed himself to be pummelled that way, his senses were hyper-alert for what was happening behind him, where the real danger was coming from.

It was a sound that gave it away, a change in the overall noise of the crowd, a sort of collective intake of breath, and then a barely registered shout of warning from Jags. Zaq knew what it meant – and he reacted. He burst out of his defensive tuck, sweeping Donny's punches aside with his left arm as he spun that way. The sweeping motion gave him the speed and power to whip his right elbow round to smash into Donny's face. Zaq felt the solid connection as hard bone hit Donny's jaw and sent him sprawling.

A quick step with his right foot, a slight adjustment of his body, and Zaq was facing the other way – just as Satty lunged, his eyes wide. He'd jumped at Zaq's undefended back but now found himself, mid-jump, facing him head-on. With no time to even think what to do, Zaq acted purely on instinct, and his instinct was to strike. There wasn't time to make a fist. With a roar, he hit Satty at the base of his nose with the heel of his palm. The impact jolted through his arm, and Satty's momentum multiplied the force of the blow. It was like smashing a tomato against a wall. The bone and cartilage in his nose popped and blood and mucus blew out of his nostrils across his face, leaving a bloody Rorschach test.

The noise of the crowd increased at the sight of blood. Satty was still on his feet, still a potential threat. Zaq advanced, hit him in the face again, then stepped in closer, grabbed Satty's wrist with his left hand and the back of his head with his right, and pulled him forward to knee him in the balls. He felt Satty sag, and dropped his head into the path of his rising knee. The impact launched Satty's head back, his body with it, and an arc of blood sprayed from his destroyed nose. He hit the floor with a jarring impact, raising a cloud of dust, and lay still.

Heart thumping, blood racing, mind awhirl, Zaq spun round to face Donny, who was getting to his feet. It had taken ten seconds or so to take care of Satty, barely time for Donny to recover and stand up again. One against one, Zaq knew he could take Donny, no problem.

Donny's eyes flicked to Satty. When they met Zaq's again, his mouth was set tight, his eyes alight with that anger that would fire up in the rich when they didn't get their way. If he felt fear, it was subsumed by his sense of entitlement.

Zaq took slow, deep breaths to get his heart rate down close to normal and help quell the charge of adrenaline inside him. He closed the distance between them. 'Just you and me now, tough guy,' he said.

Donny bit his lower lip, a sign that he was psyching himself up to attack. He was bouncing and jittery, as if he'd drunk too much coffee. Zaq kept moving towards him, waiting for him to do something. Donny was actually in a fighting stance, left side slightly forward, so Zaq expected a jab. Instead, Donny pulled his right hand back, twisting at the waist, and put all his power behind it. There was a gasp from the crowd as Zaq leant just out of range, the punch whistling past his face. It would've been a fairly decent punch if he'd known what he was doing, but it had come from a long way back, giving Zaq time to see it and react. If Donny had learnt the basics properly, he'd have jabbed with his left to distract and disorientate, and set up the big right as the potential knockout shot.

Zaq inched forward again, waiting for the next one. He left his head undefended, his guard down, inviting the shot. Donny bobbed around, feinting once, then twice, to throw him off. Then he pulled his right hand back a fraction, ready to launch it at him again.

Zaq read it correctly and saw it coming a mile off. He leant slightly to the left and, as the punch went where his head had been a fraction of a second before, he swatted Donny's hand away as he'd swat a fly. The punch sailed on into thin air, throwing Donny off balance, his right arm extended straight out. Zaq was all set to throw his own right hand over the top, which was just what he did. The punch rocketed over Donny's extended arm and hit him flush in the face, propelling him backwards, his arms windmilling uselessly. There was another gasp from the spectators.

Zaq went in for the kill. Two strides and he was in range again. He set his feet and threw a scything left hook, then a straight right, that caught Donny flush on the chin. His arms dropped to his sides, his legs gave out beneath him and he collapsed to the floor.

In the silence that followed, Zaq heard muffled shouting. Shergill was thrashing about, eyes bulging wide above the tape covering his mouth, cheeks puffed out, the muscles in his neck standing out. Zaq ignored him and went over to Donny. He was semi-conscious, moving his head and groaning. Zaq grabbed him by the front of his polo shirt, and pulled him up into a half-seated position. He drew back his fist to hit him, to do to him what he'd done to Tariq, to pay him back in kind, beat the shit out of him and leave him for dead . . .

But he didn't.

Looking down at Donny's battered face and lolling head, he pictured his brother lying in the hospital having been beaten the same way he was about to beat Donny. If he went ahead and did it, he'd be no different from Donny, Satty and the rest of those arseholes. And that wasn't him.

He'd done enough. He'd got payback and avenged his brother. Anything more would be . . . what? Wrong? Needless? Something like that. He felt the adrenaline high starting to wear off, and all the rage and anger he'd been carrying seemed to dissipate like a cloud of smoke. He took a deep breath, exhaled and released Donny's shirt, letting him hit the floor.

Fuck it, he told himself. It's over.

Chapter Eighty-Nine

'You OK?' Jags asked.

'Yeah, fine.'

Jags raised his eyebrows and gave him a searching look.

Tonka said, 'That it? You done?'

Zaq nodded wearily. 'Yeah, I'm done.'

'I thought you were going to fuck them up big-time. You hardly touched them.'

'I've done enough. What'd be the point doing any more?'

'Suit yourself. We had a deal. I'm just making sure I hold up my part of it and you got what you wanted.'

'Yeah, I'm good.' Now that it was over, Zaq just wanted to get out of there. He and Jags moved away from the others.

'Why did you stop?' Jags said. 'I thought you were going to beat them both into a fucking coma.'

'So did I. But when I had Donny there like that, and he was already out of it, I didn't see the point in carrying on. I'd already fucked him up – and I ain't them. I don't get my kicks from beating people up.'

'You properly took them out, though.'

Donny and Satty were regaining their senses. Satty was on his hands and knees, head bowed, blood dripping from his ruined nose and mouth. Donny was up on one elbow, shaking his head and blinking to try and clear his head. 'Yeah,' Zaq said, 'they weren't that much of a challenge. Guess that's the other reason I didn't batter them more.'

Zaq's gaze met Donny's father's. Shergill was giving him a withering stare. The fear and urgency that had been in his eyes before were gone now the fight was over. But the look he was giving Zaq said he wasn't about to forget him – or Jags, or Lucky or anyone else there if he found out who they were. He was probably already plotting what he would do to them. Zaq held his gaze. He wasn't the least bit intimidated by the man. He had nothing to fear from him whatsoever. Shergill was going to go down for murder; he just didn't know it.

Zaq asked Jags, 'You take care of the phones?'

'Yeah, stripped out the batteries and the SIMs, and smashed everything up. Tonka and Gugs did theirs too.'

'What did you do with the bits?'

'Chucked them in the bin bag with all the other phones and stuff.'

'What about the mics?'

'Did the same to them, to be safe.'

'Good.'

Donny, though still dazed, managed to stand, and went over to help Satty to his feet. He had to half-carry him back to the rest of their group. He fixed Zaq with the dirtiest of looks. 'You said we could go if we fought you, win or lose,' he called over. His voice sounded slightly slurred. His swollen cheek, thick lip and newly closing black eye probably had something to do with it.

'Yeah, that's right,' Zaq said. 'You can go, and I hope I never see any of you again. Far as I'm concerned, we're done.'

'We can just leave, right now?'

'I said I'd let you go. So go.'

Tonka nodded to one of his men, who strode over to the rear fire exit, hit the bar and stood there holding the door open.

Donny's band tried to get to their feet but couldn't with their hands tied behind their backs.

'Can someone get these fucking ties off, then?' Donny called to Zaq.

Zaq looked at Tonka, who signalled to one of his guys to do it. A big fella with a beard went over pulling a large hunting knife from a sheath. He went around behind the seated captives, cutting the cable ties that bound their wrists. They then peeled the duct tape from their mouths.

'What're we supposed to do with him?' Donny said, indicating his dad's big minder who'd been shot in the foot.

'What you asking me for?' Zaq said. 'He's your problem, you figure it out. Take him to the hospital or take him home, I don't give a shit.'

It took four of them to pull the man-mountain up on to his good leg, then two of them had to support him to keep him standing. The other two had to help Satty, who was still groggy and bleeding down his shirt-front. That left Shergill, Donny and Taj to walk on their own, each staring daggers at Zaq as the group started towards the exit.

Tonka and Gugs' guys escorted Shergill's bunch, while Zaq and Jags trailed along behind. When they were a few metres from the exit, the guy holding the door open grinned and slammed it shut.

'Hey, what the fuck's going on?' Donny turned and demanded of Zaq. 'You said we could go.'

'Yeah, you can,' Zaq said. 'I ain't stopping you.'

'What about these guys?' Donny waved a hand at Tonka and Gugs' people.

'What about them?'

'They're not letting us leave, that's what.'

'So . . . ? What d'you want me to do about it?'

'Tell them to let us go.'

Zaq spread his hands in a gesture of helplessness. 'Ain't nothing to do with me.'

'What do you mean? You fucking said we could leave!' Donny was almost shouting, his voice full of indignation.

'Yeah, we're done and I'm keeping my side of the bargain.'

'But they're not letting us leave.'

'Listen ... I said *I'd* let you go – *me*.' Zaq tapped his chest to emphasise the point. 'As far as I'm concerned, you can all fuck right off. But I don't speak for anyone else, not Tonka over there or Gugs over here. And, in case you forgot, you and your dad confessed, on a live video call, to killing members of their families. I got my payback; now they're going to get theirs.'

The implication of Zaq's words sank in. 'YOU LYING FUCKING BASTARD!' Donny screamed.

'I didn't lie – well, not technically – but now you got to pay the price for what you've done.' He looked at Shergill too. 'All of you.'

Shergill spat on the ground in disgust.

The rest of Donny's little gang were looking in every direction, desperate for a way out, fear plain in their darting eyes.

'FUCKING CUNT, PIECE OF SHIT!' Donny yelled at him. 'I SHOULD'VE KILLED YOU TOO!'

Tonka said something to one of his guys, who strode over to Donny and slapped him across the face. The shouting stopped instantly, the words still echoing inside the empty building. Donny held his cheek, his eyes wide with shock and surprise. Shergill took a step forward but Tonka's man turned to face him. '*Ajaa*,' he dared, and Shergill stopped where he was.

'Come on,' Zaq said to Jags, and they joined Tonka and Gugs away from the others. 'Are we all good?' Zaq asked. 'You both know for a fact now that we had nothing to do with what happened to Bongo or your brother-in-law?'

'Yeah, we're good,' Tonka said. 'You got what you wanted. Now I'll deal with these fuckers.'

Something about the iciness of Tonka's tone, or the finality of his words, struck Zaq as wrong. 'Wait' Zaq said, lowering his voice. 'You're just going to rough them up, right? Give them a beating, then turn them and the video of their confession over to the cops?'

Tonka gave Zaq a stone-cold stare.

'That was the deal,' Zaq said.

'The deal was that you'd prove you didn't kill my brother-in-law, and get me the people who did, and in exchange I'd help you get the necklace and payback for your brother. I'd also let you walk. I've stuck to my side of it. You got what you wanted, and now you can go.'

'But we never said anything about . . .' Zaq couldn't even bring himself to say it.

'What the fuck? Did you seriously think I was just going to slap them about a bit and then let them go? My brother-in-law's fucking dead. My sister's a widow. My nephew and niece have lost their dad. He ain't ever coming back. They killed him. They don't get to walk away from that. How the fuck could I ever look my sister in the eye – or any of my family – if I knew I had the motherfuckers responsible and I just let them walk away, living and breathing, while my brother-in-law's dead in the ground?'

Zaq felt sick. The realisation that he'd almost certainly delivered the Shergills and their gang to their deaths, made his stomach turn. It wasn't what he'd agreed to. 'But you've got their confessions. You could put them away for life.'

'No one's got any confessions. I didn't record it.'

'Er, I did,' Gugs said.

Tonka looked at him. 'Then you better delete it. There's got to be no evidence of what happens here tonight.' Gugs nodded.

Tonka faced Zaq again. 'There was only ever one way this was going to end, and, if you didn't see that, it's because you didn't want to.'

Was that true? Had Zaq chosen not to see how things would work out? Had he fooled himself into thinking that everything would be tied up nice and neatly, just so his conscience would be clear? Only now that it was too late, did he realise how blind he'd been. Do a deal with the Devil and you had to pay the price – as Zaq was now finding out, to his cost.

'So, we got a problem here or what?' Tonka said.

Zaq knew there was only one answer to that question that would allow him and Jags to walk out of the warehouse alive. 'No, no problem,' he said.

'You sure about that?'

'Yeah, I'm positive.'

Tonka looked at Gugs. 'What about you and your lot?'

'They killed my cousin, man. I got no problem with it at all. Only blood's going to pay for blood.'

Tonka turned to Zaq. 'You got what you came for. You going to stay or go?'

'We're going to go, if that's OK.'

'Sure, that's fine.' As Zaq started to turn away, Tonka added, 'I'm sure I don't need to tell you both that you never mention any of this to anyone else, ever.' And by not telling them, he'd told them exactly that.

Chapter Ninety

Tonka's guy let them out of the fire door and shut it after them, cutting off all sound from inside the warehouse.

'Holy fuck,' Jags said. 'He's going to kill them. What the fuck we going to do?'

'What the hell can we do?'

'I don't know – call the cops?'

'Are you crazy? We do that, we're dead.'

'What about tipping off Crimestoppers or something?'

'Listen, we're the only two people outside of this warehouse who know what's going on. Anything happens, who d'you think they'll come after? We do anything to stop them, we're fucking dead.'

'So what're you saying – we just do nothing?'

'I don't fucking like it either, but we ain't got a choice, least not if we want to keep breathing.'

'Fuck.'

'Come on, let's get out of here. I want to get as far from this place as we can.'

'Shit,' Jags said. 'How we supposed to get back? We got a lift with Lucky but he's gone. Shall we cab it?'

'Forget that. I don't want any record of us being picked up from around here.' Zaq put his hand in his pocket to get his phone, before remembering it was back at Jags' house, in the kitchen drawer. His fingers closed around something else which he pulled out. 'I've still got the keys to Shergill's motor.' They looked at each other. 'Let's just take it and get out of here.' He pressed the key fob and the alarm deactivated with a flash of lights.

They got into the car, Zaq behind the wheel. He pressed the button to start the engine and reversed out from behind the building. 'We'll dump it somewhere near your place, and walk the rest of the way.'

'You're just going to leave it there?'

Zaq thought for a moment and had an idea. He told Jags what he had in mind, which seemed to convince him. They drove in silence, not even any music playing, tension thick in the air between them. He saw Jags was staring out of the window. 'You OK?' he asked him.

'That's some serious shit going down back there.'

'I know.'

'I'm just trying to get my head around it.'

'Look, we ain't a part of whatever's going on there now. We did our bit and we're out of it.'

'We're the ones set it all up, though.'

'You don't need to tell me. I'm more responsible than anyone for getting them there. I didn't know it was going to end like this, though.'

'It's murder,' Jags said.

A sick feeling twisted Zaq's innards. 'That ain't how Tonka and Gugs see it. Far as they're concerned, it's justice. I don't agree with it, but they think it's right.'

'Sure, they deserve to pay for what they've done ... but to die ... I never thought I'd be involved in anything like this.'

'You ain't. Listen, mate, your only involvement in all this has been to get that necklace back for Lucky, and to help me out. That's it. Anything else is down to me. You got that? It's on me.'

Jags nodded, and Zaq hoped he'd said enough to prevent Jags from blaming himself. The fact that they'd left rather than stuck around to witness whatever was going to happen at the warehouse might make it easier to dissociate themselves from it over time. And if Tonka was thorough, no details would ever emerge and they might, in time, be able to shut it away and pretend it never happened.

That late on a Sunday there was little traffic around Hayes, and even less on the residential back roads Zaq took towards Jags' place. 'This'll do,' he said, as he passed a boxing club and pulled over on the other side of the road. They got out of the car. Zaq locked it and shoved the keys just far enough into the exhaust pipe that they couldn't be seen.

When they got to his house, Jags said, 'Don't know about you, but I could use a drink after all that.'

'Mate, I could bloody use one too but I have to get back to the hospital. My dad's waiting for me. I just need to grab my phone. I'll come over tomorrow.'

In the kitchen they retrieved their phones from the drawer. Jags pulled out the envelope of cash Zaq had given him back at the warehouse. 'Here, take this.'

'What you giving it to me for?'

'You should give it to Lucky. You're the one got it back for him.'

'All right, I'll give it to him, but keep it here for now. I don't want to take it to the hospital. We can talk to him tomorrow when I come over. Make sure he's put that bloody necklace back in the bank.'

'He better have, otherwise I'm going to kick him in the nuts.'

'All right, take it easy, man.' Zaq said, extending his hand. They shook firmly and pulled each other into a hug. 'I'll catch you later.'

*

It was past midnight when Zaq buzzed to be let into the ITU ward, and he had to explain to the unimpressed nurse that he was there to relieve his dad. He found his dad asleep in a chair beside Tariq's bed, snoring softly. Shit, now he was late *and* had to wake him up.

Zaq put down the bag of food he'd picked up from the petrol station and shook him gently by the shoulder. 'Dad?'

His father awoke with a start. 'Huh?' His eyes focused on Zaq and he frowned. He looked around, saw Tariq in the bed and realised where he was. His frown deepened when he checked his watch. 'Do you know what time it is?'

Zaq was well aware, but knew his dad wasn't actually looking for an answer.

'You said just for a little while, a couple of hours. It's been more than four.'

'I know. I'm sorry. Things took a bit longer than we thought.'

His dad gave him one of his patented 'not impressed' looks. 'That's what always happens when you two get together. Now I have to go home and I'll probably wake your mother up, and it's me she'll have a go at, not you.'

There wasn't much Zaq could say to that, so he kept his mouth shut. His dad huffed and puffed as he pushed himself out of the chair and collected his things together. 'All right,' he said finally. 'See you tomorrow. No, wait ... what I should be saying is, later *today*.'

Zaq just nodded. Yeah, yeah, let him have his say.

His dad left and Zaq sank into the chair, weariness settling over him like a shroud. Now the nervous energy and adrenaline had gone, he felt incredibly tired. He'd brought food but still felt too sick to eat. He took out his phone and, even though it was late, made a call.

'Yo, what's up?' Biri answered.

'Sorry to call so late,' Zaq said, careful to keep his voice low so he wouldn't get in any more trouble with the nurses.

'No worries, man. I weren't sleeping or nothing. What can I do you for?'

'Actually, I'm calling 'cause I need a favour but it's something I think you might be interested in.'

'OK, I'm listening.'

'A Jaguar SUV.'

'Keep talking . . .'

'It's pretty new, in good nick, and it won't be reported missing until tomo— I mean, later this morning, maybe midday, at the earliest. Best of all, you don't even have to worry about getting into it – the keys are with it.'

'All right, I'm definitely interested. What's the catch?'

'No catch. I just need you to do two things for me. There's a DVR player in the boot with some CCTV footage on it. I need the whole thing wiped and destroyed straight away, so there's no chance of anyone getting anything from it.'

'I can sort that. What's the other thing?'

'I need the car to disappear, for good.'

'I can make a couple of calls, have it off the road and out of sight in a couple of hours. It'll be on a ship and out of the country by Wednesday.'

'That's fine. I appreciate it.'

'I'll make some money on it. We can split it.'

'Nah, man, you keep it. You're doing me a favour.'

'All right, bruv. Nice one.'

Zaq told him where to find the car and where he'd left the keys. 'Don't forget about the DVR box.'

'Don't worry, I'll make sure it's done.'

Zaq thanked him, hung up and sat back in the chair. In the dim light of the hospital room he allowed himself to think about the events of the past week or so – Tariq, Lucky's necklace, Kang, Bongo. If the Shergills had had their way he would've been dead too, or in a coma, along with Jags and his uncle. Everything seemed to have snowballed until it had all converged and finally been brought to a head that evening. As far as Zaq was concerned, he'd got the necklace back and payback for what they'd done to Tariq – and then he'd walked away.

Had he known what was going to happen to Shergill and the rest of them?

No, he hadn't.

Should he have? Yeah, maybe he ought to have suspected and taken steps to prevent it. But he hadn't and now it was too late. That fact didn't sit well with him.

Would he be able to live with it?

He thought about it . . . and came to the conclusion that he had no other choice.

Unable to eat, he managed to have some of the drink he'd brought with him, then kicked off his trainers, pulled up another chair and tried to get comfortable, even though he doubted he'd actually sleep. He dozed fitfully at first but must have fallen into a deeper slumber because something woke him up and brought him out of it. It was a noise. Strange. Not like anything he'd heard before. He looked around the room . . . then movement caught his eye.

It was coming from the bed. He sat up and saw Tariq's hands scrabbling at his throat, the breathing tube still protruding from his mouth. Tariq was panicked, choking, trying to breathe.

'Shit,' Zaq said.

And Tariq looked directly at him, his eyes wide open.

Chapter Ninety-One

'Hold on, man,' Zaq told him. He pressed the button to call a nurse. 'Just calm down, yeah? Breathe slowly. Let me get the nurse. I'll be right back.'

He rushed out of the room, his socks sliding on the linoleum floor as he turned in the corridor. A nurse was hurrying towards him. 'He's awake!' Zaq said. When they got back to the room, Tariq was still in distress, obviously wanting the tube out so he could breathe normally.

The nurse turned the lights on. 'All right, Mr Khan – Tariq,' she said quietly but firmly. 'Just calm down and try to relax. I'm going to remove the breathing tube for you, OK?' She took hold of the tube end. 'This might feel a little uncomfortable but it'll be over very quickly. Just relax ... open your mouth as wide as you can ...' Then in one swift motion, like a magician pulling a rabbit out of a hat, she whipped the tube out.

Zaq winced as it came out, dripping with saliva. Tariq made retching noises, then coughed for a bit before finally lying back with a groan and breathing deeply.

'Your throat will be a little sore for a while but it'll be OK. Have a little water, it might help.' She poured him a glass from the jug on the cabinet beside the bed, and he took a few sips. Then she did some checks on him to make sure his vitals were OK, and updated his chart. 'Just try to rest now.' She gave Zaq a smile as she went towards the door. 'I'll turn off the light. Press the call button if you need anything.' She left, the sound of her footsteps disappearing along the corridor with her.

Even with the main lights off, Zaq could still see clearly. He pulled his chair up beside the bed. 'Shit, man, you've had us all worried sick. How d'you feel?'

Tariq looked at him but didn't say anything.

Did he remember how to talk? Did he even recognise his brother, know who he was? Zaq had to try and find out.

'Tariq,' he said, in a calm voice, 'do you know who I am?'

Tariq's eyes seemed to focus, and his lips parted like he was about to speak. Zaq leant in close to hear if he said anything. Tariq closed his eyes, opened them again and then in a raspy voice said, 'Tosser.'

'Dickhead,' Zaq said in relief, sitting back. 'You must be OK, then. I thought you might've had brain damage – more than you did before, I mean, you div.'

'Where am I?' Tariq croaked. His voice was hoarse and weak.

'In the hospital.'

'No shit? Which one?' He winced, his busted jaw making it painful to speak.

'Hillingdon.'

'What happened? Why'm I here?'

'Don't you remember?' Tariq slowly shook his head. 'You were attacked and beaten up, in Uxbridge.' Tariq just looked blank. 'You really don't remember?' He shook his head again. 'What's the last thing you do remember?'

Tariq's brow creased as he thought about it. 'Going to work.'

'When? What day?'

'I don't know. Wednesday maybe?'

That was almost three whole days before he'd been attacked. It was quite a gap.

'What day is it now? How long have I been here?'

'It's Monday. You've been here for over a week though. They had to keep you asleep so you could get better.'

'A week?' He looked shocked.

'Just over.'

'Do Mum and Dad know?'

'Know? They been sitting right here next to you every flippin' day. I been here every night. Speaking of which, I better call them and let them know you're awake. Back in a sec.'

Zaq went to the nurses' station to ask if it would be all right for his parents to come and see Tariq. It was almost five. By the time they got here, it would be about six, which was fine. Zaq went back to the room and rang his dad. The phone rang for some time before it was answered.

'This is twice in one night you've woken me up. What's the matter now?'

'Sorry, Dad. But I thought you'd want to know … Tariq's awake.'

Zaq couldn't remember the last time he'd seen his mum so happy. His parents' joy and relief seemed to fill the drab institutional room, their smiles adding to the sunlight slicing in through the half-open blinds. His mother fussed over Tariq, while his dad called their friends and relatives to relay the good news.

The doctor came in a bit later and he too was happy to see Tariq awake and communicating. They did a few more tests to check his cognitive functions and seemed very satisfied. Zaq mentioned the fact that Tariq didn't remember the attack or even the days leading up to it. The doctor frowned but said it wasn't unusual, in such cases, for people to experience some amnesia of the event in question and also to lose some time before and after. The memory might come back in time, fully, partially or maybe even not at all. It was just a question of waiting and seeing what happened. They'd keep him in for another day or so, to be certain everything was OK and that they hadn't missed anything, also to give him another scan to check the swelling had gone and to make sure there was no sudden deterioration in his condition.

Tariq might have slept for a week but Zaq felt he'd hardly slept at all in that time and he was knackered. As the morning wore on, his eyes grew heavy and he was yawning more often. Eventually, he told Tariq and his parents he had to go home. 'I just need to get some proper sleep. I'll be back later on.'

His parents were in a celebratory mood, all smiles, now that their youngest had pulled through and would, with plenty of rest, make a good recovery. His dad even seemed to have forgotten all about Zaq arriving late at the hospital the night before. '*Haah*, go home and get some rest,' he told him. His mother even hugged him as he was about to leave.

'Thanks,' Tariq said to him, 'for ... you know.'

'No problem.' Zaq nodded. 'See you later.'

'Not if I see you first.'

Chapter Ninety-Two

Later that afternoon, after he'd slept, woken, showered and dressed, Zaq went over to see Jags.

'Fucking great news about Tariq, man,' he told Zaq when he opened the front door. Zaq had messaged him early that morning to let him know.

'He scared the shit out of me, though,' Zaq said. 'I woke up thinking Darth Vader was in the room with me. Flippin' sounded like it, with that tube down his throat.'

'How is he – you know . . . ?' Jags waved a hand at his head.

Zaq sat down on the sofa. 'He's fine. Same mouthy shit as before. He don't remember getting jumped, though, or anything else about the days just before it happened.'

Jags took a seat opposite. 'Damn. I've heard about that kind of thing; people's brains blocking out trauma, wiping it clean like erasing files from a computer. Still, it's great that he's awake and seems OK.'

'It'll take him a while to recover fully but, yeah, I think he's over the worst of it.'

'Your mum and dad must be relieved.'

'They're over the moon. It was scary, man, not knowing what might happen to him. My mum just wants to get him home so she can feed him back to health. He can't go to the gym for a while, so he'll probably end up a proper fat bastard.' They both laughed, knowing how concerned Tariq was about his appearance.

'We should have a beer to celebrate,' Jags said.

'Right. I should probably eat something first, though.'

'Didn't you have anything at home?'

'Nah, I got up and came straight over.'

'Fine,' Jags said. 'What d'you want? I can whip you up some eggs.'

'That'd be great.'

Jags got up and went to the kitchen. 'You want them *desi*-style?' he called.

'Yeah, man.'

'If you're having eggs and it's pretty much your breakfast, you want tea rather than a beer?'

'Mate, tea would be perfect. We can have a beer in a while.' Zaq moved to the dining table, where he could continue talking to Jags. 'I've said it before and I'll say it again – you'll make someone a great wife one day.'

'Keep talking like that and I'll crack these eggs on your fucking head.'

Zaq laughed and watched Jags as he cooked. He seemed fine today, after everything that had happened the night before. Maybe sleeping on it had helped, given him some perspective – if he'd managed to sleep. Zaq wasn't sure whether to bring it up. Would it be better to leave it and let Jags talk about it when he was ready? But what if he didn't say anything, and it just ate away at him? In the end, concern for his best friend overrode all other considerations. 'How're you doing?' he asked. 'You know, after yesterday?'

Jags didn't look up. 'I'm OK.'

'You sure? You sleep all right?'

Jags shrugged. 'Took me a while to get to sleep, thinking

about it all, but I managed to eventually.' He tipped the onions and chilli he'd been chopping into the frying pan, where they started to sizzle. The smell made Zaq's stomach rumble in anticipation. 'You were right, though – we didn't really have any other choice. And we didn't have any part in whatever happened after we left. I got no idea about that. I thought about it plenty but I got no images in my mind, ain't heard anything about it, got nothing to go on. Far as I know, Tonka, Gugs and that lot could've shipped them all off to the Bahamas or somewhere, in one piece. Last time we saw them they were alive and well – sort of. That's all I see when I think about it. I'm just going to focus on that. Sometimes, ignorance really is bliss.'

Zaq nodded sagely. 'You'd certainly know all about that last bit.'

'You're such a tosser.'

'Funny – that's pretty much the first thing Tariq said to me when he woke up.'

'We can't both be wrong, then.'

'You spoken to Lucky yet?'

'Why don't you give him a call, see if he can come round? We better talk to him and give him that cash.'

Jags and Zaq had finished their mugs of tea and were sitting chatting when Lucky showed up.

'*Kidaah*, Zaq?' Lucky said, shaking his hand then sitting down. 'You know, you boys really had me shitting my pants yesterday. When those fuckers dragged me inside, I thought that was it, *bond pahti*, we were done for. Why didn't you tell me you had all those other guys waiting outside? I could've had a heart attack.'

'We didn't tell you because we wanted you to act natural,' Zaq explained. 'We left you out in the car 'cause we were pretty sure Shergill wouldn't come alone, and that whoever came with him would check outside. We told him, if anything happened to us, you'd call the cops straight away. Once they had you, they thought they had us all and didn't have anything else to worry about. Didn't even matter if we were trying to film or record them – we wouldn't be able to do anything with it. That's the reason they all got so talkative. They didn't figure we'd live-stream the whole thing on a group call.'

Lucky shook his head, his expression part awe, part disbelief.

'We couldn't risk you giving the game away by not being as scared as you should've been,' Zaq continued, 'or watching the doors, waiting for Tonka and the others to turn up. They might've got suspicious. As it was, you were brilliant. You played it just right, which was a massive help.' Zaq added the last bit to massage Lucky's ego, so he wouldn't stay grumpy at them. It seemed to do the trick. He was nodding, with a big grin plastered across his face. 'Anyway,' Zaq said, 'it all worked out OK in the end.'

'Tell that to the boxer shorts I had to throw away,' Lucky said. 'What did you do to Shergill and the rest of them after I left?'

Zaq and Jags exchanged a glance. 'Nothing much,' Zaq said. 'We didn't stick around long after you went. We left them with Tonka and the others. They were all OK when we went, though.'

'What d'you think those guys did with them?'

Zaq gave him a level look. 'I don't know, Uncle, and frankly I don't want to know. It might just be best if we forgot about the whole thing.'

They sat in silence for a moment, until finally Jags said, 'Uncle, what did you do with the necklace? Where is it now?'

'I did just what you said. I went to the bank first thing this morning and put it back in the safety deposit box.'

'Thank fuck for that,' Jags breathed.

'And . . .' Lucky slapped a hand on his heart, like a character in a Bollywood movie, 'thankfully, your auntie never knew anything about it.'

'Listen, Uncle,' Zaq said, 'we need to talk to you about the necklace.'

Lucky frowned. 'What about it?'

'We didn't get a chance to tell you before, with everything that was going on, but when we went to see Kang at his shop he confirmed everything you told us about it – its age, its history, all that. He also gave us a rough idea of how much it's worth.'

'*Haah* ... OK, how much?'

'He reckoned,' Zaq said, 'that it'd be somewhere around fifteen million pounds.'

Lucky stared blankly at him for a moment, as if he hadn't heard. Then he said, '*Kee?*'

'Fifteen million.'

'Fifteen ...'

'Yeah.'

'... *million?*'

'Yep.'

'*Bhen di phudi.*' Lucky sat completely still as the news sank in.

'You better leave it right where it is,' Jags said. 'Don't take it out for anything, no matter what Auntie says.'

'That ain't all,' Zaq said.

Jags twigged what he meant, and retrieved the envelope from a kitchen drawer. He gave it to Zaq, who handed it to Lucky.

'What's this?'

'You only owed Shergill ten grand for the card game but you ended up paying twenty in total and he still gave us the wrong necklace, so I made him give the extra ten back when we went to get the necklace.'

Lucky looked at the envelope, then up at Zaq and Jags. 'Fifteen million pounds?' he said.

'Yeah.'

'Then what the hell do I need this for? You boys keep it. You bloody earned it.' He shoved it back at Zaq.

'What?' Zaq said. 'No way.'

'*Haah, haah*, keep it. It's yours.'

'We can't take it,' Jags said.

'Yes, you can. I'm telling you to. You've just told me I've won the lottery and you're trying to give me pocket money.' He held a hand up, ending the discussion. '*Bus*. I don't want to hear another word about it. You're keeping it, and that's that.'

Zaq and Jags looked at each other, eyebrows raised, then they looked back at Lucky. 'Thanks, Uncle,' they said.

Now that Lucky had finally processed the news they'd given him, he was in a jubilant mood, barely able to contain himself. 'You know what this means, don't you?' he beamed.

'No. What?'

Lucky threw his arms up in the air. 'We've got to have a drink to celebrate.'

'I've got some beer . . .' Jags offered.

'*Aw, bhen chaud*, I mean a proper drink. Come on,' he said, getting to his feet, 'we're going to the pub.' He nodded at the envelope in Zaq's hand and his grin widened. 'And you boys are buying.'

Acknowledgements

Writing is a mostly solo endeavour but publishing a book is very much a team effort and I've been fortunate enough to have had some wonderfully talented people work with me on *Stone Cold Trouble*. I would like to express my sincerest gratitude to them. Firstly, to Mary Jones for all your brilliant help and advice in shaping the book and making it better than it was, and to the editorial team at Dialogue Books; David Bamford, Linda McQueen and Saxon Bullock, for helping me fine-tune the book and get the details right. You all make me look like I know what I'm doing. To Sean Garrehy for another great cover – I love it, man. To my amazing publicist, Millie Seaward, for her outstanding work in promoting the book and getting the word out. To Emily Moran in Marketing and to everyone in Sales, Production and Contracts – thank you for all your hard work, it is truly appreciated.

A massive shout out to my fearless and fabulous publisher, the force of nature that is Sharmaine Lovegrove. Thank you for believing in me and *Brothers in Blood* when everyone else had turned it down and for giving me the time and space to write *Stone Cold Trouble*. It's a joy to know and be published by you.

I am also hugely grateful to my agent, Jane Gregory, for taking me on, believing in me and fighting my corner, even when we were being told that my book would never 'appeal to a broad audience'. She even went so far as to tell one publisher they were mad not to want to publish it. I'm so glad to have you on my side and hope I've been able to prove that you were right.

My heartfelt thanks to all the newspaper reviewers who read and championed *Brothers in Blood* – you guys are ace – and to all the readers and book bloggers who also reviewed and recommended it; you're all awesome and your support has meant the world to me and still does – especially as many of you are part of that "broad audience" my books were never supposed to appeal to. I'm so happy we've proved otherwise. I hope you all enjoyed this one just as much.

I would also like to say thank you to all the wonderful authors and publishing people I've had the pleasure to meet over the last few years. You have all been so welcoming, generous and supportive. It's been such a fantastic experience to be part of the crime-writing community.

I was fortunate enough to receive a grant from Arts Council England which helped me during the writing of this book and I would like to extend my thanks to them for that and for all they do to fund the arts.

To our select little Southall posse from back in the day – you know who you are – all those weekends and summers spent hanging out with you guys are what made me want to write about the place and its people, so my thanks to each and every one of you.

To my band of brothers, Soop, Sunil, Kuldish – thanks for all your support and encouragement with this book (and Harv – who didn't have much to do with the writing but he'll feel left out if I don't mention him), and for all the other stuff that had nothing to do with writing whatsoever. I'm not going to say I couldn't have done it without you – because I could have and probably quicker too – but I'm glad you were there to share the journey with me. I love you guys.

And finally, to Joanne, for all your help and support with the writing of this book – and everything else as well – thank you. x

Bringing a book from manuscript to what you are reading is a team effort.

Dialogue Books would like to thank everyone at Little, Brown who helped to publish *Stone Cold Trouble* in the UK.

Editorial
Sharmaine Lovegrove
David Bamford

Contracts
Stephanie Cockburn

Sales
Andrew Cattanach
Ben Goddard
Hannah Methuen
Caitriona Row

Design
Jo Taylor
Sean Garrehy

Production
Narges Nojoumi

Publicity
Millie Seaward

Marketing
Emily Moran

Copy-editing
Linda McQueen

Proofreading
Saxon Bullock